D039124 9

ANDY REMIC

Soul Stealers

BOOK TWO OF THE
CLOCKWORK VAMPIRE
CHRONICLES

ANGRY
ROBOT

ANGRY ROBOT
A member of the Osprey Group

Lace Market House,
54-56 High Pavement,
Nottingham
NG1 1HW, UK

www.angryrobotbooks.com
Bite me!

Originally published in the UK by Angry Robot 2010
First American paperback printing 2010

ISBN 978-0-85766-067-1

Printed in the United States of America

9 8 7 6 5 4 3 2 1

This book is dedicated with the utmost love, affection, humour and joy to my wonderful little boys, Joseph and Oliver.

PROLOGUE
Soul Stealers

It was an ink-dark dream. A razor flashback. A frozen splinter of time piercing his mind like a sterile needle. Nienna, beautiful Nienna, his sweet young granddaughter; they stood by the edge of a wide, sweeping river, spring sunshine warming upturned faces and glinting like diamonds amongst swaying reeds. Kell was teaching her how to fish, and he guided her hands, her long tapered fingers a contrast to his wrinkled, scarred old bear paws, hooking the bait (at which she pulled a screwed-up face) then casting out the line. They sat, then, in companionable silence, and Kell realised Nienna was watching him intently. He turned, scratching his grizzled grey beard, eyes meeting her bright gaze, and she smiled, face radiant.

"Grandfather?"

"Yes, little monkey?"

"Isn't fishing… you know, unfair?"

"What do you mean?"

"Well, it's like a trap, isn't it? You dangle the worm on a hook, and the fish swims along, unsuspecting, and you whip him out and eat him for supper. It's really not fair on the fish."

"Well, how else would I catch him?" said Kell, frowning a little. He chuckled. "I could always throw *you* in – you could *swim* after all the little fishes, catch them in your teeth like a pike!" He moved as if to grab her, to toss her into the deep waters, and she squealed, backing away fast up the bank and getting mud on her hands and clothes.

Nienna tutted. "Grandfather!"

"Ach, it's only a little mud. It'll wash off."

What Kell had wanted to say was that *all life* is a trap, a deceit, a bad con trick from a clever con artist. Life leads you on, life dangles tantalising bait on a dulled hook of iron – the bait being happiness, good health, wealth, joy – and you reach with both hands, mouth gaping like a slack-brained jester in the King's Court, but Life is a *bitch* and just when you think you've found it, found your dream, the line snags and you're yanked by your balls, guts and brain. Hooked, and slaughtered. That was Life. That was *Reality*. That was *Sobriety*. But Kell kept his mouth shut. Kept it shut tight. He didn't want to spoil the moment, this simple joy of fishing with his talented, optimistic granddaughter beside the Selenau River.

Now, Kell and Saark stood on the high rooftop of the shattered, teetering tower block in Old Skulkra. This was their trap. The bait had been laid by General Graal, his Army of Iron, his disgusting twisted *cankers*, and they had been snagged like fools, like naïve hatchlings, cornering themselves in Old Skulkra with an impossible task and a terrible fight.

Kell clutched his black axe Ilanna to his chest, gore-spattered knuckles white, face iron thunder, and Saark was tense, slim rapier wavering before him, his face a shattered silhouette of half-broken fear.

Below, in the bowels of the old stone block, something ululated, high-pitched and keening and far too feral to be human. It was followed immediately by a flurry of snarls, and growls, and heavy thuds and a scrabbling of brass claws clattering and booming through velvet black.

It was the cankers... and they were coming for fresh blood.

Kell's face was a thunderstorm filled with bruised clouds. Saark's face was hard to read, battered from a beating at the hands of Myriam's men, and his blood seeped through a torn and dirt-smeared shirt from a recent stab wound. Kell took a deep breath, nose twitching at fire from distant funeral pyres in the wake of the recent battle; he lifted Ilanna, and seemed, for a moment at least, to commune with the battered axe.

The cankers drew close. The two men could hear the beasts' heavy breathing on the stairwell.

Suddenly, a *pulse* seemed to pound through the ancient, deserted city; through the world. It was subsonic, an esoteric rumble; almost an earthquake. Almost.

Saark allowed breath to hiss free between clenched teeth. His fear was a tangible thing, a stain, like ink. He glanced at Kell.

"We're going to die up here, aren't we?"

Kell laughed, and it contained genuine humour, genuine warmth. He slapped Saark on the back, then rubbed thoughtfully at his bloodied beard, and with glittering eyes said, "We all die sometime, laddie," as the first of the cankers burst from the opening in a flurry of claws and fangs and screwed up faces of pure hate.

With a roar, Kell leapt to meet them...

As the first canker leapt, so Kell's mighty axe slammed down in a savage overhead blow, splitting the head in two, right down to the twisted spine-top. Flesh, brain and skull exploded outwards, and mixed in there with muscle and bone shards were tiny, battered clockwork machines, wheels and cogs twisting and turning, clicking and shifting, clockwork gears clacking, and in a blur Kell stepped back, dragging his axe with him as the first canker corpse hit the ground and he swayed from a swipe of huge claws from the second snarling beast, Ilanna *singing* as she hammered left now, butterfly blades horizontal, cutting free the canker's arm with a jarring *thud* and a shower of flowering blood petals. The beast howled, but a third heaved and shouldered past, huge and bulky, the size of a lion, a disjointed, twisted lion with pale white skin bulging with muscle, like over-full bowels pressing against maggot flesh in an attempt to break free of a pus-filled abdomen. The canker was covered with a plague of grey fur, tufted and irregular, and its forehead was stretched right back, its huge maw five times the size of the human mouth which had formed its template, skull open like an axe-chopped pumpkin showing huge brass fangs which curled down from rancid gleaming jaws and were decorated with knurled swirls, like fine etchings in copper. The canker's body was covered in open wounds, and within each wound thrashed clockwork, a myriad of tiny, spinning wheels, gyrating spindles, meshing gears, but whereas the *pure* vachine was perfect, and noble, and secure in its Engineer-created arrogance, this canker – this deviation, this *corruption* – showed bent gears and levers and unmeshed cogs, and in a blur Kell leapt sideways, Ilanna carving a parting line of muscle across the canker's neck, like an unzipping of flesh. Despite pain and squirming, unreleased muscle, its sheer weight and bulk carried it forward across the scattered concrete beams of the tower block's flat roof, where it slammed into Saark as his rapier stabbed frantically, slashing open more huge curved wounds. They both staggered back, fell back, and Kell turned from Saark allowing the wounded man to deal with the dying canker in a hiss of steel opening flesh and a *gush* of severed arteries.

A fresh flood of cankers burst through the opening, forcing Kell towards a grim-faced Saark, and the two men stood side by side, shoulder to shoulder, faces grim and splattered with gore, weapons flickering skilfully to open savage wounds as the cankers formed an expanding wall of flesh, an arc of solid muscle, as more and more surged through the opening to reinforce their ranks until there were ten, fifteen, *twenty* of the huge beasts ranged against them, hissing and grunting.

Kell gave a sardonic snarl, teeth grinding, and rubbed his grey beard. At his feet lay five dead cankers, a feat for any mortal man – for each canker was a terrible foe. Kell's eyes glittered, dark and feral, and his gore-slippery axe lowered a little as he realised – realised with a *bark* of laughter – that they were waiting.

"What's the matter, lads?" he boomed. "Left your bollocks at home with your pus-ugly wives?"

The cankers growled, huge puddles of drool descending from wide stretched maws where brass fangs curled like scimitar blades. Behind Kell, Saark was panting, long curly hair in lank strips filled with bits of bone and flesh, his beautiful face now a tapestry of agony.

"What are they waiting for?" he whispered, as if afraid his voice would accelerate them into action.

Kell shrugged. "I reckon we'll find out soon enough."

Within seconds, the line of quivering flesh, of tufted fur and deviant clockwork was heaved aside, and a massive canker forced its way through the throng. Kell could smell hot oil, and fancied he could hear the steady, tiny *tick tick tick* of off-beat clockwork.

"Now we die," muttered Saark.

"No," snapped Kell, "for if we die, then Nienna dies, if we die, then we cannot hunt down her kidnappers, we cannot seek justice and revenge! So, Saark, will you *shut up* and focus!" Kell fixed his gaze on this new creature, this towering beast, eight feet tall, heavily muscled, with glowering red eyes and an accompanying stench like desecration. Its skin was terribly pale, corpse-flesh waxy and entirely without hair. Kell's eyes narrowed. It was almost like... almost like this *beast* was merged with the albino soldiers from Graal's Army of Iron. Kell's glittering gaze scanned the wounds in the canker's flanks and chest, where deep inside brass clockwork spun and meshed. He grinned, but his eyes were dark and unfriendly. "Gods, lad, you stink like a ten-week corpse after dysentery and plague. What the hell's *wrong* with you beasts? Don't answer that. It's nothing my axe can't put right." He gestured flippantly with Ilanna, eyes watching, and perceived the canker's understanding.

Snarls and growls echoed up and down the line, and Kell knew these unholy beasts could comprehend. They were intelligent, and that frightened Kell more than any display of corruption. It was when this huge, dominant creature suddenly spoke that Kell took a step back, boots thumping the concrete beams, surprised despite himself; although he fought well not to show it.

"I am Nesh," said the canker, forming its words with care; despite impedance from curved fangs, its accent was Iopian, and that shouldn't have been possible. The whole mass of corrupted flesh and clockwork shouldn't have been possible. It was nightmare made real. "My General, the Warlord Graal, requires the honour of your presence. Indeed, he grants you *life* in exchange for your cooperation. You may agree now, little man." The canker grinned, more saliva pooling to the shattered, ancient beams of the high roof.

Kell took another step back. Saark was beside him, and Kell glanced at his friend with hooded eyes. He muttered, "Have you found an escape route yet?"

"There's no way off this roof!" said Saark. "We're trapped!"

"We're going to have to fight our way free, then."

Saark eyed the twenty or so cankers, and could see the shadows and hear the snarls of more on the stairwell below. He shuddered, fear a dry dead rat in his throat, a snake of lard in his intestines, a fist of iron in his belly. Saark, ever the dandy, a lover of life, women, wine and any narcotic that could swell the hedonistic experience of all three, knew deep down in his darkest most terrible nightmares that he was going to die here, knew he was to be ripped apart by those huge fangs, torn into flesh shreds, into streamers of muscle and skin spaghetti, and there was nothing he could do to avert this fate.

"You're joking, right?"

Kell threw him a dark glance, and growled, "I never joke when it comes to killing. Now! Follow my lead! You understand, boy?"

Saark nodded, sweating, hands gripping his rapier tight.

Nesh, growing impatient, moved its angry red gaze from one warrior to the other, then back. Kell moved his own eyes over the waxy, pale flesh; he shivered. The creature had hints of humanity in its twisted corruption of skin and bone, but there, any similarity ended. It was a distortion, not just of humanity, but of albino and vachine; a creature of no place, despised by all. Strangely, a thread of sympathy wormed into Kell's mind. He cut it savagely with a mental blade. This beast would show no mercy, nor compassion. It was here to kill.

"So, man? Will you come?" growled Nesh, and Kell could see other cankers straining at the leash; they could smell blood, and fear, and even remnants of Saark's distant flowery perfume. Kell grinned, baring his teeth as his face screwed into a ball of hostility.

"Tell Graal he can shove my axe up his arse!"

Saark groaned… and readied himself for attack…

Winter had finally come to Falanor.

Snow fell in blankets from iron clouds beneath a pale, albino sun. Violent storms flung folds of white to cover Falanor's valleys and rolling hills, her forests and rivers and ragged, towering mountains. From the savage flanks of the Black Pikes to the north, down through recently conquered cities, from Jalder to Skulkra, Vorgeth, Fawkrin and the southern capital of Vor, winter knew no obstacle and arrived early, with a ferocity not seen in the world for two centuries.

Within three days all northern passes were blocked; an ideal situation in the normal running of the country, for it meant many of the brigands, deviants and Black-lipper smugglers who oft troubled northern towns were trapped like bears in their mountain hideouts until the following spring.

It also meant General Graal, and his albino Army of Iron, were trapped in Falanor, blockaded far from their homeland in the heart of the Black Pike Mountains, severed from the vachine civilisation occupying Silva Valley, seat of power for the High Engineer Episcopate and Engineer Council, the Engineer's Palace and revered resting place for the Oak Testament.

Graal had successfully brought his vachine-sponsored army of albino subordinates south, seizing the cities of Falanor, kidnapping Queen Alloria, murdering the heroic Battle King, Leanoric, and routing his armies, including the previously unconquered Eagle Divisions. He had done this using cunning and a merciless swift descent. And by utilising blood-oil magick.

In the wake of the successful invasion, and within hours of snow blocking the Black Pike Mountain passes, Graal's Harvesters had brought forth the Blood Refineries: huge angular machines not unlike siege engines, pulled by teams of horses and cankers and using, in a twist of final irony, of calculated mockery, the fine, wide roads built by King Leanoric for transportation of his own military divisions. Graal camped his army outside Old Skulkra, and the great blood refineries had come to rest on the plain before the deserted city just hours before heavy falls of snow rendered further transport from the north impossible.

Graal sat in his war tent, cross-legged before a low table of ivory and marble, a scatter of parchments laid out before his weary eyes. The tent flap opened allowing a swirl of snow to intrude, and a Harvester stooped low to enter. For a moment Graal stared, the uniqueness of this race never failing to occupy and twist his curious mind; he watched the tall, heavily robed figure of the Harvester with its flat, oval, hairless face, nose nothing more than vertical slits, fingers not so much fingers as long slender needles of bone used for the delicate extraction of blood from a human carcass… he watched the Harvester settle down in a complicated ritual. Satisfied, the Harvester finally lifted tiny, black eyes to focus on Graal.

"The roads are closed. We are severed from the vachine," spoke the Harvester, voice a sibilant hissing.

Graal nodded, and returned his gaze to his parchments, reports detailing the final military approach on Vor by three of his albino *Divisions*. "Then we have months before they discover the… *reality* of the situation. Yes?"

"Yes, general."

"Has the vachine-bred Engineer Princess Jaranis managed to cross the mountains south in order to inspect our situation? Although, what she expects to find other than a jewelled dagger in her guts I have no idea."

"She arrived, general. An hour ago, in fact, with her military entourage. That is why I am here."

"Entourage?" He showed interest, now. "How many?"

The Harvester chuckled, a disturbing noise deep in its long, quivering throat. "As I previously made clear, the vachine in all their pious arrogance are wholly trusting of your endeavour. Jaranis, damn her clockwork, travelled with ten men only, a unit commanded by a lowly engineer-priest. I have taken the liberty of immediate slaughter, and even now their corpses have been added to the frozen pyres of recent battle. Even now," he paused, black eyes glinting, "their clockwork halts. However. With regard to Jaranis herself... I thought it wise to allow you counsel with this twisted princess. After all, despite her pretty skin and innocent ways, she may have an inkling of our plans."

"Summon her," said Graal, without looking up from his papers.

After a few minutes there came a sudden commotion outside the war tent, and two albino warriors dragged a shackled woman into the cosy interior. Although, upon closer inspection, it was clear she was not entirely human for she sported the tiny brass fangs of the vachine – the machine vampires of Silva Valley. The vachine were a blending of human and advanced miniature clock-work, a technological advancement of watchmaking skills evolved and developed and refined over the cen-turies until flesh and clockwork merged into a beautiful, superior whole. The vachine relied on the narcotic of blood-oil, a concoction of refined blood, in order to keep their internal clockwork mechanisms running smoothly. Without blood, and more importantly, blood-*oil*, a va-chine's clockwork would seize; and they would die. Hence the necessity of vampiric feeding.

Jaranis was thrown to the ground, where she spat up at Graal, eyes blazing with fury and shocked disbelief. Her fangs ejected with a tiny pneumatic *hissing*. She climbed smoothly to her feet. She was tall, elegant, with a shower of golden curls. She was beautiful beyond the human, and as she spoke Graal could see the tiny clockwork mechanisms in her throat, miniature gears and cogs and pistons working in a harmony of flesh and clockwork. Like a well-timed vampire machine. A vachine.

Graal smiled, some curious emotion not unlike lust passing through his mind; through his soul.

"Graal, you excel yourself with stupidity and arrogance!" snapped Princess Jaranis. "What, in the name of the Oak Testament, are you *doing*?"

Graal smiled, slowly, and stood. He stretched himself and gave an exaggerated, almost theatrical, yawn. Then his cold eyes focused on Jaranis and she could see there was anything but pantomime in that shadowed, brutal gaze.

"I admit, O *princess*, that it has been considerable time since I sought to pride myself on the baser concept of… *stupidity*," said Graal, handling the word like an abortion, and as he spoke he moved smoothly to a rack of armour and began to buckle on breastplate and forearm greaves fashioned from dull black steel. "Rather, my sweetness, I seek to pride myself on the twin lusts of *betrayal* and *dominion*."

"You would betray the vachine?" whispered Jaranis, stunned. "A society you helped build from a mewling wreckage of primal carnage and bestial evolution?"

Graal smiled, and halted midway through buckling a greave. His eyes seemed distant, and as he spoke his voice was lilting, a low growl, almost musical in its harmony. "Allow your mind to drift back, like drug-smoke, for a millennium, my sweet; there were once three Vampire Warlords, maybe you have heard of them? Their names are written in iron on the Core Stone of Silva Valley, carved into the back cover of the Oak Testament with a knife used to slit the throats of babes." His eyes grew hard, like cobalt. "They are Kuradek, Meshwar, Bhu Vanesh – Kuradek, the Unholy. Meshwar, the Violent. And Bhu Vanesh, the Eater in the Dark." He glanced at Jaranis, then, head tilting. With tight lips Jaranis shook her head, and frowned, seeking to understand Graal's direction.

"These warlords," continued Graal, "were, shall we say, all powerful. I am surprised you have limited knowledge of their prowess, for they are a pivotal part of baseline vachine history." He smiled. "That is, *your* vachine history. For as we all know, the Engineer Council seek to strongly enforce a true vachine culture in which nobody strays from a pure and holy path. Is that not so?"

"That is so," said Jaranis, voice little more than a whisper. She was trembling now, and Graal felt a trickle of lust ease through his veins like a honey narcotic. Sex, fear and death, he thought, went hand in hand, and were *always* a turn-on.

"The warlords, they had clockwork *souls*," said Graal, eyes blazing with a sudden fury. He calmed himself with intricate self-control, and finished strapping on his armour with tight, sudden little jerks. "But then, you may not know this, for the High Engineer Episcopate practice and preach rewritten histories and a fictional past."

Jaranis shook her head, and Graal gestured to the two albino soldiers, who stepped forward, grabbing the young vachine woman and dragging her out into the freshly falling snow. All through the war camp tumbled jarring sounds, the snort and stamp of horse, cankers snarling, the clatter of arms, the low-level talk of soldiers around braziers. Jaranis was thrown to her knees, her fine silk robes stained with saliva, and just a little blood.

Graal emerged, striding with an arrogant air that made Jaranis want to rip out his throat. Her fangs ejected fully, eyes narrowing and claws hissing from fingertips. They gleamed, razor-sharpened brass. She considered leaping, but caught something in her peripheral vision: two figures, both female, both albino subordinates. She snarled in disgust, and turned to stare at these… soldiers.

They were tall, lithe, athletic, and wore light armour of polished steel unlike the usual black armour of the albino Army of Iron. Both women wore sleek longswords at their hips, and one had her long white hair braided into twin, wrist-thick ponytails, whilst the second had her hair cropped short. It was spiked by the snow. Their skin was white, almost translucent, and they had high cheekbones, gaunt faces, and crimson eyes. When they smiled, their beauty was stunning but deadly, like a newborn sun. And when they smiled, they had the fangs of the vachine.

Princess Jaranis hissed in shock. Albinos could not be vachine! It was not permitted. It was illegal. It was *unholy*.

Graal stepped forward, and touched one woman behind her elbow. She smiled at him. "This is Shanna, and this is Tashmaniok. Daughters, I would like to introduce the vachine princess, Jaranis." The two albino vachine warriors gave short bows and moved to stand erect, one at either side of Graal. They took his arms, as if enjoying a stroll down some theatre-lined thoroughfare in one of Silva Valley's more respectable cultured communities, and their eyes glowed with vampire hate.

"You will not get away with this… *blasphemy*!" snarled Jaranis, voice dripping poison and fury. "Not for giving White Warriors the clockwork, nor for betraying the vachine!"

"But, my sweetness, I think I already have," said Graal. He smiled down at Jaranis. "You vachine are so trusting, and so beautifully naïve. These girls, they are not some simple blending. Some back-street black-market clockwork abortion!" His voice rose, a little in anger, blue eyes glinting as his focus drilled into the vachine princess. "Don't you understand to whom you speak? Don't you recognise the birth of your death?"

"The Soul Stealers?" whispered Jaranis, in horror.

Graal smiled. He gave a slight, sideways nod, and Shanna detached from his linked arm and in one smooth movement, drew her sword and decapitated the vachine princess.

Jaranis's head rolled into the snow and blood, and blood-oil, spurted from the ragged neck stump. The body paused for a moment, rigid, then toppled like a puppet with cut strings. As blood-oil ran free, so clock-work machinery grew noisy, it rattled and spluttered until it finally faltered, and came to a premature clattering halt with a discordant note like the clashing of swords in battle.

Graal knelt in the snow, ignoring the vachine blood which stained his leather trews. He stared into the severed clockwork face of the murdered vachine; in death, she was even more beautiful.

He glanced back. The Soul Stealers were poised motionless, beautiful, deadly.

"I had a mind-pulse from Nesh," he said, voice low and terrible. "He says Kell and that puppet, Saark, are cornered in the maze of Old Skulkra."

"Yes, father," said Tashmaniok.

"Bring them to me," he said, and shifted his gaze to the Soul Stealers' bright, focused eyes, "It is the Soul Gem that matters, now. You understand?"

"We serve," they said, voices in harmony.

With the stealth of the vampire the Soul Stealers vanished, like ghosts, through the snow.

CHAPTER 1
Ankarok

Kell grinned. "Tell Graal he can shove my axe up his arse!"

Saark groaned... and readied for attack...

"As you wish," said Nesh, lowering its strange, bestial, wrenched clockwork head, red eyes shining, mouth full of juices in anticipation of the feed to come. Muscles bunched like steel-weave cables, fangs jutted free with crunches, and behind it the other cankers growled and the growl rose into a unified howl which mingled and merged forming one perfectly balanced single note that held on the air, perfect, and signified their reward.

Kell's eyes were fixed on the lead canker, his body a tense bow-string, senses heightened into something more than human. He was the delicate trigger of a crossbow. The impact reflex of a striking snake.

It was going to be a damn hard fight.

But then... the incredible happened. Nesh settled back on its haunches, eyes meeting Kell's, and the old warrior was sure he saw a corrupt smile touch the beast's lips like a tracing of icing sugar on horse-shit. Nesh stood, turned, and pushed through the cankers. The howling subsided into an awkward silence; then the cankers slowly filed after their leader, one by one, until only their rotten oil stink remained – alongside five canker corpses, bleeding slow-congealing lifeblood onto the stone roof.

"What happened?" breathed Saark, his whole body relaxing, slumping almost, into the cage of his bones. Kell shrugged, and turned, and fastened his gaze on the small boy standing perhaps twenty feet away, by the low wall overlooking Old Skulkra's ancient, crumbling remains.

Kell pointed, and Saark noticed the boy for the first time. He was young, only five or six years old, his skin pale, his limbs thin, his clothing ragged like many an abandoned street urchin easily found in the shit-pits of Falanor's major cities. The boy turned, and looked up at Kell and Saark, and smiled, head tilting.

It's in his eyes, thought Kell, his cool gaze locked to the boy. His eyes are old. They sparkled like diseased Dog Gems, those rarest of dull jewels left over from another age, another civilisation.

Kell stepped forward, and crouched. "You scared them off, lad?" It was half question, half statement. The air felt suddenly fuzzy, as if raw magick was discharging languorously through the breeze.

The boy nodded, but did not move. He shifted slightly, and something small and black ran down the sleeve of his threadbare jacket. It was a scorpion, and it ran onto the boy's hand and sat there for a while, as if observing the two men.

Saark let out a hiss, hand tightening on rapier hilt. "The insect of the devil!" he snapped.

"Look," said Kell, slowly. "It has two tails." And indeed, the scorpion – small, shiny, black – had two corrugated tails, each with a barbed sting.

Saark shivered. "Throw it down, lad," he called. "Our boots will finish the little bastard."

Ignoring Saark, the boy stepped across loose stone joists, moving forward with a delicate grace which belied his narrow, starved limbs. He halted before Kell, looked up with dark eyes twinkling, then slowly plucked the twin-tailed scorpion from his hand and secreted the arachnid beneath his shirt.

"My name is Skanda," said the boy, voice little more than a husky whisper. "And the scorpion, it is a scorpion of time."

"What does that mean?" whispered Kell.

The boy shrugged, eyes hooded, smile mysterious.

"You scared away the cankers!" blurted Saark. "How did you do that?"

Skanda turned to Saark, and again his head tilted, as if reading the dandy's thoughts. "They fear me, and they fear my race," said Skanda, and when he smiled they saw his teeth were black. Not the black of decay, but the black of insect chitin.

"Your race?" said Kell, voice gentle.

"I am Ankarok," said Skanda, looking out over Old Skulkra, over its ancient, deserted palaces and temples, tenements and warehouses, towers and cathedrals. All crumbling, and cracked, all savaged by time and erosion and fear. "This was our city. Once." He looked again at Kell, and smiled the shiny black smile. "This was our country. Our world."

Saark moved to the edge of the crumbling tenement, staring over the low wall. Below, he could see the retreated cankers had gathered; there were more than fifty, some sitting on the ancient stone paving slabs, some pacing in impatient circles. Many snarled, lashing out at others. At their core was Nesh, seated on powerful haunches, almost like a lion, regal composure immaculate.

"They're waiting below," said Saark, moving back to Kell. He glanced at Skanda. "Seems their fear only extends so far."

"I will show you a way out of this building," said Skanda, and started to move across the roof, dodging holes and loose joists.

Saark stared at Kell. "I don't trust him. I think we should head off alone."

Ignoring Saark, Kell followed the boy, and heard the battered dandy curse and follow. "Wait," said Kell, as they reached a segment of wall where a part of the floor had appeared to crumble away revealing, in fact, a tunnel, leading *down* through the wall. Kell could just see the gleam of slick, black steps. It dispersed his fears of magick, a little. "Wait. Why would you do this for us? I have heard of the Ankarok. By all accounts, they were not, shall we say, a charitable race."

Skanda smiled his unnerving smile. Despite his stature, and his feeble appearance of vagrancy, he exuded a dark energy, a power Saark was only just beginning to comprehend; and with a jump, Saark recognised that Kell had not been fooled. Kell had seen through the – *disguise* – immediately. Saark snorted. Ha! he thought. Kell was just too damned smart for an old fat man.

"Why?" Skanda gave a small laugh. "Kell, for you we would attack the world," said the little boy, watching Kell closely. His dark eyes shone. "For you are Kell, the Black Axeman of Drennach – and it is written you shall help save the Ankarok," he said.

• • •

His name was Jage, and they left him to die when he was six years old. He couldn't blame them. He would have done the same. The blow from an iron-shod hoof left his spine damn near snapped in two, discs crushed in several places, his bent and broken body crippled beyond repair – or at least, beyond the repair of a simple farming people. Nobody in the village of Crennan could bring themselves to kill the child; and yet Jage's mother and father could not afford to feed a cripple. They could barely afford to feed themselves.

His father, a slim man named Parellion, carried the boy to the banks of the Hentack River where, in the summer months when the water level was low, the flow turned yellow, sometimes orange, and was highly poisonous if drank. It was completely safe, so it was said, in the winter months when the flow was fast, fresh, clear with pure mountain melt from the Black Pikes; then, then the water could be safely supped, although few trusted its turncoat nature. Most villagers from Crennan had seen the effects of the toxins on a human body: the writhing, the screaming, flesh tumbling from a bubbling skeleton. Such agony was not something easily forgotten.

Jage's father placed him gently on the bank, and Jage looked up into his kindly face, ravaged by years of working the fields and creased like old leather. He did not understand, then, the tears that fell from his father's eyes and landed in his own. He smiled, for the herbs old Merryach gave him had taken away the savage pain in his spine. Maybe they thought they'd given him enough herbs to end his life? However, they had not.

Parellion kissed him tenderly; he smelt strongly of earth. Beyond, Jage could see his mother weeping into a red handkerchief. Parellion knelt and stroked the boy's brow, then stood, and turned, and left.

In innocence, naivety, misunderstanding, Jage watched them go and he was happy for a while because the sun shone on his face and the pain had receded to nothing more than a dull throb. The sunshine was pleasant and he was surrounded by flowers and could hear the summer trickle of the river. He frowned. That was the poisonous river, yes? He strained to move, to turn, to see if the waters ran orange and yellow; but he could not. His spine was broken. He was crippled beyond repair.

For a long time Jage lay amongst the flowers, his thirst growing with more and more intensity. The herbs had left a strange tingling sensation and a bitter taste on his tongue. I wonder when father will come back for me? he thought. Soon, soon, answered his own mind. He will bring you water, and more medicine, and it will heal your broken back and the world will be well again. You'll see. It will be fine. It will be good.

But Parellion did not return, and Jage's thirst grew immeasurably, and with it came Jage's pain beating like a caged salamander deep down within, in his body core, white-hot punches running up and down his spine like the hooves of the horse that kicked him.

Stupid! His mother told him never to walk behind a horse. The eighteen-hand great horse, or draught horse as they were also known, was a huge and stocky, docile, glossy creature, bay with white stockings, prodigious in strength and used predominantly for pulling the iron-tipped plough. Jage had been concentrating on little Megan, flying a kite made from an old shirt and yew twigs, and her running, her giggling, the way sunlight glinted in her amber curls… He ran across the field to speak to her, to ask if he, too, could fly the kite and *impact* threw him across the field like a ragdoll, and for a long time only colours and blackness swirled in his mind. Everything was fuzzy, unfocused, but he remembered Megan's screams. Oh how he remembered those!

Now, the copper coin of the sun sank, and bright fear began to creep around the edges of the young boy's reason. What if, he decided, mother and father did not return? What if they were never going to return? How would he drink? How would he crawl to the river? He could not *move*. Tears wetted his cheeks, and the bitter taste of the herb was strong, and bad, in his desiccated mouth. But more, the bitter taste of a growing realisation festered in his heart. Why had they brought him here? He thought it was to enjoy the sunshine after the cramped interior of their hut, with its smell of herbs and vomit and stale earth.

And as the moon rose, and stars glimmered, and the river rushed and Jage could hear the stealthy footfalls of creatures in the night, he knew, knew they had left him here to *die* and he wept for betrayal, body shuddering, tears rolling down his face and tickling him and pitifully he tried to move, teeth gritted, more pain flaring *flaring* so bad he screamed and writhed a little, twitching in agony and impotence amongst the starlit flowers, their colours bleached, their tiny heads bobbing.

Suddenly, somewhere nearby, a wolf howled. Jage froze, fear crawling into his brain like an insect, and his eyes grew wide and he bit his tongue, tasting blood. Wolves. This far south of the Black Pike Mountains? It wasn't unheard, although the people of Crennan were keen to hunt down and massacre any wolves sighted in the vicinity. The mountain wolves were savage indeed, and never stopped at killing a single animal. Their frenzies were legendary. As was their hunger.

The howl, long and lingering and drifting to silence like smoke, was answered by another howl, off to the east, then a third, to the west. Jage remained frozen, eyes moving from left to right, his immobility a torture in itself, which at this moment in time far outweighed the physical pain of his broken spine.

If they found him, they would eat him, of this he was sure.

Eat him alive.

Jage waited, in the darkness, in the silence, with pain growing inside him, his severed spine pricking him with hot-iron brands of agony, his heart thumping in his ears. I will be safe, he told himself. I will be safe. He repeated the phrase, over and over and over, like a mantra, a prayer-song, and part of him, the childish part, knew that if danger truly approached then his father, brave strong Parellion, would be waiting just out of sight with his mighty wood-cutting axe and he would smash those wolves in two, for surely the village was near enough for them to hear the howls? The villagers would not tolerate such an intrusion by a natural predator! But another part of Jage, a part that was quickly growing up, an accelerated maturity and a consideration to *survive* told him with savage slaps that he was completely alone, abandoned, and if he did *nothing* then he would surely die. But what can I do? he thought, fighting against the urge to cry. I cannot move!

He wanted to scream, then. To release his frustration and pain in one long howl, just like the wolves; but he bit his tongue, for he knew to do so would be to draw them like moth to candle flame.

Jage waited, tense and filled with an exhaustive fear; he eventually drifted into a fitful sleep. When his eyes opened, slowly, he knew something was immediately wrong despite his sensory apparatus unable to detect any direct threat.

Then, grass hissed, and Jage's eyes moved to the left and into his field of vision stepped the wolf. It was old, big, heavy, fur ragged and torn in strips from one flank; its fur was a deep grey and black, matted and twisted, and its eyes were yellow, baleful, and glittered with an ancient intelligence. This creature wasn't like the yelping puppies in the village; this wolf was a killer, a survivor, and it knew fresh, stranded meat when it saw it.

"Oh no," whispered Jage, eyes transfixed. Like a snake before a charmer, Jage watched the wolf pad close, then look left and right as if expecting a trap and humans waiting with pitchfork and axe. Other wolves edged into Jage's vision, growing in confidence and spreading in a wide arc. The young boy shuddered involuntarily.

They were going to eat him. Eat him alive. And there was nothing he could do.

A snarl came, low and malevolent, and those eyes never left Jage's. There was a connection between the two, between victim and killer, and Jage wasn't sure what it meant, only that he felt like a bound sacrifice on an altar; and felt suddenly, violently sick.

The wolf lowered its head, fangs baring, and the snarl elongated into a continuous threatening growl. A paw edged forward, and at the same time Jage felt a tickling across his legs which twitched as if in automatic response, and the tickling moved up over his belly and onto his chest and Jage gaped at the spider there, small, glossy, black, about the size of his hand, so close he could see the many hairs that covered its legs and thorax and he blinked, for this was the highly toxic and very, very deadly Hexel Spider, otherwise known – sweetly, ironically – as a *Lupus* Spider. Jage allowed a slow breath to escape his fear-frozen throat, and watched the spider turn to face the wolf – which had stopped, one paw extended, eyes narrowed as if in consideration.

The spider's two front legs came up, then, poised in the air, and Jage could see long curved chelicerae which he knew, even at this young age, were linked to glands carrying venom.

The wolf halted, but the growl remained, and the old creature was wise enough to recognise danger in this tiny creature. More growls echoed, and then with a shiver Jage felt more tickles spread across his body like rainfall, and his vision was *flooded* by a swathe of Hexel Spiders as they ran up him, over him, and poised, a glossy mass of legs and exoskeletons, almost covering his body entirely and certainly covering the ground around him in a bristling carpet. The wolf snarled, turned, and loped away; was gone.

Jage, however, could not breathe a sigh of relief, and his eyes roved frantically over the spiders which slowly lowered their legs from attack posture and began to move across him, down onto the ground and he was waiting, waiting for that painful bite which would bring about oblivion and this must have been why his parents left him here by a spider nest – certain of a quick, venomous end.

Jage blinked. One spider remained, on his chest, and he could see its tiny black eyes watching. Then it moved forward, and crawled up his face and he could feel each tiny footfall pressing his flesh and he wanted so desperately to scream but knew any sudden noise would bring about the bite.

The spider stopped, suspended over his mouth, and Jage gave the tiniest of whimpers.

From somewhere in the spider, whether it be chelicerae, gland or spinneret, a tiny droplet detached and fell into Jage's throat. It was warm, and slick. More drops followed, and a bitter taste flooded through him, and darkness came in a violent rage and he thought, I have been poisoned, I am dying, I was left for this, and a black swell of raging pain rushed up to meet him and he fell into and through a bottomless pit, and remembered no more.

Jage awoke face down, staring at rock. An incredible thirst still raged through him, and he had distant memories of motion but everything was blurred and his face felt sticky and he realised his skin was covered, covered with a sheen of silk honey web.

So they want to eat me, he thought, miserably. They've brought me back to their cave, so that they can eat me one piece at a time. I am a prisoner. I am food.

He struggled to move, but could not. However, there was no pain, and Jage frowned. Then he spied a flood of spiders undulating across the rocky floor towards him, each the size of his hand, many with chelicerae clicking. Some carried sacks of eggs, encased in silk, some held them in jaws but others carried their precious cargo on their backs. Jage watched, fascinated for a few moments, until he realised they had come to feed; had come to feed their young. He shuddered, and fresh tears fell, and the surging carpet of spiders stopped and several clambered over him, delicate footfalls teasing his flesh with a terrible, mocking agony. He felt the bite, directly over his broken spine, and he screamed then and would have thrashed if he could have moved... another bite came, and another, and Jage was sobbing uncontrollably as the spiders clicked and injected him with venom, and he waited for the pain to smash through him.

Instead, only euphoria eased into his veins, and thankfully he slipped into a welcome unconsciousness.

Jage awoke, propped against rock, seated in the dark, in the cold. A breeze blew, which soothed his feverish skin. He licked dry lips, and his throat throbbed raw from excessive screaming. He turned his head, surveyed the narrow tunnels which led to this small, cramped space. On a rock near his foot, to the right, there was fruit; small berries, some strawberries, several mushrooms and a potato. Jage felt an incredible hunger rush through him, and he reached out, lifting the fruit and eating it, and berry juice ran down his face staining his chin red and he laughed, and his feeding increased in frenzy until the fruit and raw vegetables were gone.

He felt stiff, and sore, and only then did realisation dawn.

He could move! He could move again.

The young boy twisted, and his back felt strange, tight and odd and *not quite part of him*. He frowned, and reached behind himself, his hand groping for his spine. What he found there made him freeze, for there was some kind of thick cord on the outside of his skin, stretching from the base of his spine all the way up to the base of his skull. His fingers traced the strange, smooth, hard substance, and as he moved, and explored, he realised the thick cord was moving with him, flexing with him. It seemed to be integral to his flesh.

What have they done to me? Jage thought, dream-like, drifting, and he saw the spiders moving slowly into his cramped cave, only this time there was something else, another spider, much bigger this time but with exactly the same markings and appearance as the tiny Hexels. Jage fixed on this large arachnid, and its graceful movement of all eight legs in choreographed coordination; it was the same size as Jage, and he realised, at least, that answered the question of how he had been moved to the cave. What was this? A queen? A king? How did it work with spiders?

The spider eased forward, ducking a little, each leg movement a forced hydraulic step, and it stopped before Jage and he looked into the four black orbs – its eyes – and the spider was watching him and he had absolutely no idea what it *wanted*. Was it going to eat him? Was it going to poison him? Did it want to be friends?

"Hello," said Jage, head tilting. His spine gave a tiny, tiny *crackle*. "Thank you, for saving me, from the wolves."

The gathering of worker spiders did not move. They were a carpet of black, all eyes on him. The large one (which he later discovered *was* the queen) stepped even closer, and Jage's nostrils twitched, for he could smell acid and hemolymph. He kept his face perfectly straight as chelicerae the size of daggers moved to his face and the spider seemed to be… sniffing him? It moved yet closer, all eight legs surrounding him, encompassing him in a strange spider-limb cocoon, and then against all odds the spider started to sing, a song without words, a high-pitched croon, a lullaby, and Jage sat there, ensnared, and she sang to him and he felt strangely at ease, a part of this family hiding under the ground and inside the rock, feared and reviled and his face formed into a strange grimace which should have had no place on a human mask and he found *acceptance* for he had been abandoned and left to die but here, here and now, with the spider queen's song soothing through his skull and veins he realised he was a part of this new family; they would look after him, and protect him, and love him, and make him *strong* again.

Deep in the caves, there was a river. The water was black, but Jage drank from it often and never suffered ill effects. He moved around the tunnels freely for a while, exploring winding tunnels and caves and caverns, many littered with bones and long, ancient drifts of web. Most of the Hexel Spiders did their hunting outside, and fed mainly on other insects, although sometimes the three larger queens who inhabited the central caves would head out into the night and return, often with rabbits or snakes, once a weasel spitting and snarling in its sack of silk; and once, even, a wolf.

Jage watched as the three queens brought the cocooned wolf into the hub of caves and tunnels; it no longer struggled, and Jage reasoned it had been given a moderate bite to sedate it. The massive shaggy beast was wrapped heavily in thick cords of restraining silk, and Jage crawled forward, curious, head tilting to one side as he realised with a start the creature was the wolf that had threatened him all those months earlier, as he lay paralysed and abandoned beside the Hentack River. On hands and knees Jage crawled until his face was only inches from the wolf, and he stared into those old, baleful yellow eyes and the wolf seemed to grin at him, panting in short bursts, and Jage felt some kind of victory and he wondered if this was sheer coincidence, or if his new family had hunted down the wolf and brought it to him.

Jage turned, and at that moment the wolf lunged, jaws snapping, slicing through his shoulder and making the young boy scream. The wolf locked jaws, and shook him, and Jage flopped to the rock and the spiders rushed over the wolf and the queen was there, small black eyes emotionless as chelicerae swept down and there came a terrible *cracking*; she snapped the wolf's muzzle in two, then a leg punched out, entering the old creature's skull with pile-driver force and skewering the brain within.

Jage fell back, weeping, pain flooding him. Gently, the queen gathered him up and a honey liquid oozed from her fangs and into his mouth and the pain eased away, closely followed by wakefulness.

Jage awoke. His shoulder felt good. It felt more than good. It felt *strong*. He looked down, and from the midpoint of his chest across his shoulder and down to his elbow, there were panels of black chitin, glossy like spider armour, and woven deep into his flesh, indeed, deep into his very muscle and bone.

The queen entered, and settled down before him. Then a foreleg reached out and touched Jage's face, and he closed his eyes and he could... *he could flow with her thoughts and feel her desperation for she was a Soulkeeper of Species and they were at war and hunted and reviled and the battle had raged for thousands of years with the Trallisk, who came with fire and poison to burn them and sting them, and battles had been fought, huge underground wars in tunnel and cave systems ranging for thousands of leagues to destroy the Sacred, and the Soulkeepers had finally been defeated in a huge bloody scourge, and since that day they moved from cave system to cave system, always running, always hiding, taking the Sacred with them, but one day they would conquer for it was their way, they were a warrior species descended from a warrior species and Jage, Jage was a human exception, a conundrum for he had shown them kindness and a form of understanding and she knew he was different and unique and they needed something unique to beat the Trallisk in war and this, this meant acceptance, for he was young and in him they could find an ally and they would strengthen him and had built him a spine from cuticle containing proteins and chitin built up in layers and fed with long protein strands into his own flesh and own spine and nerves and his body had accepted it as his own. And now. Now, after the incident with the wolf, the Soulkeepers had repaired his shoulder in a similar fashion, building him a new shoulder blade, for the wolf's fangs had torn muscle and powdered bone and they were part of him now, all a part of him, and he was part of them, and they were happy to accept Jage into their family for they knew there was no evil in his body, mind or soul and he could help them, help them protect the Sacred for its purpose was important to the world, and he, Jage, was important to the world... and one day, he would understand why they gave him the Sacred to protect.*

Jage's eyes opened, with a start. He ran his tongue around the inside of his mouth, coughed, and sat up. He flexed his new shoulder experimentally, and pressed at it with his free hand. It felt as strong as steel.

On a flat rock by his feet sat a platter of rock, with some fruit, and vegetables, and a long, slick, grey slab of meat. Jage reached out, picked up the meat, which slithered against his fingers as if trying to escape. He knew what he had to do. He had to get strong. He had to grow, and feed, and become powerful; only then could he repay the kindness of the Hexels and help them with their age-old war against the Trallisk; help them protect the Sacred. Help them *deliver* it.

Jage ate the meat, rubbing absently at his chest which itched, just over his heart, and at that moment knew he needed a new name. Something to reflect his merging with the spiders; his acceptance not just into their society, but into their very *genetics*.

From this point, he decided, he would be known as Jageraw.

General Graal rode the black stallion to the top of the hill and turned, gaze sweeping the snowy wilderness and desolate, crumbling city of Old Skulkra. "I know you," he said, eyes narrowing. "I remember you. I remember you well, Old One.'

Graal was half vachine, half albino. Accepted by the vachine society and culture because of his age, his prowess in battle, his tactical expertise as a general, and because – although their history no longer recorded it – he was one of the blood of the first vachine to walk the world, under the watchful gaze of the Vampire Warlords, Kuradek, Meshwar and Bhu Vanesh. Graal was ancient. More than a thousand years old. Ancient slave to the Vampire Warlords. And Graal was *pissed*.

He attempted to calm himself, tried to slow the thunder of clockwork in his breast. But he could not. His teeth ground together, and he tasted his own blood-oil.

A Harvester approached, eyes fixed on Graal, drifting through the fresh fall of snow like a ghost.

"You should calm yourself, Brother," said the Harvester.

"I am fucking *sick* of this charade. I want the vachine dead. I want them slaughtered! I know my destiny, by right of conquest, of kindred, of birth! I know my place, Harvester!"

"It will come," soothed the Harvester. "It will all come. You have shown great patience to this point; why do you grow so agitated? What has disturbed your mind, general?"

Graal was silent for long minutes, pale lips compressed, white face shaded by shadows, gloom, and a cascade of falling snow. His stallion stamped, snorting steam, and he turned the beast to stare across Old Skulkra. The ancient towers and palaces were rimed with snow; its cracked tenements, crumbling plazas, disintegrating bridges, all were sprinkled with a sugary ash and if Graal narrowed his eyes enough, he could imagine the city as it was a *thousand* years ago, when it was the centre of the Vampire Warlords' Empire, when it had been a Seat of Power… and of death, misery, and human desecration.

Graal leapt lightly from his mount, and stroked his pale features, lost in thought. The skin of an albino, and yet the eyes of the vachine? How little they *knew*; how little they *understood* his lineage.

"What troubles you?" persisted the Harvester, drifting close, towering over the man. A hand reached out, five long bone needles, and rested gently on Graal's shoulder.

Graal spat. "The cankers had a simple task: to hunt down an old man and his wounded companion. More than *fifty* cankers I sent, and yet they came back empty in tooth and claw. How could they not possibly find one simple old man and his tart?"

"You fear this man?"

Graal glanced at the Harvester then, and turned away. "No. Fear is not the correct word. I *respect* him, and respect the damage he may cause if left to run riot. This man is Kell, and once he troubled the vachine in the Black Pike Mountains. He and his soldiers called themselves Vachine *Hunters* – and yes, I do appreciate the irony, as sweet as any virgin's quim. They caused vachine and albino warriors alike serious trouble during a four year period. Not only did they slaughter our peoples, they disrupted the blood-oil trade and nearly killed in its entirety the smuggling of Karakan Red which, as we both know, many half-vachine rely on as part of Kradek-ka's… shall we say, experimentations."

"You were sent to deal with this thorn?"

"Yes. To pluck it free. Many times Engineer Priests, and even Archbishops, were sent with elite squads amongst the Black Pikes to hunt down and end this… problem. They returned either empty handed, or not at all. It was said these Vachine Hunters were ghosts, demons, unsavoury spirits sent by God to remove our kind from the face of the planet. Not so. They were men, highly skilled men with a talent for death and *bloodbond*," he spat the word, teeth bared like an animal, "weapons baptised in some ancient dark magick of which we had no knowledge, nor understanding. They were sent by King Searlan, a *magicker* King, after he studied an ancient text and grew afraid."

"And the text?"

"The *Book of Angels*," said Graal, darkly.

"A dangerous tome indeed. I hope it was recovered?"

"No. That was part of my reason for persuading the Engineer Council to allow me to take their Army of Iron south; otherwise, I fear they may not have trusted me with so much singular authority." He smiled. "There was, of course, also inherent panic at their impending shortage of refined blood-oil."

"Of course," said the Harvester, with a sardonic smile. "A well crafted situation. However, this... Kell? You never found him during your time In the Black Pike Mountains?"

"My soldiers tracked him, and with his few men Kell fought a retreat into the bowels of Bein Techlienain; there, the battle raged for hours in the narrow tunnels and across high bridges, until my soldiers were sure the last of Kell's men – and the man himself – were cast screaming and begging into the Fires of Karrakesh."

"And yet, it would seem he survived."

"Yes, he survived," said Graal, voice bitter. "I swear this is the same man, although I never saw his face my-self under the Black Pikes." His voice dropped an octave. "I think some of my trusted soldiers were not quite honest with me about those long, dark weeks under the Stone."

"Maybe this new and unfortunate series of events is merely... coincidence? Or possibly a foolhardy, arro-gant warrior seeking to step like a ganger into another's skin?" The Harvester seemed to be smiling, although this was unlikely through the narrow slit of its mouth. Harvesters were renowned for having a flatline when it came to humour.

"There is no such thing as coincidence," snapped Graal. He gave a bleak smile. "As I will demonstrate."

He called to a young albino warrior, and sent him to

find Nesh, the leader of the cankers sent to find Kell and Saark in Old Skulkra – and to bring them *back*. Nesh was as near controllable as one could achieve, with such an inherently uncontrollable and chaotic blend of twisted species.

Nesh arrived, huge, rumbling, mouth stretched wide open, tiny eyes filled with swirling gold as it watched Graal. The canker hunkered down, stinking of oil and hot metal. Inside, its clockwork clicked and stepped, and pistons thudded occasionally. Nesh was an example of a canker in its prime, although to be in its prime state, a canker must have regressed from both the human and clockwork that created it – to such an extent that the beautiful became ugly, the logical became parody. To be in prime canker state was to be days from death.

"Yes?" grunted the beast, its speech clipped and short. Words caused this creature, fully eight feet in height, great pain to utter. But it was a gift the canker treasured, for not all could speak through corrupted clockwork and fangs.

Graal walked down one flank, observing the open wounds, the twisted, blackened clockwork, the bent gears and pistons. He smiled, a tight smile. To Graal, more than any other albino or vachine in existence, these creatures were abomination. But like a good craftsman, he used his tools well – with Watchmaker precision. No matter the extent of his personal abhorrence.

"You followed Kell's scent? And the stench of the wounded popinjay?"

"Yes."

"And yet… you claim you lost them. In the maze of streets and alleyways?"

"Yes, General Graal. There much dark magick in Old Skulkra. Much we not understand. Much left over from… the Other Time."

"You are lying," said Graal.

There followed an uneasy silence, in which the huge, panting canker glared down at General Graal. Its mouth opened wider with tiny brass *clicks*, almost like the winding of a ratchet, and the small hate-filled eyes narrowed, fixed on Graal, fixed on his throat.

"I obey my Masters," said the canker carefully, "for only then do I get the blood-oil I require." The panting increased. Graal noted, almost subliminally, that the canker's claws were sliding free, silent, well-oiled, like razors in grease.

"My brother became a canker," said Graal, brightly, moving away from the huge beast. "For years I tried to stop it happening, tried to halt the inexorable progress of an all-conquering corruption. But I could not do it. I could not stop *Nature*. For days, nights, weeks, we sat there discussing the possibilities, of regression, of introducing fresh clockwork, of forceful medical excision. And yet I knew, I always fucking *knew*," Graal turned, fixing his glittering blue gaze on the huge beast, "when he was lying." Graal smiled, a narrow compression of lips.

"I cannot tell you," snarled the canker. "You would never believe!"

"You will tell me," said Graal, voice soft, "or I will slaughter you where you stand."

"They will *curse* me!" howled the canker, voice suddenly filled with pain, and fear, and shock.

"*Who?*"

"The Denizens of Ankarok," snarled Nesh, and launched itself with dazzling speed at Graal, claws free,

fangs bright and gleaming with gold and brass, savage
snarls erupting in a frenzy of sudden violence as claws
slashed for Graal's head and the General, apparently
frozen to the spot for long moments, moved with a
swift, calculated precision, stepping forward and ducking wild claw swings until he was inches from the
snarling frenzy of bestial deviant vachine, and his slender sword plunged into the canker, plunged deep and
Graal stepped away from slashing, thrashing claws, almost like a dancer twirling away with a stutter of
complex steps. Graal dropped to one knee, and waited.
Nesh, in a frenzy of pain and hate, suddenly decelerated
and its eyes met Graal's as realisation dawned.

"You have killed me," it coughed, and blood poured
from its mouth. It slumped to the ground, more blood-
oil flowing from its throat, and its body slapped the
damp hillside. It grunted, and there came the sounds of
seizing clockwork. Finally, the internal mechanical
whirrings died... and with a twitch, the canker died
with them.

Graal stood, and pulling free a white cloth, cleaned
his narrow black blade. The single cut had disabled the
canker more efficiently than a full platoon of armed albino soldiers. His technique was precise, and deadly. He
turned, and his eyes were narrowed, his face ash.

The Harvester was watching him closely, almost with
interest. "So, the Denizens of Ankarok aided Kell? I find
that... improbable," he said, voice little more than
a whisper.

"I also," snapped Graal, sheathing his sword. "Especially considering the Vampire Warlords slaughtered
them to extinction nearly a thousand years ago!"

CHAPTER 2
A Taste of Desolation

It took Kell and Saark hours to work their way through the narrow tunnels set within the tower block's walls. Despite Kell being broad and bulky, and Saark of a more graceful and athletic persuasion, it was Saark who really suffered – from a psychological perspective. At one point, in a tight space, surrounded by gloom and ancient stone dust that made them cough, Kell paused, Skanda in the distance ahead and below him, climbing over a series of ancient lead pipes as Kell watched; he turned, and stared hard at Saark. Saark said nothing, but a sheen of sweat coated his face, and his eyes were haunted.

"The wound troubling you, lad?" Kell was referring to the stab wound Saark suffered at the hands of Myriam – Myriam, cancer-riddled outcast, thief and vagabond, who had poisoned Kell and kidnapped his granddaughter Nienna with the aim of blackmailing him into travelling north and showing her a route through the Black Pike Mountains. So far, her scheme was working well. And so far, her brass-needle injected poison was failing to worry Kell, for he had more immediate problems; but he knew this situation would soon change. When the poison started to *bite*.

"Aye," said Saark, pausing and wiping sweat from his face with the back of his hand. He left grey streaks across his handsome, indeed, beautiful, features – or they would have been, if he hadn't recently suffered a beating. Still, even with a swollen face he had classical good looks, and once his long, curled, dark hair was washed, and groomed and oiled, and he slipped into some fine silk vests and velvet trews, he would be a new man. Saark touched his side tenderly; Kell's makeshift stitches and tight bandage fashioned from a shirt from a dead albino warrior was as good a battlefield dressing as Saark was going to get. "It's eating me like acid.'

"You should be glad she didn't stab you in the belly," grunted Kell, and looked off, behind Saark, to steep passages *inside the wall* through which they travelled. "Then you'd *really* be suffering, squealing like a spear-stuck pig long into the night."

Saark gave a sour grin. "Thanks for that advice. Helpful."

"Don't mention it."

"That was sarcasm."

"I know."

Saark stared at Kell. "Has anybody ever told you, you're an incorrigible old fart? In fact, worse than a fart, for a fart's stench soon wavers and dissipates; you do not dissipate. Kell, you are the cancerous wart on a whore's diseased quim lips."

Kell shrugged. "Ha, I get abused all the time – only not with your royal-court eloquence. But then," he grinned, showing teeth stained with age, "I reckon we walk in different social circles, lad."

"Yes," agreed Saark. "Mine is one of rich honey wine, clean and succulent women, fine soft silks, the choicest cuts of meat, and gems so sparkling they make your eyes burn."

Kell considered this. He looked around at the dust, the grime, the slime, and the stink of ancient, rotten piping. "I don't see any of that here," he said, voice level. He reached forward, and patted Saark on the shoulder. "Don't worry. We'll be out soon."

"I'm not worried," said Saark, through gritted teeth.

Kell closed his mouth on his next comment; Saark was a proud man, beaten down often in the last few days. What he didn't need was Kell pointing out his obvious claustrophobia. As Kell knew, all men had a secret fear. His? He chuckled to himself. His was the very axe which protected and yet cursed him. Ilanna. His bloodbond.

They moved on, and realised they had lost Skanda in the gloom. They reached a collage of twisted piping, ancient, slime-covered, and after climbing the obstacle, their shoulders barely able to squeeze through the narrow horizontal aperture, they came to a ladder of iron. Kell paused, boots scuffing the edge of what appeared a vast drop. The aperture, between two walls, was barely wide enough for them to descend; add into the equation a wobbling, unsecured ladder, and the descent promised to be particularly treacherous.

"Shall I go first?" said Kell, staring into Saark's open fear.

"Yes. I wouldn't like your pig-lard arse dropping on my head from above. That sort of thing can genuinely ruin a man's day."

"Let's hope I don't get stuck, then." Kell eased himself over the dusty stone, the descent lit by cracks and occasional gaps in the walls; outside, he could see it was growing dark. Kell wondered if the cankers were still waiting. Damn them, he thought. Damn then to Drennach!

The ladder felt sturdy enough under his gnarled hands, and strong fingers grasped narrow rungs as he began to descend. Above, Saark followed, his breathing shallow and fast, his boots kicking dirt over Kell.

"Sorry!" he said.

"Just don't bloody jump," muttered Kell.

They climbed downwards, the ladder shaking and making occasional cracking sounds. After a while, Kell felt a pattering of something dark and wet on his head, and scowling, he looked up to where Saark was fumbling in the mote-filled gloom.

"I hope that's not piss, lad."

"It's blood! The wound has opened. So much for your damn battlefield stitching."

"You're welcome to do it yourself."

"I think next time I will. I can do without a scar that looks like some medical experiment gone wrong. What would the ladies say? I have a perfect torso, fit only for kings, and you would massacre me with your inept needlework."

"Hold a pad to the wound," said Kell, more kindly. "And let's hope you've not infected me with the plague of the popinjay! That's all I need, irrational lust after every young woman that dances by."

They climbed, down and down, for many stories; before they reached the base, Skanda called them from a narrow ledge, which led off between the ancient, crumbling joists of another building. Like rats, they scuttled between the linings of deserted buildings; like cockroaches, they inhabited the spaces between spaces where once life thrived.

For another hour, as darkness fell fast outside, they scrambled through apertures, crawled through dusty tunnels, squeezed through thick pipes containing an ancient residue of oily film, coating their hands with slick gunk, until finally, and thankfully, they emerged from a wide lead pipe which dropped into a swamp. Skanda squatted on the edge of the pipe, watching Kell and Saark drop into the waist-deep slurry, cracking the ice. Then, with the agility of a monkey, Skanda leapt onto Saark's back and clung to the athletic warrior who frowned, and complained, but recognised that to drop Skanda would be to drown the boy. Hardly a fair exchange for saving their lives.

They waded through icy slurry, which stunk of old oil and dead-animal decomposition, despite the cold. They crawled up a muddy bank in darkness and lay on the snow, panting, before Kell hauled himself to his feet and drew his fearsome axe, Ilanna, peering around into the gloom, head tilted, listening.

"Any bad guys, old horse?"

"Don't mock. If a canker bites your arse, it'll be me you come to running to."

"A fair point."

Saark struggled to his feet and stood, hand pressed against his ribs, his slender rapier drawn. He looked down at his fine boots, his once rich trews and silk shirt. He cursed, cursed the destruction of such fine and dandy clothing. "You know something, Kell? Since I met you, I haven't been able to maintain any fine couture whatsoever. It's like you are cursed to dress like the poorest of peasants, and those who accompany you are similarly afflicted by your fashion!"

Kell sighed. "Stop yapping, and let's get away from the city. Believe me, sartorial elegance shouldn't be at the forefront of your mind; getting eaten, now that's what should be bothering you."

They moved away from the crumbling walls of Old Skulkra, away east in a scattering of Blue Spruce woodlands. Finding an old, fallen wall, probably once part of a farm enclosure, Saark built a fire using the remaining stones as shelter, whilst Kell disappeared into the woodland.

"Just like a hero to *fuck off* when there's work to be done," muttered Saark, sourly, as he struggled with damp tinder. Behind him, Skanda scavenged amongst tree roots, puffing and panting, fingers scrabbling at the snow. The noise intruded on Saark's thoughts – fine thoughts, of dancing with leggy blondes at fine regal functions, of eating caviar from wide silver platters, of suckling honey-eyed wine from a puckering quim, lips gleaming, focus more intent than during any act of war – and eventually, Saark whirled about, eyes narrowed, hand clutching his side, and snapped, "What are you doing down there, lad? You are disrupting my heavenly fantasy!"

Skanda held up three onions and a potato. He smiled. "We need to eat, yes? I am an expert at finding food in frozen woodland." The boy's dark eyes glittered. "That is, unless you wish to starve?"

"And what are you going to cook it in?" sneered Saark. "Your bloody knickers?"

Skanda lifted a small ceramic pot. "This," he said, simply.

"Where did you get that?"

"There's a ruined farmhouse, thirty paces yonder."

Saark scowled further. "Then by Dake's Balls, what am I doing starting a fire here? There's no shelter! A farmhouse will give us more shelter! By all the gods, am I surrounded by idiots?"

He explored the ruins, and they *were* ruins: ancient, moss-strewn, the original stones rounded and smoothed by centuries of rain and snow. There was no roof, only stubby walls, but at least a fireplace which shielded Saark's fire from the wind. By the time Kell returned he had a merry blaze going, and he and Skanda had pulled an old log before the flames. Saark sat, boots off, warming his sodden toes. Skanda was peeling vegetables and chopping winter herbs on a slab of stone.

Wary, Kell stepped through a sagging doorway and frowned. "What is this place?"

"It's a brothel," snapped Saark. "What does it look like? Sit ye down, Skanda's making a broth. He found some wholesome vegetables in the woods, although what I'd give for some venison rump and thick meat gravy I couldn't say." He licked his lips, eyes dreamy.

"These should help," said Kell, depositing a hare and two rabbits on the slab of stone.

Saark stared. "How, in the name of the Chaos Halls, did you manage to catch *those* with a bloody axe?"

Kell winked. "It's all in the wrist, boy." He looked to Skanda. "Do you know how to gut and skin?"

"Does a bear shit in the woods?" snapped the young lad, and Kell smiled, moving to Saark.

"He's a cheeky bugger," said Saark.

"He has spirit," said Kell. "I like that. And we owe him our lives."

"But?"

Kell looked at him. "What do you mean?"

"I've known you too long, old horse. There's always a but."

Kell's face hardened. "He's a compromise," said the old warrior, stretching out his legs and resting Ilanna by his side, butterfly blades to the ground, haft within easy reach should he need it; and need *her* killing expertise.

"Meaning?"

"Meaning I have to *prioritise*."

Saark stared at the old man. For a long moment he analysed the grey beard and the dark hair shot through with grey. Kell's face was lined and weather-beaten, appearing older, more worn, than his sixty-two years.

Saark pulled on his boots. He stood. He stared down at Kell. "Explain prioritise?"

"I must rescue Nienna."

"What's that got to do with this boy?" said Saark.

Kell's eyes hardened. He stood, looming over Saark with a sudden, threatening presence. "I will find Nienna. I will kill Myriam – and whoever stands with her. That is it. That is what my life has become. I care nothing for anybody, or anything, else. If you can't stand that," Kell's face curled into a snarl, "well, I understand *your* misunderstanding, dandy. I suggest you go back to whoring and drinking, just like you know best; that is, if you can find a place that'll let you rut and drink. After all, it looks to me like the albinos have slaughtered most of the good people of Falanor."

"Hey!" Saark thumped Kell in the chest, making the big man take a step back. "Just hang on a minute there, Kell. I stood for Nienna, and I stood for you; don't be twisting this situation around, don't be trying to say I'm no good for anything. If it wasn't for me, Nienna would be dead. Horseshit Kell, *you'd* be dead. I have my vices, yes," his face twisted a little, as if he was pained to recall them, "but I know where *my* priorities lie. And if we abandon this boy, he will die."

"Not so."

"You a prophet now, *Legend*?"

Kell's eyes narrowed. "You have been sent to torture me, Saark, I swear. I should have killed you back in Jajor Falls."

"Why didn't you?" It was such an innocent question, it caught Kell off guard. Saark persisted, clutching his side where blood wept through the makeshift packing of torn shirt. "You're the Big Man here, you're the warrior, the hero, the bloody legend of song and dance; you're the man with no conscience, the man of the fucking moment and to the Bone Halls with everybody else! Why am I still here, hey? Why am I still walking by your side? Or have you got a sneaky back-handed death lined up for me, also?"

Kell grabbed Saark's shirt, lifting him from the ground and drawing him in close, until their faces were only inches apart.

"Don't push me."

"Or what'll you do, big man? Stab me in my sleep?"

"Damn you Saark! You twist my mind! You twist my words! Everything with you is fencing, a tactical, verbal puzzle to be negotiated. And I am sick of it!"

"Listen." Saark smoothed down his shirt. "I am with you, Kell. I am not your enemy. I will come with you; we will rescue Nienna, of that I am sure. But don't let panic, don't let blind urgency cloud your vision. This boy here; he is innocent. In fact more; without him, we'd be dead."

"Maybe."

"What?" scoffed Saark. "You think you could take on fifty cankers? You dream, old horse. But what I would say to you is this; I am going for a walk, in the snow, to check our perimeter. I want you to talk to the boy. Find a peace with him – here," he tapped his own skull, "in your head. Because you have a problem, Kell, a serious problem they did not choose to address in your *Saga*."

Saark moved away from the fire, and with drawn rapier, stepped through the leaning doorway and out into the cold, bleak woods. Kell sat down for a while, the only sounds the crackling of the fire and the slithering of Skanda's knife. Eventually, as his temper settled, and recognising some worth in Saark's words, he stood and turned and crossed to Skanda, who was just slicing the final strips of meat and adding them to the broth.

"It will be a fine stew," said the boy.

"It smells good already." Kell's hand was tight on the haft of Ilanna. The axe blades gleamed cold. He was standing before the boy, just to one side, and Skanda was busy, intent on his task. An easy target. An easy death.

No, he thought.

Then: why not?

After all, he had been poisoned, infected by the vile escaped prisoner, Myriam, with the aim of blackmailing him to help her save her own worthless skin. Kell's mission was simple, uncomplicated – ride north, fast, and locate Nienna. His granddaughter had also been poisoned with the same toxin; without Kell's haste, she would die, probably sooner than he for she was young and weak. Despite Kell's age, he was as strong as an ox, he knew. But the problem here lay with Skanda. Kell

knew, deep down, that Saark wouldn't leave the boy
with so many albino soldiers and cankers scouring the
woods looking for them. But the boy would slow Kell
down. In doing so, Nienna might die… so, to his mind,
it was an easy problem to fix.

Kell scratched his beard. He realised Ilanna was still
tight in his fist. Her blades gleamed, catching the light
of the fire.

Another problem, was that if he left the boy behind,
then how long before Graal tortured information from
his spindly limbs? Saark had blabbed enough of the
story to Skanda to make the boy a threat. Which meant
only one course of action.

Kell took a step closer. Still, Skanda did not look up.
His hands moved swiftly, preparing more of the fresh
rabbit meat. The smell made Kell's nose twitch, but his
mind was working fast, one step ahead of something so
simple as animal hunger.

"You seek to rescue your granddaughter?" said
Skanda, looking up suddenly. Kell nodded, and Skanda
lowered his face again. The knife sliced and chopped.

"Yes. She will die without me. She has been poisoned."

"Saark said she was being held at the Cailleach Pass.
That's the road to the Black Pike Mountains, isn't it?"

Kell smiled grimly. Damn you, Saark, he thought.

"Yes," he said, voice barely above a whisper. The fire
crackled. Firelight gleamed in Kell's dark eyes. He no
longer appeared like a hero from legend; now, in this
ruined cottage in the midst of the night, clutching his
possessed axe and eerily silent for such a big man, Kell
was infinitely more intimidating.

"I used to have a grandfather. A lot like you," said
Skanda, innocently, oblivious to the threat which lay

within inches, within heartbeats, of his delicate and fragile existence. "He died though, a long time ago. I thought he was as strong as ten men, but age wore him down in the end until his mind snapped, and he could no longer speak. He used to sit by the fire, rocking, dribbling, and this was the man who took on a hundred of the enemy at Tellakon Gate. A tragedy."

"A tragedy," agreed Kell, voice low, and shifted his stance a little to the left, to give him better clearance for the strike. Kell licked his lips. He would kill the boy. Decapitate him. It would be clean. It would be quick. And much more humane than leaving the child to be slaughtered by the cankers… eaten alive, in fact.

Kell gripped his axe tight. His eyes went hard. He lifted Ilanna into the air. Firelight gleamed from her butterfly blades. Kell relaxed, and readied himself for the strike…

Saark moved around the perimeter of their camp like a spirit, halting occasionally to listen. The fall of snow acted as a natural muffler, but was dangerous for it hid fragile twigs and obstacles that might give away Saark's position. Still, he edged around a wide perimeter, eyes and ears alert, slender rapier in one chilled hand, and thinking hard on the problem of Falanor.

General Graal had invaded. There had been no demands. Just slaughter.

Why? What did he want?

Saark mulled over the problem as he scouted, crouching occasionally. At one point he saw an owl, high in a tree, its huge yellow orbs surveying a world which appeared, Saark was sure, as bright as daylight to the savage, nocturnal hunting bird.

Saark's mind drifted to Kell. He turned, to where he knew the ruined cottage lay. He considered Kell's motives, and thought of Nienna, but when he thought of her it made him think of Kat, and that was too painful a memory.

Only days earlier, in their pursuit to warn King Leanoric of the impending invasion of albino soldiers led by General Graal, Kell and his companions – Saark, Nienna and Nienna's best friend, Katrina, with her short, wild red hair and topaz eyes, athletic and feisty despite her youth – were riding out a snowstorm in a deserted barracks when three dangerous brigands entered. Myriam, tall, wiry, strong, short black hair and rough, gaunt features, her eyes a little sunken, her flesh a little stretched from the cancer that was eating her from the inside out. Along with her, two companions: Styx, an inexorably ugly Blacklipper smuggler with only one eye and black lips, and Jex, small and permanently angry, with a tattooed face and the physique of a pugilist.

Myriam had injected Kell and Nienna with poison, and Styx had murdered Katrina using a clockwork-powered *Widowmaker* mini-crossbow. They kidnapped Nienna during the Army of Iron's attack on King Leanoric's forces.

Kat. Murdered. Dead.

Even now, Saark brushed away a tear, and felt guilt and shame well within him. He had loved Katrina, which was ridiculous, even Saark had to admit. He was not just a dandy and popinjay, he was, even at his own admittance, one of the world's best seducers of women. He knew how they worked, how their minds operated, which dials to turn, which switches to flick, how to speak and lick and kiss and caress, and his beauty had brought him scores of lovers, many a cuckold, and so to fall in love with a seventeen year-old university student was simply *bizarre*. Ridiculous in the extreme. He told himself over and over that was not what happened; that it had been a simple tactic on his part to persuade Katrina to give away that most sought after prize, her virginity… but even Saark did not believe his own lie.

And Saark had had the chance to kill her murderer.

And failed.

Bitterly now, Saark smiled. The wounds were still fresh. The hate was still bright. He would have his day with Styx, Saark knew; one way or another, in this world or in the next. He would cut the fucker in two, and drink his blood, and toast Kat's shade towards the Hall of Heroes.

Saark stopped. Orientated himself. He had been drifting. Dreaming. He winced, clutching the pad at his side. It was still warm, and blood still leaked. Maybe he was weak from blood loss? And the recent beatings?

Saark scowled. And thought of Kell. And a sudden dark premonition swept through him.

No. Saark shook his head. Not even Kell would kill a child. Not in cold blood. Surely?

Saark's eyes narrowed.

Could he?

Flitting embers from snatches of story pierced Saark's mind. Snippets of late drinking songs, when the candles were trimmed low and coals glowed dark in the tavern's hearth. The bard would lower his voice, fingers flickering gently over lyre strings as he recounted the Days of Blood, and the atrocities that occurred therein…

All speculation, of course. Nobody knew what *really* happened all those years ago; no soldier had ever spoken of it. Those that still lived, of course, for most survivors had taken their own lives.

Kell, however… he had *been* there. He had told Saark, although Saark was sure Kell didn't recall uttering the words. However, Saark still remembered the look in Kell's eyes.

"I was a bad man, Saark. An evil man. I blamed the whiskey, for so long I blamed the whiskey, but one day I came to realise that it simply masked that which I was. I try, Saark. I try so hard to be a good man. I try so hard to do the right thing. But it doesn't always work. Deep down inside, at a basic level, I'm simply not a good person." And then, later, as Saark was sure Kell was falling into a pit of insanity… *"Look at the state of me, Saark. Just like the old days. The Days of Blood."*

The Days of Blood. The day when an entire *army* went berserk. Insane, it was said. They killed men, women, children, torched houses, slaughtered cattle, torched people in their beds and… much worse. Or so it was said. So the dark songs recounted. And Saark knew Kell didn't have the necessary streak of evil to murder a child he thought might hold him back; and in so doing, be responsible for the death of his granddaughter, the only creature he loved on earth.

"Horseshit," he muttered.

Saark limped back towards the ruined cottage, cursing his stupidity and chewing at his lip.

Saark burst through the listing doorway, eyes drawn immediately to the crackling fire which danced bright after the gloom of the snowy woodland. There was no sign of Kell. Nor Skanda.

"Son of a bastard's mule!" snapped Saark, and heard a grunt. He peered into the gloomy interior, and the darkness rearranged itself into shapes. Skanda was sat, almost hidden, stirring his ceramic pot of broth.

"Are you well?" said Skanda, almost sleepily.

"Yes, yes!" Saark strode forward, and sat on the log. He kicked off his boots and stretched out his feet, warming his toes. "Where's Kell? Don't tell me. The grumpy old weasel has gone for a shit in the woods."

Skanda giggled, and appeared for once his age. "I think you might be right."

Saark peered close. "Seriously. Are you all right, boy? For a minute, back there, I had the craziest notion that Kell might… well, that he might…"

Skanda looked suddenly wise beyond eternity. "Let us say," whispered the boy, staring into the fire, "that Kell made the right choice."

There came a crack, and Kell grinned at Saark from the doorway. "Thought you'd got lost out there, lad. Hugging the trees, were you? Digging in the dirt for more dirt? Or just having bad dreams about noble and heroic old Kell, the man of the Legend." Kell grinned, and although the destroyed cottage had little light, ambient or otherwise, Saark could have sworn Kell displayed *no* humour.

"We're safe, for now," said Saark. "No sounds of cankers, no soldiers, no pursuit."

Kell moved close. "Well don't get too comfy, lad. We eat, then we move."

"We'll freeze!"

"Freeze or die here," said Kell. "Because I'm telling you, it's only a matter of time before that bastard Graal sends someone…" his smile widened, "or some *thing*, after us."

"And the boy?"

Kell could read the pain in Saark's eyes. He sighed, and ran a hand through his thick, grey-streaked hair. "The boy can come with us. But I'm warning you, if he gets in the way, or either of you slow me down, then I'll cut you *both* loose."

"You think you can travel faster than I?" stammered Saark. "Man, I'm damn near *thirty* years your junior!"

Kell leered close. "I know I can, lad. Now get some warm food inside you. We've got a long, hard journey ahead."

They moved through the woodland and as dawn broke, wintry tendrils streaking through heavy cloud cover, so the distant walls of Old Skulkra could still be seen.

Saark called a halt, and gestured to Kell. Kell moved close, axe in fist, eyes brooding. "What is it?"

Saark pointed. Distantly, the Blood Refineries squatted on the plain like obscene bone dice tossed by the gods. "I have it in my mind to do some research," said Saark, voice soft, eyes bright. "And maybe some damage! Those machines are here for no good."

"I know what they are," said Kell.

"You do? How is that… possible?"

Kell smiled grimly. "I have seen them in action. In another time. Another place. Let's just say, Saark, that to go chasing them now to satisfy your curiosity would end badly for all of us."

"We need to know what we're fighting!"

"So, lad, now we have gone to war?" Kell smiled, but there was no mockery in his tone. If anything, he valued Saark's spirit; especially after they had been through so much.

"They brought war and chaos to Falanor. I would like to return the favour with the blade of my sword."

"A task for another day."

"You would save Nienna over Falanor?"

"I would save her over the world," rumbled Kell. Seeing the look of incredulity in Saark's face, Kell shrugged and said, "Let me quantify it thus – Graal and his soldiers are searching for us, all of us. And those Blood Refineries are their *life-blood*. They will be guarded more heavily than any sparkling gems, than any royal blood. To go there, Saark, is folly. And what would you do? Gather information? For whom? Which army will use your military intelligence? No, Saark, we must travel north. When I have Nienna, when I hold her safe in my arms, then we will turn our gaze on Graal and these white-skinned bastards."

Saark considered this. "That could, taken the wrong way, look simply like you're putting your own needs first."

"Maybe I am, lad, maybe I am. But without me, you'll never conquer these bastards. I am your lynch pin. And I have been poisoned, and even as we stand debating what to do, the toxic venom pulses through my veins. Or had you forgotten this? Without me, you will fail."

"Your arrogance astounds me."

"It is the truth."

Saark sighed, and turned his back on the giant, distant machines. "You say you have seen these Refineries working. I assume they do not bode well for the people of Falanor?"

"The battle was horrific, yes? Leanoric's slaughter devastating?"

"Yes."

"The battle was just a prologue for what is to come. Trust me, Saark, when I say we need to use cunning, use our brains; charging back into that enemy camp is the last thing we should do."

"You will not?"

"I will not. But I admire your bravado, lad. Come. We will head north. This is a battle for another day."

Saark hung his head, and they moved back into heavy woodland, tracking along in parallel with the Great North Road.

They walked all day, and Kell muttered about pains in his knees. The landscape was beautiful, with hidden hollows filled with virgin snow, woodland branches, stark and bare, pointing white-peppered fingers at the bleak, blue-grey sky. Heavy swathes of conifer forest clutched the contours of the land like a lover. Streams lay frozen like snakes of diamond. The air was crisp, cold and fresh.

Kell marched ahead often, eyes scanning the landscape for signs of enemy activity. At every hilltop he would drop and approach on his belly, so as not to silhouette himself to scouts. His keen eyes tracked the lay of the land, the contours of forest and river, of hillside and mossy nooks, of boulder fields and silent farmhouses.

At one point before midday Kell spent a full half hour watching a farmhouse; no smoke curled from the chimney, and there was no sign of life. They approached warily, driven by hunger and cold, to find the farm hastily abandoned. As they walked across a cobbled yard chickens clucked in a nearby coop. Kell gestured.

"Kill them, and bag them up. Fresh meat will do us the world of good."

Saark stared at Kell's back. "What?"

Kell stopped, and turned. "Kill the chickens. I will find us furs, woollen cloaks, dried beef. Go on, lad."

"You kill the chickens," snapped Saark.

"Is there a problem here?"

"Only peasants kill chickens! I am used to *my* fresh meat served on silver platters, garnished with butter, herbs and new potatoes, a little salt, not too much pepper, and brought to me by a plump serving wench with breasts bigger than the bloody bird she's serving!"

Kell stared hard at Saark; the swelling in his beaten face had subsided, but he was still bruised, his lips cut, his skin scratched, and he looked a thousand leagues from the well-dressed dandy Kell had met in the tannery back in Jalder. "Well," said Kell, considering his position, "here, and now Saark, you're a peasant. You look like a peasant, and you stink like a peasant. So kill the damn chickens."

"I will not kill the chickens. I am no serf!"

'You will kill the chickens or go hungry," snapped Kell, and stormed off into the farmhouse, kicking open the door and leading the way with the gleaming blades of his axe.

Saark stood for a moment, staring at the empty doorway and muttering curses. A hand touched him lightly on the arm, and Skanda grinned up at him. "It's all right, Pretty One, I'll kill them. Despite my appearance, I have a talent for it."

"Are you sure?" muttered Saark, eyes dark, lips pouting.

"Leave it to me." Skanda carried a rough bronze dagger, which he placed carefully between his teeth. He moved towards the coop and the clucking hens within.

"I'll just… find some firewood. Or something." Saark waved to Skanda, then turned and started rooting around. "What we really need are horses," he said, and crossed to the stables, knowing there would be no beasts there – in times of flight, who would leave a horse? – but willing to search all the same. As he approached, the stables were dark, and silent. Rubbing his chin, he threw open the doors to reveal a total lack of thoroughbred stallion. "Hmm," he muttered, cursing his luck. Would it have hurt, for just this once, to give them a bit of good fortune? For a change? Instead of the gods throwing soldiers and deranged creatures into the battle at every damn pissing turn?

Saark turned, leant his back against the stable door, and heard a strangled *cluck*. He winced. He had been truthful, in that his food *was* normally served on a silver platter by a wench whose breasts would suffocate three men, never mind one; but the reality of the matter, and something that shamed him, was that his life of high society had ill-prepared him for chicken slaughter. He had no idea how one slaughtered a chicken; nor any inclination to find out.

Another deranged *cluck* emerged from the coop, and Saark winced again, almost in sympathy. A sympathy overwhelmed only by his ravenous hunger. Then, suddenly, behind him something went *clack* in the gloom of the dingy stable interior. He whirled about, slim rapier drawn, eyes narrowed.

"Is there somebody there?" he snapped. "Show yourself! Don't make me come in there after you!"

Nothing. No reply. No movement. No sound.

Saark glanced back to the farmhouse, but there was no sign of Kell, and anyway, Saark resented being made to look a fool over something as ridiculous as the murder of a chicken. He pushed into the stable and lowered his head, as if this movement might somehow aid his night vision. He walked along the stalls, nose wrinkled at the stench of old dung and damp straw. The place reeked as bad as a rancid corpse. "Come out, now, before I lose my temper!" he said, voice raised, and as he neared the end stall he slowed his pace. Whoever it was, they had to be in there.

Saark leapt the last few feet, rapier outstretched, and blinked. There, huddled in the stall, was a donkey.

Saark and the donkey stared at one another for a while, and Saark finally relaxed. The donkey gave a husky bray, and tilted its head, observing the tall, lithe swordsman.

"Damn it, they left you! You poor little thing." Saark opened the door, and finding a lead on the wall, spent several minutes attaching a halter and then leading the donkey out through the stables. Kell was just appearing from the farmhouse with a collection of items wrapped in a blanket as Saark emerged into wintry sunlight.

They both stopped, staring at one another.

"You found a donkey. Well done," said Kell.

"The miserable whoresons left her! What a horrible thing to do; they could have at least set her free. Well, she can come with us, carry our provisions. I'm sure I saw a basket somewhere."

"Well," said Kell, thoughtfully, dumping the blanket on the snow-peppered ground. "I've certainly no objections to taking a donkey with us. It's a long journey, and many a donkey has surely proved its worth during my lifetime."

"Good," said Saark, rubbing the donkey's muzzle. "I think this beast has had enough mistreatment for one year."

"Yes. And I reckon there's good eating on a donkey," said Kell.

There came a long pause. "So, you'd eat the donkey?" Saark said.

"Saark, if I was starving lad, I'd eat your very arse cheeks. Now get this stuff in the basket. Did you kill those chickens?"

Skanda emerged at that moment with five birds tied together by the throat. He handed them to Kell, who took the dead chickens and glanced sideways at Saark.

"What?" snapped the swordsman.

"For shame, Saark. Getting the boy to do a man's job. *Your* job, in fact. You!"

"He offered," said Saark, miserably, and returned to the stables to find the basket.

They moved fast for the rest of the day, only stopping early evening to have a cold meal of dried beef and hard oatcakes. Saark led the donkey, which he'd named *Mary* – to a rising of Kell's eyebrows, and an unreadable expression. Saark shrugged off the implied criticism, and walked slightly ahead of the group. But on one thing they all agreed. Mary did indeed lighten their load, and the farmhouse had been a store of many provisions, from bread, cheese, a side of ham, dried beef, oats, sugar and salt, and even a little chocolate. Kell found a bottle of unlabelled whiskey, which he stowed deep in the basket. He thought it best not to let Saark know, for the last time Kell drank an excess of whiskey it had ended in a savage brawl, with Saark taking a beating under Kell's mighty fists. But, obviously, Kell had no intentions of drinking any whiskey now. He was off the whiskey. It was for medicinal purposes only, he convinced himself.

The sky stretched out, streaked with grey and black. What blue remained was thin, like a bleak watercolour portrait, and just as night began to fall they breached a hill and Kell pointed to a long, low, abandoned building made of black bricks. It had several squat chimneys, and by its overgrown look, gates hanging off hinges, missing bricks and smashed windows, had been empty for a considerable amount of time.

"You knew this was here?" said Saark.

"Aye," nodded Kell. "Camped here a few times. It's an old armoury; rumoured, or so I've heard it told, to have made the finest weapons, helmets and breast-plates in Falanor!"

"Safe?"

"As safe as anywhere else during the invasion of a wicked enemy army. I'll scout ahead, you wait here with, ahh, Mary."

Saark watched Kell descend a steep bank of tangled branches smothered in snow. The huge warrior stopped at the bottom, scanning, searching for footprints. Then, wary and with Ilanna drawn, he disappeared from view. He returned a few minutes later and waved them down, and both Saark and Skanda were more than happy to leave the biting chill of the wind behind. Despite new woollen jackets and leather-lined cloaks from the farm-house, the cold still crept easily through to the depths of their bones. Falanor in winter was not the best place to travel, nor camp.

They slid down the snowy hill, the donkey's hooves digging in deep, and Saark tied Mary up outside the de-serted armoury and ducked through the doorway, closely followed by Skanda.

Kell stood, hands on hips, looking around. They were

in a huge, long, low-ceilinged workshop; benches lined the walls, set out in L-shapes at regular intervals, perhaps fifty in all stretching off into the gloom. Also ranged around the black, fire-damaged walls were curious iron ovens, and other machines with handles and tubes and strange gears, all black iron, many now rusted into solid blocks.

"Been empty a while," said Saark, whispering, but not realising why he whispered.

"Aye," nodded Kell. "Come on, it's too cold in this room, but there's lots of side rooms. I think this place has been used by travellers for nearly two decades now. Hopefully, somebody has laid a fire."

Saark and Skanda followed Kell through the huge chamber, and their eyes wandered to abandoned benches where ancient tools rested on work surfaces. "It's like they left in a hurry," said Saark, eyes following contours of rusted tools. There were hammers and tongs, files and pincers, and other tools in curious shapes Saark had never before seen; but then, he was a swordsman, not an armourer.

Kell approached one room to the side; the door closed, and he suddenly stopped. He turned and stared at Saark, features hidden in the gloom; then he seemed to win some internal debate, and stepped forward, pushing open the door–

The black longsword slashed for his throat and Kell swayed back with incredible speed, axe slamming up, the spike at its tip carving a long groove of channelled flesh up the albino soldier's face. His chin and nose disappeared like molten wax in a spray of milk white blood, and he screamed, and Kell brought back his gleaming axe, eyes narrowed, and yelled, "It's a trap!

They saw us coming! Be ready!" He stepped forward with a mighty swing, halving the soldier's head, and then turning his back on the small room.

"They?" said Saark, drawing his slender rapier, and gaped with open flapping mouth as a flood of albino warriors raced through the gloomy old armoury; there were no war cries, no shouts, no screams of battle; only an eerie silence and thudding of boots.

A soldier fell on Saark and he parried the blow with a clash of steel, batting the ineffectual sword strike aside and drawing his blade across the man's throat. Flesh opened, parted, without blood – like slicing the throat of a corpse, thought Saark sourly – but all other images were slammed from him at the sheer number of soldiers in the armoury. Kell had been right, it was a set-up, a trap; they'd been waiting. Saark parried another blow, slammed his blade back in a shower of sparks, and exchanged several strikes before piercing his blade through the soldier's eye. Beside him, Kell's axe swung, but was hampered by the close confines fighting. He glimpsed the great blades behead an albino in a flail of long hair and gristle, and Saark *shifted* as the great Ilanna hummed past his own face.

'Kell!' screamed Saark, his face thunder, and he skipped to the side to give the old man more killing space. He spun low under a warrior's blade, and shoved his own sword up, brutally, into the soldier's groin. The albino screamed and fell, slipping on his own unspooling entrails, and Saark spun to shout at Skanda to run – but the boy had vanished. Good, breathed Saark as he prepared himself. The armoury was full of the enemy, so many he couldn't count them; what had it been? A platoon? Twenty men? Or… Saark paled, even in the gloom. If a company waited, there'd be damn near a hundred soldiers. And even Kell could not battle such odds.

There were seven down, now, and outside the sun dipped below the horizon. Darkness flooded the room. Swords gleamed. Boots stamped. The only light was a surreal glow, the sun's dying rays reflected off smashed glass; more soldiers ran at Kell and Saark, and the men defended themselves with skill, sword and axe rising and falling, deflecting blades and cutting into flesh with savage, sodden *thumps*. More albino warriors fell, and Kell slapped Saark's shoulder and pointed. They backed away across the chamber, only to hear boots thudding outside a short corridor. They were surrounded! Saark tasted fear. At the end of the day Saark was a swordsman, and an incredibly skilled one – once, he had been the King's Sword Champion, and although Saark had fought in battles before, he much preferred the consummate test of skill during one-on-one combat. In war, he hated the randomness, the chaos, the unpredictability; the threat of an axe in the back of the head when you least expected it. No, for Saark the honour and prestige was in single combat – where the victor took the spoils, wine, gold, women. But here, now... this was fast turning into a charnel house. It was out of control.

The soldiers hung back, wary. Saark could just make out their ghost-white faces in the gloom. He reckoned on about thirty, but that didn't include those coming round behind.

Thirty! If Kell and Saark had been caught on open ground, they would have been slaughtered. Surrounded and butchered like dogs. But the albino soldiers, perhaps knowing the inherent skill of their quarries, had sought subterfuge and covert attack; this had backfired, for close quarters combat meant Saark and Kell could fight a tight battle and not easily be surrounded.

"They're coming in," snapped Kell through gritted teeth. His face and beard were covered once more in blood and gore, only this time white, and glistening in what little ambient light remained. Ilanna filled his terrible hands, the edges of the butterfly blades glimmering. "You cover this side, I'll–" but his words were left unfinished, as a *blast* of blackness, of energy, a series of pulses in concentric circles like the spreading ripples in a lake after heavy impact cannoned through the confines of the armoury, and Kell and Saark were picked up amidst a surging charge of debris, old hammers, bits of battered armour, tools and dirt and even an anvil, and they seemed to hang for a moment before being accelerated in a swirling chaos across the room to hit the wall. Saark felt like his head was turned inside out, his teeth rattled in his skull, strings of bowels ripped out through his arse-hole. Kell groaned, and staggered to his feet with blood pouring from his nose. He lifted Ilanna, teeth grinding as the wall of albinos advanced… and at their core there was a tiny, ragged albino woman, with straggly white hair and bright crimson eyes and a face that was ancient, and lined, and haggard, and Kell knew upon what he looked for this *this* was an albino *shamathe*, a dreaded white magicker, and Kell shook his head and knew he had to kill her fast and put her down *in an instant* for her magick was awesome, potent, a product of earth and fire and blood and raw wild dark energy–

Ilanna slammed up, blades gleaming, but the second energy impact picked Kell up and pulped him against the wall, where the entire brickwork buckled and collapsed outwards in a shower of rubble and dust and broken beams. The armoury croaked and sagged, walls groaning, and Kell was half-buried under a pile of bricks as the air around him and an unconscious Saark rippled and surged and then was seemingly *sucked* back into normality like a rubber band returning to its original shape.

The albino shamathe cackled, and capered forward like a jester, but a tall soldier stepped to the fore, placed a hand on her cavorting shoulder and calmed the witch. "Well done, Lilliath," he spoke, words gentle, and drew a long black blade. "But… I will finish this." Lilliath nodded, hair wild and wavering.

Jekkron, tall, elegant, a warrior born, loomed over Kell who was groaning, eyelids fluttering. The old soldier had lost his axe amidst bricks and snapped timber joists. He opened his dust-smarting eyes and snarled through bloodied teeth but the albino smiled, and gave a single nod of understanding; his black sword lifted high, then hacked down at Kell's throat.

CHAPTER 3
Clockwork Engine

"So, he has betrayed us?"

Silence echoed around the Vachine High Engineer Council. The two Watchmakers present squirmed uneasily, for this entire concept was anathema to everything in which they believed, and aspired.

"That's impossible."

"Why impossible? A canker, by definition, should be impossible. We are the Higher Race, the Blessed; we are at the pinnacle of flesh and technological evolution. What then is a canker? A mockery of our genetics, a mockery of our humanity, a mockery of our vachine status. The vachine should be perfect; the cankers remind us we are not. How, then, can it be construed that Graal's betrayal is an impossibility?"

Another voice. Old. Revered. Serious. "He has served us for a thousand years. You... *young* vachine do not understand what General Graal has done for us. Without him, and without the work of Kradek-ka, we would never have achieved such an exalted state; we would never have reached our current evolutionary curve, plane, and High Altar. Graal accelerated our species.

Without him our race would be dead."

Silence met this statement. Great minds contemplated the implications of their discussion.

A voice spoke. It was young, nervous, a chattering of sparrows next to the wisdom of the owl. "The clockwork is all wrong," said the voice.

"Meaning?"

"The algorithms... they tell of the Axeman."

"What is this *Axeman*?"

"The Black Axeman of Drennach."

Again, another pause. Around the table, some of the elder vachine lit pipes and puffed on smoke laced with the heady narcotic, blood-oil. A silence descended. Several elder vachine exchanged glances.

"The clockwork engines are never specific, but they speak of a terrible killer, an axeman named Kell – but is he friend or foe? The machines will not say. They just bring up his name again, and again, and again."

"We must assume he is the enemy. Every other human to set foot in Silva Valley has had nothing but evil and destruction in their corrupt and festering hearts."

"Is that not to be expected?"

"Meaning?"

"We *feed* on them; they are like cattle to us."

"Still, we must assume this *Black Axeman* is evil, a scourge to our kind. But then, we are straying from the real problem here; that of General Graal, and what he is doing with our Army of Iron."

Silence greeted this.

"Has the report come back, yet? From Princess Jaranis?"

"There has been no communication; nothing."

This was considered. Digested. And then one of the Watchmakers stood; in the structure of the vachine

religion, only the Patriarch ruled over the Watchmakers, and the Watchmakers were few enough now to
make their rank a dying breed – only five of them left.
General Graal was Watchmaker; this was the element
of their new information which made the High Council
so nervous. Nobody wished to sound like a Heretic; nobody wished their clockwork poisoned, their flesh to be
torn and twisted forcibly into *canker*.

She was called Sa, small of stature, but with flashing,
dangerous eyes. To cross Sa was to be exterminated.
"We have little evidence," she said, voice smooth, eyes
fixing on every member of the Engineer Council in
turn. She walked around the outside of the huge oval
steel table, and stopped at the head where once, in good
health, the Patriarch would have sat; today, as on many
days, he was confined to his bed. It was rumoured he
coughed up blood-oil, and his days were numbered.
"We cannot simply condemn General Graal in his ab-
sence; he should be able to defend himself against the
diabolical accusations that have taken place over this
table. What is happening here?" Her eyes glowed. "We
used to be *united*. Now, we are crumbling. We will ad-
journ, and no more will be spoken on this matter until
Graal returns in the spring after Snowmelt. Is this agreed?"

There came a murmur of agreement, and the Engineer Council disbanded, the hundred or so members
flooding out into the warren of the Engineer's Palace,
and beyond, to Silva Valley. Finally, only Sa and Tagor-
tel, another esteemed vachine Watchmaker, were left.
Their eyes met, like old lovers on a secret tryst.

"I don't think it will be enough," said Tagor-tel. "I do
not trust the old General. And… isn't that why Jaranis
was despatched? To keep an eye on proceedings?"

"The weather is against her."

"Convenient. For Graal."

Sa puckered her lips, brooding. "I, also, have noticed *changes* in Graal. However, I do not see how one man could be a threat to the High Engineer Episcopate. To the Vachine Civilisation! Even *with* our obedient Army of Iron under his direct control. What would he do? Turn them against us?" She laughed, a sound of spinning flywheels.

Tagor-tel shrugged. "I doubt he would have the *persuasion*. The alshina have served for too long." He thought for a moment. "We need to discover what happened to Jaranis. She had the Warrior Engineers, did she not? Walgrishnacht? He is one of our ultimate soldiers. If anybody will return word, he will."

"We will see. But let us assume, for a moment – away from concepts of heresy – that Princess Jaranis has failed. That she and her entourage are *dead*. What then?"

"We can ask…" Tagor-tel paused, and checked the chamber, making sure they were alone. His voice dropped. "Fiddion."

"You think he will cooperate?"

"He has, shall we say, *passed* us sensitive information before. Graal seems to have some bond with the Harvesters; and the Harvesters play by their own rules. It is worth a try. For whatever reason, Fiddion despises his own kind."

"Do it. Contact Fiddion. Let us see if the Harvesters know what Graal plots."

Sunlight glimmered between towering storm clouds, rays of weak yellow that cast long, eerie shadows over the forests surrounding Old Skulkra. Graal strode through the camp, trailed by three Harvesters, one hand on his sword hilt, his pale-skinned face unreadable. Albino soldiers moved from his path, and he stopped only once, head turning left, as the snarls from the canker cages set his teeth on edge. Damn them, he thought. Damn their perverse twisted flesh! They reminded him, painfully, of his brother. Dead, now. Murdered, so he later discovered, by the bastard Kell and his bloodbond axe. "I'll see you burn, motherfucker," he muttered as he continued through the camp and reached the edge of the tents where albino soldiers still had campfires burning.

Several soldiers looked up at his approach, glances subservient, as if waiting for instruction. Graal did not acknowledge their existence. Instead, his eyes were fixed on the three huge black towers which sat on the plain: angular, cubic, squat, their surfaces matt black, their intentions not immediately fathomable.

"Are we ready?" said Graal.

"We are ready," hissed one of the Harvesters, sibilantly.

"Is he here?"

"He is here, General Graal."

"Good. It is about time."

Graal strode out across the plain, and the closer he moved to the Blood Refineries, the larger they seemed: mammoth cubic structures, the black surface of unmarked walls flat, and dull, like scorched iron. Wisps of snow snapped in the air as Graal strode across frozen earth, and as he came near his nose wrinkled. He blinked. The corpses, four thousand in total, stripped of armour and boots, had been laid out in rows before the three Blood Refineries. Graal glanced down, but no flicker of emotion showed across his pale face. He had more important matters on which to worry.

The Refineries towered, and he walked in their shadow. There was a man, tall and lean and bearded, reclining against the first Refinery. Graal reached him and stopped. This was Viga, Kradek-ka's personal Engineer Assistant, come to oversee the Blood Refineries and their absorption. He had travelled all the way from the Black Pike Mountains to help.

"Well met, Graal," said the man, eyes glittering, and Graal could just distinguish tiny vachine fangs, like polished brass, peeking over his bottom lip.

"I thought you would never come," said Graal, fighting hard to keep his annoyance in check. He was not used to being treated so... casually. "Was the journey difficult?"

"More difficult than you could comprehend," said Viga, rubbing at his beard. "Although I hear you suffered some disturbance yourself; something to do with an old, bearded soldier? A resident of Jalder, or so I was informed."

Graal forced a smile. "A nothing," he said. The Harvesters were watching him, waiting for his command; as if waving away an insect, he gave instruction, and the Harvesters started to lift the half-frozen corpses and feed them into long, thin slots at the base of the Refineries. It took very little effort: the instant a body touched the slot, it was sucked inside. A deep thrumming seemed to well up beneath the ground, and Graal fancied he could sense, if not necessarily *hear*, the huge but subtle clockwork engines within the Blood Refineries; mashing up bodies, extracting blood, and refining it into blood-oil: the food of the vachine world.

The bearded man turned, and watched for a while. Then he tutted. Graal stared into his eyes, and the man lowered his head.

"There is a problem?"

"Kradek-ka's daughter."

"She was always a problem."

"Do not be *flippant* with me, Graal; you know her existence is the reason you stand here now, you know the experimentation Kradek-ka performed on her was the central reason why we can *do this*; without her, without Anukis and her," he laughed, "her *jewel*, there would be no quest for Kuradek, Meshwar and Bhu Vanesh."

"You are of course, correct," said Graal, and straightened his back. Beside them, the Harvesters continued to pick up corpses and feed them into the Refineries. Deep inside, now, the meshing of gears could be heard; and huge pendulous blades working.

Graal glanced up, at the towering wall of the Refinery, and then back to Viga. He reached out to place a comforting hand on his arm, but the man recoiled.

"No. You must not touch me. I am impure!"

"We are all impure," said Graal, head tilting a little; he could see, now, that the man before him was a man ready to crack, a vachine teetering along a blade-edge of insanity.

"We should never have treated her like that. It was wrong of us to push her; to humiliate her!"

"It is too late for regret," said Graal, voice steady.

"Not so! She has escaped, gone looking for her father! Nobody should have undergone such humiliation!"

"Well, she will save us the quest," said Graal, voice hard now. This man's weakness was starting to upset him. He had great respect for Viga, especially as Kradek-ka's most trusted Engineer servant; but to whine thus? To whine was to be weak; and Graal so *hated* the weak. He placed his hand on sword-hilt.

"This whole situation is an abomination," continued Viga.

Graal drew his sword, and shook his head, and stepped close to the man and the blade touched his throat, cold black steel pressing flesh and his fangs ejected, suddenly, with a hiss of fury but Graal leant on the blade and blood bubbled along the razor edge and he felt Viga relax beside him. "It is too late to back out now," said Graal, voice little more than a whisper.

"I know that. It's just... she was an innocent vachine! We ruined her life!"

"She is in the past..." said Graal. "So be silent, and be still, and be calm; the Refineries must work, and we must build the store of energy... of magick! Only with the Refineries at optimum power can we bring about the return of the Vampire Warlords!"

"But you do not have the Soul Gems," whimpered Viga, from behind Graal's blade.

"I am working on it," growled Graal, and sheathed his weapon.

Viga had gone. Graal sat on the ground, cross-legged, and watched as the last of the bodies was fed into the huge machines. He looked around, as flakes of falling snow whipped back and forth in the wind. The distance was hazy, just like Graal's memory.

In silence, the last of the Falanor corpses were fed into metal holes. Then the Harvesters did a strange thing. They moved, each to their own Blood Refinery, and they spread arms and legs wide and shuffled forward towards blank metal walls – so they were stark contrasts illuminated against wide plates of iron. And then they – *merged*, sinking into the metal of the

Refineries, becoming for a moment at one with the machines as flesh became metal and iron became flesh,
and Graal blinked, licking his lips, nervous for just an
instant – not nervous of pain or mutilation or death,
even his own death, but nervous in case it *did not work*.
Graal blinked, and the Harvesters were gone; absorbed
into the machines. Distantly, he could hear a tick, tick,
tick, as of huge, pendulous clockwork.

He smiled grimly. They called it Interface. Where the
Harvesters used special ancient magick to refine blood,
into that chemical agent the vachine craved, and indeed
needed, to survive.

Blood-oil. The currency of their Age.

Graal sat, grimly, thinking about Kradek-ka. The vachine was a genius, no doubt; he had helped usher in
the civilisation and society they now enjoyed. However,
he was unpredictable, and a little insane. And his
daughter was another problem entirely. Graal's face
locked. She was yet just another problem he would
have to face.

General Graal sighed, and sat staring at the exhaust
pipes on one of the Refineries; slowly, the pipes oozed
trickles of pulped flesh to the snowy ground. Graal
brooded, waiting for his Harvesters to return.

If only all life was as simple as war, he thought.

When the Vampire Warlords return, there will be
more war. He smiled at that, and dreamed of his childhood… over distant millennia.

They called him Graverobber, and he lived amidst the
towering circle of stones at Le'annath Moorkelth… The
Passing Place. The name, and nature, of the stones had
long since been lost to the humans who inhabited the

land, with their curious ways and basic weaponry. But the Graverobber knew; he had researched, and learned, and been privy to a knowledge older than man or vachine.

He sat, squatting at the centre of the stone circle, watching the snow falling around the outskirts. He loved the winter, the cold, the snow, the ice, the death.

He looked down at himself, analysing his body in wonder. This is what he always did. This is what made him what he was. Narcissistic was not something in the Graverobber's lexicon, but had it been there he would have agreed; for the Graverobber loved himself, or rather, he loved what he had *become*. What had been made of him, by the Hexel Spiders, over a long, long, long period of time… a journey so long, so arduous, so painful, he no longer remembered the beginning. Now, only now, he knew that he was nearing the end.

Jageraw looked down at himself, at his twisted, corrugated body, his skin a shiny, ceramic black like the chitin of the spider, *the spider I tell you – can you smell the hemolymph? It flows in my veins and in my blood* and he stared down; his limbs thin, painfully thin, so thin you would think they would snap but Jageraw knew they were piledrivers, ten times stronger than human bone and flesh and raw tasty muscle; a hundred times more powerful yes yes. His head, he knew, for he had seen it reflected in puddles of blood, was perfectly round and bald and he had slitted eyes and a face quite feline, like the cats he used to eat, *I like those cats, tasty, all mewling and scrabbling with pathetic claws* against his ceramic armour until he snapped their little necks and ate them whole, fur, whiskers and all.

Warlords!

He almost screamed, for he had made himself jump.

He had dreamed about them. About the Warlords, the Wild Warlords, the Vampire Warlords, the precursor to the vachine that lived in the mountains; their kindred, from baby to ape and beyond, and he laughed, a crackle of feline spider and something else dropped in there like oil in water; the cry of a child.

And now! The sheer concept made Jageraw shiver. For the Warlords were an enemy to be feared, he could sense it, he could feel it, and Jageraw had played out the dream, the events to come, the promise, the *prophecy* yes I did in my mind a thousand times; and despite his strength, despite his awesome killing powers, despite his supernatural abilities of skipping and murder; well, he was afraid.

"The King is dead, the King is dead, the King is dead," he crooned to himself, voice a lullaby, voice music to his own ears, on a different level of aural capability, if not to the pleasure of anybody else. He knew it would happen, for he had seen it would happen, and the mighty had fallen, the great had toppled, and King Leanoric the Battle King was dead and his army erased and fed into the machine, the nasty black machine to make the drug for vachine.

The Graverobber rocked, chitin covered in a fine layer of snow. He heard a laboured breathing, panting, something under the hunt; interesting, he thought, because usually – in these odd scenarios – he got to feed on both hunter *and* hunted. A double feast. Lots of food for Jageraw. Lots of food including (he winked at himself and I like it, I do like it) those slick warm organs. How he did like a bit of kidney to wash down the old claret; how he did lust after a morsel of shredded lung. Tasty as a pumpkin.

The breathing was louder now, but it was hard for the Graverobber to see through thick tumbling snow; it swirled this way, it swirled that way, it swirled every damn way, but it certainly got *in the way*. Jageraw hunkered down, muscles bunching, and decided to kill the *hunted* first. Then turn on the attackers and rip off their heads, no matter how many there were. Three or thirty, it made little difference to the Graverobber; when he was in the mood for killing and feeding, then he would take his time and savour and hunt, until all of them were dead. They left a stink trail worse than any cesspit odour; it was never hard to follow.

The *thing* burst through the circle of stones and stopped, stunned, when it saw the Graverobber. Jageraw half leapt, but checked himself and twisted in mid air, landing lightly, on all fours, like a cat. Jageraw stared suspiciously at what could only be described as a *thing* in his very own circle of stones. Surely, Le'annath Moorkelth had never been witness to such a creature? But then, Jageraw had never seen a canker, and certainly nothing as twisted with clockwork and golden wire as *this* specimen.

"Help me!" growled the bulky, deviant, clockwork creature. It struggled to form the words, for its mouth was wrenched back, jaws five times wider than any normal mortal man's. Thick golden wires were wound around and *in* its flesh. Every single breathing moment looked like an agony of pain and suffering.

The Graverobber's head tilted, and he moved lithely forward, pacing, like a cat. He stopped by the edge of the stones; there was a myth that he could not, or would not, pass beyond. But it was simply a myth; Jageraw could do what the hell he liked, especially when searching for food and a sliver of kidney which tasted so fine and slick on its way down his throat, yum yum.

The soldiers were toiling up the hill under snow; but there were many. Quickly, Jageraw counted. At least a hundred. He turned, eyes narrowing at the deformed creature in his circle *his damnfire circle of stones! his home!* and he had two choices; kill the creature, or hide it. If the soldiers saw him, and they looked well armed and trained and not liable to put up the weak comedy fight of the average villager with screams and skirts and pitchfork; if they saw Jageraw, they might decide he was on the military cleansing agenda.

The Graverobber turned, slowly, and eyed the canker. Damn. That would take some killing, he realised.

So, instead, he leapt, cannoning into the shocked warped creature and in a *flash* of connection and integration and blood-oil *magick* they stepped sideways through time; skipped, simply, a few seconds *forward*. Making Jageraw and the hunted canker, effectively invisible.

The world had been, or at least *seemed*, young and wild and violent, to General Graal. Wild Warlords ruled the land with gauntlets of spiked steel and fangs of brass, and nobody, *nobody* questioned their authority. Theirs was an authority of fang and claw, steel and fire; of impalement and decapitation, where the only rule was that there were no rules: and humans were truly the despicable cattle of legend.

Graal dreamed. And in his dream, he *lived*…

Graal rode the six legged stallion through tall crimson grass towards the marshes, where blue flamingos squawked and flapped heavily into the night sky, bright by the light of the moon, recognising his inherent threat upon approach. Flamingos had far better, more primal, instincts than men. He cursed, wishing he had his power lance; he would have speared a bird for supper. He grinned at that, blue eyes narrowing, fangs ejecting, and turned his mount and rode for the nearest village. This was a new area, new settlements, and they did not know him; at the gates he leapt from his mount, head high, eighteen years of life stark on his cruel, narrow face. When they saw him, his eyes, his fangs, his talons, the five men on the gate shouted and started to heave closed the heavy timber portal but Graal strode forward, slamming a hand through the thick timbers with crunches of destruction. The men screamed, shouting for help, two grabbing long spears of black ebony and steel. Graal stepped in, batted aside a spear, pulled the man towards him and snapped his neck like tinder. He lifted the man, mouth cracking open, and plunged his fangs into the flesh, rooting for the jugular. Blood fountained, coated his pale skin, soaking his white hair, and he laughed as he drank for the blood was nectar and the high took him in gossamer wings and flew him through velvet heavens—

Pain slammed him, and he stared down at the spear protruding from his chest. Near the heart. Too damn near the heart! Graal dropped the ragdoll corpse, cursing himself, his youth, his naivety, his greed, his addiction to blood and the high which brought recklessness to feeding. He had forgotten the second man with the spear. Such a simple omission; to assume he had fled in fear and panic.

Graal grabbed the spear, embedded in his own flesh and bubbling with black blood through his fine white silk shirt; he swung it, knocking the panic-stricken guard from his feet, then snapped the haft and strode forward, towering over the man. "You want to impale me, little creature? Like this?" Graal plunged the broken spear down, into the man's eye, and

*he screamed and gurgled and kicked for a while, blood a foun-
tain, gore bubbling. Graal stood, and pulled free the broken
splinter of wood, a stake he realised, from his breast. An inch.
An inch away!*

*Graal brayed at the moon, a howl long and mournful, and
when he lowered his head it was to see the line of villagers approaching. There were thirty of them, dressed like peasants,
stinking of woodsmoke and shit and piss, their faces bubbled
with toxic disease, their hair lank, eyes lifeless, and could they
not see his sheen, could they not read the supremacy in his very
fucking skin tone?*

*They carried weapons, and coolly Graal slicked back his
hair, full of fresh blood and its heady scent, and surveyed the
array of swords, daggers, sharpened stakes, and even a few
pitchforks (oh, the fools!). One woman carried a bundle in outstretched, shaking hands and Graal nearly vomited with
laughter. Garlic. For the love of the Bone Halls, garlic? How
pure and most beautifully ridiculous! Did she not realise? Did
they not realise? Graal adored garlic. Most vampires did. It
helped take away the breath of the dead…*

*Graal pushed back his shoulders, stepped away from the
two corpses, and grinned. This seemed to shock the villagers;
maybe they were expecting him to flee. Instead Graal moved
fast, fast into them, a fist through a chest there plucking free a
beating heart, ducking a sword strike by a clumsy village idiot
with no teeth, his index finger driving into a woman's eye and
beyond, into the brain, taking a longsword from another man
and cutting his legs free in a single stroke and then Graal was
into his stride, and into the slaughter, and the sword sang and
slew, cutting heads from shoulders, hands from arms, arms
from torsos, and Graal took particular delight in slicing a preg-
nant woman in two from the crown of her head, straight
through fat chest and pumping spasming heart and belly and*

child, right down to her groin. A twin murder with a single sweep. Beautiful! Economical! Damn, in fact it was sheer Art.

Within a few heartbeats of human duration, Graal had killed all the villagers. He heard a cough, from beyond the gates, and kneeling, Graal pulled free a heart with a wrenching tear of clinging tendons and strands of muscle, then strode to the gates, where he surveyed the five stocky vampires, all mounted, all staring down at him.

"Yes?" said Graal, head high, arrogance shining in his eyes despite his youth. He bit the heart like an apple, and savoured the texture, savoured the warm slick muscle in his mouth and throat, and then squeezed the warm organ like a fruit, draining the remaining blood off into his mouth. "You caught me during a moment of indulgence. May I be of service?"

"Mount up. There's work to be done."

"Slaughter?" Graal's eyes twinkled.

"Is there any other kind?"

Graal sat, watching the Refineries, the dripping pipes, listening to the churn of clockwork machinery. All gone, he thought. Long dead, and gone. Just like his mother, the queen, and his father, the king. Killed. Murdered! *Slaughtered* like human cattle. Graal's lips drew back, making his face incredibly ugly, a baring of the vampire within him, trapped within his now weak flesh, the flesh of the combination, the pathetic shell of the vachine.

We will be free again, he nodded.

We will be free.

He stood, and stretched his back, and rolled his neck, and gazed around. Behind him, the war camp was running smoothly; the albino soldiers ran like – he laughed, a little – like clockwork. They cooked and cleaned, oiled

weapons and armour, sharpened blades, tended to prisoners and the cankers; they needed very little
organisation from Graal, for they were like insects,
workers in the hive, busy with their own little jobs and
all part of the Great Wheel.

Graal turned back to the Refineries and waited, pa-
tiently, until in the blink of an eye the Harvesters oozed
from metal walls, pulling free as if from a thick liquid.
They moved before Graal, a triumvirate of consummate evil. Graal smiled. Evil was something he could
work with.

"It is complete?"

"As you wish. The blood-oil is refined. Do you not
feel the rise in energy? The surge of usable power?"

"No. It will come to me later, in the dark hours."

The Harvesters reared up, long fingers of bone
stretching out, and to an onlooker if would have appeared – for just an instant – as if the Harvesters were
about to attack Graal, slice his head from his shoulders, peel the skin from his vachine bones. But they
did not. They prostrated before him in a low bow,
faces pressing the earth in an almost unprecedented
show, and one they would certainly never have repli-
cated before any other vachine. The Harvesters
accepted Graal as Master. He smiled, controlling his
urges of madness and almost panic-fuelled hysterics,
for these creatures were so awesomely powerful that
what Graal was actually witnessing was an acknowl-
edgement of what he was about to achieve; what was
to come, not what had passed.

The Vampire Warlords.

The Harvesters stood. One said, "What of the
Soul Gems?"

"Kradek-ka is searching for the one remaining Gem; the other two are... safe, for now. But he knows where to look. We had... help."

"Will he hold strong?"

"Yes, despite his madness."

"And yet, there is still a thorn to be plucked?"

Graal nodded. "Kell. The Black Axeman of Drennach. I know this."

"What will you do?"

"I have sent the Soul Stealers," he said. "Kell is a dead man."

CHAPTER 4
Echoes of a Distant Age

A blur slammed past Kell, whose eyes were fastened on the dark blade descending for his unprotected throat, and Kell knew he would die there, half buried by rubble, head pounding from the force of *shamathe* magic and he had never felt anything like it, so *odd*, but the blur came from the edges of his vision and connected with Jekkron, the tall albino warrior, and with a blink Kell realised it was *Skanda* the skinny little boy, and Skanda's arms and legs were wide and wrapped around Jekkron who took a step back, his face frowning in annoyance at this interruption to murder. Jekkron raised a hand, as if to slap down the annoying boy who clung to him. And then he started to scream, and he started to scream high, and loud, like a woman peeled, like an animal skewered… Skanda hadn't just wrapped around Jekkron, he was *burrowing* into the man, his head snapping left and right and chewing and tearing flesh, and his hands and feet had claws and they tore into the albino soldier, who staggered now, dropping his sword, both fists beating down at Skanda who eased *inside* Jekkron by just a few inches, and with a terrible force of magick, ripped Jekkron's skin and muscle from his chest, belly and thighs. Skanda landed, carrying the skin and muscle like a thick white cloak, and Jekkron hit the ground unconscious, seconds from death. His blood flushed out as if from an overturned cauldron.

In the sudden confusion, only Lilliath saw what happened, the rest of the soldiers simply witnessed their leader going crazy and slapping at himself; Lilliath capered to one side, over a pile of rubble, to see a donkey staring at her. Lilliath stopped, crazy hair wavering, and Mary the donkey turned slowly around, and with a vicious bray, planted both hooves in the shamathe's face, sending her tumbling back over the pile of collapsed bricks.

As Jekkron, conscious again and gasping like a fish, struggled to rise with his lack of albino flesh, so Kell grunted and hauled himself to his feet. Skanda stood before him, staring at the gathered soldiers with a face less than human, his black teeth glinting with Jekkron's white blood, and hands lifted up and held like comedy claws. Except the joke was no longer funny.

Skanda fell on the dying soldier, and ripped out his throat with his teeth, and used claws to slice down Jekkron's ribs and pull free internal organs, which he held up for the soldiers to see. Then Skanda bounded forward, and in a sudden wave of fear the albino soldiers scattered, as Skanda screeched and screamed after them, and suddenly Kell and Saark were left alone.

Kell limped to Saark, who was just regaining consciousness. Blood leaked from his ears, making his long, dark curls glossy. Both men stood, and leaned on one another weakly, and Saark gazed down at the terribly savaged, torn-apart body of Jekkron. His eyes fastened on glinting pools of milk blood, nestling in hollows and peppered with drifting brick dust.

"Did you do that to him?" coughed Saark.

"It was the boy."

"Skanda? No! No way could a small child…"

"He is *not* a small child," said Kell, and with a grunt heaved himself upright and gazed across to the unconscious body of the shamathe. Her face was black and purple. "Your mule has a fine aim."

"Mary did that? Great! And by the way, she's a donkey, not a mule."

"Same difference," muttered Kell. "Come on, we need horses. We need to put leagues between us and them."

"What about Skanda?"

"I have a feeling," said Kell, voice hard, unforgiving, "that the boy can look after himself."

Kell lifted Ilanna, and gazed down at Lilliath. He hefted the axe high, and suddenly Saark was there, hands held up. "Whoa, Big Man, what are you doing?"

Kell scowled. "She tried to kill us, Saark. You surely don't want her following? Doing *that* to us *in our sleep*?"

"You can't kill her, Kell. She's an old woman. She's unconscious! For the love of the gods!"

"She's a white magicker, and she deserves to die."

Saark planted himself between Kell and the unconscious shamathe. "No. I won't let you! It is immoral. If you kill her, Kell, then you are as bad as the enemy; can't you see?"

Kell gave a great and weary sigh. "Very well," he said, eyes narrowed, face pale from dust. "But if she comes near us again, *you* can sort the bitch out. Let's find some horses."

They moved around the exterior of the deserted armoury, Saark leading Mary by her halter, and indeed found horses tethered. Distant screams echoed through the forest. Whatever Skanda was doing to the albino soldiers, he was keeping them occupied – and their minds far away from their mounts.

There were six beasts tethered here, all seventeen-hand geldings, and Kell and Saark raided saddlebags for provisions and coin, then picked the most powerful looking horses. Saark tied Mary's lead to his mount's tail, and the men mounted the beasts under moonlight and cantered up a nearby slope, and away, into woodland, into the drifting, falling snow.

They did not speak.

They were simply glad to be alive.

They rode for an hour. Several times Saark suggested pausing, and waiting for Skanda. Kell simply gave Saark a sour, evil look, and Saark closed his mouth, aware he would not get far with Kell when the old warrior was in such a stubborn temper.

Finally, they made a cold camp, wary of lighting a fire lest it attract more unwanted military attention. Saark, in particular, was in a bad way. Whilst Kell was seemingly strong as an ox, Saark had suffered several beatings, and a loss of blood from the knife wound at the hands of Myriam; whilst better than he had been, stronger and a little more clear-headed, the constant battering was taking its toll on the man. He had deep, dark rings around his eyes, and his face was drawn and gaunt with exhaustion and pain.

"This is wrong," said Saark, as they stretched out an army tarpaulin between two trees to give them a little shelter. To their backs was a wall of rock from several huge, cubic boulders which must have tumbled from the nearby hills hundreds of years before, and this left only a single entrance from which the wind and snow could intrude.

"Which bit is wrong? Pull it, Saark, don't bloody tickle it."

"I'm pulling it, man, I'm pulling! I simply have a reduced mobility due to the wound in my side; or maybe you hadn't bloody noticed me getting stabbed?"

"I'll notice you getting stabbed in a minute, if you don't help erect this damn shelter," growled Kell. "My hands are turning blue with the cold! So go on, what's wrong, man?"

"Running away, leaving Skanda to face the soldiers, demons, and whatever else fills this magick-haunted forest."

Kell tightened a strap, and sat on a rock, rummaging in a saddlebag. Nearby, Mary brayed, and Kell scowled at the donkey. "Listen, Saark. You didn't see what I saw – the boy, he ripped that soldier's skin and muscle from his body like a rug from a floor. Peeled it off, complete! Then bit out the soldier's throat and cut out his organs. Don't start moaning to me about leaving a little boy in the woods; Skanda is no boy like I have ever seen."

"What is he then? A camel?"

Kell frowned at Saark, and motioned for the tall swordsman to sit. In a low voice, a tired voice, Kell said, "I told you what I saw. If you don't believe me, then to Dake's Balls with you! You get out there in the snow and look for the little bastard. Me, I'd rather put my axe through his skull. He gives me the creeps."

"You are incorrigible!"

"Me?" snapped Kell, fury rising. "I reckon we brought something bad out of Old Skulkra; invited it out into the world with us. I fear we may have done the world a disservice. You understand?"

"He saved us," sulked Saark, ducking into the makeshift shelter and resting his back against cold, damp rock. He shivered, despite his fur and leather cloak. "You are an ungrateful old goat, Kell. You know that?"

"Saved us?" Kell laughed, and his eyes were bleak. "Sometimes, my friend, I think it is better to be dead."

They shared out some dried beef and a few oatcakes, and ate in silence, listening to a distant, mournful wind, and the muffled silence brought about by heavy, snow-laden woodland. Occasionally, there was a *crump* as gathered snow fell from high branches. At one point, Kell winced, and took several deep breaths.

"You are injured?" Saark looked suddenly concerned.

"It is nothing."

"Don't be ridiculous! You are like a bull, you only complain when something hurts you *bad*. What is it?"

"Pain. Inside. Inside my very veins."

Saark nodded, his eyes serious. "You think it's the poison?"

"Yes," said Kell, through gritted teeth. "And I know it's going to get worse. My biggest fear is finding Myriam, and the antidote, and not having the strength to break her fucking neck!"

"Do you think Nienna is suffering?"

"If she is, there will be murder," said Kell, darkly, fury glittering in his eyes. "Now get some sleep, Saark. You look weaker than a suckling doe. You sure you don't want some more food?"

"After seeing the result of that albino's corpse ripped

asunder? No, my constitution is delicate at the best of times. After that spectacle, I have lost appetite enough to last me a decade."

Kell grunted, and shrugged. "Food is food," he said, as if that explained everything.

Saark slept. More snow fell in the small hours. Kell sat on the rock, back stiff, all weariness evaporating with the pain brought by poison oozing through his veins and internal organs. It felt as if his body, knowing it was shortly to die, wanted him to experience every sensation, every second of life, every nuance of *pain* before forcing him to lie down and exhale his last clattering breath.

The dawn broke wearily, like a tired, pastel watercolour on canvas. Clouds bunched in the sky like fists, and the wind had increased, howling and moaning through woods and between nearby rocks which seemed to litter this part of the world. On the wind, they could smell fire. It was not a comforting stench. It was the aroma of *war*.

Kell, chin on his fist, eyes alert, Ilanna by his side, jumped a little when Saark touched his shoulder.

"Have you been awake all night, Old Horse?"

"Aye, lad. I couldn't sleep. Too much on my mind."

"We *will* find Nienna," said Saark.

"I don't doubt that. It's finding her alive that concerns me."

"Shall I cook us breakfast?"

"Make a small fire," said Kell, softly. "Hot tea is what I need if these aged bones are to survive much more rough life in the wilderness."

"Ha, it's a fine ale I crave!" laughed Saark, pulling out his tinderbox.

"I find whiskey a much more palatable experience," muttered Kell, darkly.

They drank a little hot tea with sugar, and ate more dried beef. Kell's pain had receded, much to the big man's relief, and Saark was also looking much better after a good sleep and some food and hot tea. They huddled around the small fire, then stamped it out and packed away their makeshift camp. They were just packing saddlebags when Kell hissed, dropping to a crouch and lifting Ilanna before him. Her blades glittered, and in that crouch Saark saw a flicker of insanity made flesh.

Skanda walked from the trees, smiling with his black teeth. He stopped, and tilted his head. On his hand rode the tiny scorpion with twin tails. It seemed agitated, moving quickly about the boy's hand and never halting. Its tails flickered, fast, like ebony lightning.

"I found you," he said. He tilted his head. Kell rose out of his crouch, cursed, and continued to pack the saddlebags, turning his back on the boy with deliberate ignorance.

"Are you hurt?" said Saark, rushing over.

"No," smiled Skanda, "but I led those soldiers on a merry chase. I was not surprised to find you gone when I returned to the old armoury." His eyes shone. "I think I upset Kell, did I not? The great Legend himself."

Kell turned, and smiled easily, although his eyes were hooded. "No lad, you didn't upset me. But I didn't worry about leaving you behind, before you get any noble ideas about friendship and loyalty."

"Have I offended you? If so, I apologise."

Kell placed his hands on his hips. "In fact, boy, you have. You have a rare talent, don't you? The ability to kill."

Skanda stared at Kell for a long time. Eventually, he said, "It is a talent bestowed on the Ankarok. I can kill, yes. I can kill with ease. My small size and odd looks do nothing to highlight the bubbling ancient rage within."

Kell stared into the boy's eyes.

A darkness fell on his soul, like ash from the funeral pyres of a thousand children.

It is not human, he told himself.

It is consummately evil.

I should kill it. I should kill it *now*...

His hands grasped the haft of Ilanna, his bloodbond axe, and he took a step forward but a shrill note pierced the inside of his skull, and he realised Ilanna was screaming at him, warning him, and the note fell and her words came, and her voice was cool, a drifting metallic sigh, the voice of bees in the hive, the song of ants in the nest...

Wait, she said. *You must not.*

Why not? he growled.

Because he is of Ankarok. The Ancient Race. They were here before the vachine, and before the vampires before them; they invented blood-oil, and mastered the magick, and they know too much.

Kell snorted. He felt like a pawn in another man's game. I am being manipulated, he thought. But is my sweet blood-drenched Ilanna telling the truth? Or is she lying through her blackened back teeth because she *wants* something of her own...

This was Ilanna, the bloodbond axe, and she was in control, or so she liked to think. Blessed in blood-oil, and instrumental, or so Kell believed, in the Days of Blood, she offered him a tenuous link with madness, a risk which Kell readily accepted because... well, because *without* Ilanna he would be a dead man. And if Kell was a dead man, then his granddaughter Nienna was a dead girl.

He should die.

Why? Because you say so?

Kell breathed in the perfume of the axe. The aroma of death. The corpse–breath of Ilanna. It was heady, like the finest narcotic, like a honey-plumped dram of whiskey; and Kell felt himself float for a moment, lost in her, lost in Ilanna… *I am Ilanna, she sang, music in his heart, drug in my veins, I am the honey in your soul, the butter on your bread, the sugar in your apple. I make you whole, Kell. I bring out the best in you, I bring out the warrior in you. And yes I ask you to kill but can you not see the irony? Can you not see what I desire? I am asking you not to kill; I am asking you to spare the boy. He is special. Very special. You will see, and one day you will thank me for these words of wisdom. Skanda is Ankarok, he is older than worlds, look into his insect eyes and see the truth, Kell, understand the importance of what I am saying for we will never have another opportunity like this… he will help you find Nienna… help you save those you love.*

You bitch.

I am stating the truth. And you know it. So grow up, and wise up, and let's get moving and get this thing done; Lilliath is leading the albino soldiers through the woods. They are coming, Kell, you must make haste…

Kell opened his eyes. He realised both Saark and Skanda were staring at him; staring at him hard.

"Are you well?" asked Saark, voice soft.

"Aye, I'm fine."

"We can stay a while longer, if you need rest," said Saark, suddenly remembering his own sleep with a sense of guilt. He had allowed Kell to sit up all night; it had been selfish in the extreme.

"No. The soldiers are coming. We should move."

Skanda's eyes went bright. "You want me to go back into the woods? Find them? Kill them?"

"No." Kell shook his head, eyeing the scorpion perched on the boy's hand. Seeing the look, and misreading its meaning, Skanda hid the tiny insect within folds of rough clothing, and Kell made a mental note to check his boots in the morn. "We're heading north. At speed. We're going to find Nienna. We're going to rescue her... or die in the process!"

Myriam crouched beside the still pool, its circumference edged with plates of ice, their layers infinite, their borders a billion shards of splintered and angular crystal. Beautiful, she thought, breathing softly, pacing herself, and then her gaze flickered up, above the ice, to her own reflection and her teeth clacked shut and the muscles along her jaw stood out in ridges as she clenched her teeth tight. But here, she thought, here, the beauty dies.

She had short black hair, where once she had worn it long. Once, it had been a luscious pelt that made men fall over themselves to stroke and touch. Now, she cropped it short for fear the rough texture and dull hue would scream at people exactly what she was: dying.

Myriam was dying, and she still found it difficult to admit, to say out loud, but at least now she had in some way acknowledged it to herself. For a year she had harboured denial, even as she watched her own flesh melt from her bones, and she'd continually conned herself, thinking that if she ate better, exercised more, found the right medicines, then this illness, this fever would *pass* and she would be well again. However, for the past three years now she had grown steadily weaker, flesh falling from her bones as pain built and wracked her ever slimming frame. She had often joked how the rich fat bulging bitches in Kallagria would pay a fortune to have what she had; now, Myriam joked no more. It was as if humour had been wrenched from her with a barbed spear, leaving a gaping trail of damaged flesh in its wake.

Myriam had travelled Falanor, attempting to find a cure for her sickness. She eventually tracked down the best physicians in Vor, and spent a small fortune in gold, stolen gold, admittedly, on their advice, their medications, their odd treatments. None had worked. What she had gained from her vast expenditure had been *knowledge*.

She had two tumours, growing inside her, each the size of a fist. They were like parasites, but whereas some parasites were symbiotic – would keep the host alive so that they, also, could live, these tumours were ignorant, killing the host which supported them. Her one small triumph would be they would also die. Yes. But only when Myriam died.

Myriam stared into her reflection, the stretched skin, the gaunt flesh, drawn back over her skull and making her shudder even to look at herself. Once, men and women had flocked to her. Now, they couldn't stand to be in the same room, as if they feared catching some terrible plague.

I am a creature of pity, she realised sadly. Then anger shot through her. Well, I don't want their fucking pity! I just want my fucking life back! I have only existed on this stinking ball of pain for twenty-nine winters. Twenty-nine! Is that any age to die? Are the gods laughing at me, mocking me with their sick sense of humour? How fair is that, that others, evil men and women, or useless, stupid, brainless men and women, how is it they get to live – and I do not? Who made that choice for me? Which rancid insane deity thought it would be fun?

Tears coursed her gaunt cheeks, and Myriam bit back the need to scream her anguish and pain and frustration through the frozen trees. No. She breathed deep. And she did what she always did. She thought about this day. And she thought about the next day. And she knew she had to take one day at a time, step after step after step until... until she reached Silva Valley. There, she knew, they had the technology to cure her. Using clockwork, and blood-oil, and dark vampire magick.

However, persuading them? That would be a different matter.

Fear flashed through her, then, and she licked dry lips. Her mouth tasted bad. Tasted like cancer. She grimaced, and her belly cramped in pain and she brought herself back to the present with a jolt; they had not eaten for two days. And the sparse woodland in the low foothills leading to the great feet of the Black Pike Mountains contained little game. She would have to work hard if she wanted supper.

Myriam was a skilled hunter. Before her affliction, she had won the Golden Bow three times in a row at the Vor Summer Festival. Now, the cancer ate her, and had sapped her strength, made her aim less true. But she was still a devastating archer, nonetheless.

Myriam crept through the woods, her boots treading softly on hard soil and patches of snow. She picked every footfall with care and stopped often, looking around with slow, fluid movements, her ears twitching, listening, her mind falling in tune with the winter trees.

There!

She saw the doe, a young one, rooting for food. Were there any parents close by? The last thing Myriam needed was a battle with an enraged stag; if nothing else, it made the meat damn tough.

She saw nothing, and eased herself to her knees, allowing her breathing to normalise, to regulate, as she notched the arrow to the bowstring and with a slow slow *slow* measured ease, drew back the string, taking the tension with her ever-so-slightly trembling muscles.

The arrow flashed through the woodland, striking the doe from behind, between the shoulder blades, and punching down into lungs and heart. It was a clean kill, instant, and the doe dropped. Myriam felt a burst of joy, of pride at her skill; then she stood, and the smile fell from her face like melting ice under sunshine.

Death. She shivered. *Death*.

Myriam crossed the forest floor and drew a long knife; expertly she sliced the best cuts of meat and placed them in a sack, blood oozing between her fingers. Then she stood, looked around, eyes narrowing. Something felt wrong, but she couldn't place her finger on it; however, Myriam trusted her senses, they were fine honed and reliable. If the element which felt *out of key* wasn't here, it must be back at camp. Her jaw tightened.

Myriam moved like a ghost through the trees. The world was silent, filled with snow and ice, and occasionally snow clumped from trees with a tumbling rhythm.

She approached the makeshift camp, trees thinning where huge fists of rock punched upwards at the sky, dominating her vision. Myriam felt her throat dry for a moment, for the Black Pike Mountains were a panorama indeed, a line of domineering peaks that lined her sight from the edge of the world to the edge of the world. Each peak she could see reared black and unforgiving into the sky, many damn near ten thousand feet. And beyond, she knew, they got much bigger, much more terrifying, and much more savage.

Myriam stopped, head tilting. The camp was quiet. Too quiet. Her eyes scanned right, where they could see the narrow trail which led from the Great North Road to the gawping maw of the Cailleach Pass; it was along this, she knew, Kell would finally come, head hung low, poison eating him, begging her for the anti-dote, for her to relieve his pain, for her to slit his throat and end his torment. Only Kell would not; he would be thinking of Nienna, and her suffering, and how he could save her instead.

A cold wind blew, and Myriam shivered. Snow fell from the trees behind her, making her jump, and she re-alised she had dropped the sack of meat and had notched an arrow to her bow without even realising it. *Kell*, the wind seemed to whisper. *Kell. He will gut you like a fish. He will cut out your liver. He will drink your blood, bitch!*

Scowling, Myriam grabbed the sack and stalked into their small camp, where the men, Styx and Jex, had built an arched screen of timber and evergreen fronds, for pro-tection against the wind. Within this semi-circle they'd dragged logs for seats, and built a fire in a square of rocks. The fire burned low. Again, Myriam's eyes narrowed. To let the fire go out was foolish indeed; here, in this place, it meant the difference between life and death.

"Styx?" she said, voice little more than a murmur. Then louder. "Styx? Jex? Where are you?"

The camp was deserted. Myriam's eyes looked to where Nienna, their young prisoner, had been seated; there were deep marks in the snow created by her boots. A struggle?

"Damn it."

Myriam left the sack at camp, and followed tracks through the woods, kneeling once to examine a confusion of marks. She cursed; they had been using the camp for nearly a week now, and there were too many contradicting signs. Something rattled nearby. Myriam's head came up. She broke into a run, arrow notched, and skidded to a halt before a series of huge trees swathed in ivy, creating an ivy wall on two sides like a corridor; against this backdrop Nienna struggled, and even as Myriam watched Styx, squat, black-lipped Styx, with pockmarked skin and his left eye, uncovered, nothing more than a red, inflamed socket – she watched him push the blade to Nienna's throat and snarl something incomprehensible on a stream of foul spittle down her ear.

"Styx!" shouted Myriam, moving swiftly forward. She stopped, looked left at Jex, who simply shrugged. The small tattooed tribesman was not in charge of Styx; Styx was a free agent. He could do what he liked. Or so Jex's simple philosophy ran.

"She bit me!" snarled Styx. "This bitch has been nothing but trouble! Now I'm going to teach her a lesson." His free hand dropped down Nienna's side, to her hips, where he started to tug at her skirt. Nienna struggled wildly, and the knife bit her throat allowing a trickle of blood to run free.

"No, Styx," said Myriam. "This is not the way."

His head came up, black lips curling back over the

blackened stumps of his drug-rotted teeth. His dark eye glittered like a jewel. "She's trouble, Mirry, I'm telling you! What I have in store for her will break her spirit; you'll see, it'll bring her back to the real world. Either that, or one of us will wake up with a knife in the heart."

"Put the girl down," said Myriam, voice deadly calm.

"And what if I don't?"

Myriam lifted her bow and sighted down the arrow. It was aimed at Styx's one remaining good eye, and Styx knew she was a good enough shot to pull it off, despite the illness which troubled her aim.

"What are you doing?"

"Exerting my authority."

"You're being a fool, Myriam. We've been through some shit together, girl, and now you'd turn on me? I don't bloody understand! This little bitch needs taming; you've watched me rape a hundred women before, young, old, fit, fat, diseased, what's the fucking problem with you now?" He gave a nasty grin, teeth like a fire-ravaged forest of stumps. "It's not like you haven't tasted a bit of screaming young pussy yourself. You always said the bigger the fight, the better the bite."

Myriam stared at him, and she knew she was willing to see him die. Because if he harmed Nienna and Kell went *berserk* then she would never make it to Silva Valley, where the vachine technology could make her whole again, make her well again; turn her into a *woman* again. And also, only if she admitted it to herself, she was a little frightened of Kell. If they abused Nienna he would never stop till they were dead; as it was, they walked a fine line between angering the old warrior, and turning him into a permanent merciless enemy, one that would hunt them to the ends of the earth.

"If you hurt the girl, Kell won't help us reach Silva. If we don't reach Silva, then you won't get your Black-lipper contacts; remember? The ones that will make you *rich*. The ones that will lead you to the three kings of the Blacklippers and all that precious gold beyond."

That stopped Styx. His eyes narrowed. In a voice like mist in a tombyard, he said, "What do *you* know of the three Kings?"

"I know enough," said Myriam, her arrow still aimed for Styx's face. Nienna had stilled in his arms, but the blade rested against her throat, a very real threat. A bead of sweat broke out on Myriam's brow, and her elbow gave a tiny tremble.

Styx saw this. He smiled.

With a *whoosh*, Myriam released the shaft which slammed through the air, piercing the lobe of Styx's ear and rattling off through the trees. He yelped, hand coming up to his lobe, and in doing so released Nienna. She ran to Myriam, cowering behind the tall woman's legs, and when Styx looked up she had another arrow notched, ready, steel point aimed at his face. There was a snarl on Styx's face; but worse, there was hatred in his eye, deep and glittering, and although Myriam had seen that look before a thousand times, she had never seen it directed at *her*. It chilled her. Styx was a very dangerous man; and not an enemy she wished to invoke. However. If Nienna was *damaged* in anyway, then it compromised her situation with Kell, finding the vachine, and living to see the next winter. For she knew, as certain as water flowed downhill, that these were her last few months on earth.

"I think you just made a big mistake," growled Styx. He held up his hands, his knife glinting a little with traces of Nienna's blood. "But don't worry. Don't panic, little Myriam; I am no danger to you. I value the Black-lipper contacts and their great wealth *more* than I value killing you in your sleep." He glanced at Nienna. "Or tasting her foul juice."

Styx lowered his hands, and walked past Myriam and the cowering form of Nienna; he disappeared into the woodland, and Myriam released a long breath. She glanced at Jex.

"Not such a good idea," said Jex, eyes fixed on Myriam.

"You think I don't know that? You think I'm a village idiot?"

"No," said the tribesman, carefully. "But I *do* think you should have let him have his fun with the girl; it would have kept him happy, not harmed her too much, and as he says – it would have tamed her spirit just a little." He shrugged. "Now you have to watch your back. From both fucking directions."

"You can watch it as well," smiled Myriam.

Jex did not return the smile. "Some things in life, we do alone," he said, and moved off through the trees.

Myriam finally lowered her bow, and placed the arrow in her sheath. Nienna moved around to face Myriam, and her hands were shaking. She looked up, and at first Myriam wouldn't meet her gaze.

Then their eyes locked, and Myriam studied the tall girl before her. She was pretty, with a rounded and slightly plump face. Her hair was a luscious brown down to her shoulders, and her eyes bright green, dazzling with youth and vitality. For a long moment Myriam hated her, despised her, was jealous to an insane degree of her youth, and beauty, and strength, and health, whilst *she* was slowly being eaten from the inside out, turning into a husk of degenerative cells. Hate flooded Myriam, fuelled by envy, and she wanted to smash Nienna's face open with a rock; split her head and watch the brains come spilling out. But Myriam breathed deeply, controlled herself, and fought the evil in her veins, in her soul. She forced a smile to her face.

"Thank you," said Nienna.

"Don't be too grateful," grunted Myriam. "You're still my prisoner... until the mighty Kell arrives, and shows us a way through the mountains."

"Still – Styx would have..." she shuddered.

Myriam smiled. "Don't think about it. He's a bad man, aye, but at least it's nothing personal. He hates all women. Come to think of it, he hates all men." Myriam turned, and started back through the trees with Nienna close behind. Nienna was still shivering.

"Why do you travel with such hateful creatures?" said Nienna, her voice low, almost conspiratorial. "It must darken your soul to see such evil at every turn. To witness such horror, and do nothing to halt it."

Myriam stopped, suddenly, and Nienna almost crashed into her. "I saved you, didn't I, little Nienna?" Her tone was mocking, her eyes flashing angry. "Darken my soul? Child, you know nothing of me, or my life, of my horrors and pain and suffering. Don't think because of one little moment, one tiny lapse in my self-control that I'm suddenly a mother figure. You're here for a reason, and that's to draw Kell. That's why I helped you. I care nothing for your suffering. In fact, I wish I'd let Styx rape you – he was right. It would have taught you to shut your bastard mouth."

She stalked off ahead, leaving a confused and now terrified Nienna behind. Nienna trotted after her, tears on her cheeks, and filled with a complete and devastating misery.

Kell managed an hour's sleep. In it, he dreamed. He dreamed of Ilanna, his axe; he dreamed of murder; he dreamed of the Days of Blood. *He stood, muscles bulging, tensed as if pumped on drugs and violence, and his whole body quivered, and his mind flitted and could not settle on a single thought, like some butterfly caught in a raging storm. Blood smeared his face and arms and he glanced down, and Kell was naked, naked and proud and bulging with sexual arousal. His entire body was smeared with blood, and blue and green whorls of paint which were intricately complex and he frowned for he did not remember being painted, or tattooed, but then they did not matter for they were an irrelevancy… Kell leapt down from the stone wall and stood in the street, Ilanna in his hands, a snarl on his face, and refugees were streaming past him, sobbing, faces blackened with soot as behind the city burned, huge towers of fire screaming up into the skies. Kell watched the men and women and children stream past him, and Ilanna said something in his mind with a soothing caress and she sang, and Kell twitched and a head rolled, and blood fountained and Kell moved and allowed the twitching body to spray lifeblood over the butterfly blades of the great axe…*

"Ugh!" Kell sat up, shivering, and pain washed through him like honey through a sieve; slowly, an ooze, spreading gently through limbs and veins and muscles and organs and into… into his *bones*.

It's the poison, he told himself.

It's getting worse.

He pulled his cloak tightly about him. The wind

howled. Kell licked his lips. What he'd give for a drink. Gods, he'd kill for a drink. And then he smiled, face black in the moonlight, eyes glittering like some dark devil's, and he remembered the unlabelled bottle of whiskey deep in the basket on Mary's back.

It was a matter of moments to get the bottle and retire back to the phantom warmth of his cloak; the wind stirred eerily through the trees. Kell pulled out the cork with his teeth and an odour of sour, cheap, nasty whiskey filled him. He did not care. He breathed in the scent like drugsmoke; he revelled in its base oil consistency, in its hints at raw energy and amateur production. This was a whiskey made by unskilled peasants. This was a whiskey in which Kell could identify, not like the rich honeyed slop the aristocracy of Saark's social circle enjoyed. This was fire water, and Kell drank it.

He took several gulps, and it burned his throat.

He took several more, and a haze filled his mind.

The pain of the poison left him.

And Kell slept, whiskey bottle cradled like a small, adopted child.

The moon was high in a cold, crystal sky. Nienna sat, wrapped in blankets, listening to the soft snoring of Myriam by her side. The woman turned in her sleep, stretching out long legs. For a moment – a fleeting moment – Nienna considered running. She had tried twice before; the second time, Myriam had caught her and explained, using the back of her hand, what she would do the next time Nienna ran. Now, Nienna slept with her ankles bound so tight her feet would be blue by morning. And anyway, she had seen Myriam operate

her bow. She was a lethal, very deadly young woman...
who could kill over great distance. It made Nienna
shiver in horror and anticipation.

Nienna drifted in and out of sleep, as she had done
since her *kidnapping*. Such a simple word, and yet it em-
bodied day after day of a living hell. Riding in front of
Styx, and then Jex, they had shared her burden, swap-
ping her often so as not to tire the horses with extra
weight; they had ridden north, fast, as if Myriam feared
Kell would take up immediate chase. Nienna knew
Saark wasn't going to take chase; she had watched him
beaten and then stabbed with a long, sharp dagger.
Even now, Nienna was sure Saark must be dead and
she shuddered, on the edges of sleep, once again picturing the beating, hearing every crunch, every slap of
impact in her nightmares. Even now, she could see the
blade slide so easily into his soft flesh, and thought no,
it cannot be, cannot be happening, cannot be true, but
blood poured from Saark and it was true and Myriam
had come to them and they had ridden away into the
snow, without a backward glance...

Nienna thought back. Back to Kat. Katrina. Her
friend. Now dead. Now a corpse, rotting in the cold
bunkhouse where she'd been nailed to the wall by
Styx's *Widowmaker*. Nienna thought about that weapon.
Thought about it a lot. With a weapon like that, she
could really even the odds – no matter that she was a
thin, physically weak, and hardly able to lift a
longsword. With a *Widowmaker* she could punch a hole
through Styx's face and run for the woods...

No. She would have to kill all three if she expected
to escape.

But Kell! Kell would come and rescue her! Surely?

Maybe Kell was dead, spoke a dark side of her soul. He went into battle with King Leanoric – against the albino army. Maybe now he was just another corpse on the battlefield, crows eating his eyes, rats gnawing his intestines. She shivered, and gritted her teeth. No! Kell was alive. She knew it. Knew it deep in her heart.

And if Kell was alive, then he would come for her.

Nienna drifted off into sleep; coldness ate the edges of her flesh where skin poked from behind the blankets. She snuggled down as far as she could go, and her eyes suddenly clicked open. What was it? What had woken her? She was instantly wide awake – totally awake – and adrenaline surged through her system.

Nienna sat up. Her eyes searched the darkness. She turned to her right, and looked down at Myriam; the lithe woman snored softly, face lost in a haze of tranquillity that softened her features, made her more feminine. Nienna realised that when Myriam was awake her face was a constant scowl, as if she hated the world and every waking moment upon it.

Nienna turned to her left, and nearly leapt from her skin at the face mere inches from her. She felt the edge of the *Widowmaker* crossbow prod her under the blankets, and she nodded quickly as if to say, "I understand". Styx moved his mouth to her ear and whispered, "Scream, and I'll blow a hole through you, then I'll slaughter Myriam in her sleep and make my own way to Silva Valley."

"I won't scream," panted Nienna, fear a bright hot poker in her brain.

Styx pulled free the blankets, and lifted Nienna up by her elbow. Her eyes fell, and locked on that wood, brass and clockwork weapon. She was sure she could hear a tiny *tick tick tick* from within the stock. As if it was somehow powered by clockwork.

"What do you want?" she whispered.

Styx ignored the question, and eased her away from Myriam. Nienna gazed back at the sleeping woman, confused; it had been Myriam who, on both of Nienna's escape attempts, had heard the flight. Myriam slept light, like a dozing feline. Now, however, she continued to snore.

"Don't worry about her. I drugged her soup. She'll not be troubling nobody tonight."

Nienna felt icy fingers claw her heart. Realisation sank from her brain to her feet. Styx meant to rape her. Tonight. Now. And there was nothing she could do about it; not a thing on earth.

Styx marched Nienna through the woods, and he was panting hard, and he stunk of sweat and… something else. Liquor? Gin, like they used to sell in the Gin Palaces of Jalder?

Nienna was numb, not from the cold, but from fear. She allowed herself to be manhandled through the woods, stumbling. She did not complain. She could not complain. Fear had become her Master. Fear had stolen her tongue, and seemingly, her recent will to fight.

Finding a spot, Styx threw her to the ground. She landed heavy, a tree root slamming her spine and making her cry out. Even this was not enough to snap her from her cold embrace. She watched, with a mixture of horror and revulsion as Styx struggled from his leggings, one hand still holding the Widowmaker pointed loosely at her prostrate form.

Then, with the lower half of his body naked, he grinned at her and she hated him, there and then; she wanted him dead like she had wanted no other person dead in the world, ever. This man had killed her best friend. And now, this man sought to remove her chastity by force.

"If you touch me, I will kill you," she said. She wanted her words to come out strong and proud, like a sneer of contempt for this petty hateful specimen. But her words dribbled out, a mewling from a kitten, the slurred and feeble trickle of the wanton inebriate.

Kell will come, she thought with tears in her eyes. Kell will rescue me!

But he didn't come. Here, and now, Nienna was on her own.

Styx dropped his Widowmaker to the frozen woodland carpet, and pulled out a knife. The blade gleamed. He smiled, showing stubby black teeth. "I think it's time we got to know each other a bit better, pretty one," he said.

CHAPTER 5
Dark Vision

In the hills above Old Skulkra a small squad hunkered behind rocks. One, the tallest of the men, a soldier with broad shoulders and narrow hips, held a long tube filled with a series of finely shaped lenses to his eye. The delicate mechanism glittered when it caught the dying rays of the winter sun.

"Can you see him?" asked Beja.

"Yes. He returns," said Cardinal Walgrishnacht. His voice was even, devoid of emotion, but his dark vachine eyes shone. He watched, apparently impassive, as the scout approached. The man bowed low, as befitted somebody as exalted and dangerous as Walgrishnacht.

"You saw what happened?" snapped the Warrior Engineer.

"Yes," said the scout, eyes lowered to the snow. "General Graal called out his daughters, the Soul Stealers. Our Princess was..." he swallowed, then lifted his head and met Walgrishnacht's powerful clockwork gaze. "She was beheaded," he said.

Walgrishnacht stood, stunned, and when he looked around there were tears in his eyes, tears staining his pale cheeks. Never, in twenty years of combat and murder, had Walgrishnacht cried.

Beja watched the Cardinal of the Vachine Warrior Engineers, that specially chosen and infinitely deadly elite squad who had followed – secretly, in reserve – in order to protect Princess Jaranis should events turn sour. A violent blizzard had separated the two groups, and stubbornly the proud Princess pushed on regardless, no doubt eager to observe General Graal's progress and report back to the High Engineers instead of making textbook camp until the storm broke.

Now, she was dead. And Walgrishnacht could not quite believe the turn of events. General Graal was, and had been, a servant of the vachine religious culture for nearly three centuries. With Kradek-ka, he had helped usher in a new age of advanced clockwork technology, which elevated their race from savagery to high art. Graal was a founding member of Engineer Council Lore, and a harsh advocate and defender of the Oak Testament. Graal had been instrumental in the taming of pale-skinned creatures, the *alshina*, from beneath the Black Pike Mountains, and of training these soldiers in warfare and tactics; thus, he was the strategy behind many successful invasions and harvesting north past the Heart of the Mountains in Untamed Lands. After the recent breakdown of several Blood Refineries, it had been Graal who spearheaded Council and carried the vote to invade south. In High Engineer Philosophy, Politics, Ethics, History and Honour, Graal was unquestionable, and untouchable. He was Core to the Vachine Society. Integral. Like a Heart Cog.

Walgrishnacht chewed his lip, and wiped tears from his face with a long, brass talon.

"What shall we do?" said Beja, voice soft. He fidgeted. His body echoed uncertainty.

Walgrishnacht stood and stretched with a tiny *tick tick* echoing from his clockwork internals. He stared off across distant snow-fields, to the camped army of albino warriors; and he knew, in his heart, in his soul, that in an unprecedented move they were betrayed. But what was Graal's plan? What were his goals? Whatever they were, they did not involve saving the vachine race from blood-oil extinction…

Walgrishnacht shook his head. Confusion spun like a snowstorm. The whole situation was… inconceivable! Impossible! Unwarranted! And yet there had been murder, and worse, *betrayal*.

Walgrishnacht turned on Beja. "We must take the platoon back to Silva Valley. We must explain that General Graal has betrayed the vachine, and everything our world stands for."

"We may not survive the mountains," warned Beja, not through fear but tactical understanding. He was aware they may never deliver the message, and thus *warning*, to the Engineer Council.

Walgrishnacht nodded. "We will give our lives to cross," he said. "The High Engineers must reconvene the War Council and assemble the Ferals – for if Graal plans an invasion after the snows have passed, and Silva Valley is unprepared…" He left the sentence unfinished. They both understood; without warning, Graal with his highly trained, disciplined, and *experienced* Army of Iron would roll through Silva Valley like a tidal wave. In an ironic twist, it was the General who commanded the army, not the Council. But then – the General was incorruptible, was he not? Walgrishnacht's face fell into a maelstrom of hatred. "Instruct the men. We move in ten minutes."

"As you wish, Cardinal."

The Warrior Engineers readied their packs and weapons, a sombre mood descending on the platoon. Then, as they headed back north through deep snow, away from Old Skulkra and the sour betrayal that had occurred, so in the distance a howl rent the air, a long, high-pitched note that seemed to linger in the deep forests and dark places of the night.

Beja looked to Walgrishnacht. "Wolves?" he said.

The Cardinal showed no emotion. "Maybe," he said. "Move out."

Anukis, of Silva Valley, had been born to Kradek-ka, one of the founding fathers of modern vachine society. Kradek-ka, like his father before him, had risen through Engineer ranks until he attained the exalted position of Watchmaker. He had achieved this level by ingenuity, cunning, and a technical skill which far out-weighed most who lived in Silva Valley. Kradek-ka's *skill* had been with clockwork; not just the machining of parts, or the intricate assembly of clockwork components, but with the *design* of new clockwork machines – machines which, more importantly, could integrate with the vampire society, keeping the dying race alive. This engineering also formed the basis of their religion, *accelerating* them in an evolutionary arc which left them... superior.

However. With his daughter, Anukis, Kradek-ka made changes. For a start, unlike normal vachine, Anukis could not drink the refined narcotic blood-oil, which every vachine relied on to sustain their clockwork mechanisms and, it was said, lubricate their clockwork souls. No. Anukis was different. Anukis was special. Anukis could not take the blood-oil like normal vachine. She could not mate with the magick. She could not feed as a normal vachine would feed… and, technically, this made her unholy, her very existence sacrilege to the High Engineer Episcopate.

Still. Here, and now, Anukis had other problems to worry about.

She was tall, and beautiful, and in possession of long, flowing, golden curls which shone and sparkled in the sunlight. Her fangs were brass, and as she had recently found, her clockwork was built to a more *advanced* design than any in the vachine society had before witnessed. Kradek-ka had made her a Goddess – and in making her a Goddess, had at the same time cursed her, and condemned her under Vachine Law.

On a mission to find her father, Kradek-ka, whom the Silva Valley needed to repair their malfunctioning Blood Refineries, Anukis had soon found herself in position of victim, of slave, at the hands of Vashell, one of the youngest ever Engineer Priests to achieve such a rank; and a vachine who had sworn to love her until the end of time, marry her, and sire a hierarchy of proud and vicious vachine warriors. That was, until the day he discovered her impurity, her living sacrilege. After vicious humiliation, they thus set upon a mission to discover her father's whereabouts within the dangerous and daunting Black Pike Mountain range. After a series of violent events which saw Anukis discover her true nature – that she was no longer vachine, but something *more pure*, something infinitely more primal… a word which taunted her with its haunting echo of millennia – *vampire*, she was *vampire* – Anukis had been separated from Vashell, and the kidnapped Falanor Queen, Alloria, and found herself on an Engineer's Barge deep within hidden tunnels under the Black Pike Mountains, drawn inexorably towards the fabled Vrekken in the hope it was an esoteric pathway which led to her missing father, whom she believed trapped in the near-mythical world of Nonterrazake.

The Vrekken.

The Vrekken roared. It surged. And it *pulled*… nearly half a league across, and filling a cavern of such incredible scale it veered off around Anukis to impossible heights, distant sheer walls glinting with dark rock and lit by wrist–thick skeins of mineral deposits.

The Vrekken howled, like a primal giant in pain. It was a huge circular portal, a juggernaut of churning spirals leading down in massive, sweeping circles towards a savage cone depth… a whirlpool, thought Anukis, eyes taking in the scene in an instant, head tossing back golden curls as her lips came back, brass vampire fangs snarling in horror, her clockwork ticking inside with increased rhythm as gears stepped and cogs spun, twisted, clicked, and Anukis grasped the edges of the Engineer's Barge. There was nothing she could do. The powerful current had her, pulled the boat towards the Vrekken, towards its vast circular sweep and tears ran down Anukis's face for here, *here* she had discovered her true identity and suddenly realised what her father wanted of her – to help revert the vachine to the pure, to the *vampires* of old, and away from the twisted merging with deviant clockwork technology, away from a reliance on the *machine*.

Anukis breathed out in a hiss.

And sped towards the huge underwater whirlpool…

The Engineer's Barge was tugged, then flung into the Vrekken and caught like a toy. It powered in circles, nose in the air leaving a wide wake through churning waters and Anu spun down, and down, and round and down and she realised the mighty whirlpool consisted of *layers* and she passed down, through layer after layer of this oceanic macrocosm, of whirling dark energy, of raw power and violent fusion and screaming howling thrashing detonation and mighty primordial *compression*, and she thought…

There is no fabled Nonterrazake. It does not exist.

Just death. Death in this place…

Anukis screamed… and waited to be crushed, eyes closed, hunched down on the brass barge with its thumping clockwork engine, her heart thundering in her ears like the ticking of the strangest, deviant clock. Spray burst over the barge, drenching her, and she could taste salt and bitterness and the whole world was a confusion. Round and round she spun. Down down through dark layers. She felt the pressure, and heard squeals as the Engineer's Barge started to buckle, to compress and crunch and fold in upon itself and Anukis hunkered down further, a ball of foetal fear, and then there came a crash and wrenching of iron and something slammed her face and darkness rushed in like a surge of sea water into a drowning ship – and Anukis remembered no more.

A dark lake lapped a dark shore. It was raining, fat droplets pattering across the lake. Anukis fluttered open butterfly eyelids that felt stretched to the point of breaking, and wondered if she were dead. But then pain slammed her like an iron oar, and she realised she couldn't be dead; the world hurt too much, and in her experience, this sort of pain only came from being *alive*. With a tiny hiss, her vachine fangs ejected, and then retracted. This, too, told her the world was real. Only *Man* could have invented the vachine.

She pushed herself up on her elbows, and listened. Nothing, but the lapping of water and the fall of rain. She frowned. Wasn't she *inside* the mountain? Then, slowly, as if dissolving from a dream, a gentle rhythmical *hush hush hush* came to her ears, and she looked up, and her mouth dropped open. Above her, the Vrekken spun, massive and violent and dark, a whirlpool in the sky, black and blue and gold and laced with traces of occasional purple. Rain fell from the mighty whirlpool, and Anukis climbed to her knees, and then to her feet, her body aching, every joint complaining, her eyes still fixed – locked – to the truly stunning and magnificent sight above. For long minutes everything was forgotten, but slowly Anukis came round, her clouded mind clearing, and she was brought back to the present. She glanced right, to where something lay crumpled by the dark lake's shore. She began to walk, soft boots silent on slippery wet rock, and with a start she recognised the crumpled thing; it was the Engineer's Barge, crushed into a loose tangle of metal as if folded and squeezed in a giant's mighty fist. With a quick movement, Anukis looked down at herself, as if fearing, for a few seconds at least, that she had been crushed also. But she hadn't; and except for a dull throbbing in her bones, as if her internal frame had somehow taken a battering but left her flesh intact, she felt fine. More than fine. She felt… invigorated!

Glad to be alive.

She stopped and gazed around, and wondered if this was Nonterrazake, the fabled mythical underworld and, more importantly, the secret home of the *Harvesters*. She moved to the wall, which followed in parallel with the lake's shore, and began to walk, footsteps quick, urgent now, for she was certainly trapped down here, in this underground place, and of one thing Anukis was certain beyond all doubt: there was no way she could head back up through the Vrekken. It was a one-way journey.

She stopped, by a small tunnel. She would have to crawl. She got down on hands and knees and peered in. She could see light, a distant eerie glow, and began to crawl through the rock. Gradually, the mountain beneath her hands, and indeed above and around her, began to fade, a graduated change from black through grey, and finally to the colour of ivory. Of bone, bleached and old. Beneath her hands the rock was no longer black, but a rough-textured white. Her nostrils twitched, for she could smell fresh, cool air. She emerged into a larger tunnel, and saw immediately she was in a mass of inter-connected tunnels which led off, seemingly randomly. Anukis swallowed. She imagined wandering down here in a labyrinth, forever, or at least until she starved and died.

She picked a tunnel at random, and walked across rough bone floor, hand trailing against bone-smooth walls, her mind working. She looked up; the ceiling was high, vast, and it was from above cool air flowed. It caressed her skin, soothing, like a sigh from a lover.

Anukis quelled a savage laugh. That sort of life was over for her. It had been since Vashell's… *abuse*.

Vashell. She remembered his love. His words of kindness. Then his hatred, and actions of violence. Beating her. Making love to her. Fucking her. She smiled. There was a difference; a big difference. And then their quest, their journey, their *fight*. Right up to the point where she ripped off his face, and left him scarred and bleeding beyond all recognition because of her powers of newly awakened vachine dominance.

Where are you now, *lover*? she thought. And she could not keep the bitterness from her mind.

She walked. It could have been hours, or even days, for down in this bone-white place, this place of caverns and caves and tunnels, time seemed to have no meaning. And although this strange underground labyrinth of Nonterrazake was empty, and silent, Anukis could not help but feel she was being watched.

Several times she would turn, fast, a superspeed vachine flick of body and head dropping to attack crouch, fangs out and claws extended for battle. But every time she was met with a vision of simple, gleaming bone.

I am not alone, she told herself, feeling paranoid.

I am not alone…

They watched her. Hundreds of them. They glided silently through the labyrinth, but here, in this place, they were partly invisible; for these were the Halls of Bone, the place which had spawned them, the place from which they had been granted life.

They were the Harvesters. And this was their *World*.

The Harvesters watched Anukis, curious, for a very select few made it through the Vrekken alive and they wondered what elements of blood-oil magick she carried in her soul to make it so. But then, she was a daughter of Kradek-ka, and this answered much; and made the drifting Harvesters *smile* beneath their ornate robes of white and gold thread.

Shall we kill her? came the pulse through bone. It was communal, hive-mind, shared by all. It was a question asked not to other Harvesters, but to the sentient world of bone around them. They thought the same question at the same time, as if they were clones, and the answer which whispered back came from the very bone-roots of the mountain under which they ruled: Skaringa Dak. The Great Mountain.

No. Let her find her father. Let them speak.
She has much to learn.
Much to understand.

The Harvesters allowed her to drift by. There were thousands now, drawn from their blending with the bone walls and columns by curiosity, and the sweet smell of her blood... and the sweeter smell of her soul. They drifted like ghosts, long tapered fingers extended as if tantalised by her organic fluid presence. But she never saw them. For in this place, they were genetic chameleons.

Unwittingly, Anukis was guided like a pig into a trap. And eventually she found herself at a small cave, a circular opening, a wide pale interior decorated with rugs and a desk. Shelves lined the bone walls, and every single one held a tiny clock, all ticking, all transparent, so that a million cogs thrashed as one, and a million gears made tiny stepping, clicking motions. Anukis blinked, for this sight was unreal; as unreal as anything she had expected.

"Anu?"

"Daddy!"

Kradek-ka rose from the padded chair of white leather and Anukis leapt, tumbled into his arms, and his face was in her golden curls and she fell into his scent, of tobacco and clockwork oil and hot metal. He still smelled the same. His arms were tight about her, soothing away her troubles. She cried, a little girl again, her tears flowing to his leather apron, and the old Watchmaker finally moved her gently backwards and smiled, a kindly smile on the face of a wrinkled, ancient vachine.

"What are you doing here? This is a dangerous place!"

"I have come for you. To rescue you!"

"Rescue? No, no, no. Did you not read my letter?"

"What letter?" Anukis's brow furrowed, and Kradek-ka made a tutting, annoyed sound. "I left a letter for you. With Vashell. When I realised I had to come away."

"Vashell has been... evil, to me."

Kradek-ka frowned, then, and his face was no longer the face of a kindly old vachine; now, he appeared menacing, and suddenly, an infinitely dangerous foe.

"That explains much," he said, softly, and moved to a nearby bench. Idly, he lifted a tiny clockwork device and began to fiddle with the delicate mechanism. As his hands moved, so the clockwork machine began to alter and change, sections flipping out and then over themselves, rearranging like an intricate puzzle, over and over and over again in an apparently infinite cycle. Eventually, Kradek-ka placed the item down.

"What is happening, Daddy? I am confused. Why are you here? What are you doing here? The Blood Refineries are breaking, the vachine of Silva Valley – your people – are beginning to starve!"

"You must brace yourself for what I am about to tell you," said Kradek-ka, and his eyes now looked old, older than worlds, and Anukis felt a shudder run through her body. In a strange way, Kradek-ka no longer resembled her father, even though his features had not changed; suddenly, he seemed alien, an altogether different creature.

"This does not sound good," said Anukis quietly, allowing herself to be led to a low couch. She sat, and Kradek-ka sat in his chair, and their hands remained together.

"The Blood Refineries are failing because..." he looked away for a moment, eyes seemingly filled with tears; tears of blood-oil, at least. "They are failing because I engineered it so."

"What? You seek to kill the vachine?"

"*No!* That is, not directly. I had to instigate certain events. I had to make sure General Graal, or whoever else, took the Army of Iron south. Invaded Falanor. It is for a greater purpose." His voice dropped to a low rumble. "A higher purpose."

"I do not understand."

"And nor should you." He smiled. Anukis did not like the smile.

"What are you doing, daddy? You left us! Shabis is dead!"

"I know this," said Kradek-ka, face serious, eyes gleaming. "But it had to be so."

"I killed her," said Anukis, hanging her head with guilt.

"This, also, I know."

"And you do not hate me?"

"You are pure, Anu," he was suddenly smiling. "Shabis chose her own path; and it was the wrong path.

You came to me, you sought me out. I hoped it would be so. For together, we can find the remaining Soul Gems, and we can..." He stopped, suddenly, and his teeth clamped shut.

"This is too strange," said Anukis. "It is like a surreal, drug-induced dream. Have I imbibed blood-oil? Am I really hallucinating, back at my apartment in Silva Valley? Will Vashell bring a surgeon to bleed out the poisons? Tell me this is so."

"I have much to tell you, Anukis. I have much to tell. But soon, you will understand. And soon, I hope, you will choose to help me. You will help... us all."

Kradek-ka motioned, and Anukis turned, and gasped at the Harvesters standing silently in the doorway. She could see perhaps twenty, but also saw their pale bony figures spreading off into the surreal hazy gloom of the bone place.

Anukis's fangs and claws ejected, but Kradek-ka squeezed her hand. "No. They are friends."

"They have been hunting me!"

"But now you are here. Now you are safe. They do not understand the bigger game. I do."

Anukis was staring, hard, eyes narrowed, mind a maelstrom Everything was wrong. Nothing fit like it should. The world felt... *seized*, like old clockwork. Like a rusted puzzlebox.

Suddenly, Kradek-ka stood, drawing Anukis up with him. His eyes gleamed. "Don't you understand, Anu? I made you special! I made you special for a reason! The day is coming, when the vachine will regress! We will return to a time of ancient power, of ancient mastery!" His face contorted into a snarl. "Now we are second-hand, kept alive, kept whole by clockwork machines."

He spat across the desk, where thousands of tiny intricate machines lay. "It was not always thus."

"You saved the vachine," said Anu, voice small.

"I cursed them!" he said. And his eyes glittered. "And
now I will uncurse them."

"What do you mean?"

"We will bring back the Vampire Warlords, Anu," he
said. "And then you will see what a species can achieve!"

Alloria, Queen of Falanor, wife to the Warrior King
Leanoric, Guardian of all Falanor States, knew instantly
the moment her husband died. It felt as if she had been
stabbed through the heart.

She had been walking a path through high mountain
passes, not long after she left Anukis who in turn set off
in the Engineer's Barge, in search of her father. Queen
Alloria, alone now, and carrying a satchel with few provisions and extra clothing which Anukis had given her
from the Barge's stores, was navigating a particularly
treacherous path of sharp frozen rocks, a sheer cliff to
her right, a vast drop of maybe five thousand feet to her
left, down sharp, scree-covered slopes which ended in a
tumbled platter of massive cubic rocks. Her hands, once
delicate and manicured, the nails perfectly filed and
painted with tiny scenes, skin soft from rich creams and
unguents, were now hard and scabbed and ingrained
with dirt. They reached out, touching the rock wall for
security lest her vertigo tip her over the edge of the slope,
and laugh at her fall as she kicked and screamed her way
to becoming a bloody pulped carcass at the bottom.

Alloria breathed deep. She calmed her mind.

Then the pain came, slashing through her heart like
a razor, and she gasped, and heard his cry across the

miles, across the skies, across the mountains, across the void; and Alloria knew as sure as the sun would rise that Leanoric, her true love, the man she had betrayed and who had, against all probability, *forgiven her*; she knew he was dead.

Alloria gasped, and fell to her knees. Overhead, an eagle swooped, then dropped and disappeared into the vastness of the canyon. Alloria clutched her chest, and the pain was intense and she could hear Leanoric's scream which suddenly cut off – in an instant – as he was slain.

"Oh, my, no," was all she managed to whisper, and knelt there on the rocky trail, rocking gently backwards and forwards as desolation filled her like ink in a jug; right to the brim.

She knelt there. For long hours. And cried. She cried for his death. She cried for her boys. And she cried for her betrayal of Falanor, her foolish *foolish* betrayal, which sat with her, sat bad with her, like a demon smothering her soul.

It was only as darkness fell, and she heard the distant cries of wolves that she was prodded into action. She climbed wearily to her feet, drained beyond any semblance of humanity. It had all been too much; the invasion, the rape, the abuse, the kidnapping. And now that her husband was dead, and she knew in her heart he was truly gone, there seemed little left to live for. *But what about your children?* asked a tiny part of her conscience, and she smiled there on the mountain ledge, as clouds swirled heavy above her and light flakes of snow began to snap in the wind. Of course, she thought. Her children. Sweet Oliver, and handsome Alexander; oh how she missed them. She picked her way along the trail in the fast-falling gloom. But then, who was to say they had not also been slain? They had been with Leanoric as he checked his armies in those last fateful days of Falanor's rule. Surely they were still with him, in the fast-falling panic following the swift invasion by Graal's Army of Iron? The albinos had marched on Jalder, then headed south with speed, taking every city and town and village they came upon. They allowed few to escape; and those who did escape were hunted down by the terrible beasts known as *cankers*.

Alloria shuddered again. She looked up. Above her, light fell swiftly from the sky. Velvet caressed her vision. She cursed herself, cursed herself for her self-pity, and cursed herself for knowing too much. Graal. Graal. She touched her hand to her breast, remembering the gems.

Whilst she knelt, weeping, the mountain night and the savagery of nature had crept in on her. Now the Black Pikes would seek to test her mettle, her agility, her stamina and her courage.

Alloria stumbled over a rocky ledge, and nearly pitched into the chasm far below. Panting, and with hands raw from scraping rock, she moved on, telling herself constantly that Oliver and Alexander were still alive; that Leanoric would have had the foresight to hide them somewhere safe. But deep down in her heart, in her soul, she did not believe it... even if she could not feel their deaths as acutely as that of her king, her husband, her lover, and ultimately, her soul mate.

She stopped, suddenly. She turned to face the vast drop. She could no longer see it, for night in the mountains was darkness as she had never before experienced; a total immersion of vision, and senses, and soul. But she knew the drop was there; she could feel the gaping presence, the mammoth opening of space and cold, snapping air. Snow landed in her hair. She ignored it. She stepped up onto the lip.

I should die, she realised.

There is nothing left to live for.

General Graal has won.

"Wait there, little lady," came a soft whisper.

Alloria jumped, startled by the gentle voice. However, she recognised the tone, and yet the words seemed alien to her at the same time. She shook spastically, with fear, with adrenaline, with apprehension at her impending suicide.

"I cannot see you!" she hissed.

"But I can see you," came the voice, at once gentle and powerful and harsh and merciless. Strong hands took hold of her, and eased her back from the slash of precipice. Before her, waves of ice crashed down onto invisible rocks of awesome destruction.

"Vashell? Is that you?"

"Yes," came the rich, powerful voice of the vachine. "It is I."

"Have you followed me?"

"Let us say we travel the same path," came his words, at once soothing and deeply terrifying. Alloria had witnessed his cruelty first hand; and his violence. She was afraid.

"How can you see in the dark?" she murmured, heart beating a rampage in her chest. She realised, then, that she needed her blue karissia; just to help her sleep. Always to help her sleep.

"I have special vision," said Vashell. "I have clockwork eyes. Now, come, the snow is growing heavy; in an hour we will be trapped on this narrow path. I know of a cave a distance ahead where we can take shelter. By the gods, woman, you are freezing! Have you no cloak?"

Alloria struggled to free her cloak from the satchel she carried, and Vashell helped. Once encapsulated within fur and leather, she felt better; a little better. But the death of Leanoric still bit her, like wolf fangs through her heart.

"This way. Hold my hand. I will lead."

Alloria stumbled along the trail, with Vashell leading the way. She did not trust the man – she smiled, and corrected herself. The *vachine*. But then, she had little choice, and in all actuality, no longer cared. If he was going to rape her, slit her, toss her ragdoll body down the mountain, then so be it. Surely, she deserved no less? Alloria had lost the fight and fire in her heart.

They struggled on against worsening weather. The wind howled like a stabbed banshee. The snow pummelled them with padded fists. At one point Alloria fell, with a grunt and a small cry, and she felt herself reeling and sliding towards a violent chasm – but Vashell was there, strong hands pulling her back, and he held her, and she shivered and knew it was not from the cold; she was impervious, now, to ice. It was for the loss. The deep, drowning, terrible loss of her dead husband, her dead children. She knew she would never be sane again.

"Here. We are here."

Alloria could see nothing but white and gloom, but felt a sudden lessening of the wind and horizontally lashing snow. Vashell led her far back into the cave and it was curiously warm. He sat her on a stone, and using a bundle of small sticks, lit a tiny fire in a circle of blackened rocks. This place had been used by many travellers, it would seem.

Firelight filled the cave, and although little heat was produced, the illusion was enough for Alloria, for now. She moved closer, stretching out fingers to the meagre flames, and then her head snapped up as she remembered the vicious fight between Vashell and Anukis (so long ago, *drifting through ancient dreams*)… a fight which had ended with Vashell losing his *face*.

Even in the darkness, in the flickering firelight, his face was nothing less than a terrible mess; strings of flesh covered cords of tendon and visible bone; some scar tissue showed where the vachine's accelerated healing was trying frantically to compensate for such a savage wounding. But it hadn't done enough.

Vashell lowered his face; his eyes were full of pain, and shame. With head lowered, he said, "Once, my Queen, you found me beautiful." She said nothing. He looked up, glittering eyes meeting hers. "But not any more, I think."

"Beauty is more than the skin on your bones, Vashell. It is here, in your heart, in your soul, and mirrored by the things you do. And no, sadly, from what I have seen of you, and the horror of which I heard you speak, I am not prepared to think of you as a beautiful soul."

"I have done… questionable things," said Vashell, head lowered once again. His hand held a dagger. It glinted, blade black in the firelight. Suddenly, Alloria's eyes fixed on that blade, and she swallowed, tasting a thrill of raw metal fear.

She realised, with a dawning like a virgin sun, that she was antagonising a tormented man. He shuffled back a little, and breathed deeply. Here was a vachine warrior not to be trifled with. According to Alloria, he had slain children – impure, Blacklipper children – in their beds. He had no qualms about killing women. He was a predator; the ultimate predator. And he killed not to survive; but because he had an intrinsic enjoyment of the concept, and indeed, the act.

Outside, in the darkness, distant through the snow, a wolf howled.

Alloria shivered, and stared at the cave opening. She was no match for a wolf. When she had decided to head off through the mountains after her release by Anukis, she had never considered such things as wolves, or bears, or even now, as she thought about it, wild men, brigands, outlaws on the mountain trails. She shuddered. Maybe death was still the answer? But on her own terms. By her own hand. Not ripped apart by the wild.

Vashell stood and moved to the cave entrance. Then he turned to her. His destroyed face was creased in… in what? She could not tell whether it was humour, or hatred. Vashell had lost the ability to display facial expressions. Indeed, Vashell had lost the ability to show his face.

"The wolves are coming," he said.

"How do you know?"

"I can hear them. A winter pack. White wolves. They are the worst."

"Why the worst?" Her voice seemed, to her own ears at least, incredibly small.

"Because they are the most hungry," he said, with a twisted smile that showed teeth through the holes in his cheeks.

Alloria looked away.

"They are following your scent. They must have been tracking you for hours. There's precious little meat on these bare hills."

"Then I will die," said Alloria, lifting her head, eyes blazing.

"We all die," said Vashell, turning back to the cave entrance.

Outside, there came a fast padding, and a snarl. Slowly, Vashell backed towards Alloria; his athletic frame partially blocked the cave entrance, and she suddenly realised that Vashell had no sword, only the knife which she had seen him with earlier, a blade stolen from the Engineer's Barge during his escape several days ago.

Then she saw the wolf. It was large-framed but scrawny, lean and athletic and hungry-looking; its fur was a mix of shaggy white streaked with grey and black, its eyes a wide-slitted yellow, its fangs old and yellow and curved like daggers. It was far bigger than any wolf Alloria had ever seen in Falanor, and its claws rasped on the cave's floor. It stopped, head tilted, surveying the two people. Vashell, poised, did not move. He seemed frozen to the spot – either in fear, or gauging his enemy.

Then more wolves arrived, and they were snarling and hissing, drool spooling from ancient fangs as they moved as a pack into the cave which, with its too-wide opening, allowed them in three abreast. There were five, now; then eight. Then twelve. Their fur bristled with snow melt, and each wolf had a narrowed, hungry look. A haunted look. They were willing to die in order to feed.

Alloria heard herself utter a small whimper. Vashell did not turn, but she saw his muscles tense.

The lead wolf snarled, a sudden, aggressive sound, and leapt at Vashell in a blur...

CHAPTER 6
Stealers' Moon

Jageraw travelled with care, avoiding men, avoiding albino soldiers, avoiding cankers and avoiding anybody he thought might be a threat – which meant anything *alive*. The pain in his chest was worse now, and often made him gasp and he would mutter to himself, "Not pretty, not pretty," and rub at his armoured chitin as if by rubbing the area he could ease away the pain.

The canker Jageraw had saved back at Le'annath Moorkelth was gone, fled through the forest. He was an odd one that canker, yes, thought Jageraw, bitter for a moment that none wished to share his company. Did he stink? Was that it? Stink of fish? All Jageraw got out of the twisted clockwork creature was its name: Elias. Then it was gone, floundering and stamping through the forest, easy meat for soldier's crossbows yes yes. He regretted now not eating the Elias. It was a pain, spitting out the cogs, but cankers could taste quite prime.

As he moved, so he thought of the Hexels.

They had saved him.

They had honoured him.

Now, Jageraw knew his task.

140

Muttering, he stumbled on through forests and snow, stopping occasionally to hunt down some unsuspecting traveller or refugee, but even the slick feeling of raw kidneys or liver on his tongue, or even – the *joy!* – a succulent lung, did nothing to ease the pain in his chest. And the further north he travelled, the more the pain burned.

It was late afternoon, sky darkening, as Kell rode his steed up a steep hill, reins in one hand, the other on the haft of his saddle-sheathed axe. He drew rein atop the summit, and Saark came up beside him, silent, considering. Mary the donkey brayed, the noise loud and echoing, and Kell threw back a bitter scowl.

"Don't even think it," said Saark.

"What?"

"She's invaluable. And Skanda is enjoying riding her. You wouldn't take such a simple pleasure from the boy?"

Kell stared hard into Saark's eyes, and what he saw there he did not understand. Kell knew that he was good at reading men, but Saark was a true conundrum. Complex, unpredictable, Kell knew deep in his heart he would make better progress if he left Saark behind. And that was the answer, he realised. Singularity.

Pain lashed through his veins, and Kell gritted his teeth, swooning in the saddle. The world blurred and reeled, and he grasped the saddle pommel with both hands, face pale, eyes squeezed shut, and focused on simply breathing as the world in its entirety swirled down in wide lazy blood circles. He heard Saark's voice, but it was a garbled, stretched out series of meaningless sounds. And in the middle of it all there was a taste, and the taste was whiskey, and he knew that if only he could have another drink then everything would be all right again, and the pain would go away again, and no matter that it made him violent because he was in a violent world on a violent mission and the whiskey would *help him* achieve his goal; waves of pain pulsed through him, and then a moment of darkness, and then he was breathing, gasping at the cold air like a drowning man coming to the surface of a lake.

The world slapped Kell in the face, and he was gasping, and Saark was asking him if he was well. Kell took several deep, exaggerated breaths, and looked right to Saark. He gave a nod. "It's the poison, lad," he managed, voice hoarse. "When she bites, she bites real hard."

"We need to rest," said Saark. "Somewhere warm, some hot food, a good sleep. We've been through a lot." He winced, clutching his wounded side instinctively. "And we stink like a ten day corpse."

"Speak for yourself," barked Kell.

"Kell?" It was Skanda. His eyes glittered. Again, now they had stopped, the scorpion sat on his hand and seemed to be watching proceedings. Kell eyed the insect uneasily, and made a mental note to tread the bastard underboot at the first opportunity.

"What is it, lad?"

"There is a village, yonder. Creggan. I have travelled there before. It is getting late, we should move."

"Where?" Both Kell and Saark squinted, looking off over gloom-laden, snowy hills which dropped in vast steps from their position, like folds in a giant's goose-down quilt.

Skanda pointed. "Come. I will show you." He reached out, and the lead between Saark's horse and

Mary fell away. Skanda cantered the donkey forward, and the usually stubborn beast (on several occasions, Saark had had to practically wrestle the donkey into ambulation) obeyed Skanda without hesitation, nor braying complaint.

Saark shrugged, and Kell scowled. Skanda set off in a seemingly random direction from the high ground near the Great North Road. Saark followed, his gelding stamping and snorting steam. Kell waited for a few moments, pulled free the unmarked whiskey bottle, and drained the last few drops. He licked his lips, and despite hating himself for it, hoped to the High Gods that there was a tavern.

The village was small, a central square with hall and tavern and a few shops. All seemed closed and empty and dead on this cold winter evening, another apparent victim of the Army of Iron. Kell and Saark had Skanda wait by the outskirts as they rode in, weapons drawn, eyes wary as they searched for albino soldiers. Nobody walked the streets. Most of the houses seemed deserted.

"Has the Army of Iron been through, do you think?"

Kell shrugged, and pointed to the tavern where thin wisps of smoke eased from a ragged, uneven chimney. "I don't think so. No bodies in the road, for a start. But let us find out." He dismounted at the tavern, and thumped open the door. Inside was warm, a fire crackling in the hearth. A long bar supported three men, all stocky and dour, who jumped as the door opened, their eyes casting nervous to the intruders, hands on sword hilts. A tall, thin barman gave a nod to Kell, and Kell entered.

"Do you have rooms?"

"How many?"

"Two."

"Yes. It'll be five coppers a night. Will you be wanting warm water? 'Cos that's another copper."

"Warm water is a prerequisite to cleanliness and holiness, my man," said Saark, entering the tavern and smiling, leaning forward over ale-stained timbers.

The barman stared at the ragged, bruised, tattered dandy, without comprehension.

"He said 'yes'," grunted Kell, and dropped coins on the bar. Then to Saark, "Go and get the boy, and stable our horses."

When Saark had left, Kell eyed the barman. "You have a cosy little town, here, barman."

"And we would keep it that way. An army passed through, killing everyone in surrounding towns," his eyes were bleak, his mind full of nightmares, "of this we know. We would ask you to keep your knowledge of Creggan to yourselves. We have nowhere to run, you understand?"

Kell nodded, and ordered a whiskey, which he downed in one. Then, when Saark returned after stabling the horses and Mary, Kell pushed past him on his way to the door.

"Hey, where are you going?"

"Out."

"Out where?"

"Just out," grinned Kell, but it was a grin without humour.

"Old horse, I have a question. Why did you only purchase two rooms? A little odd, I thought."

Kell's grin widened. "You love that damn creepy Ankarok boy so much. Well. You can bunk with him. Maybe he'll stop you behaving like an idiot!"

• • •

It was later. Much later. Darkness had fallen, and with it a fresh storm of snow. Kell had returned, brushing flakes from the shoulders of his heavy bearskin jerkin, and now sat eating a meal at a corner table in the tavern. It was a pie filled mostly with potatoes, a little ham, and thick gravy. Kell also had a full loaf of black bread, which he sliced thickly, smothering each slice with butter. Skanda sat, facing Kell, eyes fixed on the old warrior, watching the man eat. On three occasions Kell had offered the boy food, but the thin-limbed urchin waved it away.

"You need something warm inside you, lad," said Kell, relaxing with a full belly, eyes kind now he was out of the cold, the wind, the snow, and immediate threat of battle. He was getting old, he realised. Damn it, he *was* old! And, thinking of their pursuit after Nienna, he realised just how ancient and worn he really felt. To the core.

"I am not hungry," said Skanda.

"You must eat something."

"If you could ask for a little warm milk?"

Kell nodded, and called over a serving girl. She returned shortly with a cup of warm milk, and a tankard of ale for Kell. Both Kell and Skanda sat, drinking their drinks and watching the tavern gradually fill. The village of Creggan was not as deserted as it first seemed.

"Where's Saark got to?" said Kell, after a while. He was watching a group of men in the corner, and noting their ease of movement, and how they hardly touched their drinks. They seemed like military men to Kell, but one had a taint to the lips, as if he might be a blossoming Blacklipper. Blacklippers were men, and women, who had found a taste for the illegal and hard to come by *blood-oil*, so revered and necessary to the vachine. Most Blacklippers had little idea the narcotic juice they purchased was refined from human blood. Nor did they realise it was destined for a market so… esoteric: that of the vachine civilisation deep within the folds of the Black Pike Mountains. Most Blacklippers simply lived for the moment, and took their pleasure – including blood-oil – when and where they found it; the one downside, of course, being that the more a person used blood-oil, the more their lips, and eventually, fatally, their very *veins* stood out black from their skin. When a Blacklipper's veins stood out like a battlefield map in ink, one could count their remaining weeks on one hand.

Skanda sipped his milk. "He went out."

"Where to?" Kell frowned. "He said he was having a bath."

"He said he had things he needed to buy."

"Hmm," said Kell, and placed his chin on his fist. By his boot, no more than a hand-span away, Ilanna leant against the edge of the rough-sawn table. And under his left arm lay sheathed his Svian knife; usually, his last resort weapon on the few occasions he was parted from his first love. Ilanna.

The tavern was crowded now, but curiously subdued. *They all know, then,* thought Kell. *They understand that Falanor has been invaded and they have missed the network of searching soldiers through sheer luck. No obvious roads led to Creggan. They had been overlooked.* By the villagers' demeanour, they understood what would happen if a second pass came upon this little haven.

Kell's practised eye picked out that every man wore a sword, or long knife. Even the women who came in wearing thick woollen dresses and cotton shirts were armed. This was a town living in fear. It was palpable, like ash on their skin, like plague in their eyes.

Skanda finished his milk, and stood.

"Where are *you* going, lad?"

"I'm tired. I am going to sleep."

Kell nodded, and watched the thin boy weave his way through the crowded tavern. Smoke washed over him, and a serving girl approached. She asked if he wanted a drink. Kell looked down at his ale. He looked up at her. And he considered.

"Bring me a whiskey," he said at last, voice hoarse.

Saark sat in hot water, the wound in his side stinging like the fires of the Chaos Halls, his limbs bruised like a pit-fighter's, but still happy as heat flowed through his damaged flesh and aching bones. He settled back with a sigh. The stench of blood, and sweat, and dirt, of battle, of cankers, of sleeping in the forest, of albino brains and albino gore, all were scrubbed from his now pink and raw skin. And even better, he had asked around, and purchased some rich bath herbs, and perfume, none of it as fine as the scents used in the Royal Court in Vor, but a damn sight more refined than stinking of horse-sweat and death.

Saark sighed again. The water lapped the edges of the bath rimed with excised scum. He stared happily at the new clothes – clothes he knew, in his deepest of hearts, were a wasteful extravagance, and certainly not geared for travelling across the country – but still of necessity to one such as Saark. He was addicted to buying clothes and perfume as some men were addicted to whiskey, or gambling on dog fights. Because, he knew, with fine clothes and perfume matched to his natural beauty, the whole heady mix led to one thing, and one thing only: amorous meetings with pretty young ladies.

Saark closed his eyes, picturing the many women he had conquered. And yet Katrina's face kept returning, invading his imagination, pointing a finger of accusation. I am dead, she seemed to be saying. You told me you loved me. Now I rot under the soil and you *did not stop it happening*!

Mood soured by ghosts, Saark climbed from the bath and towelled himself dry. He stood, shivering a little and staring at himself in a full length brass mirror. The wound was healing in his side; it still leaked blood occasionally, but it *was* getting better. The stitches were holding fine. The swelling in his face had gone down, so he no longer looked like a horse had danced on his features, and many of his bruises had faded to yellow, and many, incredibly, had gone.

I heal fast, he thought with a smile. But not mentally, he realised, with a grimace.

He dressed, in a bright orange silk shirt with ruffles of lace around wrists and throat, and bright blue woollen leggings. He'd also bought a new *snow leopard* cloak, long down to his ankles, fine doe-leather and lined with snow leopard fur, or so he'd been told; although he doubted it. Still, it added a nice splash of white to set off the orange of his shirt. And would undoubtedly be warm on the road.

Saark draped a cord over his neck, settling a bright green pendant at his throat, and then buckled his rapier at his side. He drew the weapon, a blur flickering silver in the mirror, a stunning display of skill and accuracy;

then he winced, slowly, and held his side. "Ouch," he muttered. "Not there yet, lover. Not there yet."

Leaving his old clothes in a pile for the tavern's serving girls to burn, Saark returned to his room and opened the door. Skanda was seated, on one of the narrow sparse beds, but his face was wide as if celebrating a rapturous applause, and something long, and brass, lay loose along his arm. Saark stepped inside and closed the door. He laid his cloak on a chair and moved to Skanda.

"What are you doing, boy?" he asked, voice low, words not unkind.

Skanda did not respond. His eyes were open, but there was no comprehension there. Saark's eyes travelled down to the brass object. It was old, very old and worn by its look, and quite ornate. Saark had seen similar objects in the houses of doctors when he'd had swordfight wounds stitched. It was a needle, a brass needle, used to inject fluids into the human body. This was affixed to Skanda's arm; or more precisely, his vein.

"Skanda," breathed Saark and moved as if to remove the needle. There came a rapid clicking sound, and his eyes moved fast and he leapt back. The scorpion was there, twin tails raised in threat, pincers flexing as it watched Saark with its many tiny black eyes.

Saark released a hiss of breath. "Damn disgusting little thing," he snapped, and drew his sword, eyes narrowing. "I'm going to cut you in two!" But then he understood the situation with a stab of insight. The scorpion was protecting its master.

How can that be? thought Saark. It's an insect! A poisonous little arachnid with no compassion or empathy for *anything*. Why would it protect the boy?

Slowly, Saark sheathed his sword and held out his hands. "I was simply going to remove the needle and put the boy to bed. You know? Make him more comfortable?"

The scorpion surveyed him for a few moments, then lowered its stings and scuttled back within Skanda's loose clothing. Warily, Saark pulled free the needle with a tiny squirt of blood, and put it to one side. Then he lifted Skanda onto the bed and laid him out, covering him with a thin blanket. "There you go," he muttered, and thought back to his own childhood, his father hanging by the throat, his mother screaming, and the long, long, long weeks of being utterly and totally alone.

Saark's eyes shone with tears. "I'll look after you, lad. You see if I don't," he said.

Saark reckoned he created quite a stir when he walked into the smoky, crowded tavern. The crowd certainly parted to allow him passage, and he ignored the many stares as he crossed to Kell and seated himself opposite the axeman, back to the crowd.

"What," said Kell, "in the name of horse-shit, are you wearing?"

"I call it *Orange Blossom in Winter*. I think it's quite alluring. I think the ladies are noticing me." He smiled a broad, happy smile.

"Mate, every bastard is noticing you, from the lowliest mongrel backstabbing thief to the dirtiest, sleaziest whore in the village. What the hell were you thinking, Saark?"

"I was thinking it's been awhile since I had some female company."

"I thought you were over that?"

"Kell, my friend, you do not understand men, nor women. This is not something I want; this is something

I *need*. I cannot control myself, no more than you control your... your swinging axe."

"Saark, we are staying one night. What possessed you to dress like a peacock?"

"It is my way."

"And you stink! Gods, it's like you've been showered with every tart's knicker-drawer lavender bottle in the country! You'll have the bastard albino soldiers on us in an instant if you step into the wilds of Falanor stinking like that."

"You are so uncouth."

"I thought you'd overcome all this crap? I thought we were on a mission?"

"What?" Saark looked incredulous. "*What?* Overcome? You confuse, old horse. Indeed, there is nothing here for which to overcome, because this is a question of breeding, this is a question of sophistication, and this is an embodiment of culture – something intrinsic, not just learned. And, because I have been forced to endure your company and travel in extraneous hardship, just because I have been forced to sleep in shit, and eat shit, and listen to shit, does not mean I thus *crave* shit. No. You know I am used to the finer aspects of life, and despite this being a poor backward peasant village," several of the men in the tavern scowled and muttered at these brash, arrogant and loudly delivered words, "filled with dirty, low-born peasants whose only knowledge is how to feed pigs and kill chickens," he laughed, a bright tinkling of crystal windchimes, "that doesn't mean to say I have to denigrate myself to the lower echelons of a rude base society. Understand?"

"You're a horse's dick, Saark."

"I rest my case."

"Meaning?"

"When faced with superior intelligence, culture and argument, you instantly revert to the base gutter which spawned you. I do not blame you for low-born behaviour, Kell, in fact sometimes I am envious; how I wish I wasn't so beautiful, and charming, and irresistible to the ladies." Saark took this moment to have a good look around, and although his eyes lingered on several buxom wenches, the sight of their moribund attire, cracked and broken fingernails and dowdy knife-hacked hair made him turn back to Kell with a scowl and deep sigh. "However. I am cursed thus, and so must make the most of my natural endowments, and indeed, the nature of my beast. And what a beast it is."

"I'd forgotten," said Kell.

"What do you mean, old horse?"

Kell bared his teeth, and drained his tankard. "We've been through some battles, Saark lad, some hard shit, and you've proved yourself to be tougher than I anticipated. You're a good swordsman, with a strong arm and keen eye, and enough mental toughness to face any enemy."

"But?"

"But the minute you touch any form of civilisation, you regress to the pig-headed sugar-mouthed hard-cocked brainless stinking village fucking idiot I've always loathed." Saark opened his mouth, as Kell hefted his axe and stood, stool scraping the straw-covered stone flags. "And if I hear another sugar-coated pile of goat's bollocks from *you*, I'll carve my name on *your* arse." Saark's mouth closed again, and Kell stalked through the crowded tavern and stepped out into the night.

"Really!" said Saark, and grinned, then winced as the stitches in his side pulled tight. He laughed, half in pain, half in joy at this simple touch of civility. He moved round the table, taking Kell's place with his back to the wall, and noticed with surprise that quite a few of the tavern's stocky peasant farmers were throwing him dark, menacing scowls. Saark waved cheerily, and they returned their dark glances and mutters to the bar, and flat ale.

"Now, what shall I do?" murmured Saark, and rubbed his chin. It was slightly pink from shaving, but by the gods it felt good to be rid of the stubble and dirt. He had groomed his moustache carefully, using a little oil supplied by Bess, the tavern master's daughter. The rest he had rubbed into his hands and smoothed through his long, dark curls. Saark knew he cut a tall, dashing, handsome figure. But after the beating by Myriam's men, resulting in a head like a sausage-stuffed pig's stomach, he had been knocked temporarily out of the womanising game. But now... *now* most of the bruises and swelling were gone, and Saark understood the dark, smoky interior would hide any remaining blemishes. Like a cat, he was ready to play. Like a lust-fuelled bull, he was ready to charge! He grinned. Saark was back, baby, Saark was back!

His eyes wandered the room, and he drank his ale and ordered another, which he also downed. Several women looked at him, and smiled. Saark graded them silently, methodically, placing them in a mental hierarchy of whom he would bed first provided no finer lass entered the premises. Such was his confidence, and experience, it never occurred to Saark that a lady might turn him down. That was something which happened to other poor unfortunates.

So intent was Saark on scrutinising the women on display, like prime beef at a cattle market, that as he was finishing the dregs from his fourth tankard of ale two men approached. He didn't register until they were standing directly before him.

"Hello, lads," smiled Saark, placing his tankard down with a *clack*. "What can I do you for?"

"The popinjay asks what he can do for us," laughed the first man. He was big, with a round head, rough-cropped hair, large ears and ruddy cheeks. In his fist, he held a longsword, point lowered. Saark's eyes followed the blade to the ground.

"That's a good question," replied his companion. "A very good question indeed. A damn fine question, if I be honest."

"Listen," said Saark, leaning forward a little as if sharing a conspiracy, "much as I'd like to sit here and trade stunning witticisms with two grand but obsequious fellows, who are both obviously the core intellectual firecrackers of this entire inbred ensemble, I really feel I must rise and circulate in order to integrate with the finer female brethren contained within this squalid den of congenital primates."

"You see," said the first man. "There he goes again. Spouting all that crap. Horseshit, I says it is."

"Aye. And he stinks like horseshit, as well." Then to Saark. "You hear that, boy? You stink like horseshit."

Saark sighed, and there came a little tearing sound. One of the men yelped, and went rigid. Saark's eyes were suddenly dark, and contained less humour, and his face and dandy clothing seemed somehow just that bit less ridiculous. "That little prick you feel against your leg, my friend – and I can *tell* you're a man who enjoys feeling little pricks against his leg – well, it's the point of my rapier. Let me assure you, my weapon is tempered from finest Jevaiden steel, and probably cost more than this entire village; indeed, I spend a good half hour a day keeping it sharp ready for the hour I need to teach some uncouth big-eared boy a lesson. Now, I'd advise you not to move quickly because the point is a single twitch from slitting your femoral artery – that's the main one, which runs through your groin and will empty your pathetic body of blood in less than two minutes." Saark leaned forward. His eyes glittered. "I've killed thirty eight men with that cut. Not a single man didn't writhe and scream like his intestines were filled with molten lead. You hearing me nice and clear, village idiot?"

Both men nodded, and stepped warily back from the dandy. Their faces had turned pale.

Saark stood, and sheathed his rapier, and turned his back on them with a show of contempt. He glanced once again around the room. His face displayed open disappointment at the sport on offer.

Saark sighed, and strode to the door. The smoke, and perhaps a little too much ale, were making him dizzy, with the added consequence of polluting his new finery with a stink like a tobacconist's smoking shed. He stepped out into the night, pulling his snow-leopard cloak tight around his shoulders and looked up into the falling snow. He leant his back against the wall and took several deep breaths, head spinning a little. Damn the grog! he thought, hand on sword-hilt.

"Hello," came a voice, a female voice, and Saark found himself staring at a tall, lithe, robed figure. In the darkness the robe seemed to glimmer like velvet, and from the edges of the hood he could see bright blonde hair, a fan of translucence. She was a little taller than Saark, but rather than intimidate, this excited him. She held herself erect with a natural nobility, and her half-shadowed features were finely sculpted, high chiselled cheekbones, flawless skin and dark, half-hidden eyes.

"Well, hello there," smiled Saark, and stroked his chin, and wondered suddenly at the capriciousness of life, the gods, and most importantly, women. "What's a pretty thing like you doing out on a cold, dark, snow-laden night like this? Surely, you must allow me to escort you somewhere warm where you might partake of drying your fine, moonlit-shadowed hair, and maybe partake of some fine Gollothrim brandy distilled from ripe plums and cherries teased from the superlative or-chards of the south."

"Oh, you speak so fine and handsome, sir. You are not from these parts?"

"Alas, no, simply riding through. But I think you may entice me to return! You live here, no?"

"My parents are dead. I spend some time with my uncle in Jangir, the rest here with my aunt. She has a small farmstead."

"Wonderful! Is it nearby?"

"A goodly trek, sir. But what of this brandy of which you speak?" She moved closer, and Saark smelt her musk. It infected him, immediately, like a heady liquor injected to his vein, a toxic narcotic injected to his brain. If I die tonight after enjoying this fabulous woman, I would die a happy man, thought Saark, as he moved close to her and her eyes were still hooded and he reached out, stroked away a stray strand of hair and she giggled, and he leant forward, intoxicated by alcohol

and her scent and their lips touched, the briefest of in-
timations, a promise of flesh and excitement to come.
The woman turned away, a teasing, calculated movement which was not lost on the dandy. He enjoyed it.
It was all part of the game.

Oh, thought Saark, you're good; you're very good.

"My room is this way," said Saark, gesturing to
the tavern.

"It would be unseemly for me to trudge through
the tavern common-room. Is there a... more discrete
entrance?"

"I'm sure we will find one, my sweet," purred Saark,
and reaching out he took her arm and they moved
through the snow, and he said, "What is your name,
my princess?"

"My name is Shanna," she whispered, voice husky
with an anticipation of impending violence.

Saark moved to the bed, and lowered the wick on the
lantern. He had taken the woman to Kell's room – after
all, the boy Skanda was sleeping deeply in their shared
quarters, and Saark knew the old goat wouldn't be
needing his bed. Well, not for the intimacies of a lady,
at any rate. The ambient air was filled with warmth,
and positive energy, and the scent of Shanna which
seemed to take Saark and spin him up and around in a
frenzy of need and recklessness. He breathed deeply,
and Shanna moved to the bed, and lowered her hood,
and removed her cloak. She wore a short, white dress,
and Saark moved to her and placed his hands on her
shoulders and she murmured, a little in pleasure, a little
in lust, a little in need, and Saark kissed the pale skin
of her neck, kissed through her fine blonde hair and

she wriggled in his embrace as if he tickled her, plea-
sured her, and it was all like a dream seen through a
distorted piece of glass. Saark stepped away, panting.
"You are beautiful and luscious indeed," he said, and
kicked off his boots.

Shanna moved to the lantern, and lowered it more.
When she looked up at him, her eyes were dark, like pools
of liquid ruby. Her face was gaunt, but stunningly beautiful. When she smiled, Saark melted like butter in a pan.
He groaned, and moved to her again, and kissed her, and
his arms were over her and touching her, and she writhed
under his touch in lustful agony and then took his head,
suddenly, in a powerful grip and stared deep into his eyes.

"I think I am in heaven," whispered Saark.

"You soon will be," promised Shanna, and there
came twin crunches as her fangs ejected and her head
dropped for his throat and a fist of insanity punched
through Saark's mind – but not enough to inhibit
twenty-five years of military training and real-world
combat. Saark swayed back, twisting fast, stepped back
and away in shock; then he leapt at her, both boots
slamming Shanna's chest and using the impact to kick
himself backwards, through a somersault to land lightly
on his feet by the door, facing her.

Shanna's hands had come up to her chest, head
tilted, the smile still on her lips. There was no pain.
Now, her visage was one of mock disappointment.
"What? You would spurn me so soon, my beautiful and
verbally sophisticated lover?"

Saark cast his gaze past Shanna, to where his rapier
stood – useless – by the window. He grinned, a nasty
sideways grin without humour as his hands levelled before him, and he stared at the vachine and took a step

to the left. Shanna followed his direction with intimacy, and eased towards him.

"You would have bitten me," he said, eyes fixed on her long fangs, and then on her eyes, and he cursed himself. Her eyes were crimson, the red of the albino warriors who hunted them. And yet she had fangs, like the vachine creatures from beyond the mountains. "What the hell *are* you?"

"You wouldn't understand, Saark, my sweet," she said, and lunged at him.

Saark swayed to one side, and cracked a right hook against her cheek, spinning away to the other side of the room. Shanna touched her face, lower lip extending a little. She pouted.

"A little excessive, Saark, don't you think?"

Only then did he realise he had not told her his name. Something chilled inside him. Some primordial instinct told him this woman, or vachine, or whatever the hell she was, was very, very dangerous. And she was looking for him. Hunting him.

Shanna leapt again, and blocked three fast punches. She grabbed his throat and groin in one swift move- ment, and hurled Saark across the room where he hit the wall, hard, and landed in a heap, wheezing, head spinning, and then she was there, kneeling beside him, and she took hold of his long fine oiled curls and snapped back his head in a vicious movement. From the corner of his eye he saw her fangs extend that little bit more. They gleamed, like brass.

"You're going to taste so sweet, my love," she smiled, completely aware of the irony.

"No," he croaked… as her fangs dropped for his throat.

• • •

Kell marched through the snow, boots crunching, the glass of the whiskey bottle cold against his skin under heavy jerkin. He stopped at a narrow crossroads, and looked about. The village was quiet, eerie, dusted with mist and falling snow, most houses sporting lights subdued behind heavy curtains. The villagers knew what would happen if soldiers from the Army of Iron discovered their little safe haven, tucked away between low hills; and they guarded their anonymity with jealous fear and an understanding of a savage retribution if discovered. Wise, he thought. Very wise.

Kell looked up and down the twisting lanes, his breath steaming. He took out the whiskey bottle. He took a long drink. Honey eased into his veins. He thought of Nienna, he felt bad, and he knew if he got drunk he was doing nobody any favours, least of all his poor, kidnapped granddaughter. He knew, then, what he really *should* do was hurl the bottle down the street and go and get his horse and ride after her to the Cailleach Fortress. But he did not. He felt his mind crumbling, disintegrating, like a mud wall before a spring flood.

He started off down a narrow street, unsure of where he was going. The whiskey tasted good on his lips, hot in his throat, and he craved more. Much more. He knew, as did all drinkers, that he could use the excuse of the poison in his veins; however, deep in his heart he realised he was only cheating himself. He needed no whiskey to cover that pain. The pain he could live with. He had lived with worse; much worse. The reality was: he needed the whiskey, because *he needed the fucking whiskey*. It was that simple.

Kell stopped. Squinted. "It cannot be," he muttered and moved to the end of the street. He barked a short laugh, and ran his hand through his beard, and then through his shaggy grey-streaked hair. "Well, I'll be damned." And he recognised the beautiful irony. If the poison went too far through his veins, seeped into his organs and heart, then he really would be damned.

It was a distillery, a long, low building built with its back against a wall of rough-hewn rock carved from a steep hillside. The windows were dark, like torn out eye-sockets. Several were smashed. Behind, in what Kell presumed was a courtyard, squatted the old boilerhouse chimney, appearing far from the best of health. Kell assumed the distillery was long out of use. His eyes gleamed. *I wonder if they left any casks behind?* he mused, and laughed. *Of course they didn't. Only a madman would do that.*

Kell moved to the door, and forced it open. He placed his half-empty whiskey bottle in the long pocket of his jerkin, and with Ilanna in both hands, stepped inside.

It was gloomy, but a little starlight from shattered clouds filtered through a broken roof, a cold silver light which emphasised shapes without giving any real form or sense of solidity. Kell squinted, and his eyes adjusted, and he smiled. He was in the tun-room, and as he walked forward realised the distillery building *dropped* beneath him allowing for a double-height interior, but nestled in what appeared a single-storey shell. It was housed in an excavation. Kell stopped, boots rasping, and peered down from the walkway on which he stood. Beneath, he could see large, solid lids for the circular wash-backs. His eyes moved, counting. There were six below ground level, and six above, surrounded by an iron frame and timber gantries. Kell tested the handrail, and it crumbled beneath his powerful fingers. He grunted.

"What a waste! Letting a fine building like this rot and die."

He walked between the wash-backs and stopped, warily, beside a rail which overlooked a lower section of the distillery reached by twin sets of iron stairs. His eyes took in the wash chargers and wash-stills, with their odd copper shapes which looked as if they'd half melted, the metal sloping towards the floor like molten candle-wax, only to harden again. They look like garlic bulbs, he thought, and took another drain of whiskey. He grunted at the continued irony. The only bloody whiskey in this entire place was the cheap, nasty blend he carried in his paws.

"Damn it. What I'd give for a single malt."

Outside, the world seemed to flood into darkness. Clouds, passing over the stars and moon. Kell squinted, for despite having incredibly acute vision, he knew age was getting the better of him and his eyesight was not as good as it once was. "I can still pin a wolf to a tree at fifty paces with my axe," he muttered, and stared down at the steps. They looked far too dangerous to descend. But beyond, he knew, was the warehouse. Would it have barrels of whiskey? He doubted it. But if there *was* some nectar stored there, it called to him, taunting, drawing him as if down some invisible umbilical.

No.

"No."

Kell took a deep breath. His fists clenched, and he stared at the bottle in his hands. It was poison, he decided. And it would kill him faster than Myriam's injected toxin.

You used to have strength, he realised.

You used to have willpower.

Once, you could have stopped. Once, you would have cast away the piss. Once, you would have been a man. A man who ruled the bottle, instead of the bottle ruling his world.

Kell hurled the whiskey bottle out over the spirit-stills, and there came a mighty *boom* followed by a clattering, skittering sound. Then silence rushed back in, like the ocean filling a hole.

"Interesting," came a gentle, feminine voice.

Kell did not turn. His senses screamed. The hairs across the back of his neck prickled, and he forced a grin between tight teeth. He reached up, and slowly rubbed his beard. "The fact that I chose to launch the bottle, or the fact that you were sneaking through the dark?"

"Neither," she said. "I was told you were dangerous, and I was simply pondering the best way to kill a fat old man."

Kell turned, Ilanna in both hands now. His eyes narrowed, and he took in the tall, lithe albino woman, her crimson eyes, her brass fangs, the silver sword sheathed at her hip. She moved elegantly, and stopped, one hip pushed forward slightly giving her an arrogant, defiant stance. She had a gaunt face, and cropped white hair. She was pretty. Dake's Balls, thought Kell, she was beautiful – but maybe forty years his junior. He grinned. "I don't die that easy," he rumbled, rolling his shoulders almost imperceptibly to loosen the muscles.

"But I'm sure that you do," she smiled, and drew her sword.

"That's what the other vachines said," he soothed, head dropping a little, eyes now pools of blackness. He was pleased to note the annoyance in her expression; not just at his recognition, and knowledge, but at his tone of voice. His was not a sermon of arrogance; his was the voice of a known truth.

"Do you want to know my name?" she purred stepping forward. Beneath her, the gantry creaked and Kell looked warily to one side.

"Not really," he said. "You fucking vachine all smell the same to me; decayed flesh, hot oil, and mangled clockwork."

She snarled, a bestial sound far from human. Her fangs slid out yet more, with tiny *crunches*. "My name is Tashmaniok. I am going to sup your blood, Kell. I'm going to savour it running down my throat. I am going to taste your most intimate dreams. I am going to drink your soul. I will lead you to the brink of despair, to a razor-edge of desolation, and you will teeter there like a maggot on a hook and then, only then, when you beg for death, when you plead with me for release... only then will I show you *real* pain."

Kell grunted. "Stop talking. Show me." But even as the words left on a hot exhalation of air she leapt, a sudden striking blur, and Kell's axe lifted deflecting the sword blow with only a hair's breadth between life and death. He stepped forward, mighty axe swinging, to deflect a second, then third blow – and as sparks flew, so the axe twisted, reversed, and swept close to Tashmaniok's face causing her to leap back.

Kell grinned at her. "You're quick, pretty one, I'll grant you that. But you talk a whole bucket of clockwork shit. Be careful, lest I spill your ticking gears over the gantry."

Tash said nothing, but lowered her head and attacked, her sword flickering in a stunning series of frenetic bursts, showing dazzling skill and a precision

Kell had rarely met in a human. But then, Tashmaniok was far from human. She was vachine.

Kell deflected the blows, struggling, sweat beading on his skin, but the whiskey was numbing his brain, and so much recent fighting had tired his mighty muscles. Blow after blow he halted, sparks showering the old distillery, only for Tash to twist her blade and attack again; slowly, Kell was forced back to the iron steps leading *down*.

Tash paused, head high, eyes gleaming. She twirled her sword, experimentally, as if loosening her wrist after a brisk warm-up session. She showed no fatigue. By comparison, Kell was sweating heavily, and he felt sick. He could taste bad whiskey and old bile. Doubt flared in his breast, but he quelled it savagely. Now was not a time for doubt. He had killed better than Tashmaniok. He had killed far better.

"You're good, girl," he said. "But I reckon you should work on your speed. I've seen one-legged whores move faster than you."

Tash smiled, with genuine humour. She lifted her head a little, and some distant beam of starlight caught her eyes, which sparkled. "Old man. Save your breath for battle. For I've not seen anything special as of yet; and to think, they call you a Vachine Hunter."

She's answered that question, thought Kell sourly. She was sent by General Graal. Their little war party had not escaped so easily. Indeed, Kell realised, now Graal felt it was personal. An intuition told him things had changed; strangely, Kell felt like Graal *wanted* something. But what the hell did he want other than Kell's head on a plate? What could Kell offer the warped general?

Tash stepped forward, fluid, sword singing a figure of eight; Kell slammed his axe horizontal, and Tash did something with her sword, a technique Kell had never before experienced. His axe clattered off down the walkway behind her, and Kell felt something large and dark fall through him, like a rock down a well. He stood, stunned for a moment, and Tash moved fast leaping, both boots slamming his chest. With a grunt Kell staggered back and fell from the steps, rolling violently down the rattling, iron construct to lie, stunned and bleeding, at the foot.

Kell groaned, and pushed himself up, then slumped to his chest once more. He rolled onto his back, tasting blood, and watched Tashmaniok walk lightly down the iron staircase. She strode, stood over him, her body framed by the sculpted shapes of spirit-stills in the gloom. Dust motes floated in the air from Kell's pounding descent, and he coughed, clutching his diaphragm, face contorted in pain.

Tash twirled her sword once more, humour on her lips. But her crimson eyes were hard. Like glittering rubies.

"Graal told me to be careful," she murmured, and lowered herself to one knee, so that she straddled him. Kell could smell her natural perfume. She smelt good.

"Aye?" he growled.

"But I don't understand why. You're nothing but a whisky-drunk old man who's seen better days." She lifted her sword high in both hands, and Kell watched the silver blade without emotion. His eyes were dark, like the soul of a canker.

Tash twitched, and her sword plunged down.

CHAPTER 7
The Cailleach Fortress

Nienna watched Styx advance, wintry moonlight glinting on his dagger. His cock was a narrow worm in the moonlight, and she realised with a start she had aroused him. Or her vulnerability had. She bared her teeth in a snarl. I'll bite it off, she thought, and images of blood descended into her mind and she knew, knew she was not strong enough to take on this man, this escaped prisoner, this *killer* but she would make him suffer, she damn well knew, and she would make him wish he'd never met her.

Styx dropped to his knees on the ground, and Nienna cringed, but she played on her fear and exaggerated her suffering and weakness, for it allowed him to grow confident and close – and then she would strike, like a viper. Styx shuffled closer, knife before him, but she could see him falling into lust and she had seen that look before, on the faces of college boys during their first encounter with a woman. They lost control. They lost intelligence. By the Bone Halls, they lost everything that made them attractive in the first place!

Nienna stayed still, like a frightened mouse.

Styx's scent overpowered her before his physicality; he stunk, of sweat, of sword oil, of excrement, of bad teeth and bad breath and the blood-oil which stained his lips from the inside out, like a parasitical disease.

He was panting. His knife lowered. His eyes half closed as he lusted towards her, lips puckered, and she hit him with a right hook, just like her grandfather had shown her, her weight dropped into it, power from the shoulder, all her strength and weight and might and hatred and fury and fear powered into that single devastating blow which rocked Styx back on his heels – and made him open his eyes, and laugh at her.

Nienna's mouth dropped open.

Styx lifted the blade. "For that, bitch, I'm going to cut you up."

Nienna felt piss trickle down her legs, and she knew she was doomed and dead and worse; a slave to this terrible man.

Something appeared from nowhere, a blur, a wrist-thick length of wood which connected with the side of Styx's head. Blood and saliva showered from his mouth, along with a tooth, and in slow motion Nienna watched him writhe sideways, body a jellied doll, and hit the earth unconscious. He twitched, and lay still.

Myriam loomed from the darkness. She stood over Styx, face contorted in rage. The tree branch descended again, smacking Styx's head so hard the wood disintegrated in her hands, separating into three discrete sections which tumbled to the earth.

Nienna sat, hands clasping frozen roots, unable to speak.

"Come here, child," said Myriam.

Nienna obeyed, scrambling to her feet to stand, staring

down at Styx. Blood ran from his ear. His lips were fluttering, and blue. Nienna looked up at Myriam, who
placed a protective hand on Nienna's shoulder.

"Have you killed him?"

"I hope so."

"You could stab him?"

Myriam spun Nienna around, and crouched, staring into her eyes. "Child, this is no place to murder an
unconscious man. I have done… terrible things. In my
past. In my life. Things so awful you could never comprehend. However. You might not believe this, but I
still have some pride. Styx did something bad here
tonight; but I have given him a warning – a final
warning. If he wishes to take it further, then I will kill
him. It's that simple. He obeys my rules, or he's food
for the maggots."

She stood. Nienna stared up at her, but said nothing.
Then Nienna tilted her head. "Are you in pain?"

"What?" snapped Myriam, eyes scanning the
dark woodland.

"You look like you're in pain. It's in your face. In
your eyes. All the time. I don't understand."

"Yes," hissed Myriam, eyes narrowed. "I am in constant pain. The gods have decided I am their plaything;
they have a task for me, and if I do not succeed then I
die, I die soon, I die in great agony, I die horribly. Why,
little chicken, what's it to you?" She forced a smile,
through her rage, to take the sting from her words. But
Nienna could still see the low-level bright agony, like a
fishing-line through her face, through her brain, and it
reached out to Nienna. To her empathy. She could not
bear to see somebody suffer.

"Where do you hurt?"

"Walk with me. Back to the camp," said Myriam. As she walked, she sighed. "It hurts everywhere, little one. In my muscles, in my bones; in my head, in my belly, in my groin."

"Should I rub your muscles?"

Vehemence flared in Myriam for a few moments, like exploding lava erupting into the ocean, but mentally she calmed herself. She hated pity. But this was not pity; this was empathy. A different breed entirely.

Myriam sighed. Nobody had touched her in years. "That would be… odd," she said, and tilted her head. "But welcome, I think."

They reached the camp. Jex was sharpening his sword. He glanced up. "Did you find him?"

"Found him and warned him," said Myriam. "Go and see to him, if you like."

"I will. We may need his skill if we meet any of those albino bastards. With just two of us, it would be foolhardy indeed." Myriam nodded, and watched Jex lope off through the woods.

"Dawn is coming," she said, and moved to the fire, throwing on a few more logs. Sparks danced. "Come and sit."

Nienna moved to Myriam, and as the tall woman sat, stretching her legs out, lifting her head with a groan, Nienna moved behind her, and placed hands on shoulders. "My grandfather taught me this," she said. She began to squeeze Myriam's muscles, and felt knots of tension there. Myriam might look cool and relaxed, but she was a tense mess of taut muscle and rigid fear. Nienna closed her eyes, and allowed her hands to follow the flow, to knead Myriam's neck and shoulders easing away tension. For a while she rubbed, and probed, and stroked, and when she opened her eyes Myriam groaned, a low ululation of almost ecstasy.

"Is it helping?" asked Nienna.

"It is wonderful," said Myriam, and turned, looking back at the girl. "It's been too long since I was touched." Then she laughed, and shook her head, her short black hair laced with sweat. "Forgive me. Ignore me. I am foolish."

Nienna saw the tears in Myriam's eyes, but wisely decided not to comment. Instead, she analysed the harsh, gaunt features, the sunken eyes, the thin white scars, the brutality of ravaged flesh. Here was a woman close to death, realised Nienna. And yet, she was a killer. She had poisoned Nienna, and Kell; did she not deserve to die? And Nienna realised. Myriam simply wanted what everybody in the world wanted. Life. A simple basic necessity, the one thing so many seemed to take for granted, the one primal commodity so many pissed against the wall with their pointlessness, their pettiness, their crime and greed and self-pity. Life. So huge, and yet so undervalued at the same time.

"What are you thinking?" whispered Myriam, her eyes locked on Nienna and there were tears in her eyes. She grinned, a young, girlish grin, and tilted her head and for a moment Nienna saw sunshine, saw youth and vitality and beauty and it all faded, crumbled into a pan of disintegration leaving Myriam's savaged face as an encore.

"I am thinking you were once pretty," said Nienna.

"And I'm thinking she'll soon be dead," snarled Styx, who'd staggered forward, blood soaking his hair, covering his face, to lean against a tree. In one hand he held a Widowmaker. Behind him, Jex stood, sword drawn, eyes unforgiving.

"So you both turn against me?" said Myriam.

"You've taken it too far with the girl," said Jex. "She's just another plaything; just like all the others. And they never bothered you before, woman. They never *got to you* before. You should have let Styx fuck her, have his fun. We would have dealt with Kell when he arrived. You are wrong about this situation, Myriam. You have changed."

"What?" she laughed, easily, fluid, eyes never leaving the Widowmaker. "I have not changed! This is about ownership, or leadership; I've got both of you bastards out of many a tight situation. Without me, you'd still be in jail. Rotting."

"Aye," nodded Styx, "that is correct. But now we're going to kill you. And take the girl. Rape her, and peel her skin from her screaming, twitching limbs. We'll have such fun, such sweet fun; she'll dance a jig a'right. Then kill her, as well, and bury her for the worms to feast. And you know something else, Myriam?"

"Surprise me," said Myriam, voice low.

"I might just fuck you. Aye. Give you one last farewell going over, before the cancer – or my knife – steals that which you think is so precious. You want to live, Myriam my sweet?" He grinned, showing stubs of teeth through black stained lips which glistened with spit. "Do you want to live, bitch?"

"Life is precious," whispered Myriam.

"So is death," snarled Styx, and lurched forward, fresh blood pumping down his bruised face, free hand flexing, the Widowmaker held high and pointed at Myriam's face. His eye was narrowed and filled with death. Behind Myriam, Nienna cowered in abject fear.

There came a *slam*, and the top of Styx's head exploded, his entire upper cranium removed in the blink of an eye by a steel-tipped black bolt. A shower of skull and brains rained down. Blood washed down Styx's face, the expression stunned for a moment, then he slammed down on the frozen soil of the woodland carpet.

Myriam lifted her own Widowmaker from between her legs, where it was concealed by her loose cotton shirt. She pointed it at Jex, and the tattooed man had gone pale despite his ink; he dropped his sword, and lifted both hands, palms outwards, showing submission.

"He was right," said Myriam, her voice a bitter epitaph. "Death is also precious. All death. Why did you do it, Jex? Why did you turn on me? We had something… special, here."

"He offered me more," came the short man's reply. He shrugged, eyes glittering, and smiled. "But now the odds have turned against him. Put down the 'Maker, Mirry. You know you don't want to do this, we've been through way too much." He looked at Styx's exploded head, which glistened crimson in a pool of blood. "Just like I *know* you didn't want to do that."

"Take your shit, and leave," said Myriam.

Jex eyed her for a while, then stooped, lifting his sword and sheathing the weapon. He shrugged again, turned, and drifted through the trees. Myriam released a long, shuddering breath, and sat back down, the Widowmaker loose between trembling fingers.

"He would have killed you," said Nienna, touching Myriam's shoulder.

"I know that! It's just – we go back. Way back. We went through some hellish times together, child. A world you would never understand." She turned and stared at Nienna. "It's not the killing that bothers me. I've killed priests with their baubled knickers round their ankles. No. It's the loss. The betrayal. I don't understand it." She laughed then, and climbed wearily to her feet, rubbing at her eyes. She stared off through the woods, which grew light with the approach of dawn. "It shouldn't have ended like this," she whispered. "We should have been stronger."

"Myriam?" Nienna reached out, touching her arm.

Myriam whirled, her face a mask of snarling animal hatred. The Widowmaker was high, pointing at Nienna's face. "Don't touch me!" she snarled. "If you touch me again, I'll remove your damn face!" With that, she stalked off through the woods leaving a shocked and chalk-white Nienna staring at the slowly cooling corpse of Styx.

Nienna sat for a long time. She watched Styx stiffen. She had never seen death like this before, close up, casual; she had never before been the spiritual prisoner of a corpse.

I should like this, she thought.

I should be filled with joy.

She pictured Katrina's face. Styx had murdered her; cut short the young woman's blossoming life. This was her revenge! This was her moment! A time for Nienna to internalise emotions and find some kind of closure.

It should have been wonderful! thought Nienna.

However, if this is revenge, why does it feel so wrong?

Eventually, she stood and stretched and moved to the packs the group had carried. Nearby, a horse whinnied. Nienna rummaged around until she found some small, hard oatcakes. She sat back on a log and ate, slowly, with small rabbit bites. As she ate, her gaze dropped, lower and lower, past Styx's shocked and destroyed face, past his narcotic-stained lips, to the Widowmaker lying on the frozen ground with his fingers still curled around the stock. Nienna continued to eat. Would it be hard to use? she thought. How hard could it be?

She stood, finishing the food. Myriam's voice cut through Nienna's thoughts of escape.

"Don't be fooled," came her softly spoken words. "It takes weeks of practice. And against somebody like me, with a deadly eye, the steady hand and eye of the hunter, and a killing edge you could never possess?" Myriam stepped forward from the shadow of the trees. "Well girl, you'd die real quick."

"I wasn't thinking..."

"Shh." Myriam held up a single finger. "Sort through Styx's pack. Save anything you think you can use, dump the rest here. We're riding out."

"I thought we were waiting for Kell?" said Nienna, her voice small.

"We will. At the Cailleach Fortress."

"I thought you said it was haunted?"

Myriam grinned, her face skeletal, and gaunt with the cancer. "We'd better make a pact with the ghosts, child; for if Jex comes back, we'll need a fortress to fend him off. He's a warrior of great skill."

"Kell will kill him," said Nienna, hope bright in her eyes.

"Maybe," said Myriam, gathering her bow. "Maybe."

They rode through a winter landscape, down narrow unmarked tracks and threading between wooded hills.

Myriam knew the trails and paths like the back of her hand; never once did she falter when they reached a fork or series of scattered trails. Nienna, riding on Styx's horse, contemplated making a break for it often, but the Widowmaker hanging close by Myriam's right hand, and indeed her skill with her yew longbow, made her think twice. Myriam told Nienna the short clockwork-powered crossbow could kill at a hundred paces; Nienna didn't want to find out the hard way.

As night approached, so did the Black Pike Mountains. They were huge, rearing from beyond the summit of a hill as they breached the rise on steaming mounts. Nienna coughed a gasp. She had seen the Black Pikes, but never this close; and when she saw the reality of their massive, stunning, brooding mass, the sheer weight of their squat and terrifying majesty, all thoughts of exploring them with student classmates went the way of campfire smoke.

"They are truly… stunning," said Nienna, almost lost for words.

"They are deadly," said Myriam, drawing rein. Her mount snorted, stamping cold, and she calmed the beast with soothing words in his ear. She gestured, with a broad sweep of her arm. "The Black Pike Mountains, thousands of leagues of impassable treachery. There is no forgiveness there, Nienna. Only hardness, and a willingness to see you die."

"One day, my friend and I were going to explore the passes. We were going to climb to Hawk's Peak. It is said to be beautiful beyond belief. We were going to camp, and paint the beauty of the scene in oils to show our friends back at university."

Myriam snorted a laugh. "Paint? Girl, Hawk's Peak is a place of wolves and bears, of bandits and blood-oil smugglers. There is beauty, I'll grant you, but there is only one guarantee; death for the unwary."

"You have been there?"

"I have travelled much in the Black Pikes."

"So has my grandfather."

"This, I know," said Myriam, eyes glittering. "It is why I need him so. Come on. We need to make camp. I can feel more snow in the air, and if it rolls down from the Pikes we'll wish we had a roof over our heads."

They made camp that night by a tumble of boulders, and Myriam cooked venison over the fire on a spit. Fat sizzled, dripping into the flames, and Nienna watched, entranced.

"Never seen meat cook before?" asked Myriam, sitting with her legs spread wide, her quiver of arrows before her, checking the length and integrity of each shaft, the quality of each tip, the helical fletching of each arrow so they would rotate in flight.

"When I lived with my mother, we never ate meat."

"Why not?"

Nienna shrugged. "She thought it was inhumane."

"How odd," said Myriam, frowning. "Animals are there to be eaten. They have no other use. What the hell did you eat, then, child?"

"Can you stop calling me child? I have seen seventeen winters pass."

Myriam grinned, and her gaunt face looked almost friendly. Almost. "Habit. And compared to me, or rather, compared to the horrors I have witnessed for the past decade, you are indeed a child; shall we say, a child of innocence? However. What did you eat?"

"Bread. Vegetables. Roots. Mushrooms."

"What a veritable platter of delights you must have

enjoyed. What about succulent meat compressing between your teeth, juices running down your throat and
chin, what about the perfect flavour of roasted venison?"
She pulled out her knife, and cut a slice from the roasting
spit. She held out the knife to Nienna. "Go on. Enjoy."

Nienna ate the venison, and it was indeed a dream.
She had eaten meat, of course; sometimes with Katrina,
or occasionally at Kell's when the grizzled old warrior
had enough coin. But it was usually dried beef, softened
in soup. Nothing as fresh and mouth-watering as this.

"It's good, yes?" grinned Myriam.

"Very good."

"See! You are my prisoner, and yet you have never
feasted so well."

Nienna looked down, then up, into Myriam's eyes.
"Why did you poison me?" she said, slowly, after a long
connection. "Why did you poison my grandfather? I
never did get a straight answer. You were too busy tying
me to a tree."

The humour left Myriam's face. She cut herself a
strip of venison, and chewed the tip as she stared into
the flames. "You have heard of the vachine," she said.
It was not a question.

"A tale to frighten children," said Nienna, carefully.
Once, in Jalder, only a few weeks previous but feeling
like a thousand years, she and her friends had laughed
about the Old Tales, the Days of Blood, and the Legend
of Three – the Vampire Warlords! And, of course, the
vachine. Ghosts from the mountains. But that had been
before the invasion of the Army of Iron; that had been
before the albino warriors, and Nienna witnessing the
cankers. She shivered, even as she thought of the huge,
terrifying beasts. Surely, in a world that contained

cankers, an ancient race that drank the blood of humans was not so hard to believe?

"They exist. In a place called Silva Valley. I believe they can make me well again, I believe their vachine clockwork technology can cure the cancers inside me."

"Clockwork technology? So that is how the vachine work?"

"They drink blood-oil. Refined blood. It is blessed with a dark magick. It is what makes the clockwork *work*. Without blood-oil, the vachine break down; they perish."

"And you would become one of these creatures? Just to stay alive?"

"Would you rather *die*?" hissed Myriam, suddenly. "Would you rather crawl under the earth, have the worms eat your eyes? You watched Styx die earlier today. Was there joy in that? Pleasure? Or are the wolves and maggots even now feasting on his corpse?"

"But surely we go somewhere… *better*, after we die."

Myriam gave a savage laugh. "You want to live with the gods? You want to travel the Elysium Halls? It is a dark comedy, Nienna, told to soldiers to make them fight in battle. There are no Halls for the Heroes. There are no rivers of nectar, no fountains of wine, no Eternal Feasts of the Martyrs. It's all a dark, savage sham."

Nienna remained silent. She did not agree with Myriam. Because, if there was nothing after life, then what reason *was there* for life? There had to be something better. Something more noble. Or it would mean people… like her father, and her best friend Katrina… it meant their deaths had been a bitter, final end.

"Why poison us, then?" persisted Nienna, eventually, after she had watched the passion slowly ebb from Myriam's cheek.

Myriam cut another slice of venison, and ate it thoughtfully. "Kell has travelled to Silva Valley. He knows the vachine."

"What? My grandfather?"

"Aye. Your grandfather."

"He would have told me," said Nienna, after a thoughtful pause.

Myriam grinned. "Told you everything, has he?"

"I know he was in the army. And I know he went through the Black Pike Mountains. But – *knows* the vachine? I don't understand?"

"He knows them, because he worked for the king; an elite group, under King Searlan, the mighty Battle King. They hunted down and destroyed vachine. They were assassins, Nienna." Her voice was soft. Her eyes glowed like jewels by the light of the fire, fuelled by passion, and a need to save her own life. "Kell knows the vachine better than any man alive; for to kill something as deadly as vachine, you have to understand it. And Kell understood them all right."

"My grandfather was no assassin," said Nienna, voice firm.

"Well, you can ask him when he arrives. For he has only days. The poison will be biting him now; he will be suffering, a great pain in his veins, in his muscles, in his bones. The worse the pain gets, the more he will strive to save himself."

"Then, why do I feel no such pain?" said Nienna, suddenly, sharply.

Myriam gave a small shrug, staring into the fire.

"It was a *lie*," whispered Nienna, eyes wide, as sudden understanding flooded her. "You told him I had been poisoned to make him come here! That was… evil!"

Myriam shrugged again. "I thought the trophy of his own life might not be enough. However you, my sweet little apple," she reached forward and cupped Nienna's chin, "you are precious enough to be worth saving."

Nienna shook her head, disengaging Myriam's grasp. "You are evil," she repeated, her eyes narrowed.

Myriam stood and stretched, a languorous movement of long limbs. She was every inch the hunter; the killer. "Maybe so. But my priority lies with myself, so don't get too high and mighty, *child*. At the end of the day, you're simply a bartering tool and to me, worth more than my soul."

"It must be savage to live in your world," said Nienna, her face dark thunder.

"Indeed it is." Myriam's face was twisted and sour. "I welcome you to try it, sometime."

They rode for long, silent hours, hooves clopping through hard-packed snow, wrapped in blankets and furs against the cold of a now mercilessly chilling winter. It was late afternoon as they appeared from the edge of scattered deciduous woodland to see the full majesty of the Black Pike Mountains rearing before them. Whereas under the woodland canopy they had been afforded glimpses, nothing had prepared Nienna for the sheer exhilaration of the Pikes.

The books and stories told of at least three thousand peaks, each a jagged tooth in a maw which split the land in two; not a single peak was under two thousand feet in height, whereas many topped seven and eight thousand, where the air was thin and crevasses seemingly endless. There were few paths which led into the Black Pikes, and of those who discovered a route, few returned. It was said all manner of creatures lived in those echoing valleys, in caves and tunnels and on high treacherous ledges; it was also said such creatures were best left to the imagination.

"Big," was all Nienna managed, awe caught in her throat like a plum stone.

"They'll take you in and spit you out," said Myriam, kicking her horse into a canter. "Come on. There's our destination."

The rugged landscape, scattered with a million jagged rocks, sloped down towards an ancient black fortress which spanned the neck of a valley. The walls were black, and seemed to gleam in the weak afternoon light. Weaving around thick grass and irregularly shaped rocks, many larger than a cottage, they progressed across the land until Nienna's eyes took the tiny toy fortress and reassessed its size and scale. The Cailleach Fortress was *mammoth*. And it was subtly ruined, Nienna realised, the closer she came. Her eyes began to pick out fault lines in the very structure of the fortress. In some sections of the towering, defensive walls, great cracks ran from battlements to foundation, and in other areas towers leaned, and the whole structure took on a disjointed air. Closer they moved, until Myriam called a halt and they squatted like tiny insects against a giant world canvas. And Nienna realised quite clearly that the Cailleach Fortress arraigned before them was *twisted*. Nothing was straight. No wall, no tower, no archway, no section of battlement.

"It is said," came Myriam's voice, a soothing whisper, cutting through the eerie silence which Nienna realised with a start had descended, "that the Black Pike Mountains, offended by this intrusion of man, sent roots under the fortress and twisted this great monument of war into a mockery of Man's achievement."

"Really?"

"Yes. Others claim a dark sorcery resided here, committing evil necrotic deeds, and the magick twisted and broke every stone used in its vast construction. Whatever the truth, there is no doubt the place is haunted. Nobody will live here. Nobody will even *camp* here."

"And we are going in?" Apprehension.

"Yes. I have learnt that if you keep your head down, the ghosts leave you be. They are nothing but sighs in the wind, the whispers of the dead in your ear, and in your nightmares. You must be strong, Nienna, but do not fear; nothing can hurt you in this place."

"You are sure?"

Myriam gave a narrow, nasty smile. "Nothing but me, that is."

Nienna returned the thin smile. "I had not forgotten. I don't think I ever will."

Night was falling fast, huge storm clouds filling the skies in a tumultuous celebration. Thunder rumbled, a deep-throated exhalation. In the distance, hailstones drummed the earth.

"Come on. At least there is shelter."

Nienna followed Myriam at a fast trot, and thoughts flitted through her mind. Escape! Turn her horse and run. But then, a sensible part of her soul realised: where to? How would she find Kell in this wilderness crawling with cankers and albino soldiers from the Army of Iron? He could be anywhere. Better to let him come to her. Better to let him take the initiative, and be prepared for chaos when he found Myriam. For Nienna knew, with a sour feeling in her belly, with images of death in her brain, it would be better to aid Kell, for she did not have the power nor the skill to finish Myriam alone. With a bitter nod to reality, she realised she had little enough will to kill in the first place. Killing was for soldiers. Killing was for assassins. And Nienna was neither; she celebrated life, and love, and honour. Death was for fools.

They moved on, and within minutes the Black Pike Mountains were swept with a sheet of pounding ice. It flooded the world, obscuring the sky, obscuring the mountains. Nienna bowed her head as hail slammed her like needles. She lifted the edge of her cloak, but still ice stung her face, and no matter how she tried to shield herself the storm always found a way in. It crept around collar and cuffs, around ankles and tiny vents at the edges of her boots that she didn't realise existed. Cold air crept into her clothing and chilled her, and she cursed it. The Black Pike storm seemed to have all the advantages.

"Not long, now," said Myriam, unnecessarily, and Nienna looked up. The fortress loomed closer, slightly askew and slick with ice and snow. The black walls seemed darker. The battlements glossy. The world was dark, except for the Cailleach Fortress – which *gleamed* with a sort of eldritch witch-light of dark energy.

"What kind of stone is that?" said Nienna, slowly, as they grew closer and closer, and the toy fortress reared above them, towered above them at an angle which made the world feel wrong. When everything was out of the vertical, it made a person's brain hurt.

"It's not stone."

"What is it, then?"

Myriam threw Nienna a dark look. *Shut up*, that look said, and Nienna's teeth clamped tight. "I don't know," she whispered, mind distant. "Something alien".

From a distance the Cailleach Fortress had appeared of normal proportions, but now Nienna realised her perceptions, as well as every vertical wall, were askew. It was big. No, bigger than big. It was *massive*, but also out of proportion. The doorways could accommodate a man twice the normal height, and every single archway or window or archer's firing slit was double the size, as if the fortress had been built to accommodate an army of giants.

They slowed as they approached the main gates, which were open, like the sleeping mouth of a waiting predator. Myriam halted, and her horse pawed the frozen earth nervously. A warm wind sighed from the gates in an easy rhythm, like breath.

Myriam glanced back, and gave a tight smile. "Do not be afraid," she said, and led the way into the corridor of darkness.

From the edges of the world shadows rushed in with a tumbling swirling hissing, like a million snakes trapped in the vortex of a storm, and Nienna's hands came up clasping her ears, clasping her skull as her eyes widened and her horse whinnied in fear, head lowering, hooves booming ancient cobbles, and as her pupils dilated to accommodate the gloom she saw the blurred shapes of the dead converge on Myriam... and then turn, blank black faces focussing and fixing and tilting, and then rushing towards her with a gestalt scream, a merged noise of agony from a thousand years past...

CHAPTER 8
Blood Taint

Kell's mind was spinning and he could taste silver – just like during the Days of Blood. Poison pulsed through his veins, through his organs, through his system, pulsed with the steady beat of his heart and the whiskey was negated, and he was sober again, and she was kneeling above him, beautiful, stunning, deadly, with her bright silver sword and bright fangs gleaming that *vampire* gleam in the starlight. This burned Kell. Burned him with shame. The king was there, old, serious, his eyes boring into Kell and the other warriors as they made the bloodpact, and blood pulsed from the wounds in their wrists, mingling in the golden bowl and flowing down channels, seeping down narrow tubes to *infuse* the weapons which seemed to glow with an inner black light. Kell stooped, lifting Ilanna, and with this dark blessing she was *his* and she whispered, *It will never be the same again, and, I will be with you forever, and I will never let you down, Kell, trust me, I will never leave you* and this touched a chord, touched every tingling nerve in his strung out, drug-infused body for *she* had left his bed, left his house, left his life, despite their vows and their promises and there and then Kell wrenched free the wedding ring and tossed it away in the darkness of the cellar beneath the temple in Vor. "I will never be a slave again," he whispered, unaware of the irony of his promise even as he spoke the words, for to become bloodbond with a weapon, to follow the Old Lore and the sap veins in the Oak Testament, a man ensured he was a slave for eternity.

"No," hissed Kell, back in the present, and he was young and strong and immortal once again, and he twisted fast, a blur, a subtle shift and Tashmaniok's sword scored a bright fire line down his cheek and struck the floor with a grinding squeal and Kell reached almost leisurely beneath his arm, drawing out his slightly curved blade, his Svian, and he thrust it up into Tashmaniok's groin and she gasped, and went rigid, and he held her there impaled on his knife and slowly crawled from beneath her straddle, so that his bearded face came level with hers. Her sword slashed at him, but he batted it aside and jerked the Svian knife, and Tash gasped again, for eight inches of steel were deep inside her flesh, deep inside her *womb* and holding her tight to Kell in an embrace. Her fangs gleamed. Kell smiled. "I was born in the Days of Blood," he hissed, and stood, and Tash rose with him for she had no option, and her vachine blood-oil ran down her legs and Kell's free hand grasped her throat and squeezed and her face, beautiful and pale and with eyes wide, crimson wide and fixed on Kell with a mixture of hate and admiration, they narrowed and Kell lifted her above his head, suspended by blade and throat, and her sword clattered to the ground, and her blood pattered like falling rain and with a *scream* Kell hurled the vachine across the chamber and she bounced from the wall, fell and landed like a cat, on all fours, then in a *blur* she was gone into the darkness; through the wall with a *crash* of buckling timber, and away into the night.

Kell staggered, then righted himself, and took several deep rushing breaths. He moved to Ilanna, aware she had saved him again and it felt bitter in the back of his mind; like an old betrayal.

He took up the great axe, and moved to Tashmaniok's spilled blood. She was a strong one, he realised. One of the strongest he had ever faced. And yet there was something else there; something more subtle. An element of the ancient.

"Saark," Kell breathed, suddenly realising his danger, and he rushed to the broken boards where Tash had made her exit, out into the snow. What greeted Kell's vision was a confused tableau, a scene from a tapestry of nightmare. Fire roared through the town. Men charged with swords. People ran, screaming. Everything seemed a sudden chaos. Kell's eyes narrowed. These were no albino warriors, no Army of Iron; these were *Blacklippers*, the amoral – no, the *immoral* criminals who once kept the trade of *Karakan Red* flowing into the vachine empire in Silva Valley. This, Kell knew. But why attack this village? Why now?

Starvation, realised Kell. The Army of Iron had invaded. Power politics had shifted. The Blacklippers could no longer ply the same trade; and they were criminals at heart, the diseased, the outcast, the toxic. Would they sit back and wait for a new harvest? Or would they flood from the Black Pike Mountains in their hundreds and take what they could?

Fire roared. Sparks glimmered in snow-heavy skies. Chaos roamed the streets. Violence stalked, screaming, on legs of iron, and arrows whistled through the gloom, punching villagers from their feet, hands clawing at fletches.

Kell squeezed from the hole, and ignoring Tashmaniok's footprints in the snow leading away, out into the forests, out into the wilderness where, within a short distance the blood droplets from her punctured wounded body *ceased*... instead, Kell moved forward into the chaos of the village, face grim, fire shining in his eyes, and with the Days of Blood reverberating in his soul like... a blood echo.

Saark screamed like a girl as Shanna's fangs descended for his throat, and he kicked and struggled and punched at her face but she held him in an impossible grip, a vice of steel, and a terrible vulnerability flooded Saark and he went suddenly limp, submissive, accepting his fate.

Fangs touched his neck. They were impossibly cold. Like ice.

"No," he whispered.

"Yes," she said, and her breath tickled his flesh.

Subliminally, he heard the door open. Kell! he thought, in a sudden triumph, with a desperate surge of energy which rushed his system like an emetic. His eyes flickered open, and Shanna's fangs sank deep, through skin, through muscle, and Saark screamed and started to struggle once more, a fish on a hook, unwilling to give up and die and a voice, a cool cold *young* voice spoke.

"Put him down," said Skanda, in little more than a whisper.

With a snarl, Shanna hurled Saark across the room and dropped to a crouch, blood on her fangs, on her chin, on her talons, and her eyes were narrowed and she hissed, "You!"

Saark hit the wall, hit the floor in a heap, moaning. His fingers came to his throat, saw his blood, and he whimpered. Outside, there came a *roar*, and a whoosh of flames. Armed men charged down the streets, and the sounds of battle swept through Creggan. Saark was confused, his mind swirling. Something pulsed in his neck like a second heartbeat. He imagined he heard a tiny *tick tock, tick tock*, like the smallest of mechanical engines. He shivered in premonition.

Skanda moved into a half-crouch, and he circled Shanna, the vachine snarling at him, Saark's blood on her teeth. She licked it, delicately, until it was gone.

"You should have died a long time ago," hissed Shanna.

"We are back," said Skanda, the young boy looking out of place, sounding out of place, as the sudden battle raged outside the tavern and people screamed in the street below. Metal clashed on metal. More fire snarled through lantern-oil soaked thatch.

"You will die again," pointed Shanna, her claw bloodied, her face more feral than human, now.

"Whatever you say, Soul Stealer, daughter of *Graal*," smiled Skanda with full understanding. And he *clapped*, and with the clap came a sound like thunder, and from beneath the floorboards flooded a surge of insects, of beetles and lice, of worms and maggots and weevils, and they spread across the floorboards as the window was suddenly *battered* by flies and wasps, by crawling things and flying things and spiders and hornets and the room was suddenly *alive* as cockroaches swept the floor and

walls like a tide erupting from the dark places of the filthy
town, and this surge of insects swept around Skanda's
feet, swirling like a fluid, a fluid of carapace shells and
wings and claws and legs and fangs and Skanda pointed
at Shanna whose face was drawn in horror, in revulsion,
and the tide of insects flowed to her and up her legs and
she turned and screamed and leapt for the window,
crashing through glass which splintered and drove into
her flesh in long jagged shards, and the insects stung her
and bit her and she fell, landing heavily, glass daggers
driving deep into her body so that blood gurgled at her
mouth and she groaned, and yet still she stood, and ran,
dodging through the battling influx of Blacklippers who
fought a cruel battle with villagers in the streets.

Skanda moved to the broken window, and tasted her
blood, wiping a smear down his tongue. Then, as the
sudden calling of insects began to dissipate, crawling
into walls and back under floors and squeezing above
rafters, heading back for the shadows and the damp
places, places of rotting food and rotting flesh, so
Skanda moved to Saark and helped the man to his feet.
Skanda touched his fingers to Saark's throat, where
twin puncture marks *glowed* like molten metal.

Their eyes met.

"You have a long life ahead of you," said Skanda,
voice sour.

"I understand," said Saark.

"I do not think that you do."

"I am still human," said Saark, fear in his eyes, in his
voice, as if by voicing the fact he could somehow make
it real. He touched his neck again, self-consciously.

Skanda nodded, features dark and hooded. "For a
little while, at least," he said.

"What will happen to me?"

"It will take time. It was not finished. You will see."

"You are age-old enemies? The Ankarok, and the vachine?"

"Yes. But we are coming back, Saark. We have been called. And there is nothing they can do."

"You can help us!" hissed Saark, suddenly. "Help us drive the albinos back, beyond the Pikes!"

"We have something more radical in mind," said Skanda, and then the small boy whirled about, and was gone, and Saark was confused but through his confusion he knew one thing was certain: this was a parting of the ways, as if Saark and Kell had brought him far enough, and now Skanda was strong enough to travel and *fight* alone, and Saark was reeling, and vomiting, kneeling there amidst broken shards of glass and the crushed shells of a hundred insects, vomiting onto the floor of the room.

Finally, he gained his feet, and found his rapier, and sheathed it on the third attempt. He staggered to the jagged window. Outside, chaos rampaged through the streets. The Blacklippers, the vagabonds from the Black Pike Mountains, were on a raid. Fire savaged the town. Saark smiled a very bitter smile; the villagers had done everything to evade the searching eyes of the Army of Iron – and in so doing, had left themselves open for a closer, just as evil, threat.

As Saark watched, he saw a great figure striding down the street. He had a full beard and wore a bearskin jerkin which made him look even larger than his natural size, which was huge enough to begin. Saark saw two Blacklippers charge Kell, swords out, glittering, and Saark wanted to shout "Watch out!" but

the words stuck in his throat like vomit and Kell turned
at the last moment and his eyes were dark death and
his axe swept up, cutting one man from groin to ster-
num in a spray of entrails and half-digested slurry, and
bone shards glimmered white in the glow of the burning houses, then the axe twisted and cut sideways and
a Blacklipper's head rolled, black dead lips tasting
frozen mud. But then Saark fell to his knees, neck pulsing, blood pulsing, his veins burning from the inside
out, and on a blanket of glass and crushed insects, he
passed into a realm of blissful unconsciousness.

Saark coughed, and floated in honey, and the world
was perfect and *he* was perfect. He sat up. His vision
swam. And then the world seemed – so clear. He stood,
crunching glass, and pain jabbed him in the neck and
he remembered the bite but even as he remembered it,
so it started to fade, as if the memory was a drift of
smoke. He had heard stories of the savage marshes to
the east of Falanor, where tiny blood-sucking creatures
swam the waters. They attached themselves to a man,
or to a stricken donkey or cow, and injected a local
anaesthetic before beginning a long, hard feast, gorging
on the creature's blood. The man, or animal, unaware
of anything amiss, was bled dry by the blood-suckers;
if three or four attached, then weakness, porphyria,
vertigo and death would occur. What struck Saark now
now was that he felt as if a blood-sucking little bastard
had attached to him; but he did not realise it. And even
as the thought entered his mind, so it became clouded,
and vanished, and he could see Kell outside and he
checked his rapier and ran to the stairs and out through
the deserted tavern.

"Where's Skanda?" snarled Kell, upon seeing Saark.

"I'm very well, thank you," snapped Saark, eyes flashing with anger.

"Where's the boy?"

"He's gone," said Saark, suddenly weary. He rubbed the bridge of his nose. Around him, fire roared and Kell grimaced at three Blacklippers, who saw his gore-stained axe and thought better of attack. "I was – ambushed, by a vachine. Skanda helped me, cast some weird ancient magick shit, and all these insects came from nowhere. I got a feeling he no longer needed us. He left."

Kell nodded. "We need our horses."

"And the donkey," said Saark.

Kell gave him a sour, twisted look. "And the donkey," he said.

In the shadows of a church tower, Jageraw watched it all. As snow fell, he'd seen the fat old warrior with the terrifying axe which spoke to him, which *knew him*, and he watched the slick dandy and the two death-cold Soul Stealers... oh how he knew them, knew them from Graal, Graal the bad man the wicked man!

Jageraw rubbed his chest, rubbed the burning there, and it was getting more urgent and it would never stop until he reached his destination. But that was a long way a terrible way, no pretty there, no pretty at all!

For hours he watched the Blacklipper raiders finishing up, and only when the cold dawn arrived and the town was deserted except for corpses did Jageraw climb steadily from the old church tower. He crept through the streets with his bag, pulling free a heart here, a kidney there, a spleen here, and some tasty precious lungs there.

Then, with his sack full of organs, full to the brim with squelching delights, he slung it over his shoulder and headed for the forests and trails no longer used by man.

It was hours later, and it was dark, and cold. Kell and Saark had rode hard for what seemed an eternity, until the blazing cottages and the vachine killers and the *danger* seemed, at least for now, far behind. It was Kell who finally pulled rein, and they sat on a low wooded hilltop, the distant fires obscured by snowfall and the haze of a welcome distance. Finally, Saark said, "How are you, Kell, old boy?" There was no mockery in his voice. Only concern.

"I have felt better. Much better."

"Back at that town, one came after you? A vachine, I mean?"

"Yes."

"Me also. She… scraped out my emotions like offal from a sack, and left them glistening on the road like so many spilled entrails. I feel unclean, Kell. I feel like she polluted my soul."

Kell turned to Saark. "They were sent by Graal, and the bastard wants us dead. Or he wants… something. Something else, although I cannot figure what." He lowered his head, and for long moments looked like nothing but a weary old man. He rubbed at his eyes, his cheeks, his beard. He sighed, and in so sighing gave in to decades of weariness, to decades of a hard life, and a harder fight.

"Are you injured?" said Saark, at last.

"Only my ego, lad. She was fast, by all the gods." He grinned then. "But if I am to be slain, then let it be by one so beautiful! She was stunning beyond belief!"

"Mine also. She hooked me like a fish. I fear I am becoming predictable." He sighed, and touched unconsciously at the collar of his cloak, beneath which lay the indelible fang-marks. He could feel them, burning. "Once, even such a beauty would have made me snarl and pucker, and flirt and push away; make her work for the privilege, you understand? Now, I fear, I am a slave to my trade."

"And what trade's that, boy?"

Saark smiled, and rubbed again at his neck. "The trade of dishonesty," he said.

They made a rough camp before nightfall, deep in the woods, and Kell risked a fire. With little food between them they ate sparsely, but took comfort in the flames.

Kell fell into a brooding silence, and winced occasionally. Saark realised it was the poison in his veins, in his organs, in his bones, and he made no comment; instead, he fell into his own weird and deviated brooding.

As Kell fell asleep, watching the fire, so Saark took a little time to move away from the camp seeking solitude. His side was still incredibly sore where Myriam had stabbed him, a bitter event which still filled his mind with dark fury and images of an almost *sexual revenge*. His fingers traced across the dried blood mask which caked his skin. He winced, and pulled up his shirt. His fingers traced the contours of the wound and he jumped, eyes growing wide, then narrowing. The wound had healed. Completely. There was not even the ridge of a fresh scar.

Saark fumbled in the darkness for a while, trying to see the wound, but he could not. And fear touched him, then. Shanna had bitten him. His fingers came up to his neck, and he realised these two wounds, also, had gone. What had she done top him? What strange va-chine magick had she poured into his veins?

Saark returned to the camp, and wrapped himself in a fur-lined cloak, and watched the fire and tried to sleep, but he was infused with a strange bubbling energy and sleep would not come. So, instead he watched Kell snoring by the fire, and wondered what powered the man: blood and gristle, like the rest of humanity? He smiled grimly. Or maybe Kell, too, was an esoteric meshing of flesh and clockwork?

Kell dreamed of Nienna. She was seated beneath the arch of the Cailleach Fortress. Strange rocks littered the ground. The Black Pike Mountains grumbled in the background, like an angry father. "I am sorry," said Kell, walking towards her, both hands outstretched, but she opened her eyes and they were blood red, and she opened her mouth and it was a vachine abomination, and her fangs crunched free and she hissed the bestial hiss of the vampire… and leapt for him, and he batted her aside, watched her roll in the dirt and dust, cracking her head against a rock. Blood flowed, but instantly healed, blood rolling backwards up her flesh as skin and bone melded, hot wax running together. "What are you?" he screamed at his granddaughter, *"What the hell are you?"* and she leapt again, long claws stretching to tear free his throat…

Kell sat up. He spat. He noticed Saark watching him and scowled. "What you looking at?"

"A grumpy old stoat?"

"Fuck off."

"You did ask."

"You didn't need to answer."

"What are you thinking about?"

"Rescuing Nienna."

"What about the poison in your veins?"

"DAMN THE POISON IN MY VEINS!" Kell screamed, face almost purple with rage, and then he realised he was standing, axe in hands, glowering down at Saark who had leant back, hands out, face open in shock.

"Calm down," said Saark, eventually, as Kell subsided.

"I am... sorry," said the big man.

"You need to learn to lighten up a little."

"You can always fu... Yes, yes, I see." Kell made a growling noise. "I am sorry. I will attempt to be more amenable. I will talk with you, Saark, and I will be a gentleman." He gave a rough cough, and pain shivered through his features.

"You are dying," said Saark, gently.

"Yes. It grows unbearable. Excuse my rage."

"We need to find this Myriam bitch."

"Yes," sighed Kell, weary with the world.

"I am looking forward to some payback," said Saark, with a narrow smile.

They rode for hours. The clouds dissipated, and the sun, although weak, was warm and pleasing on their skin. On this morning, heading north, the world seemed a much happier, warmer place.

"Talk to me," said Saark, after a while, hunched over his saddle, face lost in distant dreams.

"About what?" grunted Kell.

"Anything."

"I'm not in the mood for talking."

"I need you to take my mind off... something."

Kell stared at Saark, hard. But said nothing.

"I'll begin then," coughed Saark, and thought for a moment. "Don't you think," he paused, contemplating a myriad montage of memories in his laconical mind, "that's there's nothing sweeter in this world than a ripe, eager quim?"

Kell considered this. "Meaning?" he growled.

"It means what it says."

"Meaning?"

"Come on Kell, talk to me, confide in me, I'm bloody *bored*, mate, and you need some cheering up. I nearly died back there at the fangs of *Shanna* or whatever the shit she was called, and I want some fun. I want some philosophising. I want some banter, my man – it's what I thrive on! I want some *life*!"

Kell stared at him. He cleared his throat. "After all we've been through, after all the things we've seen, after all the battles we've endured; how can you be *bored*?"

Saark spread his arms wide, and grinned. His humour had returned. Pain no longer seemed to trouble him. He was bright as a button; brighter, in fact. So bright he *shone*. "Hey," he said, "you know me. I am a hedonist. Drink. Women. Gambling. Fighting. Thievery. Debauchery. It's a dull day when the Bone Underworld shuts its gates."

Kell coughed again, and looked away to distant mountains. Then he returned his stare to Saark. "Do you not think," he said, slowly, one great hand holding the reins of his horse, the other nestled almost unconsciously on the saddle-stashed Ilanna, "do you not think I, also, enjoy such things?"

Saark considered this. "Pah! You are Kell the Hero. Kell the *Legend*. You're idea of a good time is rescuing fair damsels in distress, hunting down vagabonds and returning stolen monies to the authorities, hell, you probably even clean your teeth before you go to bed."

"You met my granddaughter, yes?"

"Of course, a fine fillet of female flesh, she was." He coughed, and rubbed the bridge of his nose. "If you don't mind me saying so."

"I do, as a matter of fact," said Kell, voice hard. But he let it pass. "Obviously, I have a granddaughter. So then, where did she come from?"

"Your daughter would be the logical conclusion," said Saark, smugly.

"Yes. My daughter. Proof of my prowess, surely?"

"Ha. I am sure I have many daughters! One is not proof of prowess, simply a proof of simple, common luck."

"Meaning?" Kell's voice was cold.

"All I'm saying is that ale has a lot to answer for."

"And your *meaning*?"

"Well," said Saark, losing a little of his comfort zone, "I know many an ugly bastard who's sired a child. The Royal Court wine is strong, and when drank in plentiful consumption can lead, shall we say, to amorous connections best left to the annals of dreams." He considered this, as if through experience, his mouth twisting a little. "Or maybe nightmare."

Kell coughed, eyes glittering with a dangerous shine. "You trying to say something, lad?"

"Only that alcohol has sired many children. One daughter, and hence granddaughter, is no display of excellence in the art of amorous seduction."

"I'm not talking about seduction. I'm talking about love... no, no I'm not." Kell frowned, rubbing his beard. "I always was rough around talk of such things. What I mean to say is, I obviously had a wife."

"Yes?" Saark smiled politely. There were many responses he could have made, but wisely chose to utter none.

"Well," struggled on Kell, "I had a wife, and I was married, and we had a child. A girl. A little angel. I loved her with all my heart, and I was a brute I know, but it was the first time in my life I realised I would kill for somebody, and I would also *die* for somebody. That was a new one on me. That was something unique."

"I have heard it is a magical experience," said Saark, a little stiffly. "Although I have never experienced it *first-hand*, myself. *Despite* being a father many times over."

Kell grinned, and it looked wrong on his face, Saark observed. Where was the scowl? The hatred? The fury?

"Well lad, you missed out on a rare experience, for all your talk of hedonism. For nothing beats a high like childbirth – and I should know," his voice dropped to a dark realm, "I've taken every bastard drug in Falanor."

They rode in silence for a while, whilst Saark digested this information. *Well,* he thought, *there's more life in the old donkey than I realised!* "Go on," he said, finally. "What happened to your wife?"

"How did you know I was treading that particular territory?"

"I have spent an eternity in courts, with nobility, and royalty, and peasants who thought they were nobility. One thing they always want to speak about is their wives. Too fat, too thin, small tits, tits like a pig's bladder, carping, harping, moaning, whining, legs always open, legs always shut. It's all water off a greased duck's back." Saark smiled. "So, what's *your* story?"

"I was illustrating a point," growled Kell with a nasty look.

"Am I supposed to understand the point? Or does that bit come later?"

"Just listen," growled Kell. "The point is, I am no longer with my wife. She is not dead. We separated. It was the best option."

"What did you do?" asked Saark, voice a little more understanding now.

"I was a bad man," said Kell, words so soft they were almost lost in the sigh of the wind. "I was the toughest, meanest fucker you ever did meet. I maimed, I hurt, I tortured, I killed. I was infamous. My name was feared throughout Falanor. And I... I *revelled* in it, in the notoriety. Many a time we would stop at an inn, and I would leave my wife in the room and come down to the drinking bar, and drink whiskey, drink far too much whiskey, and as the night progressed so I would lie on the bar, bare-chested, laughing off challenges as a host of women rubbed ale into my hairy chest, or drank fine wine and passed it by mouth to my mouth, and then, when I was ready, I would pick out the biggest, meanest, hardest village bastard and take him outside and humiliate him. I'd never kill him, no, I was not a complete animal – although nearly, lad, nearly. But I'd always leave him with something to remember me by. Once, I punched a man so hard, when he came round he snorted two teeth out of his nose. Another time, I indented my knuckles on a man's skull; damn lucky I didn't kill him. He was unconscious for five weeks."

"And you waited by him for his recovery? Surely that was, at least, a fine and noble gesture! You showed that you had some modicum of honour. You cared enough to find out the result."

"Nonsense!" thundered Kell, filled with rage for a moment. "I met him, ten years later, when I was drunk. He showed me my knuckle imprints on his skull. Said he'd been a pit fighter for nigh twenty years, and never known a man punch as hard as I had."

"Well, your infamy was well placed, then," said Saark, coldly.

"You're missing the point, lad. The point is, I was a bastard to my wife. No. The point *is*, I was a hedonist, much like you; I disrespected my wife, I wallowed in violence, and ale, and whiskey, and the women threw themselves at me in those days, when I was the hardest fucker in the tavern and willing to take on any man in the village or town or city – and beat them all! The women were mine, they were at my disposal, they were there to be used and I used them. And my wife left me. And my daughter hated me. And I am lucky to have even a simple contact with Nienna. I am lucky to have my granddaughter."

Kell fell into a brooding hunch, and his eyes were hooded, his face dark.

"And the outcome of your sermon *is*?" said Saark brightly.

"Appreciate what you've got," snarled Kell, bitterness at the forefront of his mind. "I was like you, Saark, although you have only a limited intelligence to realise it; I was a mad man, a bad man, and I took no prisoners. Ale, whiskey, drugs, women, I took it all with both hands. But it did me no good. Ultimately, it left me hollow and brittle and broken."

"You look far from broken to me," said Saark, voice soft.

"You only see the shell," snapped Kell. "You don't see the empty cancerous holes inside. Now, be as you will, boy, do what you will with no respect for others; but I swear, one day, when you're old, and your time is spent, and you are riddled with arthritis and have no children to weep your passing, and no grandchildren to sit on your bouncing knee and ask with bright wide eyes, aye," he laughed, "they'll ask for stories of your travels with *Kell the Legend*; well, Saark, my lad, if you have been nothing but a dishonourable fellow – one day, one day you'll realise that your bloody time ran out. And you'll die, sad, and unloved, and alone. Even more alone than me." Kell smiled then, and kicked his horse forward, breaking free of the snow-laden forest and looking out and on to the looming Black Pike Mountains.

Saark scowled. Kell had touched a nerve, and his thoughts swirled like a winter storm. "You miserable, *miserable* old bastard," he muttered, and cantered after the old warrior, hands tight on the high pommel of his gelding's saddle.

Saark called a halt, and they sat under snow-heavy conifers, staring across a bleak landscape. Distantly, the Black Pike Mountains mocked them. They were getting close. As Kell grew weak, so they were getting close. And he knew Nienna was out there, just as he knew thousands of enemies were out there. Kell raged inside, and wanted to tear out his beard and his hair. It was a bad situation; a bitter situation! The world had become a savage place. But then, wasn't that what his victims thought as his great axe, his great *demon-possessed axe*, clove them from crown to crotch? You are an old man, and yet you walk with demons. You are an old man, and you converse with evil. You stalked the streets of Kalipher during the Days of Blood...

"Do you hate all vachine," said Saark, suddenly, looking back to Kell.

Kell grunted. "Eh?"

"No. Really. Do you hate them?"

"I hate what they stand for."

"Which is?"

Kell considered this. "They are not of this world by choice. They merge with machines, and in doing so, drink the refined blood narcotic of those they have slain. I reckon that's an unhealthy place to be, don't you, lad?"

"What happens when a vachine bites you?" said Saark, voice soft, but Kell, preoccupied with his own pain from the poison in his bones, and thoughts of finding Nienna, missed any subtleties or nuances which may have emerged from Saark's voice or facial expression.

"Well lad, it starts to turn you," said Kell.

"What does that mean? Turn you?"

Kell shrugged. "They give you blood-oil, and take your fresh blood. It's, not a poison exactly, but more a chemical that works in harmony with the clockwork machines inside any clockwork vampire. Without the clockwork..."

"Yes?"

"You suffer. Suffer long and hard. Until you beg for the clockwork to be inside you."

"Great. And how do you get this damn clockwork?" scowled Saark.

"You either visit Silva Valley, or a skilled Vachine Engineer. It's a religion, apparently." Kell barked a laugh, and slapped Saark on the back. "Why lad, not been bit, have you?" He roared suddenly, at his own incredible witticism, his own great humour.

"Of course not," said Saark, face straight. "Because then I'd be a vachine, and you'd want to cut off my head."

"Nonsense," boomed Kell, his mood seemingly lightened. He leaned in close. "I like you. You're my friend. For you, maybe I'd cut out only one lung."

Kell cantered ahead.

Saark frowned, a heavy dark frown like the thunder of worlds. "Wonderful," he muttered. "A vachine *killer* with a sense of humour."

Snow fell heavy, drifting in great veils across the world. Wrapped heavy in furs, they rode through day and partly through night, before finding a shallow place amongst rocks to camp. They built a fire, abandoning their subterfuge for the simple act of wanting to stay alive. Mary and the horses huddled together for warmth, and Saark sat now, face illuminated by flames, watching Kell sleep. Saark did not feel tired. He could feel his blood pulsing through his veins. Eventually the snow stopped, and the sky brightened, and looking upwards the moon seemed so incredibly bright. Saark smiled, and welcomed the cold.

He drifted for a long time, analysing his life and wondering, again, why sleep would not come. Was it the blood-oil working through his veins? Creeping through his organs? He smiled as intuition nagged him. Of course it was. He was changing, just as Kell had predicted in his summary of what happened after a vachine bit. And that meant? He had to imbibe clockwork of some sort? Saark frowned. That sounded like a bucket of horseshit. Surely Kell was wrong.

Then the pain arrived, a distant, nagging pain which grew brighter and sharper and keener with every passing heartbeat. And then twin stings shot through his mouth and Saark might have cried out, he wasn't sure, but he fell to the snowy ground and smelled crushed ice and the trees and the woodland and a rabbit shivering in a burrow and the stench of Kell, his sweat, bits of food in his bushed beard, stale whiskey on his jerkin. Saark looked up, from the snow, shivering, looked up at the moon. Again, the pain stabbed through his jaws and his teeth seemed to rattle in his skull. The pain was incredible, like nothing he'd ever felt, far surpassing the stabbing at the hands of Myriam; far outweighing the feeling of any blade which had ever pierced his flesh. He wanted to scream, but the pain swamped him, and it was a strange pain, a honey pain, thick and sweet and sickly and almost welcoming… almost.

Saark heard the sounds, then, as if from a great distance. Crunches of tearing flesh and snapping bone rattled through him, and with horror he rocked back onto his arse and touched his face, touched his teeth where long incisors had pushed through his upper jaw. He touched the fangs, felt their incredible, razor sharpness; he sliced his thumb, watched blood roll down his frozen moonlit-pale flesh, and his eyes went wide. His nostrils twitched. The smell of blood awoke something animal within him; no, not something animal, something deeper, something more feral, base, primitive, something which he could not explain.

"What is happening to me?" he said, his words thick and slurred, his head spinning. Then his head slammed right. His eyes narrowed. He fixed on Kell. Not only could he smell the detritus of human stench; now, he could smell Kell's blood.

Saark moved onto his hands and knees, and crouched, and stopped, his eyes focused on Kell, the smell of Kell's blood in his nostrils. He could smell every droplet. Every ounce. It pulsed sluggishly through Kell's veins and to Saark, here, now, the world receded, changed, and the only thing in the entirety of existence was this group of rocks, this campfire, this snow-filled moment with Kell, asleep, head back, snoring, throat exposed. Saark could see the pulse in Kell's neck. It went beyond enticement, through lust and need and into another realm which meant more than life and death. Saark wanted blood. Saark *needed* blood. If he did not drink Kell's blood he would surely die; he would surely explode into a billion fragments of pain only to be reformed again and torn apart again over and over for ever and ever and ever unto eternity.

Slowly, Saark crawled across the snow.

Under waxen moonlight, Kell slept on.

CHAPTER 9
The Harvest

The wolves crept into the cave, and Alloria stood frozen with fear, her eyes locked to the lead wolf, huge, black, yellow, baleful. "Stand back," came Vashell's voice, and Alloria turned, slowly, as if fearful the moment she presented her back it would be leapt upon, huge jaws fastening over her head and ripping it easily from her shoulders.

Slowly, Alloria retreated. The fire was warm by her back. Her mouth was dry, eyes wide, breath coming in short bursts. Her hand dropped to her lower belly, an unconscious act of protection, an act of the maternal – although her boys, if they lived – which she doubted – were many, many miles away. In a different world.

Vashell eased past her, his terribly scarred face demonic, his eyes narrowed, his clockwork ticking, gears stepping. Alloria jumped, noticing he carried a short stabbing sword in powerful grip. He had taken it from her pack. He was hunched, powerful shoulders ready for battle... which did not come. Vashell *growled*, a low animal sound, bestial and yet mixed curiously with the sounds of subtle clockwork, as if this were a gift bestowed by engineers rather than Nature. The wolves tilted heads, and under his advance they began to back away, still rumbling threateningly, but heads lower now, submissive, as if bowing down before their master.

Vashell stepped out into the storm. The blizzard whipped him. Through veils of snapping snow and ice, the mountains reared, eternal, powerful, immortal.

The wolves continued to back away, until another was set forward. It was massive, bigger by a head than even the biggest wolf. Its fur was jet black, its eyes green and intelligent. It was the prodigal, a natural born leader of the pack, a beast in its prime. Vashell stood and stared at the wolf, which carried something in its jaws. The others had made a decision, and retreated, allowing this huge creature the ultimate choice of attack or retreat.

Vashell stopped, and stared, eyes narrowed, throat still making the strange clockwork growling. And he stared without emotion at the object, the trophy, carried between the jaws of the wolf. Alloria followed Vashell out into the blizzard, arm coming up to shield her eyes, and she gasped. For between its jaws, the magnificent and powerful wolf carried the head of a Harvester.

Alloria placed her arm on Vashell's steel bicep. "Don't attack," she said, urgently. "Maybe it is a friend? Any enemy of the Harvesters is surely an ally of mine..."

But before Vashell could make any informed decision the wolf stood, a fluid blur, then stretched languorously. Its every movement held contempt for Vashell. With every nuance, every glint of those bright green intelligent eyes, the wolf seemed to say: *I know you, you are vachine, I do not fear you, I do not fear the Harvesters, I will rend you and slay you until you are no more.*

The severed head, hanging by a thick flap of skin and spinal column, was blank and white and smeared with dirt. The tiny black eyes were lifeless – but then, Alloria thought, they always looked like that. The narrow nasal slits no longer hissed with their customary fast intake of breath.

Slowly, the wolf dropped the Harvester's head to the snow. It licked its lips, again embodying contempt, then accelerated into an attack so fast it was a blur of black...

Vashell stumbled back, sword slamming up but the wolf's jaws rattled left and right, clashing bone with steel and almost disarming Vashell. He rolled, battle instinct returning, dropping one shoulder and shifting, hitting the ground, coming up fast in a crouch with sword ready, head down, eyes narrowed. The wolf's huge pads hit the snow, and it shook itself like a rain-drenched dog. It chuckled, a huge rolling rumble, turned to face Vashell, then attacked again with a savage scream, a bestial show of prowess. Vashell launched himself forward, sword held two-handed, intending to power the weapon into the wolf's lungs and beyond, into the pumping heart. But the wolf twisted, one huge paw lashing lazily across Vashell's face and sending him tumbling, skidding over snow towards the treacherous precipice. Below, rocks waited, ten thousand pointed daggers which mocked him.

The wolf paced around in a tight circle, and to one side sat the rest of the pack, a few yelping, all pelts covered in a fine sprinkling of snow, whilst on the other side stood Alloria. Her face was shocked, for without Vashell to protect her she would be dead in an instant.

The wolf moved forward, slowly, head lowering, green eyes fixed on its intended victim. "No!" gasped

Alloria, hand to her mouth, and she realised in horror
how in this savage wilderness, in the Black Pike Mountains which she had so casually underestimated, she
now relied on one who, a few days earlier, would have
quite happily slaughtered her. How mad was the
world? How ironic? A sick sense of humour, for sure.

Vashell grasped at his sword, fingers clasping steel,
and the wolf bunched for the final leap, a snarl erupting
from its muzzle as its whole frame tensed and muscles
writhed like snakes under fur and it leapt, and Vashell's
sword came up but was knocked aside, away, down,
spinning onto the rocks far far below and Vashell
rammed arms and legs between himself and the beast,
and its fangs snapped in his face, fetid rotting breath
rolling down his throat and he screamed, the vachine
screamed as clockwork gears went *click* and a surge of
blood-oil strength powered through veins and with
awesome effort he heaved, and twisted, and rolled from
the ledge of the high mountain pass. The wolf was
dragged into the gap by its own weight, and claws
slashed wounds down Vashell's throat, jaws snapping,
as it was suddenly whipped away, spinning, into oblivion. Vashell's hands snapped out, grasped rocks, but his
body slid over the edge and his fingers grappled and his
healing fingers cast for purchase. If he'd had his vachine
claws, he would have been safe. Instead, he slid for several feet on near-vertical icy rock, his movements
panicked, until his boot wedged in a narrow V, nothing
more than a crevice for hardy mountain flowers. He
caught his descent. He glanced down. The huge wolf
spun away, silent, eyes fixed on him with that bright
green gaze. And then it was gone in swathes of mist,
smashes of blizzard, and Vashell struggled for a minute

and wearily heaved himself back onto the frozen trail where he lay, panting.

Alloria was there, cradling his head, but Vashell pushed himself to his feet and turned to face the rest of the pack. He clenched his fists and snarled at Alloria to get back in the cave, his words almost unrecognisable as human, his head lowered for the final battle which he knew he could not win...

The wolves sat, watching him, then turned as one and disappeared into the storm.

Alloria helped Vashell into the cave, and he slumped, breathing harsh, blood running from the claw gouges in his throat. "Let me help you," she said, and tearing a strip of cloth from her clothing, went as if to bind the wound. Vashell caught her by the wrist, and shook his head.

"I do not need your help."

"You are bleeding."

"I've bled before. I'll bleed again. Listen, you want to make yourself useful, go and get the Harvester's head. They left it. Like I won a prize." He smiled weakly, face a horror mask of scars and weeping wounds.

"I cannot."

"You will not?"

"I *cannot* touch that thing. It's abhorrent!"

Vashell jacked himself to his elbows, then sighed and left the cave. He returned holding the dead head by the spinal tail, and he threw it next to the fire.

"What were you thinking? Cremation?"

"Not yet," said Vashell, and started warming his hands. They were battered, scratched from the fight with the black wolf, and from saving himself the terrible fall. "Look in my pack. There's some dried cat, and my hunting knife."

"Cat?"

"I caught a small snow panther. Or rather, it attacked me in a frenzy of hunger. Without a sword, it was difficult; but my dagger eventually made a good job of it, although I would rather have used vachine fang and claw." He dropped into a silence of brooding, and Alloria felt it wise to remain quiet.

She moved, and rummaged through his pack, pulling out strips of dried meat and the knife. As she turned, she saw Vashell had taken the Harvester's head and stood it on a rock. The spinal column had curled around the bloodless stump like a snake around a staff. Alloria shivered.

"It almost looks alive," she said.

"I am," came a faint, drifting, almost unheard voice from the Harvester's mouth. "Fetch me some water."

Alloria stood, frozen, but Vashell carried a small bottle to the creature's lips and poured. The Harvester spluttered, and wetted its mouth, and Alloria watched in absolute disgust as the water leaked from the creature's severed neck stump.

"But it's dead!" she cried, finally, moving to Vashell as if for protection; but he knelt before the head, and Alloria found herself doing the same thing, her eyes locked on those tiny black orbs, almost fascinated now as a tongue licked necrotic lips.

"Thank the gods you came," hissed the Harvester. "I thought I would spend an eternity in that beast's stinking maw."

"How can you still live?" said Alloria, stunned into gawping stupidity.

"Hold your tongue woman. He has limited strength." Vashell's brow was narrowed, but he did not show the surprise he ought to. Which meant he had seen this kind of thing before.

"They are immortal?" whispered Alloria.

"Not immortal," said Vashell. "Have you ever seen a cockroach?"

"Yes, once they infested the palace stores; we lost much food, and it took the servants an age to sort the problem. What of them?"

"If you take a knife, and cut off a cockroach's head, it takes the tough little bastard a week to die. And the only reason it dies? Because it can no longer eat and sustain its body as a complete entity. Harvesters are the same. Decapitation can sometimes be the end; but not always."

"That's unbelievable."

"Believe what you like, woman. But I have seen this before, once, when I was a child. Hunting snow lions with other vachine royalty; I was along for the ride, with my father. We had a Harvester with us, a tracker named Graslek. The lion surprised us in a circle of rocks, and as we fought a hasty retreat it bit off Graslek's head. My father carried the severed head back to the other Harvesters, who returned it to their world. I do not know what happened then, all I know is that the head talked the entire journey back. Gave me nightmares for months. My mother had to calm me with a strong blood-oil infusion."

"What happened to the snow lion?"

"Regrettably, it survived. Loped off into the peaks with half of a Harvester's body for a prize. Ruined the hunting trip."

Vashell sat down, cross-legged before the head. A tongue wetted lips, and at its request Vashell poured a little more water onto its eager, questing tongue. Five times more he did this, and gradually the Harvester's eyes grew bright, its features more relaxed.

"What is your name, Harvester?"

"Fiddion."

"How long ago were you…"

"Killed?" The Harvester chuckled, a low and nasty sound. "I have become arrogant, it would seem. I was performing a religious rite. I was secure in my own observation skills; I did not see, nor sense, that wolf approach. But then, maybe the Nonterrazake have removed some of my skills. In their eyes, I would deserve such a humiliating punishment."

"You have been cast out?" said Vashell, eyes wide in shock. It was the greatest show of emotion Alloria had ever witnessed from the vachine, but hard to read on his scarred features.

"Yes. And although it shames me, their treatment of me burns with hate. I would avenge myself on those who did this; I would bury their whole world under fire and ash!"

"What did you do?" asked Alloria, in awe, and Fiddion's small black eyes turned on her.

"You dare ask that of me, child? Begone! Away! I am not here to lay my soul bare before *humans*. That would be base and pathetic. But what I would seek…" he paused, small eyes blinking in a long, slow movement more to do with thought than anything else. "Yes. I would seek to give you information."

"Why?" snapped Vashell, feeling uneasy. Everything in his vachine world spoke of honour and loyalty to the Engineer Religion, to the Episcopate and Watchmakers; and they in turn, the vachine as a whole, trusted the Harvesters implicitly. They had fought wars together.

They had died together. Whatever information Fiddion wished to share, it was born from bitterness, resentment and a need for revenge. And for Vashell, this sat worse than any ten year cancer.

"I would give you information," said the Harvester, "you can make an informed choice. Would you save your race, Vashell? Would you nurture the vachine into a new millennium?"

"We can do that without your help," said Vashell, quietly, but his eyes flickered with nervousness, almost like the orbs of a hunted creature. He knew he wasn't going to like what he was about to hear; he knew, instinctively, it would change his life forever.

Fiddion laughed. Quite a feat for a severed head. His spinal column seemed to relax and contract with delicate slithering sounds, like snake scales gliding over rock.

"Listen, *vachine*," he said, and his black eyes glowed like the outer reaches of space. "Your whole race, your whole religion, your whole world is threatened. By the Harvesters. By Kradek-ka. By General Graal and his stinking Army of Iron. They work together, can't you see?"

"To do what?" snorted Vashell.

"To bring about the return of the three Vampire Warlords. They are like Dark Gods, and once they walked these lands with a malice and depravity you could never comprehend. The world shivered when they awoke; and it breathed again when they died."

"They are legend," said Vashell, head tilted, one side of his scarred face illuminated by the flickering fire. Wood crackled, and woodsmoke twitched his nostrils. Outside, the wind howled mournfully and Vashell felt a great emptiness, a bleakness, in his soul. "Even if they did return, they would do us no harm.

We are of the same blood. We are allies!" But even as he spoke the words, he could see the twisted logic of his own argument. They were not of the same blood. That was the whole point. The vachine were a hybrid clockwork deviation.

"No," said Fiddion, almost sadly, although Vashell was sure sadness was an emotion denied the Harvesters. "You are vachine. You are a dilution, my friend, of the feral wild Vampire Warlords; the vampires of old. Your clockwork is anathema to everything they believed in. Your race would be an abomination to everything they stood for; alien to their very essence.

Vashell shook his head. "We are mighty," he said. "We would fight them! We would destroy them!"

"No, because you will already be dead."

"What?" mocked Vashell. "The entire vachine civilisation? Don't be ridiculous."

"And do not be so arrogant," snapped Fiddion. "That is your curse!"

"And how would this miracle occur?"

Fiddion went silent for a while, face impassive, but then he licked at narrow lips showing his pointed teeth. "I do not know," he said, finally. "It was not introduced to our One Mind. All I know is that it involves Graal, and his army, his recent invasion of Falanor and the rivers of blood-oil now being gathered for the great magick required to resurrect the Vampire Warlords."

"You are forgetting one thing. Graal invaded Falanor on *our* instruction; on the command of the Engineers, and the Watchmakers."

"Yes. But why?"

Vashell frowned. "Because we run dry of blood-oil."

"But *why*, Vashel? Use your intellect, use your mind,

don't allow the stagnant mental decadence of a thousand years pollute your ability to reason."

"The crops began to fail. The Refineries needed fresh blood. Some of them began to break down; to become inefficient. Do you think Kradek-ka had a part to play in all of this?"

"I think we can guarantee that," said Fiddion gently.

"What must I do?" But it came to him, a strike of lighting in the thunderstorm of his raging mind. Clarity sparkled like sunlight on a raging sea. "I must find Kradek-ka. I must track Anukis. She has gone to her father; but she does not understand his betrayal of the vachine." Understanding pulsed through him in waves. Kradek-ka had made Anukis, his daughter, in a different mould; when he introduced clockwork to her, it had been different, advanced, like nothing before ever seen by the vachine. She was awesome. And now Vashell knew why. She was an instrument, somehow, a tool to be used in bringing back the Vampire Warlords.

"Kradek-ka has a larger part to play in this than you could ever believe," said Fiddion, and Vashell nodded, and he knew Fiddion, the bitter, desecrated Harvester, was right.

Vashell turned. He stared at Alloria. He blinked. "You understand all this, woman?"

"I understand thousands will die," she said, voice small and yet run through with a fine-lode of iron. Alloria took a deep breath. After all. She was Queen of Falanor. "Our fates are entwined, are they not?" she said. "The people of Falanor. And the vachine. It is not a simple case of invasion. The puzzle is far more intricate than that."

Fiddion's eyes adjusted, and focused on Alloria. She felt her breath catch in her throat; felt her heartbeat stutter and stop. "You are correct," he said, eyes boring into her like the granite and diamond drill-bits used for mining under the Black Pike Mountains.

"The Vampire Warlords will kill you all," Fiddion said, voice little more than a whisper. Then his tiny black eyes closed, and he slept.

Winter in the Black Pike Mountains was a savage, relentless mistress. The nights were long, hard, cold, the frequent storms a show of temper like nothing seen across the Four Continents. For Alloria, shivering in the corner of the cave, peering occasionally at the motionless, decapitated head of the Harvester, and fearing a return of the feral mountain wolves, it seemed to take a month just for the cold dawn to arrive.

With light came an abatement of the storm, and the mournful howling reduced to nothing more than occasional, scattered shrieks. Snow flurries decorated the cave mouth, random snaps of hail and gusts of ice-chilled wind.

Alloria sat, nearer the fire now, arms wrapped around her legs, hugging herself in a need for heat. Terrible icy draughts entered the cave, and she could feel her teeth chattering, jarring her skull. She had never experienced such savage weather in the warm southlands of Falanor. She looked over to where Vashell slept, and envied him his peace. His scarred face seemed strangely calm, his breathing regular.

What have I got myself into? thought Alloria, and gave a deep, bitter sigh. How violently her world had changed in a few short weeks. From her rape and abduction at the whim of General Graal in an effort to subdue King Leanoric, through to a nightmare journey through Falanor, and secret subterranean tunnels under the mountains, to her final accidental rescue by the vachine Anukis, Alloria's life had become a journey of insanity and confusion. Abused, both physically, sexually and mentally, she knew she teetered on the edge of breaking. And yet... and yet her country, Falanor, needed her. King Leanoric used to say: I am the Land, and the Land is me. Now, Falanor had no King and Alloria was – as far as she could ascertain – the only living member of royalty. Sourly, this led to her boys and she sank deeper into depression.

What did life matter now if her babes were dead?

Why did anything matter?

And she thought back, further. Images of betrayal flittered through her skull. She could picture a gem. A small, dark gem. With a sour taste in her mouth, she refused the memories, and pushed them away, feeling pain at simple understanding. Betrayal, echoed the halls of her memory. *Betrayal.*

Smoothly, Vashell rolled to his feet. He glanced at Alloria. "Somebody is coming."

"Who?"

Vashell ignored her and drew his knife, staring at the cave entrance. A few moments later, like a ghost from the snow, came a figure. He was tall, athletic and broad-shouldered. He moved warily into the cave with short-sword drawn, then stopped, staring at Vashell.

"Llaran!" exclaimed Vashell, and took a step forward, then paused, and lowered his face. When he glanced up, his eyes were bright with tears. Llaran lowered his sword, and his face softened.

"Vash? Is that you?"

"Llaran, little brother, it's been a hard fight."

Llaran moved closer. Icicles clung to his hair and heavy furs. His boots were crusted with ice. He stopped, staring at Vashell, his handsome face shocked, his mouth open. Llaran flexed his golden claws, and his vachine fangs ejected.

"They took your face, brother." His voice hardened a little, but then in a flurry of movement he lowered his sword and stepped in close and held Vashell. Vashell felt tears on the scars of his cheeks. The salt stung his tattered flesh.

"Aye, they took my face. But not my honour! Not my dignity! I am still more violent than you could believe possible! I am still vachine at heart, at soul!"

"I don't doubt that," laughed Llaran, releasing his older brother and moving towards the fire with an easy, relaxed, rolling gait. He stopped beside the head of the Harvester, looking down in open wonder, then with a sudden movement he slashed his sword across the Harvester's face, toppling the head into the fire. The Harvester's eyes snapped open and it began to scream, a terrible high pitched sound as flames curled around skin and licked into eyes and scorched flesh. A stench filled the cave. Vashell surged forward, but Llaran's sword came up – a swift movement. Suddenly, his eyes seemed hard and the smile had gone from his face. Noisily, and still screaming, Fiddion's head burned.

"What have you done?" shouted Vashell.

There came a clatter of noise from the mouth of the cave, and three vachine stood there, swords drawn, the bulk of their armour and furs blocking out the cold snow-light.

"We've been hunting this traitor for weeks," said Llaran, lips a narrow line of bloodless ice. "Now, as you can see, his fate is sealed. But you, dear sweet brother, you are a bonus I did not expect!"

Llaran turned to the three vachine warriors, who slid out claws and fangs in readiness for battle. Llaran stepped back towards the wall of the cave, and in a voice full of malice as he stared at his older brother, said, "Kill him. And kill the woman, too."

General Graal rode his steed to the top of the hill, hooves crunching snow and dead leaves, and scattered woodland detritus. He dismounted and calmed the beast, feeding it a handful of oats from his saddlebag. The night sky was a patchwork of black and grey clouds, and moonlight shimmered in shafts illuminating a vast city landscape below. Graal's eyes narrowed, as he watched ten thousand albino soldiers – the Army of Iron – moving into position with the precision of...

Graal smiled.

Why, with the precision of clockwork.

Silently the ranks of albino infantry assembled. To the rear, hidden by woodland, Graal knew the cankers had been released from their cages. However, hopefully they wouldn't be needed for the sleeping, unwary populace of Vor – Falanor's Capital City. The main problem with cankers was they were *too* vicious, too bloodthirsty, too brutal; they savaged a corpse without refinement allowing precious blood to pump free during frenzy and savagery. No. The trick was an ice-death using ice-smoke. Freeze the bodies of human cattle, encase them in ice – so that the Harvesters could reap the Harvest at their leisure.

Graal turned, eyes narrowing, checking the distant shapes on the Great North Road. The huge black outlines of the Refineries loomed, rumbling gently as they were dragged by teams of horses. This time, everything would come together neatly with no surprises. This time, the mission – cause and effect – would slot neatly into place. There would be no... *wastage*.

Graal returned his eyes to the waiting Army of Iron. Moonlight glinted on dull black armour, on unsheathed swords, on matt helmets. Special soldiers had been sent ahead to hunt down and silence any sentries, any woodsman, any stragglers who might alert the population of Vor to their impending slaughter – to their impending *harvest*. Graal smiled a narrow smile. After all, he didn't want to waste precious time hunting down the terrified. Not when ice-smoke could make a neat kill in the first place.

Below, Harvesters were assembling, drifting eerily, like wood-spirits, through the ranks of motionless soldiers. Graal's chest swelled with pride at his men, his albino ghosts. Graal's blue eyes sparkled, and his head tilted, and he acknowledged the *irony* of the phrase. *Albino* was not *quite* correct.

At the head of the infantry now, the Harvesters stopped. Their chanting was low, a monotone, little more than sighs on a winter wind. Their hands, with long bone fingers, lifted towards the sky and Graal felt a *pulse* of magick thump through the ground, passing beneath his boots and on down, down the steep hillside, through gullies and streams and rocks, through narrow channels of peat bog and patches of sparse woodland until it met the Harvesters and from their feet, from the soil, rose the ice-smoke. It billowed, thick wreaths and coils, like ice-snakes under the precise control of their masters. The ice-smoke grew, rising, obscuring the

Harvesters and the infantry and Graal felt a stab of pleasure as he knew, *knew* this mission would be successful,
and with its success came the total subjugation of
Falanor. After that, only one thing remained.

The mammoth clouds of ice-smoke were huge, now,
and Graal watched impassively as they rolled out, flowing down hills to encompass and swallow the first of
the buildings on the outskirts of Falanor's capital city;
there were no screams, no shouts of alarm, and this,
Graal acknowledged, was the beauty of such an attack.
It was clean. Silent. Efficient. There was no wastage.

The ice-smoke flooded across cottages, tenements,
factories, bridges, rivers, parks, a writhing coiling turbu-
lence of freezing cold with a motionless army of killers
waiting behind. This was not a battle, not an invasion;
this was simple butchery. And Graal revelled in it.

Finally, there came a scream. But by then, the ice-
smoke was moving fast as if accelerating with the
downward slope. It spread like a flood, and within a few
short minutes the entire city was bathed in white, as if
a huge blanket of mist had settled gently in the early
morning darkness. Only this time, the mist was deadly.

Graal turned to his horse, and from an oiled leather
sheath removed a slender, black battle-horn. It was said
it was made from the thigh-bone of a god, but Graal
smiled grimly at this nonsense. The horn was made
from something much, much worse.

He placed the horn to his lips, and blew a long, single
ululation which echoed mournfully across the sea of ice-
smoke. With unity and proud synchronisation, the Army
of Iron moved forward into the sleeping city streets.

And the slaughter began.

• • •

The weak winter sun had risen in a raped sky. Purple bruised clouds lay scattered, the welt-marks of the abuser. The ice-smoke had nearly dissipated, but still long coils, like dying ice-snakes, writhed in the streets. Graal rode his mount, hooves clattering cobbles, and he surveyed his handiwork. Corpses lay in piles to either side of every alley where he looked. Men, women, children, all white and blue and purple, frozen in sleep, frozen in the act of running, their bodies motionless. Some, he knew, were still alive, the ice-smoke purposefully not killing them, just seeking to retain every precious drop of blood. However, death was usually a realistic consequence. Except for those of incredibly strong disposition.

Graal rode his horse down the main thoroughfare, a wide cobbled street lined with baskets of winter flowers and where once King Leanoric, and his queen, Alloria, had ridden carriages in procession, the streets lined with cheering people, happy people, good people, unaware of the fate shortly to befall their land, their country, their species.

Graal halted before the Rose Palace, and it was a wonderful site to behold. Huge iron gates were skilfully melded into a battle scene, and protected long lawns, now piled with corpses, Graal noted, those of servants and retainers, and the King's Royal Guard, their red jackets frosted with ice. The building itself was staggeringly beautiful. Commissioned seven hundred years previously, it was built from white stone, marble and obsidian, and the mortar was mixed with silver which glinted, even now, in this weak winter sunshine. Graal cantered across a frozen lawn, hooves crunching grass, and he dismounted by the wide, flowing marble steps. A Harvester, Tetrakall, was waiting for him.

"You did well," said Graal, removing his gauntlets.

"Lambs to the slaughter," replied Tetrakall with a shrug of his elongated, bony shoulders.

"Still. Your magick is something which impresses. And I am not an easy man to impress."

"You should see the magick of my homeland," said Tetrakall, taking a bobbing step forward, his head lowering a little, his blank eyes staring into Graal's. "We weave dreams, we weave magick, we harvest souls and use them for... things I cannot vocalise, things you would never understand."

"One day, I will visit," said Graal, voice low, and he meant it. The Harvesters thrilled him in a way he found hard to express. They did not scare him – well, maybe a little – but the only thing he truly understood was that they were from an ancient time, a time before the Vampire Warlords. And this in itself was something of which to be wary. Still. They had a pact; a symbiotic agreement. The vachine got the blood for their refineries. And the Harvesters... well, they took something else.

Graal moved past Tetrakall, and Dagon Trelltongue was waiting for him. The man, once trusted advisor to King Leanoric, a man who had betrayed the people of Falanor for his own life, betrayed his king and queen, gave a deep bow and fear was etched deeply into his face as if by carefully applied drops of acid. He had aged since Graal had last seen him. He had aged considerably. Grey streaked his hair, fear squatted in his eyes like black toads, and his mouth was a trembling line of persistent terror.

"You have conquered," said Dagon, his bow lowering further, the tone of his voice unreadable. He had seen what cankers could do first hand; he did not want to be their next victim.

"Yes. And you, also, did well Trelltongue. You have–"
Graal smiled. "Why, my man, you have slaughtered
your own people. How does that feel, pray tell?" Graal
moved close. Could smell Dagon's terror. He reached
out, and stroked the man's hair, his long finger tracing
a line down Dagon's jaw. "You are responsible for the
ease of my success, you are responsible for perfectly
traced plans, responsible for the fall of Falanor. I wonder,
little man, if you sleep soundly in your bed at night?"

Dagon looked up, then, a sharp movement. "Alcohol
helps," he said, smoothly. And there was a spark in his
eyes, but Graal held his gaze and the flame died to be re-
placed by cold dread. A knowledge that every waking day
he would have to live with the guilt of betraying a nation.

"Come with me!" snapped Graal, and led Dagon
across the Welcome Hall with its gold and silver mosaics
depicting the Trials of Gerannorkin, through several
long chambers still resplendent with huge oak tables
filled with baskets of winter flowers from the South
Woods, then right, down more corridors to a huge library. Graal was sure of his path. To Dagon, it appeared
Graal had been there before. Many times.

In the ancient library, wood gleamed and stunk of
rich wax and polish. The smell of well-tended books invaded Dagon's nostrils, and a stab of recognition and
nostalgia pierced his mind; he had sat here with King
Leanoric on many occasions, as they shared coffee and
brandy and discussed affairs of state. Now, the place
seemed cold and dead, as cold and dead as the king.
And whilst it could not be said Dagon Trelltongue was
directly responsible for the invasion of Falanor – it
would have happened with or without his input, his revealing of tactics and military positions, and his

betrayal, his information, had certainly made the life of General Graal and the Army of Iron easier.

Dagon noticed a bag in the General's hand, and they moved to the centre of the library. Towering bookcases reared around them, and Graal gestured to a series of low leather reading couches. Dagon sat, on the edge of a couch, as if he might flee at any moment. Graal smiled at this.

From the bag he took a small mirror and placed this flat on a table. Then he seated himself, and stared down at the silver glass. Softly, he whispered three words of power, and the glass misted black, then swirled with sparkles of gold and amber. Then a face materialised and Graal smiled. It was his daughter. One of the Soul Stealers.

"Tashmaniok."

"Father."

"Did you find them?"

"We found them."

"Did you kill them?"

"No, father."

Graal disguised his annoyance well, with only a tightening of muscles in his jaw betraying the fact he did not appreciate such news. "What happened?"

"Kell, the old warrior, turned out more resourceful than we anticipated. He was bloodbond. But more. There was something else about him, father; something we do not understand."

"He is mortal, like the rest of them," spat Graal, suddenly losing his cool. "You must destroy him!"

"Is this pride speaking, father?" She smiled a cold smile, and Graal knew, then, he had raised her well.

"Not pride." He was cool. "Necessity. What of the other? Saark? Did he have that which we seek?"

"We could not ascertain."

"You were fought off?"

"Saark had help."

"From whom?"

"A little boy summoned insects from the wood, the floors, the air. His name was Skanda. I have read about him, in your *Book of Legends*, and in your *Granite Throne Lore*."

Graal frowned. "Impossible. Skanda is dead! The whole Ankarok race are dead! The Warlords saw to that, millennia past!"

Tashmaniok turned from the mirror, then returned to gaze at her father with unnerving, crimson eyes. Her gaze was cold; unforgiving. "Still," she said, smoothly, unperturbed. "Skanda was able to toss Shanna aside as if she were a simple village girl. And he carried a scorpion."

"Did it… have two tails? Two stings?"

"It did," said Tash. "Now do you believe us?"

"I believe there is dark magick at play," scowled General Graal. "Where are you?"

"Heading north," said Tashmaniok. "We picked up their trail leading away from the burning town. It's a long story. However, Skanda no longer travels with the two men. There is little between here and the Black Pike Mountains; we can only assume they head for the Cailleach Fortress."

"I will send some help. Something special," said Graal.

"Yes. We underestimated these men. It will not happen again. No more mistakes. We will peel the skin from their bones."

"Do it. And Tash?"

"Yes, father?"

Graal blinked, slow and lazy, like a reptile. "I love you, girls. Don't ever forget that."

"We never forget it, father."

The mirror returned to a shimmer of silver and Graal stood, stretching his spine. He moved to a narrow window in the library wall, more of an archer's slit than a true window, which had been filled with lead-lined glass. He looked down from the Rose Palace, over the vision below.

The first of the Refineries was being hauled up the main cobbled street, its darkness, and angularity, seeming to block out pink pastel light from a winter sun. Graal turned to Dagon, deep in thought.

"You know it is said this man, Kell, is blessed by the gods," said Dagon, slowly, looking sideways at Graal.

"That is not so," said Graal. "He is mortal, like the rest of you... with your *feeble* human shells."

"No," said Dagon, and his voice held a splinter of triumph. "He is Kell. He is the Legend. He carries the mighty Ilanna. He may not be a part of *your* culture, but he is certainly a part of ours."

"You know something else?" Graal strode in fury to the cowering man, and hoisted him into the air by the throat. Dagon's legs kicked and he choked, and slowly Graal released the iron in his grip.

"No, I swear!"

"Speak, or I'll rip out your windpipe and eat it before your fucking eyes!"

"All I know is what Leanoric told me! He said Kell was a Vachine Hunter, way back, years ago for the old Battle King. He roamed the Black Pike Mountains, slaying rogue vachine who troubled our borders. We did not know, back then, that these were outcast, the impure, the damaged, the unholy. We did not know there was a *civilisation!* We did not realise vachine were a discrete species, an entire race! If we had known, we would have sent our armies!"

Graal dropped Dagon to the polished, wooden floor. He moved back to the window.

"Kell is a special man. He has special knowledge."

"He knows how to kill vachine," said Dagon, rubbing his throat.

"Soon he will learn to die," said Graal without emotion, as he watched soldiers loading Blood Refineries with the first of the frozen corpses from the ravaged city of Vor.

CHAPTER 10
Echoes of a Childhood Dream

As Saark crawled towards Kell, towards his pulsing blood-stench, the hunger deep in his veins and soul, so a new devastating pain lashed through him in waves. Saark hit the ground, hard, and lay there panting, face pressing the snow, and feeling as though he was being beaten with helves. He looked up, strained to see if Kell had noticed, and then wrenched at his own face as the fangs – having made their presence known to him – retreated back into his skull. Saark screamed a silent scream of pure agony, then rolled onto his back and allowed the cold night to claim him.

At dawn, Saark awoke to Kell's whistling. He was covered by a thick blanket, and warm soup bubbled over a fire. With aching limbs, Saark stood and tested himself. Numbly, he realised there was no longer any pain. Whatever had poisoned him, blood-oil Kell called it; well, it had gone. And he still had his head, which he shook in disbelief; and *that* meant nothing had given him away to Kell.

Approaching the fire, he slumped down and Kell

smiled. "If you sleep out in the snow like that, lad, you'll catch your death."

"It was the fight. In Creggan. It took a lot out of me."

"Aye," said Kell. "Well, let's eat fast then saddle up. We have a long day through enemy-infested country ahead of us. And I dare say, those two bitches from the Bone Fields will be somewhere behind, sniffing on our stinking trail."

"Do you... do you feel all right?" said Saark, softly, not quite meeting Kell's gaze.

"I feel as powerful as ten men," growled Kell. "Come on. I want to find Nienna."

The canker stood in the shadow of the ancient oak woodland on the summit of Hangman's Hill, a natural chameleon on the outskirts of the desecrated, crumbling monastery. Snow fell, drifting in light diagonal flurries and adding a fuzzy edge to reality. The canker was huge, the size of a lion, but there the similarity ended. Muscles writhed like the coils of a massive serpent beneath waxen white skin, the smooth surface broken occasionally by tufts of grey and white fur, and by open, weeping wounds where tiny cogs and wheels of twisted clockwork broke free, ticking, spinning, minute gears stepping up and down, tiny levers adjusting and *clicking* neatly into place. Only here, in this canker, in this *abnormal* vachine, the movements were not so neat – because every aspect of the canker's clockwork was a deviation, an aberration of flesh and engineering and religion; the canker was outcast. Impure. Unholy.

As evening spread swiftly towards night, the sky streaked with purple bruises and jagged saw-blades of cloud, so the canker watched two men progress, like distant avatars, making their way gradually across the snowy plain. The small entourage zig-zagged between stands of lightning-blasted conifers and ancient, pointed stones, one stocky man leading two horses, the second, more slender and effete, master of a laden donkey. The canker shifted its bulk, aware it was invisible to the men, blending as it did with the ancient tumble of fallen stones and thick woodland of thousand year oaks, and doubly hidden by the haze of wind-whipped snow. It turned, superior clockwork eyes observing the trees, their gnarled trunks and branches full of protrusions, whorls and nubs of elderly bark. A product of ancient vegetative inter-breeding, a meshing of woodland technologies – of nature, and soul, and spirit. Like me, thought the canker, and smiled as far as such a bestial, twisted, corrupted *creation* could smile; for its mouth was five times the size of a human mouth, the jaw jacked wide open, lips pulled high and wrenched upwards over the skull with eyes displaced to the side of its head. Huge fangs, twisted and bent in awkward directions, glistened with saliva and… blood-oil.

Blood-oil. And blood-oil magick. The basis for an entire vachine civilisation; the nectar of the machine vampires.

The canker smiled again, a bitter smile as it remembered its long past, as it remembered the pretty *man*, and this time the thoughts behind the grimace were as equally twisted. For the canker was deviant, unholy, cast out by the Engineer Episcopate, and however conversely, employed by the very vachine Engineers who had condemned it. The canker could hunt. And it could kill. And in some small way attempt to find a token retribution, some faith, some hope for that entwining symbiotic battle of flesh and clockwork which had twisted the canker since shortly after its meeting with... Graal. When *clockwork* had been introduced to fresh human flesh.

Graal. Now, there was a man to hate.

The canker was obedient. It had been bribed with a future promise of returned and retuned flesh, of fresh new mortality, of assimilation into a purebreed human where it could return to a life of normality; without the eternal internal pain of battling machinery.

I can do it, thought the monster. I can *find out*.

And if not? Well, the instruction had been complicit.

I must kill, it thought.

For it is the only way to be sane.

The canker watched the two men dwindling into twilight, drifting ghosts, and even from this great distance it could smell the oil on their weapons, the sweat in their clothes, the unrefined *blood* in their veins. Hunger pulsed in the canker's brain, amidst a turmoil of gears and cogs and painful memories, *so painful*; brainmesh, it was called. And it hurt worse than acid.

In eerie silence the canker stood, stretched powerful muscles, and padded down the hill between elderly gnarled oaks.

"I thought you said there was a fortified town out this way?" grumbled Kell, stopping and leaning on his axe with a weary sigh. Snow swirled around his boots, and the huge tangled bearskin across his broad shoulders sat crusted with rimes of ice, shining silver. The two geldings halted behind him, and one pawed the frozen earth with a heavy, iron-shod hoof. "It'll be night soon;

I could dearly do with some hot food and three hours in a soft bed, away from this bastard snow."

"Ah, Kell old horse, you are so narrow-minded in your basic warrior's vision!" Saark grinned at the old soldier. As the day had advanced, he had begun to feel better and better, more fit and healthy than he had for years. It was a miracle, he realised, with a dark, grim, bitter humour. "A plate of simple peasant vegetables? Surely that cannot be your only lust? What of the warm inviting thighs of some generously proportioned innkeeper's daughter? What of her eager lips? Her fast-rising bosom? Her peasant's need to please?"

Kell hawked and spat, and focused on the dandy. "Saark mate, you misunderstand me. Exhaustion is the first thing on my mind; followed by an ale, and then a need to get to Nienna before something *bad* happens. And look at you! I cannot believe you bought such ridiculous clothes back in Creggan. You should have been born a woman, mate. Too much pompous lace and courtside extravagance. It's enough to make an honest woodsman puke."

"But Kell, Kell, dear Kell – born a woman, you say?" Saark smiled, his perfectly symmetrical teeth displaying a boyish humour that had broken many a woman's heart. "Is that because you find me secretly attractive? Through all our battles, all our triumphs, the mighty Kell, grizzled old warrior, hero of *Kell's Legend*, superior in strength and violence to all his many enemies… *secretly*, all along, he was a boy-fancier and lusted after a slice of Saark's pork pie!"

"You go too far!" stormed Kell, and lurched forward, mighty axe Ilanna held in one hefty fist, face crimson with embarrassment and sudden rage. "Don't be smearing me with your own backward deviant wants. You might enjoy a roll with a man; I do not. The only use I have for a man," he hoisted his axe purposefully, "is to detach his head from his fucking *shoulders*."

Saark took a step back, hand on sword-hilt. His smile was still there, but mistrust shone in his eyes. He knew Kell to be a good friend, and a mighty foe; honourable, powerful, but ultimately compromised by a bad streak of temper made worse by even the smallest drop of whiskey. "Kell, old boy," his words were more clipped now, for the stress of the journey – and the hunt for Nienna – was wearing hard on both men. "Calm down. I was only jesting. Soon, we will find a tavern. Hopefully, one without vachine bitches and Blacklipper raiders. And then, *then* you can satiate your own personal lust."

"What's that supposed to mean, lad?"

"I'm sure they'll have a drop or ten of Falanor's *Finest Malt*."

Kell made a growling sound, more animal than human, and took another step closer. Saark, to his credit, stood his ground. He may have looked like a rampant peacock loose and horny in the midst of a silk market, but he had been King Leanoric's Sword Champion. Many times, he had been underestimated – usually at the expense of somebody's life.

"You in the mood for a fight, lad?" snapped Kell.

Saark held up one hand, shaking his head, eyes lowered to the snowy ground. "No, no, you misunderstand." He gazed up then, reading Kell's pain. Nienna had been gone far too long, and their quest to find her seemed as hopeless now as it had when the land of Falanor was overrun by the albino Army of Iron.

Ultimately, Kell's missing granddaughter was a thorn in this great lion's paw; but one nobody could easily extract. Only Kell could do that. And the chances were, the search and rescue would be carried high on the back of mutilation, murder and annihilation. Kell was not a forgiving man.

"My friend, you are worse than any irate vachine. Calm down! I was just trying to lighten the mood, old horse."

"I'll lighten your bowels," growled Kell.

"You really are a cantankerous and stinking donkey."

"And you are a feathered popinjay, too damn fond of your own song. Shut your mouth, Saark—I can't say it any plainer—before I carve you a second smile."

Saark nodded, and they understood one another, and they moved on through the now heavily falling snow.

"There's the town," said Saark. "It's called Kettleskull Creek. Fortified with high walls. Brilliant. We might get an uninterrupted sleep! And it looks like the Army of Iron did not pass this way; probably too eager to get to Jalder, and the ripe harvest found there."

"Kettleskull Creek? What an odd name."

"It's fine, Kell. They know me."

"By the way you say 'know me', do you mean there are fifteen bastard children?"

Saark tilted his head. "You know, Kell, for you that's pretty good. No. I have only four bastard children I know of, although I'm sure there are many more in the provinces." He gave a wry smile, eyes distant, as if reliving a catalogue of pretty women. "I did a lot of travelling in the name of the king. So many beautiful ladies. So little time."

But Kell wasn't listening. He had turned, was looking down their back trail. In the distance huge brooding
hills blackened the sky through the twilight snow. Kell
searched from left to right, both hands clasped on
Ilanna. "Let's get to the town," he said.

"A problem?"

"We're being followed."

"You sure?"

Kell turned, and the look in his eyes chilled Saark to
the marrow. "Your skill is wooing unsuspecting ladies,
lad. Mine is killing those creatures who need to be dead.
Trust me. We are being followed. We need to move
now... unless you relish a fight in the dark? In the ice?"

"Understood," muttered Saark, and led the way towards the high walls of the stocky timber barricade.

Saark had spoken the truth, the villagers knew him,
and they lifted the bars on the twenty foot high gates
and allowed the two men entry. As Saark turned, smiling, he faced a porcupine of steady, unsheathed swords.

"What's the matter, lads? Did I say something
to offend?"

"Gambling debts," muttered one man with strange,
black tattoos on his teeth. He was tall and rangy, with
dark looks and bushy brows that met at the centre of
his forehead. "Let's just say that last time you was here
Saark... well mate, you made a swift exit."

Saark gave an easy laugh, resting back on one hip,
his hand held out, lace cuff puffed towards the ranger.
"My man, you have read my very honourable intention.
I have indeed decided to return in order to pay off my
substantial gambling debts." Saark moved to his saddlebag, fished out several coins, and tossed them over with
an air of arrogance. The tall man grunted, catching the

coins, fumbling for a moment, then examining the gold carefully. Slowly, the swords were sheathed by one. Saark gave a chuckle. "Peasant gold," he said, head high, eyes twinkling as they challenged the group of men. Several went again for their weapons, but the tall man stopped them, and waved Saark on.

"Go on, about your business. But don't be causing any trouble. There's enough in Kettleskull who have cause to challenge you, King's Man."

"No longer King's Man, I think you'll find."

"As you wish."

They strode down the frozen road, and Kell muttered, "'Peasant's Gold'?"

Saark gave a thin smile. "It does one no harm to be occasionally reminded of one's place."

"Surely you meant 'Stolen Gold'?"

"That as well," smiled Saark, sardonically.

The main inn, *The Spit-Roasted Pig*, squatted beside a huge, warehouse-type building, dark and foreboding, set back from the road and piled high with snow. Kell stared up at the structure, then dismissed it. He followed Saark towards the inn.

"Remember," rumbled Kell, grabbing Saark's shoulder and pulling him rudely back. "Keep a low profile in here. We restock, refuel, then we're off again to find Nienna. No funny business. No women. No drinking. You understand?"

"Of course!" scowled Saark, and held apart his hands, face a platter of innocence. "As if I would do anything else!"

Kell stared at the half-full bottle of whiskey as Myriam's poison began to eat him again. The bottle squatted on the bar, filled with an amber delight, a sugary nectar which was sweet, oh so sweet, and it called to him like a woman, called to him with honeyed words of promise. Taste me. Drink me. Absorb me into your blood, and we can be one, we can be whole. I will take away the poison, Kell. I will take away your pain.

Around Kell the noise of the inn blurred, and fell into a tumbling swirling spiral of downward descent. Only him, and the whiskey, existed and he could taste it, taste *her* on his tongue and she was delight, summer flowers, fresh honey, a virgin's smile, and how could Kell possibly say no to such an innocent invitation? How could he refuse?

Slowly, he reached out and grabbed the bottle. It was aged twenty years in oak vats. It had cost a pretty penny of gold, but the gold in his saddlebags was stolen from the albino army, the invading Army of Iron; and Kell cared nothing for their loss.

"I'm going to my room," said Kell, tongue thick, mind swirling, focus dead.

"There's a good lad," said Saark, eyes glittering with a different distraction, and watched the old warrior depart.

Saark loved many things in life. In fact, there were so many pleasures that in his humble opinion made life worth living, he doubted he could list them all. A child's laughter. Sunlight. The clink of gold on gold. The soft kiss of a woman's lips. The velvet skin on the curve of a hip. The slick handful of an eager quim. Liquor. Bawdy company. Bad jokes. Gambling…

Saark coughed, innocent and unaware, eyes on a buxom wench across the tavern who'd caught his eye. She had long red hair and a cheeky smile. Then the

heavy blow knocked him from his feet. He hit the
ground, confusion his mistress, and he swam through
treacle and felt himself being dragged. Another two
blows sent him spinning into darkness. When he came
round, groggy and stunned, a cold wind caressed his
skin, but it felt good, good against the swellings on his
face, tortured flesh battered and bruised after a pounding of helves. What happened? he thought, dazed. Just
what the fuck happened?

"Not so cocky now, are you, King's *bitch*?" snarled a
face close to his, bad breath and garlic mixing to force
a choke from Saark's lips. In the gloom he fought to
recognise his assailant, but his mind was spinning, and
the world seemed inside out.

"I'd lay off the garlic next time," advised Saark
through bleeding lips. "You'll never get intimate with a
lady when you stink like a village idiot." There was a
growl, and a boot connected with his ribs, several times.
Then he was hefted along, dragged through snow, and
over rough wood planks. He felt splinters worming into
his hands and knees, but it was all he could do to
scramble – and be dragged – along.

"Watch your footsteps, lad, wouldn't want you to
drown," came a half-recognised voice, and laughter ac-
companied the voice and with a start Saark realised
there were men, many men, and this wasn't a simple
dispute over a spilt tankard of ale; it was a lynching
party. A sadness sank deep through him, like a sponge
through lantern oil. He was in trouble. He was in a barrel of horseshit.

Saark was dumped to the ground, which echoed
ominously, and boots clattered around him. Saark
waited for more pain, but it didn't come. Curled foetal,

he finally opened his eyes and took a deep breath and
spat out a sliver of broken tooth. That stung him, that
tooth. Anger awoke in him, like an almost extinguished
candle wick. This was turning into a *bad* day.

What happened?

He was laughing, joking, there was smoke and
whiskey, they were playing at the card table. The villagers from the gate. He was taking their money like
honey-cakes from a toddler – winning fair and square,
for a change, and not having to resort to the *many* gambling tricks at which he was so good. Then… a blow
from behind, from a helve, his face clattering against
the table and taking the whole gambling pit with him.
Boots finished him off. He didn't see it coming.

But why? In the name of the Holy Mother of
Falanor, why?

"He's awake. Sit him up, lads."

Saark was dragged up, forced onto a chair, then tied
to it with tight knots. Saark tested his bonds. Yes, he
thought. There was no breaking free of those! He gazed
around, at so many faces he did not know. Except for
one. What was the man's name? Jake? Rake? Drake?
Bake? Saark suppressed a giggle. It was the rangy man
from the village gates…

"What's this all about, Stake?"

"The name is Rake, dimwit." The circle of men
chuckled.

Saark looked about uneasily, and rolled his neck. He
could still feel the press of his narrow rapier against his
thigh – but had no ability to reach the weapon. Like all
villagers, they underestimated the danger of such a narrow blade; what they considered a "girl's weapon". If it
wasn't an axe, pike or bastard sword, then it wasn't

really a weapon. Saark gave a narrow smile. Very much in the mould of Kell. They would find out, if he was given opportunity. Of that, he was sure.

"Surely I don't owe *that much* money," said Saark.

The circle of men closed in, and he could read anger, rage even, and a certain amount of *affront* on their faces, many bearded, several pock-marked, all with narrowed eyes and clenched fists and brandished weapons.

"Look around you," said Rake, unnecessarily thought Saark, although he deemed it prudent not to be pedantic. "Fathers. Brothers. Sons."

"Aye?" Still Saark wore confusion like a cloak.

"Enjoyed many a pretty dalliance during days passing through, haven't you Saark, *King's Man*? When you arrived, word went round fast. Here was Saark, an arrogant rich bastard, unable to keep his childmaker in his cheese-stinking pants."

Saark eyed the circle of men once more. Now he understood their almost pious rage. "Ahh," he said, and realised he was really in trouble. "But surely, gentleman, we are all men of the world? I could perhaps recompense you with a glitter of gold coin? I could make it worth your while…"

"You took my daughter's *virginity*, bastard!" snarled Rake, and punched Saark with a well-placed right hook. The chair toppled and Saark's head bounced from the planks. Beyond swirling stars, he saw a broad, still pool of gleaming black. More confusion invaded him. What *was* this place?

The men righted the chair, and Saark had to listen to the sermon, how rich arrogant bastards shouldn't poke around with their poker where they weren't welcome; how families had been destroyed, children cast out, bastard children born, yawn yawn. Get to the point you dullards, mused Saark, as his gaze fell beyond the men to what looked like a *lake* of black oil. It gleamed in the light of the lanterns, and suddenly Saark felt extremely uneasy. He noticed planks across the oil, resting occasionally on rusted iron pillars, and over which he had been dragged. Then he noticed, as they almost materialised from the gloom, huge, ancient machines, of angular iron, with great clockwork wheels and gears, meshing and interweaving. So. An old factory. From Elder Days. Abandoned. Derelict. With no *understanding*. But here they were, in the bowels of the old factory, the sump, where cooling oil was once stored. But one bright element drove through Saark's thoughts like a spear through chainmail.

Why bring him here?

He grinned, a skeletal grin. He wasn't leaving this place, was he?

They were going to drown him in the oil; and it would swallow him, and leave no mark of his passing.

He stared down into the black pit, motionless now, but as a man moved on the wooden planks so tiny ripples edged out and betrayed the liquid viscosity of centuries-old scum, filled with impurities and filth, and the perfect *hiding* place for *murder*…

With senses fast returning, Saark counted the men. There were twelve. *Twelve?* He didn't remember accosting twelve women, but then the nights were cold and long in Kettleskull, Saark was easily bored and so, apparently, were the local housewives and daughters. Was he really that decadent? Saark stared long and hard into his own soul, and with head hung low in shame, he had to admit that he was.

"What are you going to do?" he asked, finally, watching as Rake tied a knot in a thick length of rope. A noose? Wonderful, thought Saark. Just perfect.

"We are going to purify you," said Rake, face a demon mask in the lantern light, and moved forward, looping the rope over Saark's neck.

"No you're not, lads," came a voice from the darkness. Then Kell stepped forward, his shape, his *bulk* hinted at by the very edges of lantern light. In this gloom it mattered not that he was over sixty years of age; he was large, he was terrifying, and Ilanna held steady in bear's paws was a horrible and menacing sight to behold. "Now put the dandy down, and back away from the chair."

The men froze, helves and a few rusted short-swords held limp and useless. Rake, who held Saark in a tight embrace – a bonding between executioner and victim – stared at Kell without fear. His eyes were bright with unshed tears.

"Go home, old man. We have unfinished business here."

Kell gave a low, dark laugh. "Listen boy. I've been killing men for over forty years, and I've killed every bastard who stood in my way. Now, despite your violence on Saark here, I understand your position, I even agree with you to a large extent…"

"Thanks, Kell!" moaned Saark.

"… but this is not his time to die." Kell's eyebrows darkened to thunder. His voice dropped an octave. "I have no argument with any man here. But anybody lays another finger on the wandering peacock, and I'll cleave the bastard from skull to prick."

Time seemed to freeze. Kell's words hung in the air like drifting snow… and as long as nobody moved, the spell was cast, uncertainty a bright splinter in every man's mind. But then Rake screamed, and hauled on the noose which tightened around Saark's throat, dragging him upright, chair and all, his legs kicking, heels scraping old planks, and Kell took four long strides forward. The terrible axe Ilanna sang through the air and Rake's head detached from his body, and sailed into a dark oil pool. There was a *schlup* as Rake's head went under. His body stood, rigid in shock for several heartbeats as blood pumped from the ragged neck wound. One leg buckled, and slowly Rake's body folded to the floor like a sack of molten offal.

There was a *thunk* as Ilanna rested against the planks, and Kell's gaze caressed the remaining men. "Anybody else?" came his soft words, and they were the words of a lover, whispered and intimate, and every man there lifted hands in supplication and started to back from the chamber.

Kell turned to Saark, reached down, and with a short blade cut the ropes. Saark stood, massaging wrists, then probed tenderly at his nose. "I think they broke it."

"No less than you deserve."

"And I thought you were my knight in shining armour!" scowled Saark, voice dripping sarcasm.

"Never a knight. And no armour," shrugged Kell. He lifted his axe, heavy shoulders tense, and glared around.

"What's the matter, Kell?" Saark rolled his neck, and pressed tenderly at his ribs. "Ouch. And look at that! The bastards tore the silk. Do you know how much silk costs up here? Do you know how *hard* it is to locate and procure a fine tailor? Bloody heathens, bloody peasants… no appreciation of the finer things in life."

"Take out your pretty little sword," said Kell.

"Why?"

"DO IT!"

There came a scream. And a *crunch*. It was a heavy, almost metallic crunch. Like an entire body being ripped in half. This was followed by a thick slopping sound, and ripples spread across the black oil pool towards the men.

"That sounded interesting," said Saark, his recent beating forgotten. He drew his sword, a fluid movement. The way he held the delicate rapier spoke volumes of his skill with the weapon; this was not some toy, despite its lack of substance. Saark's speed and accuracy were a thing to behold.

"Interesting?" snorted Kell, then ducked as a limp body went whirring overhead. It hit a wall of crumbling stone, and slid down like a broken doll, easing into the black ooze. The stunned face, with ragged beard and oval brown eyes, was last to disappear. Kell and Saark watched, faces locked in frowns of confusion; then they spread apart with the natural instinct of the seasoned warrior.

The single lantern, brought by Rake and his men, spluttered noisily. Its stench was acrid and evil, but not as evil as the shadows cast by the stroboscopic wick.

Kell took a step back. More crunches and screams echoed from the darkness, then fell gradually to an ominous silence.

"What is it?" whispered Saark.

"My mother?" ventured Kell.

"Your humour is ill placed," snapped Saark. "Something just silenced eleven men!"

"Well," grinned Kell, "maybe it'll have the awesome ability to silence you! Although I doubt it."

"I am so glad we're both about to die," hissed Saark. "At least I'll die in the knowledge that you were ripped apart too."

"I don't die easy," said Kell, and rolled his shoulders, eyes narrowed, lantern-light turning his aged greying beard into a demonic visage. His eyes were hooded, unseen, but Saark could feel the cloak of solid violence which settled over Kell's frame; it felt like a high charge of electricity during a raging thunderstorm. It was there, unseen, but ready to strike with maximum ferocity.

The creature came from the gloom, moving easily, fluid, despite its bulk, despite its size. It was a canker, but more than just a canker; this was immense, a prodigy of the deviant, and Kell grinned a grin which had nothing to do with humour.

"Shit," he said, voice low, "I think Graal saved this one for us."

"It's been looking for us," said Saark, eyes narrowed, some primeval intuition sparking his mind into action. "Look at its eyes. There's recognition there, I swear by all the gods!"

Kell nodded, hefting his axe, movements smooth and cool and calculated as he stepped forward. The canker was on a narrow bridge now, a thick plank of timber which bowed under its weight. It stopped, eyes fastening on Kell, fangs drooling blood-oil to the wood.

"Looking for me?" said Kell.

Within the canker's flesh, tiny gears and cogs spun and clicked. Its huge shaggy head lowered, and Saark had been right; there was recognition there. It sent a thrill coursing through Kell's veins. Here, he looked into the maw of death. And he was afraid.

"Graal sent me," said the canker, its voice a strange hybrid of human, animal and... *machine*. A clockwork voice. A voice filled with the tick-tock of advanced Watchmaking. Its huge shaggy head, so reminiscent of a lion, and yet so twisted and bestial and deformed, tilted to one side in an almost human movement. That sent a shiver of empathy through Kell. He knew. Knew that once these creatures had been human. And it pleased him not a bit to slay them. "I am a messenger."

"Then deliver your message, and be gone," snapped Kell, brows furrowed, face lost in some internal pain which had nothing to do with age and arthritis, but more to do with the state of Falanor, the invading Army of Iron, and the abuse to *humanity* he was witnessing at the hands of the expanding vachine empire.

"He wants to speak with you. He wants you to return with me."

Kell grinned then. "He's worried, isn't he? The Great Graal, General of the Age – worried about an old warrior with impetigo and a drinking habit. Well, once I said that if we met again I'd carve my name on his arse. That promise still stands."

"He needs your help," said the canker, voice a low-level rumble. "Both of you."

Kell considered this. "Well. I bet that was hard to admit." He rubbed his beard. "And if we say no?"

"You are coming with me. One way or another." The voice was one layer away from threat; but threat it was.

Kell stepped forward, rolling his shoulder and lifting Ilanna from her rest against the floor. *Kill it,* whispered the bloodbond axe in his mind. *Kill it, drink its blood, let me feast. It is nothing to you. It is nothing but a deformation of pure.*

Kell shrugged off Ilanna's internal voice – but could not ignore Saark's. He was close. Close behind Kell. His voice tickled Kell's ear. "We can take it, brother. After all we've been through, you can't let Graal dictate. He's sent this *special messenger* and there's a reason. I'd wager it has something to do with you hunting vachine in the Black Pikes!"

"And I would second that," said Kell, and launched a blistering attack so fast it was a blur, and left Saark staggering backwards, mouth open in shock and awe as Kell's axe slammed for the canker's head. But the beast moved, also with inhuman speed, with a speed born of clockwork, and it snarled and dropped one shoulder, the axe blade missing its face by inches and shaving tufts of grey fur to lie suspended in the air for long moments. Then reality slammed back and the canker went down on one shoulder, rolling sideways and missing the pool of oil by inches. It launched at Kell, huge forepaws with long curved talons slashing for his throat, but Kell side-stepped, axe batting aside the talons and right fist cannoning into the beast's head. Again he struck, a mighty blow and a fang snapped under his gloved knuckles. The canker's rear legs swiped out, and Kell leapt back and the canker charged him but Ilanna whistled before its face, checking its charge. They circled, warily, amidst the glittering pools of oil. Saark had stepped back, to the edge of one pool, crouching beside the sputtering lantern, rapier in his fist but eyes wide, aware he was no match for a canker in single combat but willing to dive in and help at the soonest opportunity. Suddenly, he darted forward, the razor-edge of his rapier carving a line down one flank. The canker squealed, rearing up, head smashing round as flesh opened like a zip, and coils of muscle spilled out, integrated with tendons and tiny clockwork machines which thrummed and clicked and whirred. A claw lashed out, back-handing Saark across the platform in a flurry of limbs. He rolled fast and lay drooling blood, stunned. Kell attacked, but the canker snarled, ducking a sweep of the axe and slamming both claws into Kell's face, knocking the old warrior back. Kell went down on one knee, and the canker reared up, grinning down through strings of saliva and blood-oil – then turned, head twisting, focusing on Saark who had crawled to his knees, eyes narrowed.

"Don't you recognise me, Saark?"

"Yeah. I reckon you look like my dad."

"Truly? You cannot see my human flesh... the woman I used to be?"

Saark scowled, crawling to his feet, rapier extended amidst soiled lace ruffs. Then, he frowned, and his head moved and eyes locked with Kell. He breathed out, and staggered as if struck from behind. "No," he said, and moved closer to the canker. "It cannot be."

"I was a woman once, Saark." The canker settled down, a clawed and bestial hand moving back to the wound in its flank, and pushing spilled muscle into the cramped cavity. "They chose me... because of my association with you. Because... once we were..."

"No!" screamed Saark, and images flowed like molten honey through a brain twisted with rage and horror and disbelief. For this was Aline, an early love of his life, his childhood sweetheart. They had spent months wandering the pretty woodlands south of Vor, making love in shadowed glades beside burbling brooks, carving their names in the Tower Oak, words entwined in a neatly carved love-heart, whispering promises to one another, sneaking through cold castle corridors on secret love trysts – the stuff of young love, of passionate adventure; the honour of the naive. But it was never meant to be. Aline was cousin to royalty, and her arranged marriage and fate were sealed by a father with huge gambling debts and a need to secure more land and income. Their parting had been swift, bitter, and involved five soldiers holding a sharp dagger to Saark's throat. He still had a narrow white scar there, and his battered fingers came up to touch the place now. Through words choked with emotion, he said, more quietly than he intended, "Aline, it cannot be you."

"They did this to me, Saark. They knew it would hurt you. They knew it would persuade you. I must take you both back to Graal; only then, will they make me human again. Only then, can I be a woman again."

Saark's gaze shifted, from the abused deviation of his childhood sweetheart, to the fully erect, ominous figure of Kell. Kell's eyes were shadowed, but his head gave a single shake. A clear message. *No.* Saark looked back to the canker, and only in the eyes dragged back sideways over the skull, only in a few twists of golden hair which remained, only in a certain set of wrenched facial bones which, if imagination wrapped them around a normal skull could mentally reconstruct a *face*… did he recognise the woman of his childhood. "No," he said again.

"Help me," pleaded the canker, head lowering, submissive now before Saark who felt his heart melt and his brain lock and his soul *die*.

Saark, gazing down, rapier forgotten, reached out with his delicate, tapered fingers. He touched Aline, touched the pale skin, the tufts of fur, worked in horror over the merging of flesh and clockwork. And then she – it – screamed, high and long and Kell was there, looming over her, Ilanna embedded in the canker's back narrowly missing the spine. Kell placed a boot against the canker, tugging at his axe which had lodged awkwardly under a rib.

"No, Kell, no!" wailed Saark, but Kell wrenched free the butterfly blades which lifted high trailing droplets of blood and a shard of broken rib and several strings of tendon, and the canker whirled low, claws lashing for the axeman in a disembowelling stroke which missed by a hairsbreadth and on the return stroke Aline smashed a fist into Saark's chest and he was powered backwards, almost vertical, his legs finally dropping and he hit the ground, rolled, and splashed into the oil with desperate fingers scrabbling at the platform like claws...

Kell leapt again, axe whirring, and he and the transmogrified woman circled with eyes locked, then struck and clashed in a blur of strikes which left a trail of sparks glittering in the gloom. "Get out!" snarled Kell, glancing back to Saark. "Get out of here, lad, now!"

"Don't kill her," whispered Saark.

"She can never change back, don't you see?" snapped Kell, axe slamming up, claws raking the blades. He staggered back under the immense impact, and jabbed axe points at the canker's eyes. It snarled, head shaking, spittle drenching Kell. "It's a one way process! You cannot *revert*!"

The canker was pushing Kell back, claws lashing out with piledriver force, and Saark could see Kell weakening fast. Within moments, he would be dead; dead, or drowning in oil. With an inhuman effort, Saark's fingers raked the harsh boards and his legs kicked against

thick, viscous oil. He rolled onto the deck, panting, and
levered himself to his feet where he swayed. He
grabbed at his rapier, but sheathed the weapon. Kell
saw the movement, and his face went grim, went dark,
his eyes becoming something more – or indeed, something *less* – than human.

"Aline." Saark's voice was a lullaby. A song of
nostalgia.

The canker paused mid-snarl, but did not turn. Its
eyes were fixed with glittering hatred on Kell, his back
to the oil, his axe resting against wooden boards. His
chest was heaving, and his jerkin was sliced by claws
showing shredded flesh beneath.

"Will you help me?" came the voice of Aline. And
Saark could hear her, now, hear her tone and inflec-
tions entwined around the audible ejaculations of an
alien beast.

"Yes," said Saark, with great sadness. "I will help
you." He hooked his boot behind the lantern, and with
a swift kick sent the flask of oil sailing across the platform, where it shattered against the canker and flames
exploded outwards. Fire roared, engulfing the canker
which screamed a high-pitched *feminine* sound and
spun around in a tight circle, fighting the fire with claws
whirring and slashing at itself as flesh burned and fat
bubbled and clockwork squealed. Kell came at a sprint,
head down, axe in both hands, and both he and Saark
hammered down flexing planks into the darkness in the
direction of the ancient factory exit…

The canker lowered to its haunches, burning, then
glared through flames at the fleeing men. It roared, and
charged after them, its burning flesh illuminating the
way. Tufts of glowing fur fell from its burning body, into

the oil, which slumbered for a few moments after the canker's passage and then suddenly, erratically, ignited. Fire roared along the surface of the oil pools, overtaking the canker and licking at the heels of Kell and Saark, sweating now, eyes alive with the orange glow of roaring demons, and they ran with every burst of speed and energy they possessed as heat billowed around them and sparks exploded and the *roar* and *surge* of fire was something both men had never before experienced...

"We're going to *die!*" screamed Saark.

CHAPTER 11
Fortress of Ghosts

Kell ran on, and did not reply to Saark's panic, just heaved his bulk along flexing planks with fire at his boots, a stench of burning chemicals filling his nostrils and smoke blinding him. He choked, gagged, and the fire overtook the two men who ran on blindly, across yet another narrow plank into darkness and smoke and behind them the roar of fire drowned the roar and screeches of the burning canker and suddenly both men slammed into the welcome ice-cold night air, flames belching from the orifice behind as they hit the snow and rolled down a gentle slope to finally slide together, turning slowly on ice, to a stop, Kell's great bearskin jerkin glowing and smouldering.

The two men coughed and choked for a while, entwined like scorched lovers, then untangled themselves from one another. Kell staggered to his feet and hefted his axe, staring up at the factory doorway, brows furrowed, fire-blackened face focussed in concentration as his eyes narrowed and he readied himself in a centuries-old battle-stance.

"Surely not?" whispered Saark, climbing to his feet and spitting black phlegm to the snow. His fine clothes were blackened, scorched tatters. Beneath, his flesh was burn-pink in places. He patted his head, when he suddenly realised his hair was on fire.

Kell did not reply. Just stood, staring at the doorway where an inferno raged. And then something moved, a huge cumbersome ill-defined shape within the shimmering portal, a demon dancing in the fire, an image of molten rock against the stage of a raging inferno, and Saark thought he saw the shape of the canker, of his twisted childhood sweetheart, of Aline, stagger within the opening and then slump down, clockwork machines *glowing* as they finally succumbed to the heat and ran in molten streams. Then the roof of the factory belched and slumped, and with a great groaning roar it collapsed bringing part of the walls down with it, and burning rubble filled the doorway and all was gone and still, except for the bright fire, and the demons.

"How could Graal do that?" whispered Saark, eyes still fixed on the blaze. All around the factory, snow-steam hissed like volcanic geysers.

Kell stared at him.

"To a woman, I mean," said the scorched dandy.

"Graal will do what he has to. To get the job done."

"I want his head on a fucking plate," snarled Saark, suddenly. "I want that man dead."

Kell gave a curt nod, and turned his back on the inferno. "We all want him dead, lad." He sighed, then. And gave a narrow smile which had nothing to do with humour. "But at least he's showed us one thing."

"And what's that?"

Kell's face was a dark mask, his eyes pools of ink. Unreadable. "He thinks we're a threat. He went to a lot of trouble to bring us in. And that means we are a

danger not just to Graal, but to the whole damn vachine invasion. And… I think we have something he
wants. Ilanna, maybe? I do not know. But we will find
out, I promise you that." Kell began to walk, back towards the stables. It was time to leave. It was time to
leave Kettleskull Creek *fast*.

Saark stood, stunned, watching Kell's back.

Fire crackled, and sparks spiralled up into a clear and
frozen night sky.

Kell turned. Grinned a sour, twisted grin. So much
for a warm, soft bed! "Come on, lad. What're you waiting for? We have to make *General Graal* earn his coin.
And he'll have to move faster than that to catch us."

In silence, and with sombre heart, Saark followed
Kell into the night.

It was a day later, and darkness was spreading fast, a
vast jagged purple shroud easing out from the towering
blocks of the Black Pike Mountains, questing knife-
blades stealing into the real world like a disease
spreading from its host. Kell reined in his horse, and
climbed stiffly from the saddle. The pain from the poison was with him again, in his blood, in his bones, and
he grinned with skull teeth. At least this fresh agony
took away the lesser evils of arthritis and torn muscles
from battle. At least it focused him – *focused him* – on
impending death.

Nobody lives forever, old man, he thought to himself. And I wouldn't want to! But by the gods, it would
be sweet to taste life long enough to see the bastard
Graal dead and buried.

Saark's boots hit the frozen ground, and he rubbed
his eyes. "I ache like a dog in a fighting pit."

"You look just as rough."

"Thanks, old friend."

"If I was your friend, I'd hang myself."

"You're a regular old charmer, Kell."

"There she is." He pointed, and Saark took in the majestic sweep of the mountains, an endless block of vast peaks, sheer and violent and ragged. Cold wind and snowstorms swept down from the Pikes, as if it was some epicentre for gratuitous weather and intent on inflicting misery across the civilised world.

"They're just so… big!" said Saark, eyes once more sweeping the mammoth portrait before him. It was an oil painting, a violence of blacks and greys, purples and reds. "And beautiful," he added, voice touched with awe. "Totally beautiful."

"You ever been here before?"

"Once, in my younger days. Alas, I believe I was pretty much drunk for the entire trip. And I rode it in a fine brass carriage with two women of, shall we say, dishonourable disposition. One had a poodle dog. What tricks that yapping snapping little canine could conjure!"

Kell snorted, and started over the hillside. Rocks lay strewn everywhere, building in intensity as the ground rose towards the vastness of the sky-blocking Pikes. Saark followed, still talking.

"One of the women, a ripe peach named Guinevere, had a neat trick whereby she would take a long, thin block of cheese, and upon removing her corset…"

"Stop." Kell turned. "There's the fortress."

"Cailleach?" Saark gave a tiny shudder. He glanced around, at the fast-falling gloom. The wind howled in the distance like slaughtered wolves. "Hadn't we better wait till morning?"

SOUL STEALERS

"No. We're going in. Now."

"It's turned dark," warned Saark.

"I'm the worst fucking thing in the dark," snapped Kell.

"I'm sure you are, old boy. But my point is, the rumours state this place is, ahh, haunted. And correct me if I'm wrong, but more specifically, haunted at night. Yes?"

Kell chuckled. "I thought you were a modern hedonist? I didn't think you'd believe in ghosts."

"Well, yes, I don't, but when you hear so many fireside tales..."

"Popinjays drunk on watered wine," snapped Kell, and surged forward, allowing his horse to pick a trail through the rocks. Muttering, Saark followed at a reasonable distance, telling himself that if wild beasts or haunted *things* attacked, then at least it would take them time to consume the bulk that was Kell, thus giving *him* time to flee.

As the hill dropped to a flat plain, so the rocks became not just more intense in their regularity, but larger, more ominous. Many were smoothed by centuries of weathering, and bands of precious minerals ran through many a cottage-sized cube.

The hugeness of the subtly twisted fortress came ever closer, and as darkness fell through the sky, so Kell ran his gaze over the dark stones, the cracks, the jigged walls and battlements. Above the battlements, leading back to the keep and the rocky valley beyond, which the fortress seemed in some way to *protect*, stood several slightly leaning, slightly twisted towers. Most had no roof, just great blocks which had shifted and settled, to give the appearance of some puzzle – or at least, a madman's example of architecture.

"It's depraved," said Saark, eventually.

"It's old," said Kell.

Staring at the warrior's broad back, Saark, said, "The two go hand in hand, Kell, old wolf. But what I mean is, look at it, the whole thing, it's – well, it's not straight, for a start. I thought they would have brought in some decent builders. Architects who could draw a straight line. That sort of thing. Not some epileptic draughtsmen who spilled the ink and let idiots loose with a trowel!"

Kell stopped and turned. His eyes were glinting. "*Shut up,*" he said.

"Yes, fine, no need to be rude. You only needed to ask."

There was an old road, made of the same strange dark stone. Many cobbles were missing, and filled with dirt and frozen weeds. Much was obscured by wide patches of ice. Kell picked his way carefully to the road, and they moved down it, towards the huge maw of a leering archway. The Cailleach Fortress reared above them in the gloom, defined by moonlight and foregrounded by the immense power of the sentinel Black Pikes.

"The archway is a guardian," said Kell, voice little more than a whisper. "Listen. She will speak to us…"

"What?" snorted Saark, voice dripping sarcasm. Yet as he stepped forward, so warm breeze rolled out to greet him and he halted, shocked, hackles rising on the back of his neck. "What's going on?" he growled. "What kind of horse-shit is this?"

"Be quiet, boy," hissed Kell, glancing at Saark, dark eyes glinting like jewels. "If you value your bloody life. Follow me, say nothing, do nothing, do not draw your weapon, don't even shit in your kerchief unless I give you permission. I've been here before; and there are rules."

"Rules?" whispered Saark, and despite himself, despite his new found… strength, from impure blood, he moved closer to Kell. "I don't like this place, Kell. It has a stench of evil, in its very rocks, in its very bones."

"Aye, lad." They moved beneath the huge gateway. Beyond, darkness wavered like the oesophagus of some huge, breathing creature. "So follow me, be a good lad, and we both may get through this alive."

"You really think so?" whispered Saark, and the final dregs of light were cast from the sky.

"No," said Kell, "I'm just trying to make you feel better." And with that, he disappeared into the void.

Saark walked, his eyes narrowed, his mouth shut, his fist wound tight about his mount's reins and his arse puckered in terror. Behind, he heard Mary the donkey braying and he wanted to turn, to shout "Shut up you stupid donkey!" but he did not; he had neither the nerve nor the energy. Fear coursed through him like raw fire. It filled his mind with ash.

They walked, boots echoing on cobbles. Shapes seemed to drift around them, ghosts in silk, sighs caressing cold skin, and Saark realised he had new, heightened senses. He could feel more, sense more, smell more. He could smell his own stench of fear, that was for sure.

Something brushed his cheek, like a kiss, and he fancied he heard a giggle of coquettish laughter. Something tightened in his chest. It had not occurred to him the ghosts – or whatever depraved spirits, or dark magick these creatures were – it had never *occurred* to him they would be *women*. He felt a caress down his thigh, and another kiss on his cheek. His resolve hardened. The whole thing felt wrong, and then he caught sight of a figure ahead and she walking towards the two men.

She was tall, eight feet tall, and very slender and narrow, both of hips and limbs. Her skin was dark, and shined as if oiled. She wore a black silk robe which rustled, and the hood was thrown back to reveal an almost elongated face, high and thin with pointed features and narrow, feline eyes. Saark looked into those eyes and realised the pupils were horizontal slits. They looked wrong. Saark swallowed. The tall woman stopped, and only then did Saark realise she was both insubstantial, like a drifting haze in the darkness; and that she carried a black sword strapped at her hip. Ha, thought Saark. A ghost sword? And yet he knew, in his heart, it would cut just like the finest steel.

"Who passes in my realm?" came her voice, and it was note-perfect and absolutely beautiful.

"I am Kell. Once, I served your people."

"Kell. I remember. You slew the vachine. That was good."

Kell bowed his head, as if offering obeisance to royalty. He stayed like that for what – to Saark, at least – seemed an exaggerated length of time. Then he stood, and back straight, stared into the ghost's eyes.

"May we pass, lady?"

She lifted a ghostly arm, and pointed at Saark. He shivered, and felt suddenly light-headed as if... *as if his brains were rushing out of his ears and a million memories flowed like wine like water and he was dancing and laughing and drinking and fucking and he was watched from a million years away by eyes older than worlds and he felt himself judged and he felt himself wrenched through a mental grinder and then–*

Saark was kneeling on the cobbles, panting, and his head pounded worse than any three-flagon hangover.

Slowly, Saark climbed to his feet, and ignoring Kell and the ghost, unhooked a water-skin from his saddle and took a long, cool draught.

"That hurt," he said, eventually.

"There is a taint on this one," said the ghost, pointing to Saark but talking to Kell.

"Aye. I know. But he's with me."

"It runs bone deep," said the ghost, and Saark froze as he realised what she meant. His infection. His bad blood. His newly acquired and gradually transforming *nature*. What had Kell said? He'd killed *vachine* for these creatures? So they were enemies, and she knew Saark for what he was – or at least, what he would become.

"He's still with me," said Kell, staring at the apparition and, with his traditional stubborn streak, refusing to back down. Eventually, the tall, dark lady gave a single nod, and glided away, disseminating as she moved into spirals of black light which eventually whirled, and were gone.

"What a bitch," breathed Saark, releasing a pent-up breath.

"Halt your yapping, puppy, lest I cut off your head!" snapped Kell, and strode forward, leading his horse.

Saark clamped his teeth tight shut, and followed Kell. Behind him, Mary brayed, and Saark scowled. To his ears, it was an abrasive, mocking, equine jibe, and if there was one thing Saark hated, it was being laughed at by a donkey.

They emerged into the courtyard before the twisted, disjointed, deformed keep. Behind them, the tunnel was dark as the void, sour as a corpse. Saark breathed cool ice air, and thanked the gods he was alive – and not just alive, but with his *affliction* still his own.

Kell was panting, and they looked up at the sky in wonder. Hours had passed, and strange coloured starlight rimed the frozen mountains and peaks.

"Grandad!" screamed Nienna, and sprinted across ice-slick cobbles from the doorway of a small, stone building. She leapt at him, wrapping herself around the old warrior and he hugged her, buried his face in her hair and inhaled her scent and welcomed her warmth, and her love, for without Nienna, Kell was a bad man, a weak man, a lesser man; a dilution. With her, he was whole again. Filled with honour, and love, and an understanding of what made life and the world so good.

Kell dropped Nienna to the cobbles, and she half turned as Myriam appeared at the doorway. Myriam gave Kell a curt nod, eyes bright, head high, proud and wary and strong despite the cancer eating through her. She gave a smile, but it was an enigmatic smile and Kell could not read her intent. She looked past Kell, to Saark, and he saw her eyes glow a little.

"How are you feeling, dandy man?"

"Better now your knife is no longer in my guts. But be warned, Myriam, your time on this planet is finite. You made an enemy of me for life; one day, I will slit your throat."

"But not now?" She moved forward, still athletic despite her gauntness. "Why not, Saark? What's stopping you? The poison which eats Kell even as we speak?"

"Enough!" bellowed Kell, and stomped forward, loosening Ilanna and swinging the great axe wide. For a moment only fear shone like bright dark flames in Myriam's eyes, then she shook her head and strode forward to meet him. If nothing else, she had spirit, and courage enough to match her cunning and evil.

Myriam halted before Kell, and looked into the huge warrior's eyes. She was tall, and proud, and she matched Kell for height. "Do you want to live, Kell, or do you want to die?"

"I don't die easy," he growled.

"You never answered the question."

"Where's the antidote?"

"Close by. However, I have another insurance policy I need to show you; otherwise, what's to stop you cutting me in half with that huge axe? Ilanna, she's called, isn't she?" Myriam smiled, then, and Kell did not like the smile. There was knowledge there, but more. There was an intimacy.

"You are playing games," said Kell. He glanced over to Nienna. "Did this woman hurt you, girl?"

"No, grandfather. And much as I hate to say it, she saved my life. Styx wanted to rape me, and kill me. Myriam murdered him. Jex left."

Kell nodded, and leaned in close to Myriam, aware her hand was on her sword hilt but knowing, as he had always known, that he could cut her in two before she cleared weapon from scabbard. "You play a dangerous game," he said, threat inherent in his tone.

"Yes. The game of life and death. And I choose life. And so should you. Don't be a hero, Kell. Don't be a jangling, bell-adorned capering village idiot."

"I say kill her," said Saark, and he moved closer, his slender rapier drawn. There was a quiet, dormant rage bubbling beneath the surface of his foppishness. "If we let her live, she'll stab us in the back. Again. And this place isn't so big; we can find the antidote to the poison."

"Stab you in the back?" laughed Myriam. She focused

on Saark. "I'd save that pleasure only for you, my sweet." She smiled, easily.

Saark growled. Kell held up a hand. "Enough." He focused on Myriam. "You have bought a truce for now. I will take you through the mountains. But the poison is seeping through my system. If I do not have the cure soon, I will be useless. And the Black Pike Mountains is no place where a warrior should be useless."

"I will give it to you – soon," breathed Myriam, calmer now that imminent threat was gone. But she knew; Kell was like a caged lion, one moment passive, submissive even, the next a raging feral beast. "But first, you must see this." She lifted her hand, then, and turned it so her palm faced upwards. Across her skin danced a tiny flame, and the flame grew until it was an inferno of silver flames all contained on the palm of her hand. The flames twisted and curled, and then formed themselves into a vision. In the tiny, glittering scene Kell stood on a high mountain pass, with Nienna behind him, cowering against frozen rocks. Saark was nowhere to be seen. Huge beasts loped forward, their fur white, their fangs terrible. They were snow lions, there were three of them, and they were mighty, their fur bright white, three males with bushy manes and yellow eyes. Kell roared and charged the snow lions, and claws smashed aside his axe. In the scene, the third lion circled Kell, leaping nimbly up the rocks and then dropping down before Nienna. She screamed, her scream tiny and a million miles away. The lion grinned, and lunged for her, but Myriam rushed past, her sword sticking into the lion and making it rear, blood gushing from a savage throat-wound and spraying bright crimson against snow and fur. The lion stumbled back, and went over the cliffs – and in the tiny vision, Myriam took Nienna in her arms and cuddled the terrified girl.

Slowly, the image faded, and Myriam closed her hand.

"You are a magicker!" gasped Saark, taking several steps back. "A witch!"

"Nothing so dramatic," snapped Myriam, scowling. "But I have certain prophetic skills. I may not be able to use magick for pain and destruction, as some can and do; but I see things. This was my vision. And yours, too."

"Clever," said Kell, face dark.

"If you kill me, then the lion kills Nienna." Myriam tilted her head. "You see how the puzzle pieces are coming together? To make a whole?"

"The game is not finished. Not yet."

"Still. We are a partnership."

"Is that why you killed Styx? Because you worked out another way to persuade me?"

"Yes. The power of the Black Pike Mountains brings out the magicker in me; but you are correct. I knew none of this when I poisoned you, and as we drew close to the Pikes then the dreams began, the visions, the pains in my heart."

"I will take you where you want to go," said Kell.

"To Silva Valley? Through the Secret Trails? The Worm Caves?"

"Yes."

"You swear?"

"If you save Nienna's life, as in that vision, then I swear. Now get me that damn antidote! I feel as if you have my balls in the palm of your hand, and I don't bloody like it!"

"Maybe one day I will," soothed Myriam, and turned, and disappeared back into the small stone room at the foot of the keep. She emerged with a tiny vial, and tossed it to Kell. He shook it. There was a small amount of clear liquid within.

He unstoppered the vial, and stared at Myriam. Then knocked it back in one.

"It will take a day or so, but will cleanse the poison from your system. This, I swear."

"And what of Nienna?" growled Kell, voice dark.

"I was never poisoned, grandfather!" smiled Nienna. "That was a lie. A lie to bring you here."

Kell stared for a long time at Myriam. She hid it well, but she was terrified. Eventually, Kell blinked, and relaxed his hand from the terrible haft of Ilanna.

"Now, we can kill her," smiled Saark, and glanced to Kell for support. "Yes, Big Man? Is that what you have in mind?" He was too eager. Too eager for death.

"No," said Kell. "You saw the magick."

"Pah!" snapped Saark. "She conjured that from thin air; it is an empty ruse, a courtside conman's trick, a slick cock up your arse, my friend. Do you not see?"

"It may or may not be real." Kell had a stubborn look on his face. His voice was low. "And maybe I have my own business now, in Silva Valley."

"Your own business? Like what?"

"That would be my business."

"You are worse than any mule," frowned Saark, and sheathed his rapier in disappointment. "Listen. Can we at least rest before we set off on some foolhardy mission through the most treacherous mountains the world has ever known? I stink. I stink worse than the donkey. In fact, I stink worse than you, Kell!"

Kell stared at Saark, and realised the man was saving face. He urgently wanted Myriam dead, and it was still there in his eyes, a burning coal. But for now, Kell could rely on Saark not to unbalance the equilibrium. But long term? Whether Kell believed in the vision or not, whether Kell chose to kill Myriam or not, Saark would one day have his way. And that sat bad in the back of Kell's mind, like an old bone buried by a dead dog.

"We have time," said Myriam, and stepped aside, pointing back into the small room – which in turn led to a small complex of apartments, empty and cold now, but which once must have housed a gatemaster and his family. "We can build a fire. Heat water. It is better than camping in the snow and ice."

Nienna led the way inside, followed by Kell, who struggled to squeeze Ilanna's huge butterfly blades through the opening.

Saark looked at Myriam. She smiled, and tilted her head.

"I have one question."

"Which is?"

"Where was I in the vision?"

"But you don't believe in it, dandy."

"That doesn't matter. Where was I?"

Myriam shrugged, and moved into the building.

"Playing damn games with my head," Saark muttered, and followed with a certain amount of apprehension.

The main guard room was small, but Myriam had built a fire in the hearth filling the limited space with heat. The group slept on under their travelling blankets, but the stone plinths in the chamber used as beds were hard and unforgiving, uncomfortable and deeply cold. Outside, the wind howled from the high passes of the Black Pike Mountains, rasping and ululating through

guttural corridors and wide, slightly skewed battlements. Even in the guard room, every line was just a
little bit out of square. It made for many complaints, as
each bed seemed to be trying to roll its occupant to the
floor, or twist them into an unsubtle heap.

Kell slept a deep sleep without dreams, his rage at
last satiated in his quest for Nienna. For this simple
pleasure, he was thankful. It was also a sleep of recovery, as the antidote to Myriam's poison went to work
on the toxins in his blood, in his muscles, in his organs,
eating away at the chemicals that would make Kell a
dead man. But at the back of it all was the secure
knowledge that Nienna was unharmed, and that he
was by her side, his axe in one hand, his bulk and ferocity and skill a barrier to any who might now
threaten her.

Nienna slept uneasily. The Cailleach Fortress was not
just unwelcoming, but deeply unnerving. As she lay,
thinking about her dead friend Katrina and all the good
times they'd been through, and contemplating the
young woman's death for the thousandth time, so she
would hear gentle whispers like draughts from the
higher reaches of the chamber, or hisses and bangs, like
popping stones in the fire. Nienna thought of her
mother, a long way distant, lost and lonely – possibly
even dead. Had she fallen when the Army of Iron invaded Falanor? Was she dead and buried, food for
worms? Or had she found an escape? After all, she was
a very resilient woman. She was the daughter of Kell.

Saark, on the other hand, tossed and turned, his
teeth hurting him, his blood hurting him. His heart
raced through his ears, pounded at him with hammers
as his body fluctuated from a heart rate of one beat per

minute, leaving him gasping for oxygen, then shooting up to two or even three hundred beats, racing through his chest like a steam-powered clockwork engine and making him claw his blankets in panic, the world a swirl of weird colours and surreal smells and sounds as his senses adjusted, and he felt himself dropping into the world of the altered human…

Eventually the feelings passed, and Saark was just falling into an exhausted sleep after three nights of wakefulness when he sensed somebody close to him. A hand touched his chest, lightly, and Saark's eyes flared open in panic. It was Myriam. He remembered the last time she had been this close; the stab of the knife, the wound in his guts, eating soil. Saark grabbed her wrist, a savage hard movement, but Myriam did not complain. She was there, beside him, her breathing slow, her eyes glittering.

She leaned close, so that her words tickled his ear, and Saark was a split second from drawing his punch-dagger and feeding it to her eyeball. "I would speak with you," she said, words gentle.

"Last time you wanted to speak with me, you stabbed me in the belly."

"That was different." She seemed to be fighting something, and her face twisted. "I am… different."

"Really? That is a surprise."

"Damn you, Saark! Come outside."

She stood, and he let go of her wrist, leaving enraged marks where his surprisingly powerful grip had scoured her flesh. He watched her leave, a cold wind and curls of snow entering the warm guard room on her departure. Cursing, Saark rolled from his hard bed and pulled on trews, boots and cloak. He stepped outside, closing the door quietly behind him, and was hit in the face by a snap of wind-driven snow. He gasped. The cold reached into every gap in his clothing and bit him like a piranha. He cursed. Then cursed again. He saw Myriam further ahead, sheltering under a huge towering buttress of stone. Saark put his hand on the hilt of his rapier, and walked towards her, grimly. If there was any foul play, he would gut her like a fish.

The sky was dark, but a glowing edge to the horizon signified the beginnings of dawn. Snow and wind whipped and shrieked. Saark gazed up at the massive keep, huge and black, slick with ice and slightly jigged from the vertical.

Walking towards Myriam, one hand holding the neck of his cloak together, he snapped, "What the shit do you want, woman? It isn't normal to be out in this."

"You'd better get used to it. We have a long way to go."

"What do you *want*?"

Myriam met his gaze, then. "I wanted to say I am sorry. About before, in Falanor, when I…"

"When you stabbed me in the guts? You bitch."

"Yes. I was. I was fuelled by hatred, by need, by a lust for life. It has made me irrational. Unpredictable. And I confess, a little… insane." She took a deep breath. Looked off, over the skewed fortress battlements. "I would make amends. I would say that I am sorry. That is all."

"Kell is taking you to the Silva Valley. We are here because of you."

Myriam shook her head. "I cannot explain it, but you are here for a greater good. This is what the magick has shown me, taught me, revealed to me."

Saark's eyes were hard. "You'll not con me with your half-penny tricks, bitch. I've seen plenty of part time conjurers in my time; and in my experience, the only thing they crave is silver coin. Amazingly, this impending accrued wealth always coincides with a 'greater good'. Crazy, wouldn't you agree?"

"You can believe what you wish. But Kell believes, and that is for all our benefit."

"Yeah, well, the old goat's a rancid fool."

"I will say it again. I am sorry. You can take it with grace, and acknowledge that I may have changed – that, bizarrely – spending time with Nienna has, shall we say, *altered* my view of the world. She has touched me. She has changed me. And now, because I have changed, the magick runs deeper through my veins. In sacrificing my hate, in stepping away from my rage, I can see more clearly."

"Good for you, girl! What do you want? A big sloppy kiss?"

"Curb your cynicism," she snapped, and he could see tears on her cheeks. Saark chewed his lip, and considered stepping close to her, holding her, hugging her, telling her he forgave the vicious stabbing back in the woods. But his mind shifted. She was a chameleon. She was out for self-preservation. He did not believe she had changed, but still sought personal profit at their little group's expense.

"Ha! I'm going back to bed. Save your sob stories for Kell. He's a sucker for a dying woman."

"But you, Saark? What do you care about?"

Saark gave a dark smile under the glowing edges of a rising winter sun. "Why, I'm a soft touch when it comes to myself."

"So we are the same, then?"

Saark stared at Myriam, stared at her hard as the

truth of her words bit him. He opened his mouth to speak, then closed it again. She was correct. They were *exactly* the same. Saark used people for his own ends. He always had, and he always would. He was vain, narcissistic, and totally enveloped with furthering his own pleasure – and life. Shit, he realised. Shit. In Myriam's position, would he have acted the same? Would he have stabbed somebody, poisoned another, in order to force them to help? And he knew, deep down in the glowing embers of his ruptured heart, that he probably would.

With shame touching him, he turned and went back to his cold bed. And the pounding of the rampant vachine blood-oil in his veins echoed right down to his soul.

Soon after dawn they followed a narrow alleyway through the fortress, winding between towering dark walls which exuded not just cold and gloom and abandonment, but an inherent *dread* which seemed to be a part of this long-deserted fortress. People had not only died here, it felt as if their souls had been sucked into the very stones, distorting them, tearing them free.

Kell led the way, walking his skittish horse with Nienna in the saddle. He didn't want to let her out of his sight. Nobody would take his granddaughter from him again; not without stepping over his dead body first. Next came Myriam, dressed in warm winter garb, her face seeming more shrunken on this freezing morn, her eyes ringed with purple and black, her breathing rasping and shallow. And behind came Saark, a wary eye on Myriam, listening to her ragged cancerous breathing and wondering how long she really had left. She wanted to reach Silva Valley, but according to Kell it was a hard, brutal journey and Saark could not quite puzzle out why he was still agreeing to do it. Surely, he could turn around now? He had Nienna. He had the antidote. And even if he believed Myriam's magick, her supposed prophecy, if he headed away from the Black Pikes then surely he would never see a pride of snow lions. How, then, could he lose Nienna to attack? It was strange. Saark decided to question Kell in private when the opportunity arose.

Within the hour they were free of the Cailleach Fortress, and in a narrow valley which ran beyond, through a narrow pass with massive, sheer towering walls. It was terribly gloomy in the pass, and huge rocks littered the floor, in places rising in piles which the group had to scramble up and over, slipping and sliding on wet rocks and ice. The horses struggled on gamely, and with pride Saark watched Mary – more agile than them all, despite carrying a heavy load on her back. The donkey did not complain, but willingly climbed each hill of loose rock to stand, staring down at the cursing humans with an almost equine arrogance.

After a while, Kell called a halt. "It's no good taking the horses any further, unless we intend to eat them."

Everybody stared at him. "You can't *eat* a good horse," snapped Saark. "What a waste of a fine creature!"

Kell grunted. "It's meat, like anything else. But the path will grow ever more treacherous; best now to let them free. They will soon start to slow us down. If we release them here, there's a chance we may find them on our return."

"Our return," said Myriam, softly, eyes distant. She smiled a skeletal smile. "Maybe some of us won't return? Instead, we will find paradise."

"In your dreams, Myriam," said Saark unkindly, and slapped his mount's rump, watching the beast slither back down the pathway and canter to a halt. The group emptied saddlebags, and then Kell stared meaningfully at Mary.

"No," said Saark.

"She'll be a pain in the arse."

"Nonsense! Mary is a fine beast, agile as a goat, the stamina of a lion. Where I go, Mary goes."

Kell peered close, and grinned. "Is there something I don't know about you and that mule?"

"Mary is a donkey. And don't be so crass."

"Why not? You've fucked everything else in existence."

"I resent that, axeman."

"Why so? I've never seen one so rampant. You'll be chasing Myriam next!" He roared with laughter, some good humour returned, and slapped Saark on the back. "Come on lad. Walk ahead with me. I wish to talk."

They moved on after releasing the horses, and Saark led Mary, her rope wrapped around one fist. Behind, Nienna walked with Myriam, and Myriam smiled down at the girl. "Is it good? Good to be back with your grandfather?"

"Yes. I have missed him terribly. I knew he would come for me."

"I... I wanted to apologise, girl. For the way I treated you. And treated him. I have been selfish beyond reason."

Nienna shrugged. "What I don't understand is why we are still here. Why we are heading through the mountains. I thought he would leave you when you gave him the antidote; in fact, I thought he would cut you in half." She smiled, a weak, cold smile, her eyes glittering.

Myriam sighed. "I have done... bad things, Nienna. I admit that. And I deserve Kell's hatred. And even yours."

"I don't hate you," said Nienna, smiling gently. "I see your pain, understand your agony. I pity you, Myriam, not hate you."

Myriam's eyes went dark. "Well girl, sometimes pity is far worse."

Ahead, Kell had halted. The towering walls were silent, looming, filling the narrow pass with shadows. Water trickled and gushed in various places, and had frozen solid in others, either in fingers of sculpted, corrugated ice, or in vast, hanging sheets. Occasionally, stones rattled down the sheer iron-stained flanks of this interior slice from the mountain range.

"We must move with care," said Kell. "There have been many rockfalls here over the years. Any loud noise could bring down the Pikes on our bloody heads. We all understand?"

"Aye," nodded Saark, rubbing Mary's muzzle.

They set off again, down a rocky slope, boots slithering. Eventually, Saark said, "Kell, I have a question."

"It better not be about sex," growled the huge warrior.

"No no. Not this time. I was simply wondering why we are still here?"

"Think about it."

"About Myriam?"

"No, you dolt. About the two vachine who Graal sent to kill us. I was thinking about them; thinking a lot. Graal has invaded Falanor, wiped the whole damn army of Leanoric under his boots. So then. What next? We stumble through his camp like blind men through a brothel, and by some bloody miracle manage to escape. What *should* Graal do? Continue his expansion in the name of vachine blood-oil gathering? Or spend considerable resources sending killers after us? Why? Why hunt us down? He knew we were heading north. Why waste two of his best killers? Surely he has more important fish to fry."

Saark considered this. "He knew your history, Kell. About being a Vachine Hunter for the old Battle King."

"Exactly. But that should not worry him; what's the worst I could do? Harry a few stray vachine scum in the mountains? Hardly a threat to his war effort, don't you think?"

"What are you getting at?"

"Graal knows I was heading north. He knows I know the Pikes. Maybe – and this is just a thought – maybe he thinks I'm heading for Silva Valley. The homeland of the vachine. But then, surely I would be slaughtered the minute I arrived?"

"So you think Graal wants to stop you finding Silva Valley?"

Kell nodded. "Yes. He thinks I know something I don't. There is some great mystery here, some puzzle we need to unravel. I think Graal is not playing for the vachine; I think he works his own game, I think the conniving bastard is up to his own bowel-stinking tricks. But what? What could he possibly be doing? And *why* would he think I was a threat to his plans?"

"I see your reasoning. And now I see why we're heading north, instead of south back to the relative comfort of Falanor – such as we'd be able to find. If Graal doesn't want you here, this is probably the best place for you to be."

"Exactly!" growled Kell. "Silva Valley, that is where the answers lie. The more we travelled north after

Nienna, the more I realised that Myriam's goal is our goal. She wants immortality; I want answers. Our only chance of stopping this damned invasion is to confront its source. We need to know more about these Harvester bastards, we need to know where the albino soldiers come from – but more importantly, we need to find the source of the vachine."

"You cannot take on an entire nation of clockwork killers," said Saark, hand on Kell's shoulder.

"You just do it one head at a time," snapped Kell. "You'd be surprised what a pyramid you can build."

"I think, old horse, that sometimes you are crazy."

Kell nodded sombrely. "I'm just the way the world made me."

More snow fell, a light scattering making rocks treacherous and slippery. After several hours of the narrow pass they emerged into a circular valley with a frozen tarn at its floor. All around reared jagged teeth peaks, and Kell put his hands on his hips, breathing deeply, staring out at the stunning, desolate beauty of the place.

"Kingsman's Tarn," said Kell. He pointed, and the others followed his gaze. "Up that way is Demon's Ridge, the first of our trials. If we can get up there by nightfall, we'll be safe from anything that follows."

"You're being followed?" said Myriam, eyes narrowed, hand straying to her longbow.

"I guarantee it," said Kell. "Graal seems to have a passion to make me dead. Well, as he's going to find out, I don't die easy."

"You keep saying that," snapped Saark.

"Ain't it true, lad?"

"I'm not disputing its truth, just pointing out that it grates on my nerves every time you say it."

Kell laughed, seeing Saark's uneasiness. A cold wind howled down over the tarn, and rushed past them like a phalanx of cold angels. "I understand now! You are so much out of your natural environment, it hurts."

Saark frowned. "What do you mean?"

"The royal court," Kell sneered, "with its golden goblets, bowls of honey fruit, its randy middle-aged courtiers with powdered wigs and silk panties and glossy leather boots – that's your world, Saark. The world of easy sex and animal sex, of whiskey-wine and the best cuts of meat full of thick fat juice and spiced herbs from a different continent! The world of the dandy. The fop. The rich idiot with too much gold and nothing between his ears, nor his legs, I'd wager. That, Saark, my favourite horny, perfumed goat, is the world to which you belong. Your natural setting. But this. This!" He stared around, at the wilds, the rugged ridgelines, the whipping flurries of snow, the ice, the storm-filled skies; a place of natural wonder, and brutality, and death. "This is my place," he finished quietly.

Saark pushed ahead, leading Mary. "That way, you say?"

"Yes. Across the heather. There's a rocky path we can follow further on, an old stream bed leading up to Demon's Ridge. You'll struggle with that damn donkey, though."

"I'm not leaving her behind. Not here," said Saark, patting her fondly.

"Aye. Well, I suppose there's good eating on one."

"What?" Saark's voice was ice.

"Her meat will be a bit stringy, but it'll do when we're starving on the crags."

"She's not for *eating*," scowled Saark. "That would be a crime!"

"Aye. A crime to my belly, is what I'm thinking. But come on. We have a long way to go."

They rose from Kingsman's Tarn in the basin valley, and within an hour the wind was howling across the rock faces and cutting through their clothing. Each pulled on extra woollen shirts and dug out thick cloaks, as high over the ridges snow danced and threatened heavy falls.

"I expect," said Saark, grunting as he jumped down into the old stream bed and turned to guide Mary, "that the snow can easily block our passage. Render our journey impossible. That sort of thing?"

"Aye," said Kell, panting, putting his hands on his hips to gaze up the narrow incline ahead. Although snow was present, it was surprisingly shallow and banked to one side of the old stream bed. Kell picked a path to the left where his boots could still grip the stones, and he led the way up the slope.

Their progress was slow, and before long all four were panting, and struggling to move forward. Despite cold and ice, the small rocks of the old stream bed shifted under boots, making the scramble difficult.

Still, they pushed on.

Out of the wind it was hot work climbing, and they played an annoying game of removing clothing, then suffering the bite of wind and putting it back on. Saark cursed more than the others, and Nienna was silent, her face strong, eyes focused on the task, pushing herself on much to the silent pride of Kell. *She is definitely of my blood*, he thought. *She has the strength of ten lions!*

Darkness was gradually falling as they reached the final section of the steep trail, which grew worse for perhaps the final hundred metres of ascent up to Demon's Ridge. The ridgeline had vanished now, and all they could see was rock and ice, boulders and channels in the mountain rock.

Saark stopped, and glanced back at what they had climbed. He grinned over at Nienna. "You're doing well, girl." She nodded, but no smile came to her face. She was exhausted, hands cut, feet sore, the cold seeping into her bones, the wind shrieking in her brain. "I am trying, Saark. Really trying." Her voice was the voice of a child again, and weariness her mistress.

Now, the climbing got harder and they struggled on, clawing at the frozen rocks, dragging themselves up steep inclines and past huge boulders. Mary the donkey was, as Saark predicted, surprisingly agile, but as he peered further and further up the trail, he wondered for how long she'd be able to manage.

They struggled on, sweat pouring down faces, making their hair lank and skin chilled by the wind. Myriam suffered the worst, for with her savage cancer she had grown weak, and grew weaker with every passing day. Her face and eyes were fevered, and she drank water often, hands shaking with fatigue and dehydration. At one point she stumbled, and Saark was there in the blink of an eye, moving with incredible agility and speed, grabbing her arm before she toppled back down the steep road of stones. She smiled in gratitude to him, leaning on him heavily as she fumbled for her water bottle again. Saark scowled, and let go.

"I should have let you go," he snapped.

"You're still sore about that knife wound, aren't you?"

Saark said nothing, but moved ahead. Myriam watched him with bright fevered eyes.

Kell was first to reach the summit and stand on the heady heights of Demon's Ridge. He planted a boot either side of the ridgeline, hands on hips, hair and beard caught by the wild, whining wind, and gazed out over the stacked ridges and endless teeth of the Black Pike Mountains. They filled his vision like nothing else ever could, and Kell caught a breath in his throat, filled with emotion, filled with dread, and filled with a deep certainty, an intuition that this was his last time in the Black Pikes. He knew, as sure as night follows day, that he would die here. The Pikes would claim him. For Kell, this time, there was no going home.

Melancholy hit Kell like a fist. He helped Nienna climb up and stand beside him on the high ridge, gazing out across the staggered realms of hundreds of mountains which stretched off to a distant, dark horizon. Trails of dry snow curled in the air, and each mountain was subtly different, many purple or black or grey, many with snow on flanks and peaks; but they all shared one thing in common. Each was a savage barbed pike, a threat to life and love, and without an ounce of mercy in the billions of tonnes of rock which carved out passes and channels, gulleys and scree slopes. These were the Black Pike Mountains. All they brought to humanity was suffering and death.

Saark arrived next, panting, his dark curls drenched with sweat. Mary the donkey followed him, struggling up the last section, but once on the ridge was sure-footed and seemed unconcerned by the vast drops surrounding them. Saark patted her muzzle and looked to Kell. "You move fast for an old fat man," he said.

"And you climb well for an effete arsehole."

Saark gazed out. "I don't like the look of that. Too many places to die!"

"It's beautiful!" said Nienna, voice filled with awe.

"Yeah," muttered Saark, taking in great lungfuls of air, "as beautiful as a striking cobra. Girl, this place is no place for mortals. The Black Pikes were put here by the gods to keep us away from the Granite Thrones!"

"The Granite Thrones? What're they?"

"Tsch," scowled Kell. "That's a myth."

"In my experience, nine times out of ten myths are based on fact."

Kell shrugged. "Whatever. That does not concern us. What *does* concern us is getting to Silva Valley; it's a long, hard haul my friends."

Myriam climbed the final stretch, and stared at the donkey's arse blocking her path. Saark clicked his tongue, and Mary moved out of Myriam's way, eyes flared, ears laid back along her dark-haired skull.

"This is no place for an ass," said Myriam acidly, stepping up onto the ridge.

"I wish everybody would stop complaining about my donkey," moaned Saark.

"Who said I was talking about the donkey?"

They laughed, and stared out in wonder. The world seemed much larger, a vast sweeping canvas. Nienna turned a full circle, eyes absorbing the magnificent splendour as the wind swooped and howled, crackled and snapped.

Kell laid his hand on Nienna's shoulder. "Is this what you wanted, girl?"

"What do you mean?"

"That day, when the Army of Iron invaded Jalder. You said you were bored. You wanted a taste of adventure. Well, you've been given adventure all right. You've been given adventures enough to last you a lifetime!"

"It's not what I expected," she said, in a small voice, remembering the evil people she had met, the pain she had endured, the friends she had lost. And most of all, she pictured Kat, a victim at the hands of Styx's Widowmaker crossbow. Nienna realised she was glad Styx was dead. He was a bad man, and had deserved everything. "I realise now. I did not understand. It would have been better to stay at home, go to university, raise a family." She took a deep breath, and looked up into Kell's eyes as the wind whipped her dark hair. "But I am here now, and this thing is happening to our world. The Army of Iron will not stop, the vachine will not stop – not unless we stop them, right?"

Kell chuckled. "An old man, a haunted child, a cancer-riddled woman and a foppish dandy. What chance, in the name of the Bone Underworld, have we really got?"

"You sell us short, old man," said Saark, smiling, his eyes twinkling as his gaze moved back down the trail they had traversed. The smile dropped from his face, as if he'd been hit by a helve. Distant, by the tarn, where the pass led from the Cailleach Fortress, something moved. "We have company," snapped Saark, hand on the hilt of his rapier.

The group turned, looked down, and stared.

Distant, two pale-skinned figures emerged. They were tall, lithe, athletic, and moved with a balanced ease across uneven ground. Even from this great remoteness it was clear they were Graal's daughters, the vachines who had attacked Kell and Saark earlier. They were the Soul Stealers. And they still hunted Kell's blood.

"I thought we'd scared them off," said Saark, voice little more than a whisper.

"No chance, lad," said Kell, eyes hooded. "And look. This time they brought friends."

Behind the two women, on long chain leashes, came the cankers. There were three of them, but these were smaller than previous beasts and appeared, almost, like bow-legged horses. Only these seemed to have no skin. Bloody, crimson flesh gleamed, even from this distance. One of the skinless cankers screeched, and the sound echoed through the basin valley like a woman being stabbed, reverberating on high spirals of wind. It was a chilling sound.

"Time for us to move on, I think," said Saark, mouth dry, voice a whisper.

"Let's go," agreed Kell, and they headed down the opposite side of Demon's Ridge as far below, in the valley, the Soul Stealers sniffed the air and started forward in pursuit.

CHAPTER 12
The Black Pike Mountains

General Graal knelt on luxurious rugs, his body naked and oiled, and grasped the black sword in shaking fingers. He had imbibed drugs, the leaf of the Truaga Plant, and allowed his blood to be filtered through KaKa Leaves. And although he was considered an amateur in circles of magick, this simple spell taught by Kradek-ka, this simple mind-to-mind communion using blood-oil as a signal carrier was something at which Graal was becoming peculiarly adept. For he knew he would need this skill when the Vampire Warlords returned…

Kuradek, Meshwar and Bhu Vanesh.

It had been an age since they walked the lands. An age since they sat on the Granite Thrones. But their time was about to return, and Graal could feel their apprehension in the Blood Void; could feel their frustration and eagerness, and ultimately, their desire to return with their toxicity, with their plague.

"Kradek-ka?" he whispered.

"I am here," said Kradek-ka, the telltale *tick tick tick* of his vachine clockwork filling Graal's mind and making it difficult to concentrate over such distance.

"I am finished here. Falanor is a conquered land."

"Yes. You have conquered it, Graal; you have brought a bloody retribution for their past; for the times of Ankarok. Servants they again shall be! And, as a consequence, we have enough blood-oil for the Summoning. But still, we need the third Soul Gem. Without it, we will have no control of the Vampire Warlords. With all three Soul Gems, we will be Masters." He laughed, a cold cruel laugh.

"Does Anukis know?" said Graal.

"No. She is a simple fool. She believes me, and she trusts me; after all, I am Watchmaker, I am Engineer! She was polluted by her mother as a child, I fear, fed simple morals and indoctrinated in the way of vachine; she wishes to see the vachine society expand and prosper, despite what they did because of her impure nature; despite what Vashell was forced to do – by coercion, and by magick. But she will come round, Graal. She will deliver the Soul Gem voluntarily… And if she does not? Well, I will rip the Gem from her chest with my own teeth. The Engineer Religion must end here. It is time for a new Empire. An Empire based on Blood and Sacrifice and Vampire Plague!"

Graal said nothing for a moment, and thought of his own daughters, Shanna and Tashmaniok. If they had carried a gem of infinite power, of destructive soul magick buried deep within their own flesh, if they had carried a key to controlling the ancient vampire gods – would he sacrifice them? He smiled then. Of course he would. For they were only flesh, and bone, and what Kradek-ka and Graal planned… Well, that was immortality. Power. And total control.

"What of the second?" said Graal, then. "Have the three moons aligned?"

"The moons are aligned," confirmed Kradek-ka. "And even as we speak, Jageraw is in the mountains on his strange deviant course. As the Book of Angels decreed, the Gems had to be implanted in Guardian Souls. When released, only then would they have the true power to control the Vampire Warlords."

"So we have Anukis. We have Jageraw. Our *lady*, our *contact* implanted the third... have you found her, yet? Have you found the Guardian?"

"Yes." Kradek-ka's voice was soft. Clockwork gears stepped and clicked with a vague, background buzz. "I know the Guardian now."

"Did she choose well? Is the Guardian known to me?" said Graal, voice grave.

"Let us just say this answers a puzzle which has haunted us for many a day, General Graal."

The brass chamber in the Engineer's Palace was cold, and eerily quiet at this hour of the night. Sa entered, pulling a high-collared shimmering iron gown tight. Her eyes burned with annoyance. "This had better be good," she snarled, striding across the metal floor, boots ringing. Then she stopped. She stared at Walgrishnacht and the three remaining members of his platoon.

The Cardinal and his vachine warriors were in a sorry state. Their flesh was cut and burned, by weapons and by ice, and their armour and clothing was in tatters showing signs of many a battle. The vachine warriors wore bloodied bandages with pride.

"You came through the mountains?"

"Through the Secret Paths," said Walgrishnacht.

"And you have news," said Sa, briskly.

"Princess Jaranis is dead. General Graal had her murdered. I assume this precludes invasion."

"It is not your duty to *assume*," snapped Sa, eyes narrowed. "You were pursued?"

"By cankers," said Walgrishnacht, voice level. Tagor-tel gave a short hiss, air rushing past his vachine fangs. He gestured to Sa, who nodded. For cankers to attack vachine was unheard of. Unbelievable! Even to utter such a breath was heresy in the Engineer's Palace.

"You can prove this?" said Tagor-tel, voice low and filled with poison.

Beja stepped from the shadows, and he carried a sack. Unceremoniously, he upended the cloth and a huge, deformed canker head rolled out, leaving blood-oil smears on the chamber floor.

Sa took an involuntary step back. She met Walgrishnacht's steel gaze.

"We are not the enemy here," said the Cardinal, and she noted his hand was on his sword-hilt. He had a finger missing.

"Do you realise to whom you speak?" hissed Sa, invoking her Watchmaker status.

"Yes," said Walgrishnacht. "But it looks to me that Graal intends to invade. You must call the War Council. If you do not pull our troops, and our *Ferals* back from Untamed Lands, we will be defenceless. Silva Valley will be defenceless!"

Sa gave a nod. She turned to Tagor-tel. "Any news from Fiddion?"

"No. He has been strangely silent."

"Then call the War Council," said Sa, voice bleak. "Come the spring, it appears we go to war."

● ● ●

Kell and his fellow travellers made a hasty descent into a narrow pass which led through the mountains. Tension was eating them, now. On their trail were two cross-breed vachine albino killers. Which meant... what? That the vachine and albino soldiers were breeding? Saark shivered at the thought as he moved lithely across rocky ground, and a cold wind laced with ice caressed him.

"You're going to have to leave the donkey," said Kell, finally, as they stumbled through a narrow inverted V, leading to a rocky ravine.

"No."

"It's not up for debate, Saark. With those bastards on our tail, we need to put down more speed. She's slowing us down." Kell placed his hand gently on Saark's arm. "My friend. If Mary is with us when the cankers come, they will tear her to pieces. You know this."

Saark nodded, and with a tear in his eye he patted the donkey's muzzle, removed the heavy load from her back and took a few essentials from the bags, before slapping her rump with the hilt of his rapier. With a startled "eeyore", Mary cantered back down the trail, then turned and stared at Saark reproachfully with large, baleful eyes.

"Go on. Shoo!" he yelled. Looking back to Kell, he grinned. "I love that beast," he said, and Kell nodded, eyes hooded, hand on the Ilanna's matt black shaft.

"Let's move," said Kell, eyeing the high ridgeline above. Distantly, he fancied he could hear canker snarls, but shook his head. It was the wind in the crags. But they were coming, he knew. The albino women and the cankers. They were coming, all right. He could feel it in his bones. In his very soul.

Kell had been right to abandon Mary. They moved with more speed now, although both Nienna and Saark complained bitterly at the pace; and Saark more-so than the young woman. On Kell's direction, they angled right, up a steep rocky slope filled with flat plates of granite and slate, boots stomping and sliding to send yet more rocks scattering and clattering to the valley below. Kell pushed them hard, and after fifty minutes or so all were streaming with sweat, pain flashing bright patterns through their brains. Saark paused, and gazed down the scree slope.

"I can see Mary!" he said, almost triumphantly. Then stopped dead, as from a narrow chimney in the opposite wall of rock loped the three cankers. They stopped, snarling and drooling, and spread out, circling the donkey, great paws padding and claws drawing sparks from the hard ground, eyes fixed, travelling in lazy pendulous sweeps. Mary eeyored in panic, eyes wide, ears laid back on her terrified skull. Saark found his heart in his mouth, terror running through his veins. "No," he muttered, gripping his rapier as Mary hunkered down in terror, bunching her hind quarters to do the only thing she knew how; to kick. "Not the donkey!" wailed Saark. But, after a few brief circles, the cankers broke away like a squadron of hunting falcons, and padded along the bottom of the valley floor.

"Shh!" said Kell, motioning for the others to lower themselves to the ground, killing their skyline. Then he glanced up. Above them reared a high wall of granite cut through with lodes of glittering quartz, diagonal bands that gleamed and sparkled. He fancied he spied a narrow aperture. A narrow squeeze would be good to slow down the cankers – or at least force them to come through in single file. But they hadn't been spotted yet; if they stood and ran now, it would draw the cankers to them immediately. If they were lucky, the cankers would lose their scents.

"They're heading off down the ravine," whispered Saark.

Kell nodded.

Myriam shifted, and a rock rolled down the slope, bouncing as it reached the bottom to send a hollow clatter reverberating through the rocky wilderness. The cankers stopped, a sudden movement, and all three heads turned to stare up at the hiding adventurers.

"Well done, bitch," hissed Saark.

Kell stared at the cankers. He had never seen anything like them. Their skin was translucent, showing the crimson of thick muscles cut through by clockwork machinery within, all twisted and deformed just that little bit – a characteristic which set them apart from pure vachine. It was a twisted merging of clockwork technology and flesh made real.

Their eyes were blood red, faces elongated almost into horse muzzles but much wider, much larger, showing curved fangs which twisted and bent in seemingly random directions. They moved on all fours like huge lions, but as they turned and bounded up the slope Kell and Saark blinked, realising they had hooves.

"Mother of Mercy," whispered Saark, drawing his rapier.

"Run!" screamed Kell, suddenly, breaking the spell. Nienna and Myriam sprinted, sliding up the scree, with Saark and Kell close behind. Kell pulled free Ilanna and kissed her butterfly blades. "Don't let me down this time," he muttered.

I am here for you, Kell. Here to kill for you. As you know I always will.

They sprinted up, as best they could. The cankers moved fast, faster than a human, and spiked brass claws emerged from hooves sending showers of sparks scattering down the scree slope. Myriam reached the narrow aperture first, and lifted free her long bow. She notched an arrow and touched a fletch to her cheek in one swift movement. An arrow flashed through the gloom, hitting a canker high in the shoulder. It squealed then, with a high-pitched whinny, twisted and corrupt. The cry of a dying horse.

Nienna ran into the gap in the rocky wall. It was the width of a man, the walls green and slick and slimy. Moss lined the floor in a thick layer, and above, about twelve feet from the ground, several large fallen rocks had formed a wedged, uneven roof.

"Come on!" shouted Nienna, fear etching her face and voice like acid. She pulled free a long knife, and stood, waiting, watching.

Saark reached Myriam's side and turned. He was an agile and quick man, made faster by his bite at the teeth of the albino vachine. He had left Kell behind, labouring, for once his prodigious size and strength working against him. Kell was panting hard, sweat running in rivulets down his face, into his beard, and he powered on, Ilanna in one mighty fist as the first of the cankers came up fast behind him... at the last minute Kell screamed and whirled, Ilanna slamming through flesh and knocking the canker back down the slope, where it rolled and thrashed past its sprinting comrades. Kell came on a few more steps. He was twenty paces from the aperture, but the cankers were too close. Another arrow flashed, close over Kell's shoulder and into a canker's throat – the beast reared, emitting the strange screaming horse-shriek, but dropped to the ground and charged on. Kell's axe slammed in an overhead sweep, connecting as the canker leapt for his throat with long brass claws, and Ilanna bit through muscle and flesh, snapping bones with terrible crunches. The canker twisted, trapping the axe and rolling away, tearing the great butterfly blades from Kell's sweating grip. The third canker leapt, but Myriam's arrow flashed, striking the beast through the eye. Kell shifted left as the beast hit the ground beside him, thrashing, and he leapt on its back, great hands taking hold of its long equine head and wrenching back with all his strength, his muscles writhing, and for a long moment they were locked, immobile, a bizarre double-headed creature from a deformed nightmare – then there came a mighty *crack* as Kell snapped the beast's neck. The canker fell limp, mewling, and Kell ran back to his em-bedded axe, taking hold of the shaft and wrenching the weapon free. Panting, and covered in huge globules of canker blood, he turned and ran for the crevice.

"Well done, old horse!" beamed Saark, as Kell reached the wall of rock. The old warrior glanced up, lips tight, saying nothing. He turned, and watched the two injured cankers climb to their feet. Even though Ilanna had cut a huge chunk from the beast, breaking bones within, it shifted itself and they could see the huge *open* wound – enough to fell any bull or bear – and watched as *inside* the wound thin golden wires seemed to flow, twisting and entwining around broken bones, pulling them with little cracks back into place, into alignment, then wrapping around and around and around, binding, strengthening, as all the time the ominous *tick tick tick* of slightly offbeat clockwork clicked across the empty rock space.

"Inside," growled Kell, squaring himself up.

"They can fit," said Saark. "The cankers are smaller than others we've met. Kell, the bastards can follow us."

"Not if I have my way!" he hissed, eyes like glowing coals. Myriam and Saark followed Nienna into the narrow gap, and Kell lifted Ilanna above his head as the cankers orientated themselves on the man and dropped their heads, growls emitting on streams of saliva.

Kell swung his axe, striking the rocky wedge above. The wall *boomed*, sparks spat in a shower, and above the rocks trembled. Again Kell struck the wall, and again, his huge muscles straining, Ilanna shrieking and singing in simple joy and the cankers charged, their brass claws raking the rocks and for a final time, Kell slammed his axe into the wall and above there came a rattle, followed by cracks as three huge rocks shifted, and one fell, the second fell atop it, and their combined weight brought a wall of granite tumbling into the gap as Kell leapt back, stumbled back, dust billowing out and slamming him like a wall of ash. Kell coughed, choking for a moment, blinded, dust in his beard and eyes. He dropped his axe, rubbing at his eyes and coughing some more, and Saark patted the old man on the back.

"Well done, old boy."

Kell picked up Ilanna and surveyed the blockage, his eyes following it upwards. He grunted in cynicism. "Let's see how long that holds. Not long enough, I'd wager."

"You're ever the sweet voice of optimism."

"Get to chaos, Saark. And next time, try using that pretty little rapier instead of standing by watching me fight!"

"Hey!" Saark spread his hands. "You seemed to be doing such a fine job! You didn't need my little prick in the middle of your hero battle; after all, you are *Kell the Legend*. They wrote poems about you."

Kell stared beadily at Saark, then pushed him heavily in the chest. "Go on. Follow Nienna and Myriam. Let's get out of this shit hole before a mountain of rocks comes down on our heads."

"Don't push! You'll wrinkle the silk."

Kell shook his head and sighed. "Some things will never change," he rumbled.

They moved as swiftly as they could through the gloom, and more snow began to fall. They found a cave, and Kell allowed Myriam to build a small fire. "They know where we are, anyways," he said. "And I think we all need something warm inside us."

Myriam made a thin soup in a shallow pan she carried in her pack, and as they sat shivering in the small damp cave, warming hands over the meagre flames, Myriam stirred the soup, and fixed Kell with an odd look.

"You know, Kell, when I was younger I was a student at the University of Vor. We had many texts there; it was during that time I found I had a small affinity for magick."

"Illusions, you mean," snorted Saark.

"Even so. There were many texts I studied before… before my affliction."

"And?" Kell had made a mug of coffee, and held it between his great bear paws. It looked a little ridiculous. Out of scale. He drank the bittersweet brew, and sighed, feeling caffeine and sugar fire through his system. That feeling was closely followed by a ravening hunger. How long since they had eaten? How long since they did anything except grab a sleep of exhaustion, or a meal of dried meat as they fled yet more danger? Oh, for a fine steak, a tankard of honey-mead, and new potatoes garnished with herbs and butter. Kell found his mouth watering. Horse-shit, he thought. Things were going to get a lot worse before they got better, that was for sure.

"I think I know these two women who follow, in pursuit. These, as you say, blend of albino and vachine. Of what you speak is a rarity; if the texts are to be believed."

Kell stared at her. "They had texts on the vachine at Vor University?"

Myriam gave a strange smile. "Yes. They were kept under lock and key, obviously. King Searlan, as his father and grandfather before him, did not want the vachine made common knowledge to the populace. It was bad enough having Blacklippers running blood through the mountains, feeding any impure vachine willing to buy Karakan Red, without further adding to dark legends."

"And that's where you found out about merging human with clockwork?"

Myriam nodded. "Yes. When I contracted my…" her face contorted a little, and her eyes darkened despite the fire, "my *cancer*, when I had exhausted my funds on employing ridiculous and pointless physicians who took my money and made recommendations, none of which worked, then I turned to *knowledge*, I turned to those secret books I knew existed in the Vor Vaults. I knew which Professors held the keys. I persuaded them, one way or another, to give me access."

"You mean you used sex?" blurted Nienna, meeting Myriam's gaze.

"Don't look at me like that, girl. I did not – and do not – want to die."

"None of us want to die," said Nienna. "But we don't always get a choice." She bared her teeth in what might have been a smile; a smile tainted by memories of Kat.

"You say you think you know these women? Explain."

"They fit a description I once read. In an ancient text."

"Hold on," said Saark, holding up his hand. "I've been close to one of these killing bitches. Real close. And I'm telling you she wasn't a day over the age of twenty."

"That isn't the way it works," growled Kell.

Myriam nodded. "They do not age; or not as you and I understand the ageing process. A vachine with regularly updated clockwork – well, they could live for hundreds of years. And these two – Shanna and Tashmaniok they were named – they were famous for many dark deeds. They were known as the Soul Stealers! And they were there at the Siege of Drennach. They were there during the Days of Blood."

"They were?" said Saark, eyes wide. He glanced at Kell. "Hey. *You* were at the Siege of Drennach! It's in the poem. It's part of the Legend!"

Kell licked his lips, eyes down, and sipped his coffee. He leant forward with a grunt, and stared into the pan. "Is the soup ready?"

Myriam tasted it, then reached into her pocket and added more salt. "Soon. Let the meat soften. I, also, find it hard to chew."

Kell sat back, and as he stared into the fire he said, "The Siege of Drennach was a bad time. Many died there. Nobody cared about Drennach, back then. We felt like we'd been deserted, by the King, by the people of Falanor. We were left out there to hang. There were only three hundred, a quarter what the garrison should have been, especially in a place that big. When the savages came from over the rolling desert dunes, wearing flowing robes and carrying tulwars and spears with golden heads that shimmered in the sun... well, each man on those walls knew he was dead meat. The savages had War Lions on leashes, huge beasts trained to fight in pits and then, at Drennach, trained to attack the defenders on the walls." Kell shook his head, and sighed. "It was a bad time; a time of death." He looked up. "I did bad things, then. I was a cruel man." His face hardened, eyes narrowing. "A very bad man."

"But you never saw these *Soul Stealers*?" asked Saark.

Kell shook his head. "Never heard of them, lad. And when I had my little encounter back at the distillery, I did not know the bitch. She seemed to know me, but I assumed that was because they were hunting us – sent by Graal, no less. If there was anything deeper, anything from back at Drennach, well, she gave me no sign."

"One thing is for sure," said Myriam.

"Oh yeah?" snapped Saark.

"They are deadly."

"I think we should eat, now," said Kell.

"Grandfather?"

His face cracked into a smile. "Yes, little monkey?"

Nienna returned his smile. "You said you were a bad man. Were you... were you *really* bad?"

"Only to the bad men," lied Kell, shivering as he spoke the words, shivering as flickering red images of gore and torture rampaged through his mind; shivering, as he remembered his daughter.

Kell forced the memories away. No. Not now.

Now, he had a different agenda. To keep Nienna alive.

And to end the madness in Falanor.

He could only do that by remaining calm, and thinking things through, and not drinking whiskey and losing his temper. He could only do these things by *not* being Kell the Legend. His Legend came from his evil, dark deeds, from blood-oil and whiskey, and from the Dog Gem soul of Ilanna. From Ilanna.

Kell coughed, and accepted soup from Myriam.

"I should be dead," he said, and sipped the hot, thin broth.

"But you are not."

"I deserve it," said Kell, fixing eyes on Saark.

"That's up for debate," smiled Saark, weakly. "You continually claim to be a bad man; and yet I see you perform good deeds all the time. Good deeds that help people; look at Nienna. You *saved* her, Kell."

"To save myself," he grunted.

Saark laughed, a tinkling sound in that strange cold place. "You are indulging yourself, old man, you have this image of yourself and you will not, *can* not admit that good exists inside you. Well, mate, whatever you say. But you and I both know, even if you had not been poisoned, you would have strode across this world with your axe in hand, slaying any bastard who got between you and your granddaughter."

"There you go," said Kell. "You admit it. I would have slain any who stood before me. That is not honourable. That is not strong. That is weak, Saark; I am a weak man. A strong man would not use his physical strength as do I. A strong man would not... *abuse* his gift."

"The only abuse here," said Saark, "is your lack of table manners. Look! By all the gods, you're spilling soup down your jerkin. You're a scruffy bastard, Kell.

It's in your beard and everything! Can you not connect hand to mouth? Can you not retain a simple soup in your orifice?"

"I'll shove my fist in your orifice if you don't stop mewling."

"Ha, and there was I defending your honour and integrity."

"I need no man for that," said Kell.

Myriam had been watching bemusedly as the two men squabbled, then sat, staring at Kell. "Kell."

"Yes, lass?"

"I am confused. And a little worried."

"Spit it out."

"Well, as to why you are still guiding me to Silva Valley – to the vachine. I don't want to wake up – or not wake up – with an axe in the back of my skull. I am tired of looking over my shoulder. Weary of living in fear. And I recognise I have earned this by my actions. To you, and to Nienna. I am deeply sorry."

Kell grinned, looking down into their meagre fire. "You have pushed me a lot, Myriam. Pushed me beyond the boundaries of accepted behaviour." He glanced up. His eyes glittered, then he shifted his gaze sideways to his granddaughter. Nienna was looking up at the cave walls in fascination, as if she'd found a particularly original composition of poetry embedded in damp stone. Kell shook his head. He could not understand her continual enthralment. "The thing is, lass, if you'd pulled that trick on me a few years back, with the poison – well girl, you'd now be dead. The minute the antidote touched my lips I would have split you down the fucking middle like a log." He rested back, soup finished, hands on his knees. He sighed. "However. I am

trying. I am trying to be… not good, but *better*. I am trying to be a *tolerable* man, for Nienna, to show her a fine
example. Ironically, I am trying to do this in the midst
of an invasion. But a man must strive." He ran his hand
through his thick, shaggy, unkempt hair. Then
scratched at his beard, rubbing away a smudge of soup.
"And we have the same goals. The same destination.
Silva Valley seems to be the place with answers. I am
Kell. And I sorely want some answers."

"I have a trade."

"Another one?" growled Saark. "The only trade you
deserve is a blade between the ribs."

"Quiet," snapped Kell, scowling. "She's done bad
things. We all agree this. But then, Saark, you are
hardly the angel. I have not forgotten what you did
with Kat. You are a predator. What did the men say
back at the village? At Kettleskull Creek? 'Saark, an arrogant rich bastard, unable to keep his childmaker in
his cheese-stinking pants.'"

"Oh. You heard that, did you?"

"I heard it, lad." He glanced at Myriam. "What are
you thinking?"

"Information. About the Soul Stealers."

"Go on."

"You promise not to kill me?"

"If I'd wanted to kill you, you'd already be dead."

Myriam nodded, realising that her life hung by a
thread, and that thread was called Nienna. She swallowed.

"The Soul Stealers. They are creatures of the Black
Pike Mountains. That is what I read."

"Yes?"

"Their father is said to be an ancient servant of the
Vampire Warlords. They do his bidding. I read that for

hundreds of years the Soul Stealers have been employed in an attempt to bring back the Vampire Warlords – and if they do, these Warlords will use the vachine and the albinos and the Harvesters... all will be subservient, all will turn the world into a dark place of chaos."

Kell considered this. "I have heard this tale before," he said. "About these Warlords, although under a different name; it is a fiction used to frighten little children by the fire. It is a nonsense."

Myriam shrugged. "There is a place, Helltop, a mountain-top hall, a sacred place of the vachine. It overlooks Silva Valley, from thousands and thousands of feet up. It is said to be the home of the Soul Stealers. It is said that they cannot be killed except in that place, for it is a source of their power, the source of their own collective soul. And when they kill, every soul they take flows back to the Granite Thrones which reside there."

"I have heard of the Granite Thrones," said Nienna, suddenly. "It is where the Blood Kings once sat. We did it in Classical History in preparation for Jalder University." She went quiet, then. She was continually reminded of a life she no longer had.

Kell nodded, remembering shoving his Svian deep into the vachine who attacked him. He should have pierced her core, with a blow like that. He should have destroyed her clockwork engine. "You think we'll have big trouble with these Soul Stealers?"

"I guarantee it," whispered Myriam.

With the dawn they set off through an icy valley, and a stone path rose in a series of switch-backs for perhaps two thousand feet. They climbed this narrow pathway in silence, hands cold and tucked into furs and pockets, and with faces tortured by the biting, howling, bitter mountain wind. Kell led the way in grim silence, brooding. When Nienna asked how long they had before the Soul Stealers and the cankers caught up with them, he just smiled grimly and shook his head.

At the rear travelled Saark, and Myriam dropped back, boots kicking loose rocks. She walked along beside him for a while, in silence, as jagged walls reared around them and far above, an eagle soared.

"Have you forgiven me yet?" she said, smiling.

"No. Fuck off."

"Harsh words, Saark."

"Not as harsh as sticking a knife in an unsuspecting man's belly."

"That was a mistake. I admit that now."

"Not easy to forget, nor forgive."

"Still, I am sorry. I apologise. I would never, ever do it again." She met his eyes. "I mean it, sincerely, Saark. It was a mistake." She gave a short laugh, like a bark. "I must admit, the more I have got to know Kell, the more I admire him. He is so strong, powerful, a giant to walk the mountains with."

"Careful girl, I think you're getting a bit wet down there."

Myriam looked at him, her face humoured. "You think so? Because of Kell, or because of you?"

Saark stopped for a moment, staring at her, then continued to walk the steep trails, calf muscles burning, feet throbbing inside his boots, his pack a dead weight across his spine – as if he carried a corpse.

He shook his head. Smiled. "I must admit, girl, I do tend to have that effect on young women." He considered this. "And middle aged women. Hell, even grannies. It's rare I've met a woman alive who doesn't want a bit of the tender Saark loving."

"Do you really think that much of yourself?"

"No. Women think much of me. I am simply along for the ride."

"Have you ever been in love?" Saark's smile fell, and immediately Myriam realised her mistake. "I am sorry," she said.

"No. No, don't be. I shouldn't bottle my guilt and self-loathing inside; it's an unhealthy combination. Yes, I have been in love. Twice. One was taken away from me, for an arranged marriage."

"And the other?"

"The other was married to another," said Saark, voice a croak, eyes filled with tears. He waved away her concern. "Ach, both were a long time ago, although some bastard seems intent on reminding me of past miseries. Have you ever been in love?"

"No," said Myriam, tilting her head to one side. "I admire men, for looks or physique, but if I am totally honest, then no man has ever grabbed my heart. And then, well, I became ill, and it has eaten away at me, robbed me of youth and my looks, even my body-weight. It is a savage punishment. The gods have a sick sense of humour, don't they? They seem to use most of it on me. No wonder I became so bitter."

Saark was watching her. "I admit," he said, voice soft, "once, you must have been a bonny lass."

"Enough to turn your eye, Sword Champion!" she snapped, "But no more."

"I'm sorry. I did not mean to offend."

"None taken," but her voice had become more brutal, more desolate.

"It must have been difficult. Watching yourself fading away."

"Yes, Saark." Her voice was little more than a whisper, and they came to a narrow set of large boulder-type steps, blocks carved from the mountain trail. Kell had helped Nienna up, and was ahead. Saark leapt lightly up, then turned and as Myriam climbed, she slipped... Saark moved so fast he was a blur, and caught her wrist. He lifted her onto the stone step, her hand in his, one hand on her hip. They stood for a moment, looking at one another, then Saark stepped back and coughed, releasing his hold.

"Watch your step, girl. That's a three thousand foot drop. And I bet you don't bounce much on the way down."

"Thank you."

"Pleasure."

They moved on. "Imagine," said Myriam, "if you suffered a horrible scarring to your face. Or you were trapped in a fire, and ended up with face and hair on fire leaving you brutally burned and ugly. How would you respond?"

Saark shivered. "It is a fate worse than death," he conceded. "I would be an easy victim for a torturer. This is my weakness, I admit. The minute he touched my face, I'd whimper like a girl and spill any and all secrets I carried."

"Vanity is a curse," said Myriam.

"Ahh, but only when you're not as beautiful as I."

"You are a real romantic," said Myriam, voice hard.

"I try," preened Saark, missing the irony – or choosing, at least, to ignore it. "I try, my sweet."

● ● ●

At the top of the climb they came to a plateau coated in hard-packed snow. Their boots crunched and, despite their ascent, a world of further, higher peaks spread around them in a glorious, full panorama. Nienna spun in circles, giggling, and Kell breathed deep. The wind was curiously still on this mountain summit, and Kell pointed with Ilanna, across a high ridgeline peppered with ice.

"Wolfspine," he said, simply.

"Looks dangerous," muttered Saark.

"It is," replied Kell, darkly. "We must take great care." He ruffled Nienna's long, dark hair. "And especially you, little monkey." But Nienna did not reply; her eyes were wide at the sight of the ridge they were to traverse.

Wolfspine. A half-league in length, a narrow, undulating ridge perhaps a foot in width, and with sheer four thousand foot drops to either side. The path itself was an inverted V of stone, black, slippery, frosted with lace patterns of ice.

Kell led the way, across a slightly curved plateau of snow, boots crunching. The air was still, and calm, brittle and cold, and bright light glared painfully from white snow.

Saark caught him up. "We are wonderfully ill-equipped for this," he said.

"You think I don't realise that, lad?"

"Just thought I'd mention it."

"Just try not to fall off, eh?"

"I'll certainly do my best on that account."

They stopped, where the mountain plateau rose and narrowed to the Wolfspine. Distant, through a haze of low cloud, they saw the next peak, the next Black Pike connected by this insane walkway of treacherous, icy rock.

"Is there no other way?" whispered Saark.

"No. The next five peaks are impossible to climb, and this ridge rises and dips, but links each peak together; without it, there would be no way to Silva Valley. The mountains form a protective barrier. In deep winter, this place is impassable – to all but the mad."

"Ha, and I suppose you're going to tell me you've done it?"

"I have," said Kell, voice low. "But I had ropes, and boots with spikes, and proper ice-axes."

"Can we do it now, do you think?"

"We're going to find out, Saark. There's no point going back. And... I want you to go first."

"Me?" squeaked the dandy, his fear palpable. "Why not you? You've all the damn experience. What do I know? I just drink wine and fuck pampered plump beauties. This is out of my bounds, Kell old horse. This is so far out of my world I should be paddling among the stars."

"I must take the rear," said Kell.

"Why?"

"In case those bastard cankers come back."

"Oh. Yes. A fine reason."

Kell stood, staring along the ridgeline. He glanced back at the near-flat plateau. It stretched off, then fell away into a darkness of seemingly endless valleys and tumbling mountain slopes. Beyond, he could see Falanor stretching away, see her hills and distant villages, her frozen rivers and snow-covered forests. Here, he knew – here was the point where Falanor fell behind, vanished, was eaten by the mountains. Here was the point of no return.

He remembered his time before, in the Black Pikes, hunting vachine.

"Damn," he said, and his gaze swept the world. Everything was clear and still and unbearably dazzling. It was like the gods had painted the world in pastel shades. Kell watched Falanor, and felt as if Falanor stared back. Help me, she said. Purify me. Make me proud.

"I'll be back," growled Kell, turned his back on Falanor, and started to climb up to the Wolfspine ridge.

"They're coming."

Nienna's voice was high in panic. Kell turned, glanced back over the undulating ridge. They were picking their way carefully over the narrow ribbon of stone, and clouds had shifted, a mist enclosing the small group, muffling sounds and at least, for a while, hiding the heart-stopping sheer drops to either side.

Kell drew Ilanna, and stood. He heard the snarls. The mist moved in patches, sometimes clearing, sometimes thickening. Then it cleared on their back-trail, and Kell saw the two crimson equine cankers. They moved fast along the ridge, sure-footed, drooling, their eyes fixed on their quarry, on fresh meat, on palpable fear.

There came a *whoosh* by Kell's ear, and an arrow punched into the lead canker, just below its face. It roared, feathered shaft erupting from its flesh, and pawed at the buried arrow for a moment, snapping the shaft. It roared again, and charged, pace increasing.

"Saark," growled Kell. "Go on. Get Nienna to the next peak. There is a resting place on the top of the mountain, a stone shelter. It would be easier to defend than here."

"And what about you?"

"I'll stay awhile, see what happens."

Another shaft hissed from Myriam's bow, and hit the lead canker in the eye. It reared then, screeching an impossibly high screech, and toppled from the mountain, sliding down the terrible slope at first, then connecting with a large rock and soaring out into the void. The mist swallowed the canker, and the monster was gone.

Now, as the mist cleared in patches, from further down behind the cankers strode the Soul Stealers. One lifted her bow, and too late Kell focused and *realised*. An arrow flashed, and Ilanna rose – but too slow. The arrow nicked his cheek, leaving a fine line of blood as it continued its trajectory... behind Kell, and into Myriam's throat. She gurgled, gasping, clawing the shaft and staggering back. She hit the ground, pitched sideways, and before Kell could grab her, slid off the ridgeline and into the vast, swallowing mist of the mountain void.

Nienna screamed.

Kell scowled, and turned back. Another arrow flashed for him, but with a rising rage and casual arrogance Ilanna snapped up and the arrow was deflected, cracking off into the mist.

Kell faced the final, charging canker.

And the Soul Stealers beyond.

"Come on," he growled, lowering his head. "Come and eat my fucking axe."

CHAPTER 13
Kindred

Vashell stared at the three vachine warriors, and heard Fiddion's Harvester head crackling in the fire as flames consumed flesh, and felt Alloria move away, behind him, giving him combat space. Vashell breathed deep, and settled into a rhythm of battle. They were underestimating him, he knew, because he had no face or claws or fangs, but Vashell was a warrior born. He hefted his knife, and stepped forward as the first of the vachine attacked...

It moved fast, leaping almost horizontally at Vashell who dropped his shoulder in a blur, knife ramming up into the vachine's belly and ripping savagely sideways as he took the vachine's short black sword in his fist, and twisted allowing the moving body to slam against the wall with a splatter of blood. With a short hack, he severed the vachine's head and blood-oil flowed free from the neck stump. Nobody else had moved. Vashell squared himself to the other two creatures who stared, stunned at what they'd just witnessed. They separated as far as the cave would allow, and as the wind howled mournfully outside, Vashell caught sight of his brother from the corner of his eye; Llaran was smiling.

"What's funny?" snarled Vashell. "The fact I'm going to sever your spine?"

"You cannot stand against us."

"Watch me."

With a battle shriek Vashell attacked, ducking a sword strike and slash of claws, elbowing the vachine in the face and front-kicking the second, leaping figure back to the wall. He leapt himself, and sword blades clashed, and he reversed his sword thrusting it under his own arm and into the chest of the vachine leaping at his back. The creature gurgled, and clockwork whined and clicked, and Vashell withdrew the blade, turned fast and lopped off the second man's head... continuing the fluid move with a roll of hips, drop of one shoulder, his left arm bearing the knife coming up, a clash of steel sending sparks scattering through the cave as the short black sword came high overhead to slam through the third vachine's shoulder, and deep down into lungs. Clockwork machinery, spinning and moving, could be seen through severed, wide-open flesh. Vashell tugged free his blade, and split the vachine's head clean in two showing a cross-section of skull and brain – closely meshed with fine gold wire and tiny, micro-clockwork. The head peeled in two, like fruit-halves, and Vashell heard the sounds and turned fast – but Llaran had gone. Fled, into the snow.

Alloria was standing, hands before her, panting hard. Vashell leapt to the fire, and using the tip of his sword flicked Fiddion's head from the flames. It was a blackened, crisped ball, a globe of stinking fried pork and fat ran from orifices, and steam rose from the cooling, over-cooked meat.

"Hell," hissed Vashell, his vachine blood-fury still

raised as his eyes narrowed, and he contemplated following Llaran into the snow. To be betrayed by his own brother! He could not understand it. But then he thought about it, and he could. Vashell was no longer beautiful vachine; and he had lost his fangs and claws, that which made him holy, that which endeared him to Engineers and Watchmakers alike. If they had taken him back to Silva Valley, he would have been executed as impure. Burned, like a common criminal. Quartered, like a captured Blacklipper. Vashell spat into the fire. "Bastards." Now, he could never go home, and that burned worse than any loss of face.

"Listen… to… me…" croaked Fiddion.

Vashell moved to the cooling head, and knelt. He reached out, touched the scorched flesh. He shook his head. "I cannot believe it. You tough little bastard. Can you hear me, Fiddion?"

"Listen carefully. Vashell. The Vampire… the Warlords, they will return. Kradek-ka and Graal, they will make it so. A… summoning. They will…" He coughed, then, and a tiny raw pink tongue darted against scorched, blackened lips. "They will take Anukis. To Skaringa Dak. Helltop. To sit on the Granite Thrones. She has the Soul Gem, you see? You must stop this." He coughed – or at least *choked* – again, ejecting a long thick black stream of gore. "Help Anukis," said the Harvester. "Help the vachine race."

"You don't know what you ask," said Vashell, eyes full of tears which stung his tortured face. "She has taken everything from me; my fangs, my claws, my vachine life. She took my pride and my dignity – stripped me of everything and left me as outcast! Even if I saved Silva Valley, saved the entire vachine civilisation – they would still turn on me and execute. Don't you understand?"

"That is why you must help," said Fiddion, quietly. "Now put me back on the fire. None, none must know my secrets."

Vashell obeyed, placing the Harvester's crisped, smouldering head back into the flames. The fire roared for a moment, bright green flames soaring to scorch the roof of the cave. Then the head burnt fiercely; in minutes it was nothing more than an outline of ash, which crumbled, vanishing into glowing embers.

Alloria was there. She placed a hand on Vashell. He looked at her.

"What will you do?" she said.

He glanced back at the vachine corpses, their blood-oil staining rock and ice. Then he stood, and shook free the queen's grip. He lifted his short black sword and examined the blade. Then he bared his teeth, where once his vampire fangs had sat.

"I will fight," he said, eyes lost in shadow.

It was like a dream. A dream watched through fog. A dream watched through refracted glass. Kradek-ka took hold of Anukis by the throat and he pinned her down, and she screamed and struggled and the Harvesters helped, long bone fingers piercing and cutting her flesh and the brass needle was long, and dripping with globules of amber fluid, of sweet sweet *honey* and Kradek-ka, face twisted in animal hatred, plunged the needle into Anukis's neck and her struggling slowed and ceased and she watched the scene from outside her body, and felt good, and felt warm, and memories faded and everything in the world seemed cosy and kind and simply *right*.

• • •

It had taken days of preparation, but Anukis had grown strong, had grown calm, had filled herself with yet more love for her father. He sought to make the va-chine strong, to accelerate their civilisation; his was a noble cause. And when he pioneered new technology, she would be accepted back into Silva Valley, no longer blood-oil impure, no longer outcast. She could return to her old life. With Kradek-ka, her father, by her side.

Now, they travelled ancient mountain tunnels. The walls were of purest white, and the Harvesters who travelled with Anukis and Kradek-ka, numbering per-haps thirty strong and making her shiver when they crept up behind, smiling curiously with long bone-fin-gers extended, carried small white globes which lit the way with a dull, feverish light.

Kradek-ka led, with Anukis usually one step behind. Occasionally he would smile back at her, at his eldest daughter, at his *special* daughter, and her mind swam a little as she tried to remember why she was there. The gold liquor the Harvesters gave her in the morning and evening, it seemed to have dulled her senses and made the world flicker like beautiful candlelight, and yet it confused her at the same time. It was most strange.

"You are a delight to behold," said Kradek-ka, re-membering her earlier struggle, her fight, her animosity. But then, all emotions were easy to control with a subtle infusion of drugs. Just like all physical as-pects were easy to control with a little introduction of melding clockwork.

They walked, through endless tunnels. Sometimes the walls were smooth and curved, corridors wide and paved as if used by great armies or royalty; other times they became angular, the white tiles gleaming and slightly off centre, awkward to look at as if they were plucking to unravel your mind. Then they would walk across rough hewn stone, sometimes dry as desert sand, other times slick with water or a clear, viscous slime. But two constants remained; the walls were always white, and the tunnel floor always sloped up.

They climbed. For hours, they climbed.

Occasionally they would come across rest rooms, low-ceilinged and scattered with beds. Kradek-ka would allow Anukis to sleep, to regain her strength. Kradek-ka never slept and would stand at the foot of her bed, watching her, staring at her, until she drifted into a world of dreams, of before the horror and bloodshed, when she used to sneak at night through the city streets of the Silva Valley, avoiding Engineers on her way to the Blacklippers for a bottle of Karakan Red.

When she awoke, Kradek-ka was always there, the Harvesters like ghosts in the background, or out in the tunnels, watching, drifting around, their purpose esoteric and unfathomable. Anukis often wondered if Kradek-ka stood watching all night; or if, when she slept, he would move away and entertain himself. However, he was always there when she awoke. Once, she might have found it creepy. Now, however, she found it comforting. Her father, the Watchmaker, was watching over her. He was all-seeing, all-strong; he was the backbone of the Vachine Empire. He had invented the Blood Refineries. He would save the vachine. He would expand the vachine. He was immortal. He would care for Anukis, forever.

They travelled on, and sometimes they would pass huge caverns, high up on narrow stone walkways with golden wires to grasp in order to steady oneself. Below, the white ground appeared soft, and pulsed with an inner white light. Harvesters collected there, and looked up in their thousands. Sometimes they watched these intruders – for that was how Anukis felt – and they would pass beyond the massive cavern confines. Other times, the Harvesters would lift their long, bone fingers and Anukis could not tell whether it was in salute, or in condemnation.

On crossing the fourth or fifth cavern filled with thousands of soundless Harvesters, Anukis turned to her father. "There are so many of them," she said, face ashen, strange pains in her chest, deep down in her clockwork.

"Yes. Nobody from Silva Valley, no Engineer, no Watchmaker, not even the Episcopate have seen these Halls. They are a holy place, and we are lucky indeed to pass through and remain unharmed. Usually, they would descend on us in thousands, and we would be instantly husked."

"Why, then, do they allow us passage?"

"Because we have something important to do," smiled Kradek-ka. "Something that will benefit them immensely."

"What do we have to do?" said Anukis, face a little slack. The drugs were starting to wear off, and the pains in her clockwork were increasing, and so strange, she thought, so odd that she needed the honey liquor more often now. She thought of the past; had she always needed the honey liquor? She did not remember taking it before, when she was a free vachine of Silva Valley... but then, the entirety of her early life was fuzzy and just a little bit twisted, and she let the memories go, let them slide away as more of the honey drug slid down her throat and eased into her veins and she was at peace.

Kradek-ka patted her hand. "Don't worry about it, sweet little Anu. You will see. Everything will be fine in the end. I promise."

Anukis nodded, and then they came to a sleep chamber, and she slept.

Anukis sat in a white place. The trees were blinding, dazzling, their white and silver leaves shimmering. Water tinkled nearby, white water in a white-rock stream. It was filled with natural music. It calmed her.

Looking down, she sat on spongy white heather, her legs curled beneath her. She was naked, except for marks under her skin; dark imprints of clockwork which made her grimace at the mechanical. Anukis slid her vampire fangs in and out, revelling in the slick smooth movement. Yes. Kradek-ka had made her well.

Anukis peered around for a long time, her mind sleepy, the world a strange place, her ideas not connecting, her memories fuzzy and distorting, reverberating like a skewed dream. It may have been a thousand years. It may have been a micro-second. Time seemed to have no time, here.

Anukis heard a sound, and through the white woods strode a woman, tall, naked, stunningly beautiful. Her long hair shone in the diamond light. She smiled when she saw Anukis, who hissed in fear...

It was Shabis! And Shabis was dead.

"I killed you, sister," she said, voice impossibly soft, eyes lowering in shame.

"No. Vashell killed me," Shabis said, and embraced Anukis, kissing her cheeks and lips. "You tried to warn me. I would not listen. I should have listened to you, sister." Tears shone in her eyes. "I was drunk on his love like wine; I was addicted to his lies, like I was to the blood-oil of our corrupt society."

"Father will make it good again."

"Do not listen to him!" The sudden flash of anger in Shabis's eyes shocked Anukis, and she took a step back. Her feet sank into soft moss. She was stunned by the ferocity; the sudden change.

"Why not?" Anukis was gentle.

"Because! He is a liar. He has always done things for his own ends. We have never factored into his equation; I know that now. I can see clearly. I understand Kradek-ka as I understand no other, and he is evil, and he will destroy our vachine civilisation."

"No, he will make it strong again! He loves the vachine, he has nothing but honour towards the Episcopate and Silva Valley." But Anukis felt suddenly hollow, as if she had been scooped empty by a giant claw. Somehow, she recognised the truth in Shabis's words. Somehow, she glimpsed through the encompassing lies.

"You are wrong, Anu," said Shabis. "We were always his tools. His weapons. Only I was the expendable one. He used Vashell, used Vashell to drive you *here*."

"Where is here?"

"You are in the Harvester's Lair. They are a created thing, like a machine, like a clockwork engine. They were created by the Vampire Warlords... created with only one purpose."

"Which is?"

"To harvest blood. Yes, now they help the vachine and help convert the blood to blood-oil; but that is only to keep the dream alive, to keep the workings of the machine alive. Soon, you will see the power of their onslaught. They will turn against the vachine, Anukis. And they will be led by Kradek-ka."

Anukis frowned. "Once, not long ago, I was cast out by my own people. The vachine of Silva Valley humiliated me, and I was destined for death. I set out with Vashell to find our father – he was captured by the Harvesters. I swore I would seek vengeance on the vachine, for never had I felt such pain. Surely, if Kradek-ka seeks to destroy the vachine... no, it is all too confusing. It is all too insane!"

"The vachine are your race," said Shabis, gently. "You cannot destroy a whole race because of what they did to you. Genocide is never the way, no matter how unholy you perceive the enemy, Anukis. Our father intends to kill the vachine. All of them. And that includes you."

"Now you are being ridiculous. Father would never hurt me."

"Not yet. Because he needs you. But the time will come."

The scene started to fade around Anukis, and she swallowed, mouth dry with fear. She was being dragged away from this ethereal plane, away from whatever bright, shining existence Shabis inhabited. And she had no control. No control at all.

"Needs me?" she said, speaking quickly, lethargy leaving her momentarily. "In what way does he need me?"

"Ask him about the Soul Gems," whispered Shabis, even as she faded away and was gone.

Anukis awoke. The walls pulsed white. Kradek-ka was watching her. He smiled, but his eyes were dark, his fangs gleaming gold. Kradek-ka was vachine. And yet, now that she thought about it, she had never, ever, ever seen him take blood-oil. And when Anukis was considered *unholy*, he had not just known about Karakan Red and the Blacklippers... he had known Preyshan, the *king*.

"Tell me about the Soul Gems," said Anukis, moistening her lips with her tongue.

There was a flicker in Kradek-ka's face, but then it was gone. He smiled in serenity. "I don't know what you mean."

"The Soul Gems. Why do you need me, father? Where are we going?"

"We are going to celebrate a holy ritual. On behalf of the Harvesters. We are giving thanks that they help the vachine with blood-oil; that we are all holy together."

"Something is wrong. You are their prisoner."

"Yes. A prisoner of sorts. Only until I help them... perform a certain ritual."

You don't need me."

"You are coming," said Kradek-ka, his voice hard and brittle as iron. Then he softened a little. He took a deep breath. He reached out, and helped Anukis rise from the soft, white bed. His hands were gentle. His claws gleamed, sparkling like silver in the diffused light.

"I will stay here. I feel weak. I need to sleep."

"No. Time grows short. You will come now."

Anukis met her father's gaze. "No, father. I will not," she said, voice icy, breaking free of the honey drugs in her veins and mind and wondering just what game was being played here. Anukis was sick to the heartcore of being pushed around, told what to do, used and abused and taken advantage of. She had come through the Vrekken, risked her life for her father, and yet this did not *feel* like her father; he felt like an imposter, a chameleon, something which changed its skin to please and was yet different inside. A different organism.

Kradek-ka, still smiling, slammed out his fist. At the end, his claws were extended and they were impossibly long, huge curved silver and gold blades which pierced Anukis's throat, driving through her windpipe and neck muscles and spine, appearing at the back of her neck in an explosion of blood that decorated the white walls. With the force of the blow Anukis's body danced like a dropped corpse in a noose, and Kradek-ka stood there, holding Anukis in the air, a punctured ragdoll. Anukis gurgled and kicked, not quite believing the strength of Kradek-ka, not quite believing her own weakness, and not quite believing what had just happened.

"My girl," said Kradek-ka, eyes glowing impossibly dark. "You will do exactly what you are told," he said, and retracted his claws.

General Graal moved to the Blood Refinery. The cold night breeze cooled his naked body. Without clothing and armour, he was tautly muscled and very, very lean. Graal's skin was perfectly white, like fine porcelain, and when he turned the moonlight caught his features and gave him a surreal, dead look. As if carved from stone.

"The Sending Magick is ready, general," came the sibilant hiss of a Harvester, bobbing as it walked towards him. Graal nodded, and moved through the snow, feet crunching, to where the huge Blood Refinery squatted, fat and black and bloated, like a burnt corpse in the sun, like the full belly of a corpse-fed battlefield raven. He turned back, looked at the Harvesters, and beyond, down into Falanor's capital city of Vor. Many buildings burned fiercely. The temples. The libraries. Smoke spiralled into the dark winter sky, fireflies of ash dancing like insects. Graal's nostrils twitched, and he could smell distant smoke. He turned back to the Blood Refinery. It reminded him of an overfull insect.

"We are finished here," he said, voice low. "You know what to do."

"Yes," hissed the Harvester.

Graal stepped forward, and pressed his naked body against the Blood Refinery. He started the incantation, and felt the Sending Magick flow through ancient iron and *into* his veins and flesh and bones, and he flowed with the magick and was absorbed by the magick, and it smashed his skull with a sudden bright pounding and he flowed with it, and the destination was clear and he felt every component atom in his being broken down and disseminated then reintegrated into a whole, and Graal laughed for this was what insanity must feel like and he revelled in it, this was what being a god must feel like and he bathed in it, gloried in it, and lost his own mind to it all, and it was Good.

Graal swam. He leapt. He flowed. It took a million years.

He eased like a blood cell through the veins of the universe.

He trickled through time, like a virus through an organism.

Graal no longer existed, for his matter was part of all matter, and the magick *tugged* at him, and *directed* him and only through the bindings of the spell did he retain some semblance of identity and was not spread across an infinite plane.

And then everything was dark. And it was over.

• • •

It felt like being born. Pain lashed him with a million stings in every atom of flesh, and Graal would have screamed but the pain was too great. He squeezed from something soft and slick, pus-filled and flexible and yielding. He slapped to the floor, trembling as if suffering a violent seizure, and cold fluid poured out after him and covered him with thick ice ichor. He felt hands on him, or felt *something* on him, and they were hard and pointed and pierced his flesh accidentally. He was man-handled into blankets and he realised, with a moment of panic, that he was blind. Towels rubbed his body, rubbing life back into his flesh, rubbing gooey liquid from his eyes, and gradually a soft diffused light began to wander into his eyes and skull. Only then did Graal cough, and disgorged a huge stream of thick pus which pooled on the floor to lie, quivering, like dark blood.

"You did well," said Vishniriak, and the Harvester patted him gently in a rare moment of connection.

Graal focused on the Harvester, but could not speak. His vocal chords were raw, as if rubbed by a grater.

"I felt like God. I felt like Death," he finally managed.

Vishniriak nodded, in understanding. He had travelled The Sending. He understood exactly what Graal meant. To travel the Lines of the Land by magick was to be a part of the earth, of the mountains and oceans and forests and bedrock. It was to lose identity. Without powerful bindings, a mind would snap. But Graal was strong. Graal was very strong.

Graal stood, and clothing and armour were brought for him. He dressed slowly, feeling old, feeling more old than the Black Pike Mountains. Finally, he strapped well-oiled armour into place, and a short black sword by his side.

He nodded at Vishniriak. "Has Kradek-ka arrived?"

"Yes, general."

"And he has the girl?"

"He has, general."

Graal smiled then, his eyes gleaming. "Kell is coming to us. We must prepare," he said. "The time is ready for the Vampire Warlords to return." And he strode confidently, arrogantly, from the chamber deep within the bowels of Skaringa Dak.

CHAPTER 14
Wax Nest

The world was shrouded in mist. Kell stood, poised on the high mountain ridgeline, the world around him a blanket interspersed with vast drops and glimpses of the rearing, Black Pike Peaks.

Ahead, the mist thickened momentarily, obscuring the two Soul Stealers. Only the canker came on, and more vachine longbow shafts whistled from the mist and Ilanna slammed left, then right, cutting arrows from flight... as the canker, close now, and amazingly nimble for its bulk, bounded along the narrow, undulating rock path and leapt at Kell with a savage snarl, an ejection of saliva, and Kell's axe slammed left but the canker ducked, equine head swaying back. Claws hammered at Kell but Ilanna deflected the blow on a fast return sweep, and he took a step back, the mist suddenly parting around him to reveal vast drops from nightmare. He ducked another swipe of curved claws and set his chin in a grim line as he clenched teeth hard, brows furrowed, and felt himself descending dropping plummeting into a blood red rage...

I will help, said Ilanna.

Yes, said Kell.

A flickering staccato of images rampaged through his mind. It was the Days of Blood – again. And he welcomed it. *He stood, muscles bulging, tensed as if pumped on drugs and violence. His brain ached, and random chaos bounced around the cage of his brain. He lifted Ilanna, and she sang, she sang a high beautiful song only this time THIS TIME the world could hear her lullaby and the people running down the street fleeing the insanity of the army they stopped, and turned, and listened to the stunning ethereal voice of Ilanna as the perfect hypnotising notes reverberated through fire and smoke and sounds of slaughter, and the fleeing refugees paused and Kell strode amongst them Ilanna cutting left and right, and they did not flee, and they did not retaliate, they simply stood staring at this blood soaked figure at Kell's rage and his fury and his madness as Ilanna slammed left and right with economical accuracy, and they had love in their eyes, love for Ilanna's Song, and they welcomed death and in welcoming death their blood fed the butterfly blades and when they were all dead, all cut up in pieces on the muddy cobbles, so Kell fell to his knees amongst the men and women and children, and he cried, his tears running through a mask of blood and he cast Ilanna away and screamed "WHAT HAVE I DONE?" and he knew then, that he was cursed, that he was evil, that ultimately he was trying to be good and just and honourable; but deep down, he was simply a very bad man.*

Kell blinked.

The canker was on him, fangs an inch from his throat and his eyes met the mad crimson gaze and he dropped Ilanna between them, and thrust her up and *out*, blades punching a huge hole up through the beast's great, cavernous chest, and Kell's legs braced and his teeth ground, and he stood there, strong, a powerhouse, with the

impaled canker kicking on the end of his axe and with
neck muscles and arm and shoulder and chest muscles
bulging, his face purple with effort, and he lifted the
kicking squealing canker up, high up into the air and
stood there, feeling a wonderful power flooding through
him, feeling strength and godliness teasing through flesh
like a divine orgasm. Ilanna began to sing and the canker
kicked, like a lizard on the end of a spear. Kell jerked the
axe, blades cutting deeper into the huge beast, fully twice
his size, great equine head thrashing with teeth gnawing
invisible bones, and Kell thrust forward again, the blades
so deep now that thick gore flowed out, over his head
and torso, drenching him in entirety. With a final thrust
Ilanna severed the canker's spine. It went suddenly still
on the end of the axe. With a mighty scream, Kell
wrenched Ilanna sideways, half severing the dying
canker's body into two discrete pieces, which flopped
with slaps of thick dead meat. Bloody clockwork components scattered, many tumbling down the mountain's
flanks, clattering, brass and crimson gears still stepping,
wheels spinning, cogs shifting. Kell lifted Ilanna in the
air, one-handed, as the mist parted and the Soul Stealers
locked eyes to him and he grinned, grinned through his
mask of canker blood and Ilanna began to sing. She sang
a high beautiful song, which rang out across the mountains and valleys, echoed across snowfields and frozen
tarns. It was long and eerie and mournful, a song about
murder, a song about death. And as she sang, so the Soul
Stealers paused, and they stood for a long time listening
as the dead canker slowly shifted, and slipped from the
mountain ridge, vanished into the abyss. Eventually, Kell
lowered Ilanna. The Soul Stealers turned, and disappeared into the swirling white vapour.

"Grandfather!" came Nienna's shout. They were far across the ridgeline now, Saark guiding the young woman. Kell turned, moved away from the canker's blood pools and stopped. Gazing down where Myriam had fallen, he tried to differentiate her corpse from the distant slopes and jagged rocks. He could not.

"Damn it," he snarled, then loped across the ridge at great speed, showing no fear of heights, showing no worry at the vast slopes veering off to either side. For Kell, vertigo was something that happened to other people.

Saark and Nienna moved on, through the eddying haze, and Kell eventually caught them up as they climbed towards the next mountain top. As they breached a rise, a savage steep scramble which did its best to cast all three back down the mountainside, so a wind snapped around them and the mist cleared, and the world of the Black Pike Mountains opened like God peeling the top off the world.

"Stunning," said Nienna, simply.

Kell grunted.

Saark helped the old warrior up the last scree of rocks, and they stood in silence staring at the black granite wilderness, and the sweeping fields of snow. It was quite light where they stood, although the wind bit into them like ice knives.

"You did well," said Saark.

"I reverted," said Kell.

"Meaning?"

"Something happened to me. Something happened to Ilanna. Something bad."

"I don't understand."

"I think only Ilanna understands. I think, sometimes, she plays her own game, Saark. She sang to the Soul

Stealers – there was a connection there, what kind of connection I am not sure. But they retreated. They fled."

"You killed the canker. Maybe they were scared of you?"

"No," grunted Kell, rubbing his beard and leaning on the axe. Her blades gleamed black in the harsh winter light. "No, they were frightened of Ilanna. I think."

"Where do we go next?" asked Nienna, hunkering down in her clothing. Her face was drawn, ashen, her eyes red from crying. The death of Myriam had stunned her.

Kell pointed, to where a huge mountain reared high above the others. It was formidable, even at this distance, with twin horns of overhanging rock rearing near the summit and spreading out, so the beast in its entirety resembled the skull of a ram.

"Skaringa Dak," he said. "Otherwise known as Warlord's Peak."

"That's one ugly mountain," said Saark. "And it's big. Too big, Kell. Look at the distance we have to cover! We can't be dragging Nienna all that way."

"We must. But rest assured, we go *through* the mountain, not over the top."

"Kell, that's Silva Valley you're talking about. It's an entire *civilisation*, by all the balls of the gods! You cannot fight the world, old friend."

"One step at a time," said Kell.

Saark sighed, and Nienna moved to him, hugged him. "I can't believe Myriam is gone," she said. Saark nodded, but said nothing. It did not surprise him, and he had to admit, he had wanted her dead. However, now the deed was done, guilt stabbed him like a tiny knife in the belly. She had been a victim of the cancers eating her body, her bones. She had given in to madness to chase an impossible dream. And her only reward now was lying dead and broken, a smashed doll, at the foot of the terrible Black Pikes.

"Yes," he said, finally, and hugged Nienna tight. It was a simple connection, a simple sharing of warmth and humanity. And in this dark place of stone and ice, it felt necessary.

"Come on," said Kell. "We have a long way to go."

"You're mad, old man."

"Maybe," he said, face dark. "Let's get moving, before those bitches forget Ilanna's song and come back."

She swam through darkness, and at last there was no pain. It had happened so suddenly. The arrow in her throat, rolling from the high ledge, then... a long, rattling descent. She hit rocks, and was conscious for a while of great darkness hanging over her like a guillotine blade waiting to drop. Then, she supposed, she died. There was a long period of nothing. And then fire seemed to rage through her veins, potent and raw, the most powerful injection of energy she had ever, ever felt. She felt something cold against her chest, and with a jerk she shuddered in huge lungfuls of cold mountain air. Only then did she feel the pain at her neck, and everything came rushing back and she opened her mouth to scream but a hand clamped over her face, muffling her. She thrashed for a while, arms and legs kicking in chaos, but something immeasurably strong pinned her down, holding her still, and she felt the fire raging through her and it hurt, hurt so bad, hurt worse than anything she'd ever felt and seemed to rage for a million years. Then her eyes flickered open and she

stared into a gaunt, pale, beautiful face. The face of the
Soul Stealer. She tried to struggle in sudden panic, but
Shanna held her tight and smiled a hollow smile and
showed her fangs, which were stained with blood.

"Be still, child," she hissed. "It will not take long."

She looked to the left and Tashmaniok came into
Myriam's plane of vision. She carried something and
Myriam frowned. Then another punch of pain spun
through her and she convulsed, unable to breathe, her
heart filled with pure white agony as she slammed into
cardiac arrest.

"Now," said Shanna.

Tash knelt, and in her hand was a tiny device, a cross
between the innards of a watch and an insect made
from gold wire. It scampered from Tash's hands, and
moved across Myriam's skin as she stared down at it,
pain slapping her in waves, her eyes following the tiny
clockwork machine in terror. "This is the latest technology," came Tash's soothing voice, as the clockwork
spider paused over Myriam's spasming, fractured heart,
lifted a leg, and with a high-pitched screeching drilled
a hole through her breastbone.

Myriam screamed, thrashing, and again Shanna
clamped the woman's mouth, cutting the sound off
with a sharp slap. The tiny clockwork machine cut
downwards, opening a dark hole in Myriam's chest,
and then climbed in. It reached back, and did something – as if closing a zip. Then it crawled into Myriam's
heart and long tendrils of gold wire ejaculated from tiny
needles, encircling Myriam's dying, fluttering organ
and encapsulating it. Tiny sections of the clockwork
machine broke away, and began to travel through Myriam's body. She spasmed, and convulsed, her limbs

twitching, her eyes rolling back, froth foaming from her mouth, fingers and toes clenching and then suddenly *erupting* with brass claws, and her teeth broke out with *snaps* as fangs pushed from her own gums. They were made from gold. They gleamed.

Finally, Tash threw Shanna a knife. Shanna slashed her wrist, and allowed a gush of dark blood-oil to spill into Myriam's open mouth. She convulsed again, as if taking poison, her teeth stained crimson, and black, her tongue lolling around like a fat eel. Then, finally, she went still.

Shanna wrapped a cloth around her wrist, binding it tight, then climbed from Myriam's still, lifeless body. She moved to Tash, and placed her hand on the Soul Stealer's shoulder. They waited, motionless, watching Myriam with interest.

"Did it work?" said Shanna, finally.

"If they do not bind, she will soon fall apart," said Tashmaniok without emotion. "Like succulent cooked meat pared from the bone. Like a desecration of all that is human." Then she turned, and stared up the mountain flanks to Wolfspine. Her eyes narrowed, still remembering the pain of Ilanna's song piercing her skull. It had skewered her brain like a spear. Her soul. Even now, she was shivering.

We will find you soon enough, old man, she thought.

We will see how long the magick lasts in your axe!

All pain fled. It happened in an instant. Myriam sighed, and breathed out. She felt, ultimately, at peace. Devoid of the agonies which had wracked her for so long, the cancers which had eaten her and supplied constant pain. She had suffered an eternity, the pains fading to a background agony, a persistent throb which just became normal to everyday existence. Only in sleep did the fire sometimes abate; and there was always a vast disappointment in the morning when Myriam awoke to find she still suffered.

But... Not now.

She felt it, as an emotion, as injected knowledge. The clockwork had moved through her body, combining with blood-oil, combining with the virus of the vampire, and all three had worked in harmony. Cancers were obliterated in a moment. The arrow wound in her throat had bubbled, and slowly healed as she slept. Her pain had gone, all pain had gone, and she floated in a warm secure place not unlike a womb.

Her eyes opened. It was dark. They were in a small, warm cave. Shanna and Tash sat on rocks by the fire, watching her.

Slowly, Myriam sat up. She was wary. These were the enemy.

Then she looked down at her hands, and a thrill of fear and excitement flooded her. Her fingers ended in claws. She blinked. She reached up to her throat, remembering the savage arrow-wound which had, effectively, punched her from the summit of the ridge. The flesh was smooth, uninterrupted by wound or scar.

Then her hands moved to her teeth, and touched gently at the fangs there.

She looked at the Soul Stealers.

"You have made me vachine?" she said, softly.

Shanna nodded.

"You have removed the cancer from my body?"

Tash stood, and crossed to her. She held a shard of mirror, which Myriam took and stared into. She sank into that mirror, then, sank into the silvered glass as if being sucked down into a lake of beautiful mercury.

Myriam stared at her own face. Her flesh had filled out, and although she was pale, she was radiant with health. No longer did gaunt eye-sockets dominate her face with purple rings. Her eyes sparkled like fine-cut gems. When she smiled, her teeth were white and strong, not knuckle-dice wobbling in a corrupt jaw.

Myriam looked down at herself. Her clothing was battered and tattered and torn, as befitted somebody who had slid down the mountainside. But her hips were full, legs powerful, her fingers strong, the flesh filled out and defined by muscle.

"There is one more thing you must do," said Tash-maniok, kneeling beside Myriam.

"Anything," she wept, "anything at all."

"You must swear your soul to us," she said, voice gentle. "You must swear it by the blood-oil that flows in your veins, by the blood-oil that lubricates your clockwork."

"I will swear with all my heart!" cried Myriam, and put her face in the palms of her hands as she thanked the vachine for giving her health, strength, and ultimately, her life.

"Good," said Shanna, also leaning in close. "Now, my little virgin vachine, we have a job for you."

They walked through the darkness, down a narrow rock trail.

"This is insane," said Saark, for the tenth time.

"Shut up," growled Kell, for the tenth time.

"We'll break our bloody ankles, man!"

"What, so you'd wait here for those vampire bitches to hunt you down, would you?" snapped Kell.

"Stop being such a court jester, and get on with the job, lad."

Saark shrugged, and moved on. In truth, the dark held no problem for him. Not now. Since Shanna bit him, his eyesight, and especially night vision, had increased tenfold. Now, the night was like a green-tinted summer's day. No longer would he have trouble falling over things drunk in the night. Now, there was no night.

However, despite increased strength and vision and stamina and healing, Saark was having other problems. Like the stench of blood. Here, and now, walking the mountain trails in snow and ice and whipping, freezing wind, he could smell Kell's blood more than anything. But Nienna's was also there, a more subtle, more gentle sweet fragrance; like the scent of roses, when compared to nettles. But with great force of will Saark was learning to master this weakness, or what he saw as a flaw in his new-found gift – or maybe curse? – and was able with great strength of mind to suppress the urges to extrude his still-growing vampire fangs and leap on Kell, devouring his throat and heart-blood.

The only problem had come when Kell killed the canker, lifting the beast up on the end of his axe and shaking it over his head, emptying its blood and blood-oil and guts over himself in a carnage orgy of gore. The sheer stench hit Saark like a wall, rolled over him like an explosion of rampant forest fire, and it was all he could do to hide his crazy rolling eyes, his extending claws, and not jump on Nienna's back and tear out her spine. In that moment, he wanted Nienna more than anything on earth, with a feeling of emotion and raw need greater than anything he had ever had to endure.

Forget sex; sex was as rancid milk to thick clotted cream. This desire for blood, this urge this lust this mockery was more powerful than the sun and the moon. Brighter than the stars.

Nienna had turned, seen him advancing on her, and smiled weakly, meeting his crazed eyes. It was the smile that did it; broke the spell and caged the savage beast growing inside Saark. Without that *connection* of love and trust, he would have leapt on her and chewed out her soul.

Now, Saark fought himself.

He fought the new urges which drove him, using internal logic to battle the growing needs of a blossoming half-infected vampire. All he needed was clockwork integration to make him whole, and he would be a changed person, he realised. All he needed was a Watchmaker, and he would no longer be Saark. Saark would be dead. A stranger would stand in his shell. He would be corrupt. He would be lost.

"Damn it," muttered Saark, clawing himself, a thrashing of internal turmoil.

"What's it now, dandy?" snapped Kell, turning and scowling. Saark could see him as clearly as in daylight. He could see the pulse of blood at Kell's throat. It made his mouth go dry with longing.

"These damn vachine," snapped Saark irritably. "Don't you just fucking hate them?"

"Every last one," said Kell, turning back to the trail. "They need exterminating like a nest of cockroaches." He moved on, picking his way with care and helping Nienna when she needed help. Behind, Saark's eyes gleamed with malevolence.

• • •

They rested two hours before dawn, eating dried salted beef and rubbing warmth back into limbs bitten by cold. Saark had wandered off for toileting, and Kell sat close to Nienna, looking down into her eyes with concern.

"How are you, girl?"

"Frightened," she said.

"We have to do this, you understand?" he said. She nodded. "We have nowhere else to run. The bastards have taken over Falanor; we must fight the invasion at its root."

"What will you do when we arrive?" she asked.

"I will find these Watchmakers, I will find those who control the Army of Iron, the people who rule Graal. First, I will ask. And when they snarl in superior arrogance, then, then I will fight, and I will take their top Watchmakers hostage, force them to withdraw their soldiers from our land."

"Do you really think you can do this?"

Kell nodded. "I'll give it my best damn shot," he said.

"A fine plan," said Saark, approaching from the path to the large ring of rocks where they were seated, "with, I can see, only three major flaws."

"You heard all that?" said Kell.

"Aye, I heard some."

"What did you hear?"

"About finding the Watchmakers, holding them hostage, that sort of thing."

"By God, lad, you've got some incredible hearing."

"No, no," said Saark slowly, "I was on my way back."

"You were all the way over there. Shitting behind that rock. I could smell you. You stink worse than any boy-lover's perfume." Kell shook his head, frowning. "And lad, you move quiet. Did you say you used to be a thief?"

Saark shrugged, and stroked his chin. "Is it time to move?" he said. "I have a feeling those Soul Stealer bitches are close on our trail."

"Yes. Not far now," said Kell.

"Not far from what?"

Kell stood, and stretched, and his mood visibly darkened. "The Worm Caves," he said. "So don't get too comfortable, lad, because we have a lot of sneaking to do. The Worm Caves are no place for mortals. They ooze death."

"You can't be serious," said Saark, eyebrows rising. "You mean the *Valentrio* Caves? Shit. No, Kell. I've heard the tales, about the white worms which inhabit that place. In fact, they were from the same bloody bard who sang about your bloody maudlin *Kell's Legend*. Which just goes to show what a barrel of donkey-shit those songs really are." He grinned, a sour grin. "Maybe there's no danger after all?"

"Funny," said Kell, and threw Saark his pack. "Believe me, there's danger all right. So empty yourself now; this is no place to be needing a shit break. Let's go."

Shivering even more, and far from pacified by their talk, Nienna followed Kell, and Saark brought up the rear. The aroma of their blood twitched his nostrils, more tantalising than ever, now. He scowled, eyes narrowed. Damn this curse, he thought bitterly. Damn it to the Dark Halls! Damn it to the Bone Underworld!

The archway was small, and carved in a blank wall of rock with no other noticeable features. It would have been easy to miss the opening, if you hadn't known it was there.

Saark stood back from the black arch and looked up at finely carved script. His brow furrowed. "I've never seen lettering like that, before," he said, then wrinkled his nose. "Gods, it stinks in there."

"The *leski* worms," said Kell, voice soft.

"Have you even seen one of these worms?"

"Only once. From a distance. They have teeth as long as your forearm – but that's all I saw, I was too busy running in the other direction. They have a poisonous bite, lad, so don't get too close."

"That's comforting. What does the writing say?"

Kell shrugged, and started removing unnecessary kit from his pack. "Empty your pack of junk. You're going to need to travel light. There are some narrow places in there, tight places. Places a man could get easily trapped."

"But I thought you said the worms were big? Fangs as long as a horse's dick, or something?"

"They are, but they compress their bodies to squeeze through narrow apertures. Like a rat, Saark." His eyes twinkled. "You should know all about that kind of vermin, coming from your Royal Court background. And anyway, to answer your question, the script reads, 'Seek Another Path'."

"That's it? That's the warning?"

"That isn't good enough for you? With a stench of death like Dake's arse pumping out?"

"You have such a way with words, my man." Now, with his pack somewhat lighter, Saark drew his rapier and ran a finger along the blade. He re-sheathed the weapon. "Let's get going. Before I change my mind."

"You can always head back. Woo those vampire killers with your charm."

"What, and have them bite me, turn me into one of them? That would be insane!"

"Yes," said Kell, eyes glinting, "we wouldn't want that, lad, would we? Then I'd have to cut your head off!" He gave a low rumble of laughter, and slapped Saark on the back.

As they moved to the entrance, and Kell stooped to enter, Ilanna before him, Nienna touched his arm. "Grandfather?"

"Yes, monkey?"

She smiled at that. "I'm scared," she said.

"Don't be. I'll protect you."

"I know you will. But… I'm still scared."

Kell turned, and righted himself. He lifted Ilanna, looked at her curious matt black butterfly blades – so unlike any other weapon he had seen. She was older than the mountains, so the legend went. And indestructible. He kissed the blades, then bent down, and kissed Nienna on one cheek. "Just stick close to me, little lady. Don't be frightened of the dark. Kell walks beside you."

Nienna nodded, eyes full of tears. Her adventure was not quite what she'd expected. Not when so much blood and death was involved. Not when good women like Katrina had to give their life for nothing; for the honour of thieves and murderers. She sighed. And followed Kell into the gloom.

The Valentrio Caves were dark for perhaps a hundred metres, and then the floor seemed to shine with a very pale, sickly light. The darkness closed in fast, with claustrophobia in one fist, and haunting echoes in the other. Within minutes Saark had closed the distance from his rear guard, and was almost treading on Nienna's heels.

"Kell," he hissed, after perhaps ten minutes where they followed a level, winding passage.

"What?" said the old warrior.

"The light. On the floor. By Dake's Balls, what is it?"

Kell grinned, face a skull in the pale, ethereal glow. "Slime. From the worms. They must secrete it. Or something."

Saark's face fell. He looked ill. "Shit," he said. "I wish I'd never asked."

"Don't worry," soothed Kell, seeing Nienna's face from the corner of his eye. "This tunnel system is vast; it stretches for hundreds of miles under the mountains, vertically as well as horizontally. You can travel here for weeks and never see a worm. The *leski* are primitive, they have no understanding. They just eat and breed."

"Sounds a bit like us sophisticated humans," muttered Saark.

"Come on. Let's get moving. We have a long way to go."

They walked, boots making odd sounds on the sticky, luminescent ground. Saark realised, unconsciously, that he had his rapier drawn. He cursed himself, and sheathed the weapon, frowning. At least his rising fear and claustrophobia were good for one thing; they were taking his mind off the sweet, cloying smell of Nienna's blood, distracting him from the ever-present rhythmic thumping of her heart. He shook his head. What are you becoming, Saark? he asked himself, and didn't like to consider the answer.

They moved for hours, and sometimes the glowing floor would end and they would ease through deepest gloom, guided by mineral veins in the rock and marble walls. Sometimes, the corridors would narrow as Kell predicted, so that both Saark and Kell had great difficulty squeezing through and only Nienna was able to pass with ease. Occasionally, they came to areas where huge boulders had dropped, crushing part of the tunnel and making it near impossible to pass. Several times they had to squeeze beneath a chunk of mountain that, if it shifted, would crush them like an ant beneath a boot. At one point the crushed section was extended, and Saark found himself on his back, scrambling along with limbs scratched and dust falling in his eyes and his panting coming in short, sharp bursts. Panic was an old friend clutching his heart, and he was coughing and choking and pushing up at the immeasurably huge rock above and wondering if he was going to die until Kell's rough hands grasped his scruff, and hauled him the rest of the way under the obstacle.

Saark sat there, choking, covered in grey dust and looking pathetic. He wiped his sweating, dirt-streaked face, and glanced up at Kell. "Thanks, old boy."

Kell gave a single nod, and stood, stretching his back. "It's going to get more enclosed ahead."

"Just what I need," said Saark.

"I'm just warning you."

"Well, don't! I'd rather have a sour, nasty, bad surprise."

Again, they picked up the trail of glowing passageways, this time rising steeply until the tunnel emerged onto a small platform overlooking a cavern. As they approached, they could see the slime-glow increase in intensity, and this warned the group; they moved slow, hunkering down as they broached the rise. The small platform was just wide enough for the three of them; and what they saw left them crouched in stunned silence.

Below, in what appeared to be a naturally carved cavern, a massive affair strewn with stalactites and stalagmites, there were pods; corrugated, white, each pod about the size of a horse and divided into six or seven bubbled segments. They lay, motionless, not glowing but pale white, almost luminescent. And there were hundreds of them. Thousands. Littering the cavern, many of them packed in tight, crammed together.

"What," said Saark, with a completely straight face, his voice low and carefully neutral, "are those?"

"I don't know," said Kell.

"But you said you've been here before!"

"Yes, but I've never *seen* those before!"

"Are they, you know, something to do with the worms? Maybe they hatch, or something? Like eggs?"

"Possibly," said Kell, giving a small shiver. If they hatched, the group would be immediately overrun.

"Look," said Nienna, pointing. Kell lowered her finger. "I can see it, girl."

They were *pulsating*. As if they were breathing.

"What now?" whispered Saark.

"I reckon we could go down there and cut one open," said Kell. "Then we'd know exactly what was inside. Exactly what we're dealing with."

"*What?*" snapped Saark. "Are you out of your mind, you crazy old fool? You might set them all off, then we'd be fucked for sure. And here's another thought – if they are eggs, then what in the name of the Grey Blood Wolf laid them?"

Kell nodded. "I suggest we circumvent."

"I would second that," agreed Saark.

They moved to the right, still watching the thousands of pulsating, segmented cocoons, or eggs, or whatever the organic objects were. They looked dangerous, and that was enough for the party.

Taking a right-hand tunnel, Kell led the way once more, wary now, Ilanna in his great fists. He was more alert, eyes straining to see ahead, ears listening for sounds of any approaching enemy. He wouldn't let Saark or Nienna speak now, and they travelled in morbid silence, ears pricked, nerves suspended on a razor wire.

The tunnel wound on, ever upwards, crossing many more in a complex maze. Kell chose openings with a sure knowledge, and Saark made a mental note not to get lost down here. The Valentrio Caves were a maze like nothing he had ever witnessed.

Eventually, the low-ceilinged corridor ended in a small chamber. It glowed. There were eight of the slowly pulsating, slowly *breathing* pods blocking their path.

Kell halted, and held up his fist. Saark and Nienna froze, peering past him. The chamber, floor lined with sand, was small. The pods filled it entirely, leaving nothing but narrow passages between each throbbing slick body of luminescent white. Nienna shivered.

"I don't want to sound like a pussy," whispered Saark, "but is there another way around these... these *blobs*?"

"It'll be all right," said Kell. "I'll lead. Nienna, stay close behind. Saark, bring up the rear."

"Why do I always have to go at the back?" he whined. "What if one of the quivering little bastards wakes up and jumps on me?"

"Well," smiled Kell, "it won't be the first time you've taken it from behind."

"You are a jester, Kell. You truly should be capering like an idiot in the King's Court."

"Can't do that," growled Kell. "The king is dead."

They moved into the narrow spaces between the segmented bodies. Each cocoon was tall, as tall as a man, and most at least as long as a horse, high in the centre and then tapering down in staggered segments towards the tips, which seemed to glow, changing suddenly from pale white fish-flesh to jet black, and then back.

Saark shivered. Kell moved with his jaw tight. Nienna desperately wanted to hold somebody's hand, for she could feel the fear in the air, smell the metallic scent of these pulsing cocoons. Kell brushed against one, and for a moment the pulsating ceased. In response, Kell, Saark and Nienna froze, staring in horror at the huge bulbous thing.

"You woke it!" mouthed Saark, urgently, face screwed into horror.

Kell gripped Ilanna tighter, but after a few moments the regular rhythm of the creature resumed. The group seemed to breathe again. They crept past, six, seven, eight of the cocoons, and then Kell stepped out into the opposite tunnel and breathed deeply, shoulders relaxing. Nienna stepped out behind him, and Saark turned to stare back at the corrugated pods. "Well thank the bloody gods for that!" he grinned, as his rapier swung with him, tip at knee level, and the point of his decorative scabbard cut a neat horizontal line across the nearest pod's fleshy surface. There came a hiss, a bulge, then a thick tumbling spill of white splashing out like snakes in milk. A scream rent the air, so high-pitched the group slammed hands over ears and grimaced, then ran down the tunnel as the scream followed, perfectly in rhythm with the pulsing of the *thing's* body.

"You horse dick!" raged Kell. "What did you do that for?"

"I didn't do it on purpose, did I? Can I help it if their skin is as flimsy as a farm maiden's silk panties? I barely touched the damn thing!"

"Come on," said Nienna, pale from the screaming, and she led them on a fast pace up a steep corridor. Suddenly Kell lurched forward, grabbing Nienna and bundling all three into a side-tunnel. They stood, in the gloom, and watched the albino soldiers pounding past. Kell counted them. There were fifty of the very same black-clad albino warriors who'd invaded Falanor.

"So, this is where they hide," whispered Kell, face grim.

"I am assuming," said Saark, in a quiet, affable voice, "that this place wasn't crawling with *either* egg-pods, nor albino soldiers, the last time you came through?"

"It was twenty years ago," snapped Kell. "I've slept since then."

"And got drunk many times," responded Saark, voice cool, eyes shaded in the gloom. "You've brought us into a hornet's nest, old friend. How many albino soldiers are here?"

"Let's find out," said Kell.

They moved back up the tunnel, which rose yet again on a steep incline that burned calves and sent shivers through straining thighs. They travelled for an hour, and three times more they came across squads of albino warriors wearing black armour and carrying narrow black longswords. And several times they passed along the lips of vast caverns, each full of pulsating segments, glowing, quivering cocoons. The third time they did so, Saark called for a stop. Down below, they saw several albino soldiers moving through the chamber, and one stopped, resting a hand on a quivering flesh segment.

"They're changing colour," said Saark.

"Eh, lad?" said Kell.

"The pods. They're no longer translucent. Now they are a deep white. Like snow. Look."

Kell peered. He shrugged. "So what?"

"And their pulsing is slower," said Nienna.

"So what?"

"You're an irascible old goat," snapped Saark. "The point is, each chamber seems to be some kind of birthing pit. That's my opinion. And these things are looked after by the albinos."

"Why would they do that?"

"Maybe they like to hatch worms," said Saark. "Maybe they are building a worm army!"

"That isn't even funny," said Nienna, eyes wide.

"Who said I was joking?"

"Shut up," said Kell. "Look. Something is happening."

They watched. A hundred soldiers marched into the cavern, and arranged themselves around a circle of five pods. A tall albino warrior stepped forward, and drawing a short silver dagger, he cautiously inserted it into the nearest pod and, with intricate care, cut a long curve downwards. Flesh bulged, and was followed by a flood of white which sluiced across the stone floor. There followed a tumble of cords, like thin white tree roots, and then there was a shape nestled amongst the mess, amidst the thick strands and gooey white fluid. It slopped, spread-eagled to the floor, and several of the soldiers stepped forward and...

"Holy Mother," said Saark, mouth open.

"So this is where the bastards emerge," growled Kell.

"What are they?" whispered Nienna, stunned by what she saw.

The soldiers wrapped the newly born, nearly-adult albino soldier, naked, flesh white and pure, scalp bald and glistening with milk, limbs shaking and unable to stand without support, in a blanket. The man was like a newborn foal, weak and quivering. The surrounding soldiers led the blanket-trussed newborn down a corridor in almost reverent silence.

"They're hatching," said Saark, without humour. "The human maggots are hatching."

"They're not fucking human," snarled Kell.

"Well," continued Saark, in the same cool, level voice, detached and not quite believing as he tried to comprehend the magnitude of what he was witnessing, "what actually *are* they, then?"

"They're the enemy," said Kell, "here for us to kill."

"An interesting viewpoint," came the smooth, neutral voice of the albino warrior. He stood, and behind him were thirty soldiers. All had bows bent, arrows aimed at the three peering intruders. "They are, in fact, our alshina larvae. As you so quite rightly put it, young man, we are not human. This is where we are hatched – eggs laid, implanted, and hatched by our queen." He drew a short black sword, and used it to point. "Ironic, that you refer to us as the *albino*. That would be *your* arrogance speaking. To think we are simply humans without pigmentation. Man, we are a different *species*."

He turned, then, and surveyed the bent bows of his warriors. Several smiled.

"What do you want?" growled Kell, and slowly stood. He flexed his shoulders, and his face was thunder. Saark stood next, and he placed a warning hand on Kell's shoulder.

"Look," said Saark. "They have Widowmakers."

The dandy was right; some of the warriors carried the same weapon that Myriam and her little band had used back in Falanor; the same weapon which had taken Katrina's life.

"If you know what these Widowmakers *are*," said the leader, smoothly, with no hint of fear or panic, "then you obviously know what they can *do*. I suggest you drop your weapons. My soldiers have been primed to kill the girl first."

"Why, you bastards," frowned Kell, stepping forward. The Widowmakers lifted in response to his antagonism. They were surrounded, heavily outnumbered, and even the mighty Kell could not fight with thirty arrows in his chest.

"We have to do it," urged Saark, and was the first one to lay down his rapier. Nienna, wide-eyed, fearful, threw down her own sword and reluctantly Kell knelt and placed Ilanna reverently on the rocky ground.

"Take care of her, lads. I'll be wanting her back real soon. And if there's a single mark on her, I'll be cracking some skulls."

"Fine words," smiled the leader, but then the smile fell like plague rain. "Restrain them."

They had hands tied tightly before them, Kell grumbling and growling all the time, facing out into the great hatching chamber where yet more newborns were eased from their larvae pods and into the cool air of the chamber; into the real world. Like insects, thought Kell with a shudder. They are hatched like insects.

He was spun round by surprisingly strong hands, and a huge white-skinned soldier smiled at him, crimson eyes fixed on his, hand on the hilt of his short black sword. "You'll be cracking skulls will you, Fat Man?" he hissed.

Kell's head snapped forward, delivering a terrific head-butt that dropped the albino warrior in a second, and had him crawling around in circles, blinded.

"There's the first one," growled Kell. "Any more fools want to try me out for size?"

The leader pressed a razor dagger to Nienna's throat. He still retained his air of calm, of clarity, as he stared down at his disabled soldier who – even as he watched, died on the floor. His skull was indeed cracked. Broken, like a raw egg.

"Anything else, Kell, anything at all, and I'll cut her up. A piece at a time."

"You've made your point, lad," said Kell, showing no surprise that the leader knew his name. "Just as I have made mine. So tell me – what happens next in this vile and acid-stinking albino piss-hole? You got any more surprises for us?"

"Just one," said the leader, words soft as he caressed Nienna's trembling throat with his blade. "Somebody wants to meet you."

"And who would that be? My mother?"

"No," said the leader. His crimson eyes twinkled. "His name is Graal. He's been expecting you."

CHAPTER 15
Soul Gems

Skaringa Dak was a huge, evil mountain, even by the usual standards of the Black Pikes which in themselves had a reputation for being huge, evil, merciless and downright impenetrable. Skaringa Dak towered over surrounding peaks, and to one side, between hooked crags and violent obstacles, if one was to stand *just right* between jagged teeth, a person might, when the mists and snowstorms cleared, see the distant, widening spread of Silva Valley, home of the vachine, home of the engineered vampire race.

Near the summit, surrounded by glossy knives of rock sat ragged slopes containing millions of glossy, polished marble daggers, impossible to traverse on foot and a natural – or maybe not so natural – barrier to the flat circle of Helltop, five hundred metres beneath the mountain's true summit.

Helltop.

A place of mystery and magick for ten thousand years, surrounded by walls and fissures, crevices and crags, hooks and knives, and accessed only by a narrow, sloping tunnel which led deep inside the

bowels of Skaringa Dak, and welcomed the foolish
to explore.

Helltop.

A five hundred-metre circle of flat rock, polished
marble, inlaid with natural lodes of silver and gold so
that it twinkled under snow-melt. The surrounding
peaks lay deep in snow, but not so the circle of Helltop.
Helltop was immune to snow. Some said it was a volcanic fissure from deep within the mountain that
channelled heat from unfathomable places; others said
it was acts of evil magick which had taken place there
over the centuries, ranging back past even the Vampire
Warlords of Blood Legend – and which lingered, invisible, like esoteric radiation.

Set in the centre of Helltop and criss-crossed with
thick bands of gold and silver in the glossy floor, sat the
three Granite Thrones. They were ancient, and hewn
by primitive hand-tools centuries before. They were
jagged, and rough, and basic. And they were *old* beyond
the comprehension of modern civilisation. Before the
three Thrones there was a small, circular pool of liquid,
like a glass platter of black water. This natural chute fed
down, *down* through a thousand vertical tunnels, natural fissures and chutes and stone tubes cutting through
the rock to the very roots of the mountain. These were
the arteries of the mountain. These were its *life*.

Graal stood beside the Granite Thrones dressed in a
white robe. Wild mountain winds whipped his fine
white hair, and his unusual blue eyes surveyed this, the
scene he had awaited for nearly a thousand years.

A mournful howling echoed through the mountains.
Graal smiled. He could feel the *pull* of so much blood-
oil and its associated magick of the soul. Now, all they

needed were the Soul Gems and the Sacrifice to finalise and bind the spell. To bring back the Vampire Warlords. To *control* the Vampire Warlords.

Graal looked left. Kradek-ka, Watchmaker of the Vachine, gave him a single nod. He checked on Anukis, his daughter, who stood, swaying, blood-oil on her lips, her eyes rolled back, the honeyed drugs in her veins flowing thick now with a necessity of oblivion.

Graal opened his arms, and he opened his mind, and he *felt* the mountain beneath him *within* him and he felt its great veins of silver and gold, and they were one for a moment, he, Graal, and Skaringa Dak, and he knew this was the mountain of the Vampire Warlords: Kuradek the Unholy, Meshwar the Violent, and Bhu Vanesh, the Eater in the Dark. *Can you hear me, children?* he whispered, flowing through the mountain's vast caverns and tunnels, flitting like a ghost through the hatching chambers of his Army of Iron.

We hear you, sang the Soul Stealers.

Have you brought them to me? he whispered.

We have brought them to you, sang the Soul Stealers.

Then we have the final Soul Gem, he said. His eyes flickered open and he stared at Kradek-ka. "We have all three," he intoned, voice like a lead slab, the flesh of his face quivering as if in prelude to a fit.

"Then we must prepare," said Kradek-ka, and placed his hand gently over Anukis's chest where her heart, a heart entwined with the clockwork augmentations of the vachine, beat with the ticking of a finely engineered timepiece.

Under her skin, something glowed in response to his touch, in response to Skaringa Dak, in response to Graal and Helltop and the Granite Thrones. Beneath

Anukis's skin, beating with the pulse of the clockwork machinery which kept it alive, glowed the implanted Soul Gem.

Snow whipped Vashell as he crouched, hidden in a narrow V of rock, and stared with open mouth down at the plateau of Helltop. "I cannot believe it," he hissed, and glanced back down to Alloria. She was weak with cold and fatigue, even wrapped in furs from the wolves Vashell had skinned to keep her warm. "Fiddion was right. They seek to bring back the Vampire Warlords!"

Alloria tried to creep under an overhang of rock, out of the wind and the blizzard. She was dying, Vashell knew, and guilt tore at him. But this was different. This was the vachine. This was Silva Valley. Now, in this place, he realised what evil magick they were about to perform... and more importantly, what sacrifice they needed to make it work.

Blood-oil was not enough.

Graal needed the souls of the clockwork vampires.

Thousands of clockwork vampires.

But *how* could he do it? None of the Old Texts spoke of the Ritual of Bringing, or the Summoning. And pages had been savagely cut from the Oak Testament, so it was said, by the First High Episcopate Engineer in order to stop evil filling the world. The pages had been burned. It was the only way.

So how did Graal *know*?

You bastard, thought Vashell. You would sacrifice our people.

You would sacrifice the entire vachine civilisation! And for what?

To rule beneath the Vampire Warlords? But understanding eased into Vashell's mind, then; a deep and
intuitive understanding. No. Graal was too arrogant.
Too power hungry. He would seek to rule the Vampire
Warlords. To control them. Not to *become* one of them,
but to be their Master.

"You are insane," Vashell whispered. And he knew
what he had to do. He had to stop them. When the Soul
Gems were presented to the Granite Thrones, he had
to stop them – to kill the carriers. Or at the very least,
to kill the Soul Stealers. For only with the Soul Stealers
could the Soul Gems be extracted and used for the
Summoning. So it was written in the Oak Testament.

Vashell watched, as *something* tied tight with golden
wire was dragged onto the platform. It had black, corrugated skin and was making feeble mewling noises. It
was big, and powerful, but – impossibly – subdued.

Vashell felt sorrow. And he felt pride. He felt guilt. And
he felt an incredible compression of the mind. He had always loved the vachine. He had been a prince of the
Vachine Empire, and yes, since his impurity at the hands
of Anukis he was outcast and could never return to the
place he loved; the place which folded neatly around his
heart and soul like a fist. But he could do something. He
must do something. He was the only one who *could*.

He stared, through tears, at the mewling creature.
And blinked as he recognised, there beside the gleaming chitinous monster, Anukis. Sweet Anukis! And the
puzzle pieces fell into place. Anukis carried a Soul Gem.
That was why Kradek-ka made her so special, so *advanced*, and used his technically brilliant vachine
engineering to keep her alive; to create a *prime*. That
was why he allowed vachine society to turn against her,

so that when this time came, when the need to sacrifice so many of Silva Valley came, then Anukis –

Vashell went cold.

Anukis would be ready, he thought.

Ready to kill. Ready to murder.

Ready to sacrifice…

Vashell realised with a sick feeling in the pit of his stomach that the whole thing had been a game, a clever strategy, instigated and plotted by General Graal and Kradek-ka in order to bring back the Vampire Warlords. They had planned, and plotted, and hijacked the Blood Refineries, necessitating orders from the vachine to invade Falanor in search of new fresh blood-oil… when in reality what they did was gather raw materials to allow the rebirth of the Vampire Warlords.

Thousands of humans. Thousands of vachine.

All dead, and about to die, just so the Three could walk again!

He would stop them. He would halt their plans.

Vashell reached for his bow, and with freezing fingers notched a deadly arrow to the string. He turned and peered back over the ridge. Who to kill? Who was the most effective target? If he only had *one shot*? Kradek-ka? Anukis? Sweet Anukis… tears stung his eyes, and he brushed them away. Or Graal. If Graal was dead, surely they could not continue?

Vashell heard the tiniest of sounds, like metal claws on rock, and he turned, and went terribly cold.

Two women stood, almost nonchalant in their easy posture. Their fangs gleamed, and their claws gleamed, and one had long white hair tied back into tails, and one had short hair spiked by the blizzard. They carried swords. They were smiling.

"What on earth," said one, tilting her head so as to accentuate the beautiful curve of her face, "are you doing up there?"

Vashell moved fast, bow smashing round, shaft releasing like a striking cobra.

There was a snarl, a slam, and a tearing of flesh.

Alloria whimpered, and backed away through the snow.

The Soul Stealers ignored her as they briefly fed.

Now, weaponless and bound, a squad of ten from the Army of Iron marched Kell, Saark and Nienna without relent through the underground tunnels of Skaringa Dak. Their commander, tall and arrogant, was an albino named Spilada, and he led the way – in fact, seemed the only one in the group to *know* the way. They marched all day, sweat pouring down faces, muscles burning and screaming during internal tunnel ascents, many of which were scrambles, extremely dangerous scrambles when hands were tied tightly before them. At one point Nienna slipped, stumbled, and began to slide down a long slope of scree towards a gaping black chasm. One of the soldiers grabbed her by the scruff, hauling her whimpering body away from a sheer, vast, underworld crevasse.

Kell turned to Spilada. He smiled, a warm and amiable smile, only the fury raging in his eyes telling a different primal story. "Anything happens to the girl, and I'll eat your fucking eyes out," growled the old man.

"And receive ten swords in your back," came Spilada's terse response.

"Yes," grinned Kell. "But *you'll* have no face, and eyeballs dancing on your open cheekbones."

"Shut up. And walk."

"Whatever you say," growled Kell, and with a nod and courage-building smile to Nienna, started up the scree slope.

At the top they stopped for a short rest on a ledge of black rock. Below, the scree slope led off to a massive drop which fell away into echoing blackness. The air was strange, at some times freezing cold making the group shiver, at others bearing wafts of raging hot air which brought them out in streams of sweat. Kell and Saark were kept seated apart, but Nienna was allowed to sit near Saark.

"How you doing, girl?" grinned Saark after he had regained his breath.

"That was incredibly hard," she said.

"Yes, we're not mountain climbers, right?"

"No." There came an awkward pause. Around them, the white-skinned soldiers sorted out their kit, all the while keeping a close eye on the prisoners. Kell sat to the left, legs dangling off a small drop, face calm but eyes murderous. They could sense his violence from a league away. "What's going to happen, Saark? I'm frightened."

"I don't know, Little One," he soothed. "What I do know is that it was a mistake coming here. Kell thinks he can take on the world; yet now, here, he's just a broken, captured old man."

"He's still Kell," said Nienna, voice soft, pride and belief shining in her eyes. "He is The Legend. He slew Dake the Axeman. He was the Hero of Jangir Field. He turned the tide at the Battle of Black Beach, carrying Dake's head back to the King. He was at the Battle of Valantrium Moor. He's a hero, Saark. He cannot be beaten!"

"He is still a man," said Saark, gently, thinking of the other side of Kell, the dark side of Kell, the murder in his eyes, the murder in his axe, and ultimately, his part in the Days of Blood. Unreported massacres. Cannibalism. Torture. The rape of the dead...

"He's more than just a man," said Nienna, hope in her breast. "He is Kell."

Saark nodded, not willing to remove her spark, her hope, but staring around at the ten warriors with a sense of painful reality. He smiled, still thinking of these soldiers as albino. But they were not. They were... Saark shivered. Shrugged. He had no idea what they were. Part insect? They were shells, he realised. Something else, something *old*, living inside a human shell.

Kell stood, and stretched, back still to the soldiers. He turned, and two looked up from honing swords, watching him closely. He smiled in a friendly fashion, and moved over to them. "I need a piss," he said.

"Over there," gestured a soldier, with a nod.

"And how do I get my cock out? You've tied me tighter than a fishmonger's purse strings."

"You'll not be untied, old man."

"Better come and hold it for me, then."

"No. I have a better idea." The soldier smiled, a wax, fake smile. "Just piss in your pants. You old warriors all stink of piss anyways; it's said you make incontinence pads out of leaves in the forest, but I don't believe it myself. I think you just line your britches with old shit. It all adds to the rancid stench of the legend."

Kell shrugged, easily. "No problem. If that's what you want." A pool of piss leaked out from one boot, forming a puddle of glistening yellow and Kell stepped closer to the men, trailing a stream of piss and both soldiers, with backs to the scree slope now, dropped their gazes in disgust.

"Not here, you dirty old fool!" snapped one soldier, and glanced up –

Into Kell's boot. It was a massive blow, catching the soldier under the chin and lifting him high into the air, and backwards. He tumbled down the scree slope in a clatter of rocks. The second man rose fast, started drawing his sword, but Kell stamped on his hand and he let go of the blade; twisting, Kell stamped down a second time, boot catching the pommel and striking it downwards. The sword blade punched through scabbard, a diagonal strike down through the buckling man's left calf muscle, right through flesh and into his right foot, pinning his legs together. He toppled, screaming, clawing at the bloodied blade.

At the edge of the scree slope there came a short scream as the sliding soldier was ejected into the abyss. He took a clatter of stones with him. Then silence followed his long descent into oblivion.

The rest of the soldiers leapt into action, drawing swords and Kell turned on them, eyes glowing, teeth bared. "Come on, you heaps of walking horseshit! Let's see what you're made of! Let's see if the maggots fight as well as they breed!"

"No," came a soft voice. Spilada held Nienna, one hand clamped around her throat choking her, the other with a short skinning knife, blade gleaming. Even as Kell watched, face thunder, Spilada let go of her throat, grabbed her hand, lifted it before the group and with a swift, tight cut, snipped off the little finger of her right hand. Nienna screamed, there was a spurt of blood and she went down on her knees weeping, cradling the mutilated limb, rocking. Her finger lay on the ground, like a tiny white worm.

Spilada stepped forward, and as Kell surged at him he lifted a finger and placed the skinning dagger against Nienna's throat. He smiled a cold smile. Kell stopped. He lowered his face. The flat of a sword smashed the back of his skull, and he went down on one knee. Boots waded in, and they kicked him, eight soldiers kicked him, but he did not go down. He simply took the beating, blood on his teeth, eyes never leaving Spilada even under the heaviest of blows.

Saark leapt to Nienna, cradling her, tearing off a section of his shirt and binding her cut finger as best he could. He glared up at Spilada. "What are you doing? She's just a child!" he snarled.

Spilada shrugged. "Next time, I'll cut off her hands. You men, you listen, you *will* cooperate. This is no game we play." He turned back to Kell, who had stood now the beating ended. The soldiers backed away from him warily, as if they surrounded a wild caged bear. In the background, the man whose legs were pinned together by his own sword whimpered. Spilada made a strange tight gesture, a flicker of fingers, a signal, and another albino slit the wounded man's throat in a rush of white blood. He gurgled for a while, twitched, and was still.

"I will kill you," said Kell.

Spilada shrugged. "You will cooperate. Do I have your cooperation? Or shall I fetch my bag of razor-knives?"

"I will do as you ask," said Kell, gently. He lowered his head. He did not look at Nienna.

"Hush girl," said Saark, and the soldiers now bound Kell's feet – a loose binding, an effective hobbling which allowed him to walk, clumsily, like a prisoner. Saark hugged Nienna. She was crying in pain and shock.

"He cut off my finger!" she wept, staring at the bloodied section of shirt tied tight around her stump. "He cut it off! What kind of men are these? We should never have come here!"

"They're men who'll do much worse if we don't co-operate," said Saark, nostrils twitching at the stench of blood which filled up his nose and mouth and mind with a whirling red vortex of sudden lust. "Come on." Saark helped Nienna to her feet. She swayed, with pain and shock.

"Can she walk?" snapped Spilada. "If not, we'll toss her into the canyon."

"I can walk, you bastard," Nienna snarled, suddenly venomous. There was pure hate in her eyes. Spilada smiled at the vision.

"We have a little Hellcat here, I see."

"A Hellcat who'll cut your throat."

Spilada's smile dropped from his face like a stone down a well. "Enough talk. Walk or die."

Nienna nodded, and Saark helped her to stumble to her grandfather. Kell looked at her then, sorrow in his eyes, tears on his cheeks and in his beard.

"I'm sorry," he said.

"It's not your fault!" wept Nienna, and tried to hug him, clumsily due to her bound wrists.

"I caused you injury. I will never forgive myself."

"You were trying to get us free," she said.

Kell scowled. "I should never have brought you here, child. This is a place of death." His voice dropped, turning to a growl. "Or very soon, it will be." His eyes strayed to Ilanna. She had been placed in a sack with other weapons, and one soldier carried it over his shoulder. But Kell could see her outline. And he could hear her voice.

In time, she said. *It will come.*

I promise you that, Legend.

Kell nodded, and the group moved into another narrow tunnel which led, as ever, upwards.

After many more hours, during which they were allowed only short rests – mainly for the sake of Nienna, who had dropped into a subdued, bitter silence – they emerged from another steeply-climbing tunnel onto a platform in a vast subterranean cavern. Now, the soldiers carried lit torches, for the glow of worm slime had faded behind them. Fire sputtered and whipped in wild underground breezes, howling from unseen high places, crags and hollows, high tunnels and caves. The platform led out over a narrow stone bridge, wide enough to let three men walk abreast but with no guard rails. It arched slightly over a vast abyss, and disappeared into darkness which the torchlight could not penetrate.

"There's somebody on the bridge," said Saark.

"You've better eyesight than me, lad," said Kell.

"You first," grunted one soldier, and prodded Kell. Kell climbed a few short rough-hewn steps, and out onto the windy, underground bridge. It was damp, and looked slippery. Wary, Kell stepped forward, but the bridge was solid under his boots. He walked with care, followed by Saark and Nienna, and then the soldiers from the Army of Iron spreading out behind with Spilada at their core.

"By all the gods, it's Myriam!" said Saark, voice rising a little in surprise.

SOUL STEALERS

369

"Does she have her bow?" snapped Kell.

"Yes! She must be here to help." His voice dropped. "But... something is wrong," he said, head tilting to one side. "How could she have survived that fall?"

"Probably got stuck on a ledge," muttered Kell. "Don't think about that now... what we need to think about is *escape*."

"If we fail, we die," said Saark, looking into Kell's eyes.

"Then we die," said Kell softly. "I have a knife in my boot. When we get close to Myriam, follow my lead."

"Stop the talk!" snapped Spilada from the rear. He drew his sword. "Unless you want ten inches of steel in your spine!"

Kell and Saark were quiet, moving forward across the slick stone bridge. The wind snapped at them with hungry jaws. The abyss loomed. Myriam was smiling as they came close.

Kell gasped, for her hair was thick and lush, her gaunt face no longer gaunt, but finely chiselled and defined by beauty; her figure, her limbs, her hips, all were powerful and athletic, and her flesh was healthy, even in this cold subterranean hollow, not the waxen pallor of the near-dead. Now, she was beautiful again. Myriam was no longer a slave to cancer and the fear of death. Myriam was a woman in her prime.

"Kell..." warned Saark.

And Kell knew, knew the risks, knew Myriam might not be *with them* but the opportunity was too good and the location too neat not to use for his own ends, his own plan, and battle rage swamped him and he could not be a prisoner, could not be bound like an animal heading for predicted slaughter and yes they might all die, but better to die fighting! He stumbled, tripped on

the bindings which locked his legs together in a prisoner's hobble, and went down on one knee. The tiny
knife in his boot cut up, through leg bindings and wrist
bindings with one swift harsh movement and as Kell
arose in a blur of action Saark had turned to him, and
Kell slashed his bonds, in the same movement his arm
snapping back and launching the blade which embedded to the hilt in Spilada's eye. The soldier screamed,
grappling at his face and Kell leapt down the bridge, fist
slamming one man to break his cheekbone and send
him rolling, to topple from the span. Another drew his
sword but as it left the scabbard Kell was in close, head-
butting the man and taking the weapon neatly. A
back-handed swipe cut his head from his shoulders, the
short blade rammed through another's man's chest to
the hilt, and Kell tossed the soldier's blade to Saark who
leapt to Kell's aid. They cut their way through three
men in as many seconds, leaving the kneeling figure of
Spilada behind them on the bridge. The clash of steel
on steel echoed through the vast cavern. Nienna,
shocked by the sudden violence, the acceleration of battle, blinked, then stared at the kneeling figure of
Spilada. He held the hilt of the small knife, gently, as if
readying himself to pull it from his eye-socket. With a
growl, Nienna leapt forward and slammed the heel of
her hand against the hilt of the blade, driving it deep,
through Spilada's socket and into the brain within. Spilada slumped back, legs kicking, and Nienna dropped
to her knees and was sick on the bridge.

　　Saark battled the remaining soldiers, and Kell
dropped to one knee, opening the sack in the hands of
the dead soldier. Slowly, reverently, he drew out Ilanna.
She squirmed in his hands, her haft almost like *skin* to

the touch, and Kell stood and his eyes were fire and his mouth was a grim line. "Saark, step back," he said.

Saark stopped, and backed away. Kell strode forward, rolling his shoulders.

The enemies stared at him, and their eyes moved to the axe. So, thought Kell, they know her. "Come on," he said, voice little more than a whisper of mountain breeze.

The remaining soldiers turned and fled, dropping their swords, sprinting along the bridge and disappearing into the black.

The wind howled, increasing in fury. Kell turned back to Saark, and Nienna, and the figure of Myriam who had not moved during the battle. However, she had not drawn an arrow to aid them. Kell scowled, and strode forward, with Saark joining him.

He stopped short of Myriam. He placed Ilanna against the stone of the bridge with a dull iron clank.

"You're looking well, lass," he said, calm, meeting her gaze which now shone with good health and bright vitality. Myriam laughed, the tinkling of a summer brook over marble pebbles.

"You can see what happened," she said, and as she spoke they could spy her tiny vachine fangs. Her nose twitched. Nienna came to stand behind Kell and Saark, peeping at Myriam, face confused.

Myriam made eye contact. "Nienna." She smiled, face radiant. "It feels wonderful, Nienna… truly, I am whole again, truly, I am at the peak of my physical prowess!"

"Step aside," sighed Kell. "I can see you're not here to help, and I have not the will to fight you."

"What?" mocked Myriam, suddenly. "The great Vachine Hunter, not willing to fight the terrible, evil vachine which stands before him? I thought you were Kell? I thought you were a Legend?"

"What do you want?" said Saark, voice soft.

"Ahh, the suckling vachine speaks!"

"*What?*" snapped Saark, face pale, etched with worry.

Myriam looked past Saark, to Kell, meeting his iron gaze. "He didn't tell you? The dandy didn't share his great secret? Back in the town, he was *bitten*, Kell. I can smell it! He's half-turned, but without the clockwork it's a slow and painful process." She dropped her gaze back to Saark. "Had any strange pains, boy? In your fingers? In your teeth? In your heart?"

"Shut up," growled Saark.

"Or what?" grinned Myriam. "You'll rip out my throat with your fangs? Go on Saark, show your friends your teeth. You can't hide it now, can you? Only the dark down here has been concealing your shame. But there's nothing to be ashamed of, Saark! Nothing, it's wonderful, it's a rebirth! Don't you feel your senses singing? Can't you hear the beat of the Mountain's Heart?"

"What do you want?" said Kell, voice level, refusing to look at Saark. Saark took a step away from Kell. Fear etched his features like moonlight.

"I am to escort you," said Myriam, returning her gaze to Kell. "I was to take you from the soldiers, but you had to have your little sport. Still. I said you would come quietly." She winked, and her tongue licked her vachine fangs. Somewhere, almost unheard, there came the *click* of changing gears. "For old time's sake."

"Stand aside, Myriam," said Kell, lowering his head and the rage of battle welled in him again and he was finding it harder to control, and he could hear the screams of the dying and the mutilated, the burned and the raped during the Days of Blood. And their blood ran in his mouth and down his throat, and he was eating their raw meat with the others, with the damned, with the possessed. That wasn't me, said Kell. But he knew different. And a hundred souls screamed from his past and pointed at him with cold dead fingers.

"No," said Myriam, still making no move for her weapon.

"So be it," said Kell, and hefted Ilanna – as a *whoosh* hissed through the air, and something unseen slammed past at incredible speed and Kell was knocked to the ground with stunning force. Kell was up, a blur of movement, blood on his mouth and eyes narrowed. He whirled on Nienna and Saark. "Get back!" he screamed. "Back along the bridge! They're here!"

"This is a place of blood-oil magick," said Myriam, gently, and drew her own short sword. It was silver, and it glowed, just a hint, but enough to show it was no ordinary weapon of base metal. "And the Soul Stealers are strong here, Kell, so strong… stronger than you could ever comprehend."

Nienna and Saark were running, and Kell turned back to Myriam. His intention was obvious. Never leave an enemy behind; especially not one with a bow. Ilanna came up, black butterfly blades dull by comparison to Myriam's silver sword, but infinitely more threatening. He launched at Myriam, but she danced back, silver sword parrying the blow. Again, something whistled past Kell, so fast he did not see, and something fine and hard wrapped around his face. With Ilanna in one hand, he clawed at the substance, pulling at it but it wriggled, and he saw it was a fine gauge golden wire. More whistles and moans of wind surrounded him, and

suddenly there was a flurry of activity as the Soul Stealers passed, their flight one of magick, and the gold wire
wrapped around Kell's face and head and neck, and the
wire was around his arms, pinning them against him
and strapping Ilanna to him, and he fought and struggled, but they drew tight and he screamed as they cut
through clothing, cut into his flesh, then they were
squirming, moving, writhing as if they had a surreal intelligence, a form of metal life, and Kell's legs were
tightened and he hit the bridge, watched the wire as it
seemed to *expand* and grow and wind around him, and
around him, until he could not move, could barely
breathe, locked to his axe like a dark lover.

Kell watched, witnessed Saark and Nienna hit the
bridge further along. There came light slaps as the Soul
Stealers landed on the stone, vachine fangs bared, eyes
crimson and burning. They moved close to Kell, and
Tashmaniok knelt, and stroked his face and beard in-
terwoven by gold wire, and she smiled, then turned
back to Myriam who had sheathed her sword.

"Bring him," she said, and in raw agony Kell passed
into darkness.

CHAPTER 16
Warlords

Vor, capital city of Falanor, sat in silence, desolate, a ghost town. Fine snow whipped along the dead streets. Darkness bled into corners like leaking ink. Occasionally, lightning cracked the sky like a bad egg.

On a hill overlooking the city squatted the Blood Refineries. They were dark, brooding, terrible in their monstrous design and purpose. The wind hummed around the huge vachine-built edifices, as if conveying a lament for the slaughtered, the drained, and the desecrated.

Above this gentle storm of snow, there came a crackle of high electricity. Not lightning, but a web of incandescent fingers which trailed across the sky in bursts, illuminating the clouds, melting the snow, filling the sky with a lightshow of wonder and bestial primitive ferocity. The only audience were encamped soldiers from the Army of Iron left behind to guard the Blood Refineries, and they emerged from tents and shielded eyes, gazing up in wonder, heads tilting, mouths forming lines of compression... and of understanding.

"So it begins," said one, his words a whisper in the storm.

More crackles leapt across the sky, this time blood red and turning the night into an electric storm of crimson. The Refineries started to hum, to vibrate like caged animals in shackles desperate to break free. The horizontal bursts of electricity filled the sky, no longer bursts but sheets of sparks and webs and fire, which finally *discharged* with tornadoes of bright burning light against the Blood Refineries... and the world was filled with noise and concussion and raw energy as General Graal, hands raised in the Black Pike Mountains, on Helltop, on the Vampire Warlords' Seat of Power, so he drew this source of blood-oil magick and allowed it a channel *home*.

They had assembled on Helltop, and Graal walked along the line of Granite Thrones, his back to them, showing contempt for their weakness, but also hiding his joy at their capture. Kell was dumped to the slick smooth ground, and he grunted as he hit the floor and glared up at Graal with undisguised loathing. Nienna was weeping, the wires which bound her cutting into flesh and drawing blood, and Saark said nothing, his mouth a bloodless slit. Graal turned.

"Stand them up."

Unceremoniously, the Soul Stealers dragged Kell, Nienna and Saark to their feet, and they shivered as the cold mountain wind kissed them, and gazed around at the silent dark gathering. There were soldiers from the Army of Iron, a silent honour guard for their General and Watchmaker, Kradek-ka. Of the three Granite Thrones, two were occupied. The first, by a young woman with long, golden curls and the fangs of the

vachine. Her face was slack, drugged, her eyes rolled
back in a skull which showed the marks of a beating.
Her throat still sported a huge puncture wound, half-
healed by advanced vachinery, and softly through the
silence, the tick-tick-tick of her clockwork could be
heard. On the second throne was a strange, crumpled,
black-skinned creature, his skin more like insect chitin
than real flesh. He was tied, as were Kell and Saark,
with tight golden wire and although they could read no
expression in his face, his eyes held a deep and ancient
rage... and yet also understanding, and submission, and
cooperation. For Jageraw, this was the culmination of
his purpose and his existence. This was his destiny, and
they needed no bonds.

Kell hawked, and spat on the ground. Distantly,
thunder rumbled through the mountains, the Black
Pikes displaying unease and raw, limitless power. He
scowled at Graal, and looked slowly around, at the soldiers, at Kradek-ka who displayed a facial expression of
intense focus, and then to the Soul Stealers and Myriam,
their vachine subordinate, who had helped capture
them and truss them like goats ready for sacrifice.

"At last. Kell. You have arrived. We have been waiting for you."

Kell growled something incomprehensible, and spat
again. "I made a grave mistake the last time we met,
Graal. I should have carved you out a skull-bucket and
pissed in it. However. The error is mine, but one I'll not
make again."

Graal gave a low, level laugh, but his eyes held no
humour. He looked up at the torn sky. Then back to
Kell. "Can you not feel the *shift* in power, Kell? Old
man, can you not feel the vibrations in the air, and

smell the sickly-sweet blood-stench of a hundred thousand victims? They are coming back, tonight, and all we lacked was the final Soul Gem. My beautiful daughters, here," he moved around Tashmaniok, his hand sliding around her hips as he walked, and she tilted her head to smile at Kell, a dazzling show of beauty, "they did well to find it and deliver it to evil."

"What horseshit is this?" snarled Kell. "We have no Soul Gem!"

"But you do," said Graal, voice lover-soft, moving close to Kell, "and it is buried inside," he touched his own chest, "integrated with the heart, and it will be such a shame to cut it free because, sadly, a side effect of removing the Soul Gem is… death."

He turned and moved back to the Granite Thrones. He reached out, and touched the huge solid artefacts, face serene, for he knew everything was ready, everything aligned, in place, and nothing – not even Kell – could stop them. Nothing on earth could stop the Vampire Warlords.

Graal raised his arms to the sky, and the sky crackled with horizontal sheets of crimson electricity. The Soul Stealers moved to him, stood slightly back, pale faces bathed in a glow of blood-oil magick. The wind shrieked through Helltop like a million banshees. The snowstorm whipped and snapped, and the sky, still full of awesome primal power, an awe-inspiring *Summoning*, turned red and black as it filled with blood-oil streaks of energy. The snow itself turned red, into frozen blood snowflakes, and crimson flakes fell around Helltop like tears from the slain, which is what they surely were.

"They are coming," said Graal, and looked to Kradek-ka. "Are you ready?"

"I am ready," said Kradek-ka, face impassive.

Kell struggled against the wires which held him, then glanced across at Saark. "Lad? Can you hear me?"

Saark looked at Kell, weariness and defeat shining in his eyes like emerald tears. He gave a single nod.

"Can you help me get free?"

"I doubt it," whispered Saark. "And even if I did, you would slay me."

"What are you talking about?" hissed Kell, face a contortion of effort and fury. Around them, the bloody snow thickened, and more discharges rent the sky. The wind howled like death, moaned like a widow, screeched like a castrated priest.

"I was bitten. I am changing. I will become like her." He gestured to Myriam with a nod of his head. His voice was as bleak as a midwinter sacrifice. Then he looked at Kell, full in the eyes, face contorted in fear. "You are the Vampire Hunter," he said, voice almost sardonic. "I will never sleep soundly again." His eyes dropped to the floor, his dark curls whipped by the savage wind.

"Listen, lad," growled Kell, trying to control his temper, "the only one I'm going to kill around here is that annoying fucker Graal. So get your claws out, or your vampire fangs or whatever, and get me free of this fucking wire! You hear?"

"I cannot," said Saark. He was filled to the brim with melancholy. He had resigned himself to death. He sighed, like a tumbling fall of worlds.

"You will not!" snapped Kell, and watched uneasily from the corner of his eye as Kradek-ka drew a long, curved, matt black blade. "Help us get free, you dandy bastard! Look. I promise I'll not kill you. There. I've said it. You can't let them do this…"

Saark shook his head, tears running down his cheeks. "Truly, Kell, it is out of my control."

Kell stopped his struggling. The gold wire bit his flesh like razors. He was pinned to Ilanna, the greatest of slayers, and the irony was he could not get a hand free to wield the mighty weapon. *If only I could get one arm free*, he thought. *I would welcome the orgy of violence! I would bathe in blood again. Just like the Old Days.*

Suddenly, the energy and horizontal sheets of lightning and fire died, along with the wind and the snow. The sky was a terrible, flat black, as if they gazed up into a slab portal of nothing, a huge and endless void. Silence settled like ash. The world became an incredibly still place.

"What's your next trick?" shouted Kell. "You going to pull a rabbit out of a horse's arse?"

Graal stared at Kell, as if seeing him for the first time. Then he gazed down, down at a small pool of black which nestled at floor level before the Thrones. The Arteries of Skaringa Dak. The life-blood of the mountain itself. Kell blinked, seeing the pool for the first time; it was black, black as ink, black as moonlit blood, black as the Eternity Void.

Graal spoke, and when he spoke it was as if he communed with the mountain, with Skaringa Dak Herself. "Mighty Vrekken, hear my call, rise up for me, rise up and do my bidding!" and his hands crackled with blood-oil magick and Graal knelt, and plunged his hands down into the pool and his eyes were closed and blood ran from his eyes and ears, staining his pale white skin red, and his body vibrated and twitched as if in violent epileptic spasm, and then Graal kicked backwards, sprawling to the ground at the foot of the three Granite

Thrones, but quickly stood, coughing up blood and spitting it to the rock. He grinned over at Kell, teeth stained, then towards the motionless figure of Kradek-ka.

"We need the Soul Gems," he whispered.

Kradek-ka approached Anukis, and her eyes seemed suddenly normal and sane as she gazed into the face of her father, the father who had nurtured her from womb to womanhood and whom she had trusted with all her heart. "No," she said, golden curls trembling, vachine fangs baring as the dagger plunged into her chest, tearing through white cotton and cutting deep through to her heart... Anukis screamed, and started to thrash madly despite her golden bonds, splashing blood upon the Thrones, and Kradek-ka grasped her throat, steadying her, and cut a deep circular hole in her chest, the tip of the knife slicing through skin and breast-bone to prise free the Soul Gem which had lain dormant inside her, a parasite, beating with her heart since birth.

Kradek-ka took the Soul Gem, and turned to Graal, and behind him his daughter writhed on the Granite Throne in the throes of death, blood bubbling up her throat and down her chin like a crimson mask. But Kradek-ka ignored his kindred, and lifted the Soul Gem for Graal to see. It was small, the size of a thumbnail, and a perfect cylinder of matt black which gleamed under a coating of Anukis's blood-oil.

"And the next," said Graal, blue eyes shining. His words, although softly spoken, carried across the surreal, impossibly quiet plateau of Helltop.

Kell's head snapped left, to Saark, then down, to Nienna, who was watching with a kind of morbid fascination as Kradek-ka approached the corrugated black creature that was Jageraw. *They think one of us carries a Soul Gem!* screamed his mind, suddenly. But which one? And something pierced his mind like a splinter, and he smiled a sour smile as he realised what made him special, what made him such a terrible, evil killer. There was something alien inside his flesh. Something which had corrupted him. Something in his heart, put there during the Days of Blood.

In silent shame Kell replayed his past, the horrific deeds he had committed, and surety settled in his mind like honey in a pot. The Soul Gem was inside him. It had polluted him. Turned him bad, like an alien cancer. And now they were going to cut it free. And then he was going to die... but at least die a pure man, at least die a *good* man. Now, he truly understood.

Kell struggled against the wires, and Nienna looked up at him and she smiled, and it was a terribly sad smile that filled him with an empty, rolling void. He could not stand for this! He would not stand for this. But the more he struggled, the more the golden wires bit his flesh until he was slick and slippery with his own blood and his own lacerated skin. "Bastards," he was growling, "bastards!" he screamed, his voice booming across Hell-top and the Black Pike Mountains but it did not matter, it made no difference as Kradek-ka's blade sawed through Jageraw's chitinous armour and the creature made no sound, made no struggle, even as the blade bit flesh and cut through to his heart, prising out the Soul Gem on its tip to lie, nestling in Kradek-ka's palm like an excised insect.

"The Hexels hid you well," said Kradek-ka, and his eyes were locked to Jageraw's and he smiled, head tilting. "The Soulkeepers gave you the weapons to live, little boy. They turned you into something... something *else*. So you could protect this Soul Gem, the First Soul Gem, until the time of the Summoning. We owe you a great debt."

Jageraw nodded, and closed his eyes, and died in silence.

Something seemed to sweep across Helltop. It was an *emotion*, a *pulse* of energy. "They can feel us," said Graal, licking bloodied lips. "The Vampire Warlords acknowledge us."

"One more," said Kradek-ka, and turned towards Kell, and Saark, and Nienna.

"One more," nodded Graal, and walked slowly forward, the Soul Stealers close behind, their footsteps matching his, their white hair glowing in the odd light from an unseen moon.

"You were the hardest to hunt down," said Graal, his smile crooked, his words hoarse.

"Let me fight you!" raged Kell, struggling with all his might, blood slick across his entire body and soaking his clothing as the golden wires bit. "I'll not die like this, you fucking whoreson! Not on the end of a butcher's knife! Let me fight, I say!"

Graal tilted his head, and turned, and stared strangely at Kell. Then he laughed, a chuckle so base and evil it sent Kell into a paroxysm of fury. But his words stopped Kell dead.

"Not you," said Graal, and reached out, and stroked Kell's bearded cheek. "You do not have the Soul Gem, old man. Whatever gave you that idea?"

And it was like a hammer blow, for if Kell did not carry a parasitic evil within him, something which had polluted his humanity, made him carry out evil acts like no other... then the fact was, he was simply a bad man.

But this mammoth shock was followed by a realisation.

"Gods, no!" he hissed, as Graal moved to Nienna and Kell's mouth dropped open and how could it have happened, how could the girl carry something like that inside? Without anybody knowing? Without showing any adverse signs? And now Graal was going to carve her up like a pig on a block, and she would die in this desolate lonely terrible place so that *They* might live… and Kell could not stop it.

Graal looked down at Nienna. "Be still, little one. This will soon be over," and he smiled and reached out and touched her skin and tears were coursing down her face, and Kell was frothing at the mouth in rage and frustration and he was the greatest warrior of Falanor, the greatest *Legend* of the age and he could do nothing to save his beautiful, innocent granddaughter…

Graal moved on, past Nienna, and took hold of Saark who jumped, as if waking suddenly from a dream. Graal dragged the tightly wired dandy across the platform and Kell hissed, mouth dry, eyes blinking fast.

"Kell, hey, what's going on?" yelled Saark, starting at last to try and struggle, shocked from his reverie and maudlin coma by the very real events about to unfold. "What are you doing?" he shouted into Graal's face. "Get off me you fucker!"

Graal paused, then sat Saark on the Granite Throne, stepping back as if to admire a fine sculpture. "Didn't you realise?" said Graal, voice little more than a whisper but carrying clear across the silent, reverent platform. "I thought she would have told you?"

"Who? What the hell are you talking about?"

From the cave entrance came Alloria, only now her skin glowed and her eyes dazzled and her fingers ended in brass claws. Tiny fangs protruded over the Queen's lower lip and she walked slowly, languorously to Saark, to the King's Sword Champion, to her ex-lover, and she moved beside the Throne and looked down at him with a mixture of pity, and love, and understanding.

"I'm sorry it was you," she whispered.

"What have you done?" said Saark, voice dropping low, dangerously low. "Oh Alloria, you have betrayed everything, what have you done?" And it fell into place, puzzle pieces tumbling into position, and that was why Graal went for her after the initial invasion of Falanor – not just as a bartering tool against the King, but because... she was *his*.

"It took a while for her to love me," said Graal, crossing to Alloria and kissing her, and she responded, one hand coming up to rest against Graal's cheek. "But once infected with blood-oil, once a slave to the clockwork, once she became *vachine* she grew to know her place, she grew to understand the world with open eyes. She was a great tool in leading Vashell here, and in finding the traitor, Fiddion. But then, I digress." He motioned to Alloria, who moved to stand alongside Myriam – both women changed by the blood-oil bites, the infection of the Soul Stealers. Both watched, fascinated, as Kradek-ka approached Saark with his small black knife.

Saark glanced over, at the other thrones. Anukis was dead, slumped to one side. Jageraw was a motionless mass of bloodied insect-armour woven with dark human flesh. And now... now it was his turn!

"No!" he yelled, and started to struggle. "Kell, Kell do something! But Kell could do nothing, and their eyes met and Kradek-ka reached forward and with his iron vachine grip, pinned Saark back against the Granite

Throne. Saark could not move. He was motionless, not just in Kradek-ka's hold, but in horror, and terror, and his eyes were on the tip of the curved blade which moved slowly, inexorably toward him; and he thought back, thought of Alloria and what they had together, the love they had together and it had all been fake, all been an act and she had been charged with *implanting* the Soul Gem into a host for safe-keeping, and he had been that host, their love a mask to hide her real intentions, and Alloria had been a spy for Graal and a traitor to her husband and the people of Falanor and hate ran deep through Saark's veins, then, as he understood; maybe she had not been willing at first, but what had fuelled her? What in the name of the Seven Witches had fuelled the Queen of Falanor to betray everything she loved? As the knife cut deep, and Saark gasped, and ice forced into his flesh and cut into bone with a grating, grinding sound Saark's eyes met with Alloria's and she smiled at him and there was no sorrow there and she was completely *vachine*, she was no longer human and rage and hate flowed strong in Saark but he could not move and pain flashed up and swamped his mind and the knife cut deep and carved a circle the size of a fist from his flesh, and he gasped, unable to breathe as he was mutilated, and he did not struggle and did not scream and the pain and ice were everything, all consuming, swamping his vision and he gasped, again, and saw as if through a veil of blood the Soul Gem excised from his own savaged body and he coughed, and blood splattered from Saark's mouth, and he felt everything and the world fall away and down into a blood red pool of darkness.

Kradek-ka turned, in silence, as Saark slumped to one side behind him, blood running down the Granite

Throne and onto Helltop. "No!" screamed Kell, struggling pointlessly, and Nienna was weeping and
Kradek-ka handed the three Soul Gems to General
Graal, who took them, took the three small matt black
cylindrical jewels – the source of so much agony and
pain and blood and death and power.

"Now, we call the Vrekken," he said.

Skaringa Dak was huge and brooding and ominous,
once volcanic with a million natural arteries and channels and tunnels and veins, now dormant but home to
the swirling underground whirlpool, the Vrekken; it
overlooked Silva Valley to the North, dominating the
skyline of the vachine civilisation and controlling the
flow of the Silva River from deep inside the Deshi caves
and beyond, where the Silva River flowed deeper into
the heart of the Black Pike Mountains.

Now, as General Graal's blood sacrifice and blood-oil
magick Summoning sent ripples of energy through the
natural arteries of Skaringa Dak, so the Vrekken, that
mighty underground whirlpool, roared a noise so loud
it made the mountain tremble and there came a distant
boom boom boom as water pressure increased a million-
fold and with the power of the ocean, the power of the
mountains, the fury of the *land*, the Vrekken reared
from its deep bottomless pit and water heaved through
tunnels millennia deserted, black and cold and shimmering like blood. It pounded through corridors and
caverns, smashing up through a hundred breeding
nests of Graal's white-haired soldiers, up up up through
thick arteries as the mountain trembled and the world
trembled and billions of gallons were forced under
enormous pressure into the Silva River, out through the

gaping maws of the Deshi Caves, out with such incredible pressure and a wall of water reared like the rising head of a striking cobra and slammed at once down Silva Valley crushing houses and temples, warehouses and palaces, and thousands of vachine were slammed with such force they were crushed, compressed down into a mash of flesh and corrupted clockwork components. Thousands ran, streaming down pavements and jewelled roadways, but the wall of water pounded along and they were gone in an instant. The Engineer's Palace was torn in two, one half picked up like a toy and dashed along the expanse of Silva Valley, bounced from mountain wall to mountain wall as tens of thousands of screams rent the air and the mighty force of the Vrekken crushed the occupants of Silva Valley... and the vachine civilisation therein.

The roaring seemed to last a thousand years. It echoed deafening through the Black Pike Mountains, like mocking laughter. And... as soon at it had come, the might of the Vrekken was gone, leaving Silva Valley flooded, a churning platter of dark black waters. Where once the valley had sat, now was a surging, seething lake.

Slowly, the violence faded and the new lake settled, calming, to be still.

Silva Valley was no more.

And the dead screamed unto eternity.

On Helltop, they stood in silence. The roaring of the Vrekken, the flooding of Silva Valley, the extinguishing of the vachine civilisation had taken perhaps five minutes. Kell, eyes narrowed, stared hard at Graal. "What have you done?" he said.

"It was a necessary sacrifice," said Graal.

"You exterminated their colony like insects."

Graal's eyes gleamed. "And soon, you will see why!" He gestured to the Soul Stealers, and Shanna and Tashmaniok moved to Anukis, and tossed her corpse aside. Then they did this to Jageraw, leaving smears of dark blood on the Granite Thrones. Finally, they grabbed Saark, who was wheezing, eyes closed, the huge fist-sized hole in his chest showing shattered breast-bone and the open cage of smashed ribs. Within, his heart beat with a slow, irregular rhythm – like a fist opening, and closing, and opening, and closing. They tossed him to one side, where he rolled over and Nienna ran to him, and nobody stopped her.

"Saark!" she said, face wet with tears. But she could not hold him, for she was bound too tight.

"All is well, Little One," he grunted, and forced himself into a sitting position. He looked down at his open chest in horror, and when he smiled blood glistened on his teeth.

"Saark, don't die," she wept.

"I don't think I have much choice in the matter," he managed, voice hoarse. Then he winked at Nienna, and coughed, eyes closing in pain. "Did I ever mention you're a stunning young lady? A real catch."

"You'll never change," laughed Nienna through tears.

"I wish…" he winced again, the agony plain on his face, "I wish I had just a few more years. So… so many women, still left, to please." His head slumped forward, and breath rattled from his lungs.

Kell gazed out over the distant, flooded Silva Valley, and turned back to Graal. Graal and Kradek-ka stood before the Granite Thrones. The pool before the Granite Thrones – down through which Graal summoned the

Vrekken – was an empty hole, deep and bottomless, all water sucked free when the Vrekken threw its hydraulic fury at Silva Valley.

Graal and Kradek-ka stood, either side of the hole. They faced the Granite Thrones. They seemed to be waiting. Kell glanced left, to Myriam and Alloria; both were entranced by the sight, by the Summoning, and the air crackled with dark energy. The Vampire Warlords were coming. It was written in the sky. Written in the stone. Kuradek the Unholy. Meshwar the Violent. Bhu Vanesh, the Eater in the Dark. The world would descend into chaos. And the Vampire Warlords would build a *new* Empire.

Kell looked right. The Soul Stealers were entranced, their bright crimson eyes fixed on the Thrones. This was the moment. This was the time. If Kell could break free now, he could... what? A cold realisation dawned. The Summoning magick had been cast. The spell was done. All the deaths, the blood-oil, the sacrifice... the Soul Gems had done their work, summoned the Vrekken, destroyed the vachine, killed enough vachine souls to bring back the Vampire Warlords from the Chaos Fields – from the Blood Void.

What could Kell possibly do? Even if he murdered Graal and Kradek-ka, it would make no difference. The Summoning was *happening*. It was an unstoppable Force of Nature. Of Chaos. Of *Magick*.

I can help you, said Ilanna.

No, you cannot, said Kell.

He is coming, be ready, said Ilanna. Kell scowled. His gaze swept the platform. He could see the stars again, but a blackness like smoke rolled out against the night sky, blocking out the stars in three hazy patterns. Kell blinked. Was he imagining this haze-filled sky? He lowered his eyes, and shook his head, and all the fight had gone out of him. They were here, Saark was dead, he and Nienna had failed. They had thought they were so powerful, so clever, bringing the fight to the enemy – when in fact, all they did was deliver Saark and the Soul Gem to Graal.

And he came, from the edge of the scene, from between the rocks where before there was no passage, and he stepped from smoke and he was barefoot and danced on the glossy slick surface of Helltop. He was six years old, with thin limbs and pale skin, he was ragged and tattered, wore torn clothes and had black, shiny teeth. His eyes, also, were black, and they shone with an ancient wisdom, with the decadent wisdom of the Ankarok. Skanda danced, twirling and weaving, a slow dance to unheard music, perhaps the music of the stars and the magick and the Summoning itself, and Kell watched the little boy with his mouth open, and a sour needle split his brain and Kell scowled, for Skanda was part of this evil too and if Kell could get his axe free he would make them all pay, for the blood and the death. Kell watched Skanda dance, and the Soul Stealers turned and fixed eyes on the little boy, and they drew their silver swords and leapt at him with sudden violent snarls and the world seemed to *tilt* and come rushing back into place and Kell watched in awe as Skanda danced between the impossibly whirling sword blades, and he leapt and twirled and danced, and the blades hissed and sang around him, a glittering web of death and Skanda lifted his eyes and they met with Kell's, there was a *connection* and Skanda smiled and he lifted his hands and from his hands flowed... insects. They

came in a flood, crawling and skittering, flying and
buzzing and stinging, they poured from Skanda's hands
and now his mouth opened and they flooded from his
throat and rushed past the startled Soul Stealers who
dropped to their knees in defensive crouches as Graal
suddenly turned, realised what was happening and his
face turned from bliss to fear, his eyes darkening, his
mouth opening to scream but the insects flooded out,
over the plateau and over Kell who panicked, squirming in his bonds as worms and maggots and
cockroaches and wasps flowed over him, smothering
him with their insect noise and acid and...

Kell blinked. The gold wires fell away, eaten by insects.

Kell looked down, at Ilanna grasped in his mighty,
lacerated, blood-drenched hands. Slowly, he looked up,
and saw the Soul Stealers, and Graal, staring at him.
Skanda danced on, a mournful dance, insects still pouring from his mouth and his little boy's feet slapped
pitifully on the slick ground. Graal pointed at Kell. "Kill
him!" he screamed, with a sudden insane fury and the
Soul Stealers stood, then leapt at Kell who brought
Ilanna up in a savage sweep and stream of sparks, batting aside both swords and knocking the two female
killers back.

Kell took a step forward. He lowered his head. "I am
Kell. And I am mightily pissed off."

The Soul Stealers leapt again, and Kell moved with
awesome speed, a blur, an age of pent-up rage and frustration unleashed in a few swift heartbeats. Swords
struck Ilanna, were cast aside and she sang as she cut
for Tashmaniok's neck but the Soul Stealer back-flipped
away, too fast, and her fangs came out and her claws
grew long and they could hear the *tick tick* of stepping

gears and clockwork wheels. She leapt at Kell, snarling, and was caught on the flat blades of Ilanna but twisted, one boot between the axe and herself, and pushed herself away into a roll as Ilanna sang a finger's breadth from her throat. Shanna attacked, sword slashing, claws trying to gouge Kell's eyes. He stumbled back, and she came on, snarling and spitting and Kell was forced further back until the rock wall halted him and he fought a short, furious battle, axe and blurring sword flickering to a discordant song-clash of steel. Kell ducked a sword strike, jabbed with his axe but Shanna shifted, avoiding the blow. Tashmaniok came in on Kell's right, and sweating now, slowing, the old warrior back-handed an axe strike at her face which she easily avoided.

"You're getting slow, old man," taunted Tash.

"You're going to die, old man," laughed Shanna.

"Then we'll eat your granddaughter," said Tashmaniok, all humour gone. She was neither sweating, nor panting; she showed no signs of exertion. Kell, on the other hand, was a sack of shit. He was covered in his own blood, in lacerations from the tight cutting wires, and his sweat was stinging his many wounds and fuelling his fury. But the vachine killers were right; he was old, and he was tired, and he was tiring. Fury and rage could only last so long. Kell had only minutes... *seconds*... to live. They knew it. And he knew it.

"Catch," said Skanda, from between the two Soul Stealers, and he threw the twin-tailed scorpion and Kell tried to dodge but the scorpion landed lightly on his chest, just under his throat, and before he could do anything both tails flexed and struck like the twin heads of a striking snake. The scorpion stung Kell, who yelled in surprise as the Soul Stealers turned on

Skanda for a moment, distracted, swords a blur as they frantically attempted to kill this boy of the Ankarok, but he danced, tantalisingly, forlornly, between their blades. Then there came a sharp *crack*, and Skanda smiled an ancient blood-oil magick smile and watched as *time* cracked and Kell stepped in two, and looked at himself, looked at his twin, his clone, his double, one a few steps out of time meaning he was not one, but two. The Kells stared at each other, stunned into silence, and the Soul Stealers stood still with mouths hung agape. The two Kells turned, like a mirror image, and with roars that shook the air launched themselves at the Soul Stealers, twin Ilanna axes singing a curious humming chorus of axe-blade death. Swords and axes shrieked, and now that each Kell fought only one enemy his confidence and speed and agility returned, and with savage necessity the original Kell forced Shanna back against a wall, his axe strikes accelerating as she grew more and more frantic, and she called out for help, "Tash!" a shriek of the condemned as Ilanna batted aside her sword blade for one last time and with a mighty roar, a bestial battle-scream Kell lifted the butterfly blades of his bloodbond axe and they came down in a savage vertical strike that cut Shanna from skull to quim, and slopped her bowels and clockwork components to the Helltop plateau. "No!" wailed Tash, distracted by her twin's destruction, and Kell's axe cut through her neck, sending her head rolling along the stone ground, slapping slowly to a halt by Graal's boots.

Skanda smiled, and clapped, and the twin-tailed scorpion ran onto his hand and up his arm. He clapped again, and there was a second *crack*. The air felt greasy, full of smoke, and the second Kell disappeared as time jigged into synchronisation, into a linear snap of reality.

"Don't ever do that again!" snarled Kell, turning in rage, his head pounding as if struck by a mallet, but Skanda had gone. He ran to Nienna, and Graal was shouting orders to the soldiers surrounding the Granite Thrones. Even now, dark smoke was coalescing on all three Thrones, and Kell shook Nienna, dragging her away from Saark's body. "We must go," he growled, eyes wild.

"Bring Saark."

"I reckon he's dead!"

"Bring him!" she shrieked.

Kell grabbed the limp body of Saark, grunting as he slung him over his shoulder for the dandy was heavier than he looked, then dragging Nienna behind, he sprinted for the only exit available – the empty pool, the hole, sitting stagnant before the three Granite Thrones. Graal had drawn his sword, and as Kell charged so he turned and his face was death, his eyes twinkling sapphires, and the sword came up and Kell screamed and hurtled towards him, axe coming up and smashing Graal's sword aside as Ilanna cut a long streak down Graal's left cheek, peeling his face open like a fruit, and Kell's last glimpse before they were swallowed by the hole was that of three tall, smoke-filled figures seated on the Granite Thrones. Their eyes were blood red, and they were watching him. Kell, Nienna and Saark fell into the chute, into the vertical tunnel below, and in the blink of an eye vanished from Helltop.

They fell.

Fell, towards the distant, booming Vrekken.

• • •

On a high peak above the flooded Silva Valley sat four Vachine Warrior Engineers and two Watchmakers. Walgrishnacht's eyes were bleak, his face drawn and haggard as he surveyed the destruction of Silva Valley below. Their escape had been a miracle. Many had died following.

"Nobody could have predicted this," said Sa, voice gentle.

Tagor-tel placed his arm around her shoulders, and they sat for a while, thinking of the thousands who had died, smashed and drowned below them in the echoing caverns of the Vrekken.

"We must call what remains of the vachine armies," said Walgrishnacht, standing, and he turned and stared at the distant peak of Skaringa Dak. Above it, blackness swirled like evil personified. "We must summon the Ferals."

"It is too late!" wailed Sa. "Can you not feel it? Can you not feel *them*?"

"I do not understand," frowned the Cardinal.

"Graal has summoned the three Vampire Warlords," said Sa, tears running down her cheeks. "With or without our armies, this means the end of our civilisation."

Walgrishnacht drew his sword, which gleamed black in the moonlight. "Only when I am dead, and my proud blood-oil stains the battlefield, will I believe this is so," he said, and gestured to the few remaining members of his massacred platoon. "Let's move out," he said, brass fangs gleaming.

The wind crooned across the peak of Skaringa Dak. Graal, pushing his peeled cheek back into place with a squelch, turned and faced the Vampire Warlords. They were huge, and dark, their skin swirling smoke, their eyes raging blood, and they stood – in unity, as one – and first Kradek-ka knelt, and then, slowly, General Graal knelt and a chill terror flooded him like nothing he had ever felt. For the Vampire Warlords were terrible, and they were death, and they had changed and brought something *else* back with them from the Chaos Fields, from the Blood Void, from the Halls of Bone. All around the platform soldiers knelt to show terrified obeisance, and Myriam and Alloria knelt also, the wave of total fear washing over them and making piss run down their legs.

"General Graal," said Bhu Vanesh, the Eater in the Dark, and blood eyes tilted in a smoke face to survey his subordinate, to survey his slave, and Graal nodded, unable to speak, the terror like thick flowing ash in his mouth and his brain and he was a child again – how had he thought they could control these ancient, bestial, primitive Warlords?

Kuradek stood on the Granite Throne, and peered off across the desolation of Silva Valley. He smiled, face swirling gently, every feature a blur, every breath a rattle of chaos. "Silva Valley is destroyed."

"Yes," managed Graal, forcing words between clenched teeth.

"You have done well, slaves."

"Yes," forced Graal.

Meshwar the Violent stepped away from the Granite Throne, and for a moment Graal thought he might disappear; like this whole Summoning was a bad nightmare, and the magick which had brought the Warlords back might restrict them to the Thrones. But it did not.

"Gather your soldiers," said Meshwar, surveying the warriors from the Army of Iron, heads bowed, fear and chaos worms in their rotten, spinning brains. Mesh-war's gaze was bleak. His voice was an intonation from a different realm. From a world of chaos. "Gather them all. Now is time. Now we go to war."

"Against whom?" trembled Graal.

Blood eyes glowed. "Against *everyone*," he said.

ACKNOWLEDGMENTS

This novel was a hard one to write due to many elemental factors. My gratitude goes to Sonia, for being such a little prima donna in front of (and away from) the camera lens; to Ian Graham for the helpful and highly amusing "Stinkling" sessions, and his esoteric windswept Facebook comedy; to Marc Gascoigne, for his encouragement, faith and witty banter; to Lee Harris, for his perverse humour and lack of military comms; and to all those fellow writers and fans who attend the cons, making life so very entertaining. And thanks, finally, to all those who take the time to write with words of encouragement. In this cynical world of negativity, it does make a difference.

ABOUT THE AUTHOR

Andy Remic is a British writer with a love of ancient warfare, mountain climbing and sword fighting. Once a member of The Army of Iron, he has since retired from a savage world of blood-oil magick and gnashing vachine, and works as an underworld smuggler of rare dog gems in the seedy districts of Falanor. He is hard at work finishing *Vampire Warlords*, the next bloodsoaked instalment of the life (and legend) of Kell.

Find out more at:
www.andyremic.com

An exclusive extract from
VAMPIRE WARLORDS
The Clockwork Vampire Chronicles III

PROLOGUE
Portal

The wind howled like a spear-stuck pig. Black snow peppered the mountains. Ice blew like ash confetti at a corpse wedding. The Black Pike Mountains seemed to sigh, languorously, as the sky turned black, the stars spluttered out, and the world ceased its endless turn on a corrupted axis. And¬ then- the Chaos Halls flickered into existence. Like an extinguished candle in reverse.

A sour wind blew, a death-kiss from beyond the world of men and gods and liars, and smoke swirled like acid through the sky, black and grey, infused with ancient symbols and curling snakes and stinging insects. The smoke drifted down, almost casually, to Helltop at the summit of the great mountain Skaringa Dak. The Granite Thrones, empty for a thousand years, were filled again with substance. With flesh.

The three Vampire Warlords, as old as the world, as twisted as chaos, formed against the Granite Thrones where they were summoned. Almost. Their figures were tall, bodies narrow shanks, limbs long and spindly and disjointed, elbows and knees working the wrong way. Their faces were blank plates on a tombstone, eyes an evil dark slash of red like fresh-spilled arterial gore, and yet their worst feature, their most unsettling feature, was in their complete physical entirety. For in appearing, they did not settle. Did not solidify. Their nakedness, if that was what it was for the Vampire Warlords wore no clothing, was a diffusion of blacks and greys, a million tiny greasy smoke coils constantly twisting and writhing like an orgy of corpse lovers entwined, cancerous entrails like black snakes, unwound spools of necrotic bowel, and their flesh relentlessly moved, shifted, coalesced, squirmed as if seeking to strip itself free of a steel endoskeleton forged from pure hate. Their skin coagulated into strange symbols, ancient artefacts, snakes and spiders and cockroaches and all manner of stinging biting slashing chaos welcomed into this, The Whole. They were not mortal. They were not gods. They were something in-between, and oozed a lazy power, terrible and delinquent, and none could look upon that writhing flesh and wish to be a part of this abomination. Their skin and muscle and tendon and bones were a distillation of entrapped demons, an absorption of evil souls, an essence of corrupt matter which formed a paved avenue all the way back to the shimmering decadence of the vanishing Chaos Halls.

The Vampire Warlords turned their heads, as one, and stared down at the two men... the two vachine, who had summoned them, released them, cast them into ice and freedom.

And the Vampire Warlords laughed, voices high-pitched and surreal, the laughter of the insane but more, the laughter of insanity linked to a binary intelligence, a two-state recognition of good and bad, order and chaos, pandemonium and... lawlessness.

"You," said Kuradek, and this was Kuradek the Unholy, and his skin squirmed with dark religious symbols, with flowing doctrine oozing like pus, with a bare essence of hatred for anything which preached the word of GOD upon this decadent and putrefying world. In the history books, the text claimed Kuradek had burned churches, raped entire nunneries, sent monasteries insane so that monk slew monk with bone knives fashioned from the flesh-stripped limbs of their slaughtered companions. Kuradek's arm lifted, now, so incredibly long and finished in long fingers like talons, like blood-spattered razors. General Graal, mouth hung open in shock and disbelief, hand pressed against his face where Kell's axe had opened his cheek like a ripe plum, nodded eagerly as if frightened to offend. Fearful not just of death, but of an eternity of writhing and oblivion in a tank of acrid oil.

"Yes, Warlord?" Barely more than a whisper. Graal bent his head, and stared in relief at the frozen mountain plateau beneath his boots. Anything was better than looking into those eyes. Anything was better than observing that succulent flesh.

"Come here, Slave."

"Yes, Warlord."

General Graal straightened his back, a new anger forcing him ramrod stiff and his eyes narrowed and he stepped up onto the low plinth where the Granite Thrones squatted like black poisonous toads. Kuradek was standing, and the other Warlords, Meshwar the Violent and Bhu Vanesh, the Eater in the Dark, were seated, gore eyes glittering with an ancient, malign intelligence.

"You sought to control us, just as the Keepers controlled us," said Kuradek.

Silence flooded the plateau, and all present lowered heads, averted eyes, as a wind of desolation blew across the space, chilling souls. Graal, teeth gritted, did well to maintain that gaze. Now he was close, he could make out finer details. The skin, the flesh of coiling smoke, of writhing symbols, of constantly changing twisted imagery, was glossy – as if wet. As if oiled. And now he could see the Vampire Warlord's vampire fangs. Short, and black, like necrotic bone. Not shimmering in gold and silver like the vanity of the vachine. Graal ground his teeth. Oh how they must have laughed at the narcissism of the vachine sub-species. How they must now be revelling in such petty beauties the vachine had heaped upon themselves.

"No, I..."

Graal stopped. Kuradek was staring at him. Foolish. He could read Graal's mind. Kuradek made a lazy gesture, and for a moment his entire being seemed to glow, the smoke swirling faster within the confines of its trapped cell, Kuradek's living flesh. General Graal, commander of the Army of Iron, was punched in an acceleration of flailing limbs across the granite plateau. He screamed, a short sharp noise, then was silent as he hit the ground and rolled fast, limbs flailing, to slap to a halt in a puddle of melted snow. He did not move. Kuradek turned to Kradek-ka, who half-turned, as if to run. He was picked up, tossed away like a broken spine, limbs thrashing as he connected with a rearing wall of savage rock. He tumbled to the ground, face a bloody, smashed mask, and was still.

Now, the other Warlords stood. They moved easily, fluid, with a sense of great physical power held in reserve. All three gazed up as the Chaos Halls gradually faded and the stars blinked back into existence, one by one. Now, the wind dropped. Total silence covered the Black Pike Mountains like a veil of ash.

"We are here," growled Meshwar, and as he spoke tiny trickles of smoke oozed around his vampire fangs, like the souls of the slain attempting escape.

"Yes," said Bhu Vanesh. Also known as the Eater in the Dark, Bhu Vanesh was a terrible and terrifying hunter. Whereas Meshwar simply revelled in open raw violence, in pain for the sake of pain, in punishment without crime, in murder over forgiveness, Bhu Vanesh was more complex, esoteric, subtle and devastating. Before his imprisonment, Bhu Vanesh had prided himself on being the greatest vampire hunter; he would and could hunt anything, up to and including other Vampire Warlords. Before their chains in the Chaos Halls, Bhu Vanesh had sought out the greatest natural hunters in the world and let them free on forests and mountain landscapes, himself as bait, himself as hunter. When the hunt was done, with his captured victims staked out, he would gradually strip out their spines disc by disc, popping free of torn muscle and skin and tendons, and he would sit by the camp fire as his hunted victims screamed, or sobbed, or simply watched with stunned eyes as Bhu Vanesh savoured his trophy, licked the gristle from the spine in his fist, sucking free the cerebrospinal fluid with great slurps of pleasure. Bhu Vanesh was the most feral of the three Vampire Warlords. He was the most deadly. An unappointed leader...

Bhu Vanesh was the Prime.

Meshwar pointed, to an albino soldier. "You. Soldier. Get Graal." The man gave a curt nod, and crossed to the General, helping him wearily, painfully, to his feet. Graal leant on the albino soldier, panting, blood and snot and drool pooling from his smashed mouth, his battered face. His pale vachine skin was marked as if beaten by a hammer.

Kuradek strolled across the clearing, and a cool wind blew in as the world was restored to normality, as blood-oil magick eased from the mountains like a back-door thief slinking into the night. Kuradek climbed up a rocky wall, his thin limbs and talons scarring the rock. Pebbles rattled down in the wake of his climb. Then he stood, on a narrow pinnacle of iced slate, and gazed out over Silva Valley, once home to the vachine civilisation, now flooded, thousands of vachine drowned to seal the magick that would return the Vampire Warlords to the mortal realm.

Shortly, his brothers joined him, and the three tall, spindly creatures, their shapes a mockery of human physiology, their flesh constantly shifting in chameleonic phases of smoke and symbols, stood tall and proud and surveyed the world like newborns.

"The vachine are dead," said Kuradek.

"Mostly," observed Meshwar.

"Those that live need to be hunted," said Bhu Vanesh, a smoke tongue like a rattlesnake's tail licking over black fangs. He anticipated the hunt in all things. It was what gave his existence simple meaning.

"Not yet," said Kuradek. "We are new again to this world. We are weak from escape and birth. We need strength. We need to build the vampire clans. Like ancient times, my friends. Like the bad old days."

"Suggestions?" Meshwar turned to Kuradek, narrow red eyes glowing with malevolence.

"I remember this country," said Kuradek, looking back over hundreds of years, his mind dizzy with the passage of time, coalescing with images of so many people and places and murders. "This is the homeland of the Ankarok."

Bhu Vanesh made a low, hissing sound.

"They were imprisoned," said Meshwar. "Just as we."

"Yes. We must watch. Be careful. But until then, I feel a stench in the air. It is an unclear stench. It is the stench of people, of men and women and children, meat, unhealthy and unclean, with no pride or power or natural dignity. We must separate, my brothers, we must head out into the world and," he licked his black fangs, eyes glinting by the light of the innocent moon, "we must repopulate."

"So we go to war?" said Meshwar, and his voice held excitement, anticipation, and... something else. It took little for Meshwar to become aroused.

"Yes. War. Against all those deviant of vampire purity!"

VAMPIRE WARLORDS
Coming soon from Angry Robot
www.angryrobotbooks.com

ANDY REMIC

KELL'S
BOOK 1 OF THE CLOCKWORK VAMPIRE CHRONICLES
LEGEND

"Remic delivers in the action stakes." — SciFi Now

"A novel of power and scope, able to stand as a
worthy successor to the Gemmell crown. 5*****"

Fantasy & SciFi Books

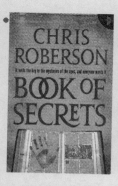